HARD QUESTIONS

HARD QUESTIONS

IAN WATSON

VICTOR GOLLANCZ

LONDON

First published in Great Britain 1996
by Victor Gollancz
An imprint of the Cassell Group
Wellington House, 125 Strand, London WC2R 0BB

© Ian Watson 1996

The right of Ian Watson to be identified as author of
this work has been asserted by him in accordance with
the Copyright, Designs and Patents Act, 1988.

A catalogue record for this book is
available from the British Library.

ISBN 0 575 06189 8

Typeset by CentraCet, Cambridge
Printed in Great Britain by
St Edmundsbury Press Ltd, Bury St Edmunds, Suffolk

96 97 98   5 4 3 2 1

Acknowledgements

For assistance and advice I warmly thank John Cramer, Howard Davidson, Bill Froud, Jonathan Vos Post, Rudy Rucker and Michael Ward. All misuse of their advice is my doing, of course.

1

Built on earlier cemeteries and sand dunes, the Richmond district of San Francisco between the Golden Gate Park and the Golden Gate Bridge became home after the Russian Revolution to thousands of refugees. Forty years on, the golden onion-domed cathedral of Saint Mary the Virgin in Exile arose. Beneath its floor was laid the body of the priest-become-bishop known as John the Barefoot, who had campaigned for a new home for those exiles.

But émigrés grew old or drifted away to suburbs. Instead, many Asians moved in to the Richmond district. Chinese, Cambodians, Koreans. And then the collapse of Soviet Communism caused a new influx of Russians, escaping from hard times and from the new gangsterism, or simply to do business.

When three men who called one another Night and Dawn and Noon met in a small apartment in an unassuming townhouse on an avenue in the mid thirties off Geary Boulevard, no one would have paid much attention.

White venetian blinds obscured the half-open window through which a slightly salty breeze blew from the ocean a mile away. A computer was scrolling as its program trawled. Key words were being highlighted and tagged. *Quantum. Chip. Encryption.*

Maps were thumb-tacked to walls. Files and journals and directories were stacked around the floor, along with some unopened packages from Gump's and FAO Schwartz, gifts to take home to Russia. A bottle of Stolichnaya and glasses and an ashtray of Marlboro butts weighed down news clippings on a low table.

Both Night and Dawn had the high cheek-bones, dark

7

wiry hair and lack of fold to the eyelids denoting the Mongol blood which flows in so many Russian veins. These two might easily be mistaken for native Americans. Fair-haired Noon was Caucasian. Noon and Dawn were burly; Night was rangy and lean. All three were entering middle age, bitterly.

They spoke softly in Russian. Even when arguing, they would do so quietly.

'The agency must be stupid sending us something like this,' said Dawn. The news clipping was illustrated by a photograph of a young woman standing nude on a beach. Her groin was blurred. '*National Investigator* is full of bourgeois shit. I was raped by an alien from Venus. Elvis Presley is on Mars.'

'Think again,' said Night, whose real name was Andrei. 'Look at the Matsushima connection. Quantum computers. She's due to attend a conference shortly in Tucson. *This woman knows things.*'

'Cambridge ... in *England*, not in Massachusetts ... However did those journalists come by this story? And the pin-up photograph too!'

Night shrugged.

On the computer screen a message flashed: **Invitation only.** Immediately to be overlaid by: **Please wait.** Without much delay the software invaded a private bulletin board.

'I have a hunch about this,' said Night.

Noon nodded. 'It's a wild card. But maybe you're right.'

They talked about the recent boating accident which had put Tony Racine in hospital. Strong rumours were that Racine's QX Corporation in San Jose were edging very close to a prototype quantum computer. Supposedly so were Motorola's corporate research laboratories in Phoenix. Matsushima likewise, at their labs in Japan and in England.

'If we agree,' said Night, 'I'll fly to Phoenix—'

'But we already tried to penetrate Motorola—'

'—and I'll drive down to Tucson to check out this conference and this young lady. I do have a feeling.'

Dawn nodded. Night's hunches had sometimes paid off handsomely. Noon filled three glasses.

Since Night would fly much of the way, he wouldn't be taking a gun which could show up on airport scanners. The young woman should be a soft touch.

2

Seen from the air the desert had resembled pale cracked cardboard. Driving down the interstate from Phoenix in a rented Pontiac, under a sky too bright to be quite blue, the widespread ugliness of raped landscape offended Andrei's eyes.

Whole zones were wired off. Former farmland, perhaps, to judge by sporadic decaying buildings. Abandoned now to bales of tumbleweed. A sign proclaimed something about a water authority. It came to Andrei that this land had been bought and forsaken for the sake of whatever water was underground. He had heard that the cities and their sun-dwellers were draining the desert even drier than it was already. And over in the west, wasn't the Colorado river a pygmy compared to its former self?

A few bullet holes had pocked that sign. Other signs along the route had been shot into illegibility. No drivers of cars or rigs currently cruising the route were acting as if they were on a firing range, but obviously some people did, presumably at night.

In the midst of nowhere, a vast half-completed housing development loomed. It looked like a colony under construction on one of the dead seas of the Moon, or on Mars.

Once during the drive Andrei stopped and got out to stretch his legs and smoke. As soon as he left the artificial chill of the car, he was smitten by heat and light which seemed quite interchangeable. The light was sheer heat; the heat was luminous. Air trembled, faintly tainted. Since the air was so dry, the haze must be pollution drifting from dozens of miles away.

The droning of crickets seemed like tinnitus within one's own ear. Shrubs were razor-wire. Bushes were bundles of dried rubbish. Mountains in the distance were two-dimensional. The mountains might have been merely cut-out backdrops, a studio set for an amateur cowboy movie, or the scenery of a hostile alien planet.

A huge bronzed rig powered past, hooting mournfully. Following it was a long silver fuel-tanker. The tanker could have been a ballistic missile condemned to roam the interstates of America horizontally forever. Along came a truckload of volcanic cinders, destined perhaps for landscaping.

Andrei felt sick at heart, then angry.

Much of Russia's wilderness had also been ravaged – in the service of society. Yet to no ultimate profit. Futilely! And then the servants of the state had been betrayed, impoverished, while only gangsters thrived.

Coming closer to Tucson, Andrei passed a great oasis of a golf course. A few miles further on was yet another golf course. Aquifers were being drained so that people could knock balls across greens.

3

The Convention Center was simultaneously hosting a motorbike fair and a convention of tax consultants. In fact the upcoming conference about consciousness wasn't slated for the main building with its vast exhibition hall and galleria and ballroom and its arena which could seat nearly ten thousand people, but for a theatre adjoining the complex which would comfortably house the expected five hundred attendees.

Registrations and accommodation for the conference were being handled by the University a mile to the east. Before heading there, Andrei took Polaroid pictures of the Leo Rich Theater and its surrounds. Each picture which emerged was paled by the drenching light.

The immediate vicinity included a score of parked Harleys and their owners. Almost all of the tanned young men were dressed in baggy jeans and leather bomber jackets. Shades hid their eyes. Blue bandanas soaked up sweat from their brows. Baseball caps were turned backwards. Chubby-cheeked and hard-jawed, those fellows. Even though Andrei hadn't pointed his camera at any of them, someone assumed so. While Andrei waited for a final picture to appear, four bikers spread out at a trot to bracket him.

'Why you taking our photos without permission?'

'What you up to, man?'

'I'm interested in architecture, that's all, guys.'

Dozens of other people were around. Surely enough bystanders were present for him to be safe from assault. However, a biker snatched the picture from his hand and glowered at it. Only then, when some of the other men in bomber jackets moved, did Andrei spy an item of graffiti upon the theatre wall. In bold black zig-zag letters: *Inzane Nation*.

A biker eyed Andrei's part-Mongol face. He raised his shades, revealing slanted eyes.

'What *nation* are you, man?'

Had they figured Andrei for a foreigner? Oh no, these were Indians, native Americans. They thought that he was one of them, but of an unfamiliar tribe – working as a plain clothes security employee for the Convention Center, capturing evidence of vandalism with his camera.

'I'm a tourist,' Andrei protested. The biker tore the photo in half.

'Hey—'

A young white patrolman, in jackboots and short-sleeved blue shirt and vizored helmet, was approaching.

'What's going on?'

His hand hovered by the side-arm in its holster. Such a mood of menace, in the glaring sunshine.

'It's nothing,' Andrei replied. 'A slight misunderstanding, officer. They thought I was taking their photograph.'

The patrolman grinned.

'Oh, you mustn't do that – not unless you pay them a dollar each.'

Was the patrolman in collusion with this gang of bikers against the foolish foreigner? Maybe he was trying to

11

appease the bikers to ease the tension. Their attitude was sullen. The patrolman continued to grin.

'Dollar's the going rate on the reservation, right?'

Should Andrei take the hint, and hand over money as if paying a fine?

The bikers' spokesman scowled at the patrolman: 'Navajo *Nation*, man, not reservation!'

Was the patrolman a racist? Andrei had seen so many swarthy faces on the streets. It was as if he had actually crossed the nearby border into Mexico.

'You boys are a long way south.'

'Come to see the bike fair, what else?'

The officer scanned the assembled Harleys. If he noticed the phrase upon the theatre wall, he chose to ignore it.

'Thinking of changing your wheels, then, boys?' Was he being ironic or appreciative? The incident seemed to be subsiding. Onlookers were losing interest. The officer advised Andrei: 'Move along, mister.'

4

Towards evening, a sudden storm briefly freshened the city, and Andrei too. The heat had begun to sicken him.

Clouds boiled forth from the mountain range to the north like sulphurous smoke gushing from a volcano in eruption. A ten-minute rain shower lowered the temperature a bit and settled some of the smog trapped in the valley. In the aftermath the sunset was gory – and fleeting. Within what seemed a few minutes the sky was a gloomy lavender; then indigo. Streetlights were a myriad hovering fireflies. Headlamps hurried by, the eyes of prowling beasts. A coyote began to yip somewhere in the city, its voice carrying eerily through the evening. From elsewhere, another wild urban animal answered.

The rapid disappearance of daylight had surprised Andrei. Still, an almost-full moon was up, so he took numerous Polaroids around the Desert Hacienda, where a certain young Englishwoman was scheduled to stay the following week.

The Hacienda was much more up-market than the cheap hotel which Andrei had chosen for himself. Twenty minutes' leisurely walk, at most, from the Convention Center, the Hacienda's spread boasted luxury adobe cottages set around semi-private garden patios. Palm trees shaded walkways, illuminated discreetly after sundown by occasional low mushroom-lamps. With its lawns and bushes and low walls of sun-baked brick, the Hacienda was easily accessible to a prowler – who might, after all, merely be using its cocktail lounge or its gourmet restaurant.

When Andrei had visited the University earlier, to register for the conference, he had pretended to be a psychologist from a clinic in Zürich. He was on vacation, he'd said. He'd come to Tucson because of his hobby. His private passion in life, so he claimed, was cacti. He had intended to spend a whole week exploring the Saguaro and Organ Pipe national monuments. Only by chance did he learn about the conference.

Glancing through the list of delegates in a secretary's office, he was surprised, delighted to come upon the names of three or four old acquaintances. Oh, and here's another one: Dr Clare Conway from England. *Where's she staying during the conference?*

Oddly, he was the second person to have asked that same question today, though the previous enquiry had been by phone. Another old friend. An American.

A subsequent phone call by Andrei to the Hacienda had confirmed Dr Conway's reservation. *No, sir, not a double. The Visitors' Bureau definitely told us a single. Yes, sir, Cottage 12's a single all right . . .*

Cottages 11 and 12 shared a veranda fronting on a littie lawn. A white plastic table and chairs stood under a graceful paloverde tree. The camera whirred as it produced another Polaroid of the adjoining moonlit chalets.

A stiff metallic finger pressed against Andrei's neck.

'Don't move.'

His first thought was that a security guard had crept up on him. When a second person in jeans and thin leather jacket relieved him of the camera, he briefly imagined that a couple of members of the Navajo Nation had trailed him. The thin-faced individual was no Indian, though. The gun muzzle stayed against the base of Andrei's skull while his wallet slid free, and then the keys to the Pontiac. Were the two men muggers?

'Where are you parked?' a voice whispered.

Andrei told them, hoping that the men would run off and steal his car.

'We'll take a walk to your car. We'll have a conversation.'

5

It was a conversation about his interest in the chalet. And about the conference literature which was in the glove compartment. And about a photocopy of the clipping from the *National Investigator*.

While unheeding traffic drove past the parked Pontiac, Andrei nerved himself to ask, 'Who are you?'

Facing Andrei in the back of the Pontiac, the thin man had pushed up the sleeves of his jacket. On his left arm above the wrist, passing headlights revealed a tattoo of an angel in flight carrying a naked woman. Bearing a bare soul away up to heaven in his embrace. A typical motif from a medieval painting – except that this was modernized and erotic.

The other man – who had sat in the driving seat and searched for documents – was chunky, freckled and ginger-haired. He wore a military combat jacket with many pockets, open over a thin T-shirt emblazoned in psychedelic script with the phrase LOVE THY LORD.

'Who are you?'

The ginger man grinned into the driving mirror.

'We're Soul Brothers, you could say.'

But they weren't blacks.

14

'Maybe we can co-operate,' suggested Andrei. 'Who are you representing?'

'Oh, you'll co-operate,' the thin man assured him. His companion started the engine.

They drove to a cemetery on the far side of the interstate. There, his captors relocated Andrei into the trunk of the car. They wrapped parcel tape around his wrists and ankles and stuck some over his mouth.

Andrei guessed that the car returned downtown. Several times it halted, presumably at red lights. Then the engine died. Doors opened and shut. About ten minutes passed before the pair returned. Had they stopped at Andrei's hotel to collect his belongings? The cheap hotel wasn't hot on security.

When the car stopped again a short while later, only one door opened and closed. One of the two must be transferring to their own vehicle.

A hideous journey followed, during which Andrei lost all track of time. Despite some draughts, the air in the coffin-like trunk became stifling. By day he would surely have died. After an interminable distance the route became rough, bruisingly so. The Pontiac must be negotiating a track through wilderness.

6

On that hot serene Sunday morning in the first week of September, a punt glided along the Cam under the mellow seventeenth-century stonework of Dame Elizabeth's Bridge. Decorative cannonballs on the parapet railing seemed to balance precariously. The girl with the pole ducked low. As she crouched on the platform of the punt, trailing the pole as rudder, her sandy hair cascaded and her short bleached jeans skirt rucked up her tanned freckled thighs.

Lolling against a cushion, eyeing her, Orlando Sorel quoted suavely in French, '*La chair est triste, hélas! et j'ai lu tous les livres.*'

Georgette translated promptly, 'The flesh is sad, alas,

and I've read all the books. Mallarmé's poem, "Sea Breeze". You aren't tired of *me*, Orly, are you?'

As she straightened, shaking her mane, the punt drifted onwards. Across the lawns the knobbly Gothic spires and pinnacles of King's College Chapel rose high against a sapphire sky. Half a dozen other punts, several with camera-ready tourists, lazed along the next stretch of the narrow river. A large dragonfly darted and hovered by the punt, then veered away.

'So I come up to college specially, weeks early,' declared Georgette, 'and suddenly the flesh is sad! Is breakfast in bed such a bummer? Croissant crumbs in the sheets!'

Orlando brushed at his blue velvet jacket as if to dislodge phantom flakes of pastry. His floppy bow tie sported purple polka dots on a mustard background. The black hair which lapped his collar gleamed, somewhat oily. From beyond King's, the University Church clock started to sound the chimes which had been copied at Westminster and all over the world; Orlando consulted his watch.

'Don't be *touchy*.' He wouldn't tolerate petulance in others. 'Actually, I feel the need to get away. Not from you, my dear, but from Cambridge. A week in Paris might be amusing.'

Georgette began to pole enthusiastically along towards the next low bridge.

'Catching Le Shuttle tonight. I do have some things to look at in the Bibliothèque Nationale. The fact is, I've done something slightly naughty.'

'Do tell!'

Orlando pouted his lips.

As their punt neared King's Bridge, back at Dame Elizabeth's Bridge a wrought iron gate clanged shut. Through the Scholars' Garden a man came running alongside the river. Orlando gazed, hoisting himself higher on the cushion. The man's tweed jacket flapped. He clutched a newspaper like some baton which he must presently pass on to another hand.

'Oh, *precious*,' drawled Orlando.

In his late forties, the runner. Neatly trimmed chestnut

16

beard and moustache, receding curly hair. If he had been a few inches taller, he might have seemed robust. Being of less than average height, the impression was of a certain squat portliness. Still, he must possess stamina to keep up his pace – although his mouth was open, sucking in oxygen.

When the runner noticed who was upon the water, Orlando raised a limp hand in ironic salute. The man came to an abrupt halt. Puffing, he brandished the newspaper and shouted out, 'You *bastard*! You did this, didn't you—?'

Idly, Orlando swivelled his hand and hoisted his index finger.

Since the bearded man was unable to walk upon water to reach his taunter, he could only glare and resume his sprint. Another wrought iron gate swung open and shut. He dashed across the bridge.

'Goodness, Orly,' said Georgette. 'Jack Fox seems pretty steamed. What *have* you been up to?'

'Oh, it's *definitely* time for a trip to la belle France for me and my favourite pupil . . .'

It was also time for Georgette to crouch again, to pass under King's Bridge, but Orlando's attention was scarcely upon her.

7

His pace telling upon him by now, Jack Fox emerged at a jog-trot from the pinnacled gateway of King's College and turned right along King's Parade. He dodged ambling tourists. He angled across Trumpington Street, almost colliding with a bicycle.

Presently he was passing barred mullioned windows set in a wall the hue of honey fronting directly upon the pavement, before arriving at a castellated gateway. Coats of arms surmounted the Tudor arch. The statue of a bishop in red robe and golden crown prayed up above, sheltered by a portcullis-like half-canopy of intricate stonework. The stout oak double-doors were shut, but a wicket stood open. A knot of Japanese were eyeing the notice advising that

Spenser College was closed to the public until the afternoon. They peered into the deserted main court. In the centre of the lawn a fountain sprayed from a conch shell clasped by Neptune.

Jack cut across the grass to the far corner of that front quadrangle. Another archway led to cool flagstoned cloisters surrounding an inner lawn. Panting, he dodged into a stairway.

On the second-floor landing, he paused to recover himself outside a door over which the name *Dr C. Conway* was neatly lettered. Chest heaving, he banged with the fist that clutched the newspaper.

'Clare,' he called, though not too noisily. 'It's Jack.'

Briefly he rested his brow against the oak.

He was soon admitted.

He almost hustled a slim woman in her late twenties back into her study. Fawn slacks. Thin beige turtleneck sweater, with a saffron motif of Rodin's Thinker cradling his chin on his fist in cogitation. Her fair hair was swept tight into a ponytail.

'Clare, have you seen this—?'

'The *Sunday Scoop*? Of course not – why have you bought that rubbish?'

On the third page of the newspaper loomed her photograph. She was standing upon a beach, naked, looking carefree. Her breasts were pale little compact apples. Her hair hung loose. Her groin was vague, an unfocused plastic doll's. The story was titled: CAMBRIDGE PROF-ETTE SAYS YOUR COMPUTER WILL COME ALIVE.

Seizing the paper, she read falteringly, 'If anyone can make your hard disk lively, Clare can, says the *Scoop* . . .'

She started shaking, and subsided into a black leather armchair over which her academic gown with scarlet hood was draped.

'Jack, I don't understand—'

Bewilderment in that dainty oval face. Snubby nose wrinkling like a rabbit's. Tears of distress, or even terror, in her pale blue eyes.

'I popped out to the newsagent for a carton of milk,'

explained Jack. 'Heather wanted to make a sauce, and if we waited for Luke to unglue himself from his computer we'd wait forever ... Mr Singh in the shop said to me, "There's a Cambridge story in the *Sunday Scoop*, Dr Fox." It's Orlando's doing, without a doubt! I actually saw him along the Backs – in a punt with some doting darling. He gave me the finger.'

'South of France, last summer, that's when. I remember! He only snapped one shot of me like that. I was an idiot to let him.'

'You were feeling blithe.'

'What a fool it makes me look now.'

'The jealous petulant bastard! He's trying to screw up our trip.'

Clare gaped blankly at the newspaper. 'How bad *is* the write-up?'

On her desk a computer screen displayed the first page of the final draft of the talk Clare would be giving in Tucson. *The Brain as a Computer of Light* was the title. Books on anatomy, neurology and psychology populated shelves. Files had colonized half of a black leather sofa. One window stood open over a midget balcony occupied by blood-red geraniums in small terracotta urns. The door to her bedroom was open, the bed still unmade.

'Fairly bad,' admitted Jack.

'Oh God,' as she forced herself to read, 'a journalist phoned me a few days ago. He said he was from the *Guardian*. Now it's all here in this rag. Not in any sensible form, of course! Buzz words and juicy bits. "Brilliant Junior Research Fellow at Spenser College, Cambridge..." "Funded by Matsushima electronics giant..." "Fierce race for the quantum chip..." "Computers thousands of times faster..." "Quantums use alternative universes to do their thinking in..." "Prof-ette Clare says *human* brains use quantums – that's how we're conscious of being alive."' She groaned. '"So if computers use quantums, they'll become alive too...." "Clare's off to the Hard Question Conference in the Arizona desert to hammer this out. We hear it's hot in those parts. Our hard question is: will she be stripping off there too?" I'll sue them,' she said. 'Do you think I can sue?'

'At least they air-brushed you a bit. Family newspaper.'

She thumped a fist on her knee as if to swat a fly. 'I confirmed that bloody reporter's queries, but not in these words. He sounded legitimate. Quantums, indeed! As if they're tiny trained fleas, jumping around in a box. And this damned photo! What next? Do I pose for *Penthouse* in my gown? Sure route to academic esteem.'

'If Orlando took the photo, I think he owns it.'

'It's *my* body.'

'You mustn't knot up, or you'll get a migraine. May I?' Jack moved behind Clare to massage her shoulders. She flinched, then she let herself relax.

'Oh God,' she murmured, 'will he send Heather a clipping?'

'Anonymously, like that wretched phone call . . .'

'I'd much rather you stayed here, Jack, but what about the milk?' The milk was a familiar item she could fasten upon.

'I'll tell Heather I bumped into, oh, Phil Martingale. He wanted to know all about which groovy gurus I'll be interviewing in California after the conference. I have to indulge the head of faculty, don't I?'

'Wasn't it Martingale who approved your travel application?'

'Oh, back in May. He'll probably have forgotten the details by now. What else can you expect from an expert on memory functions?'

Clare almost smiled. 'I do need a friend right now – and *you're* that friend – but you'd better hurry home.'

Jack squeezed her shoulders.

She sighed and smoothed the newspaper over her knees. 'Behold,' she said, 'my breasts, which Orlando has seen.' Seen, and more than seen, as Jack knew achingly well. His glance towards the open bedroom was wistful indeed.

'It's inhibiting, isn't it, this photo?' she continued. 'It acts as negative pornography – for us! I'm sure it's part of Orlando's scheme. To make me feel sick about sex.'

'Surely he must believe we've already been to bed together—'

'He *did* make me feel sick about sex. Specifically with him – so dominating of my feelings! I'm damned if I'll have my emotions manipulated by him while I'm away in another continent!'

Jack could still hope. But another anxiety loomed.

'What about the Matsu people, when they read this? I mean, the publicity aspect?'

'*They* certainly won't try to pressure me to cancel our trip at the last moment.' She darted a glance at the computer screen. 'But now I suppose I'll have to cut out any speculative bits about quantum computers achieving self-awareness! I'll stick to the main theme of quantum effects in the human brain.'

'How can you be so sure Matsu won't pressure you?'

She dithered. 'You really must go, or Heather will smell a rat.'

'The rat,' he said, 'is Orlando.'

'Don't get into another fight with him. Please, even if he tries to provoke you. It would only make matters worse.'

Jack nodded. 'I might end up in court for assault rather than flying to America.'

Before Jack could make his departure, on her door there came several brisk rat-tats.

Jack opened the door to discover a burly elderly man with short grey hair dressed in black suit and crested college tie.

The head porter peered past Jack, disapproving stolidly as only a senior servant could.

'Dr Conway,' he announced to Clare with a blunt politeness, 'the Master asks that you call upon him, as soon as is convenient. May I tell him you will do so?'

As Clare rose, the newspaper slid to the floor. The porter's gaze followed it. 'I see that you appreciate the reason, Dr Conway.' So saying, Rogers departed.

Jack half closed the oak door.

'Does Rogers scan all the newspapers in his lodge?'

'Only the rubbishy ones. He never liked it when the college accepted women members.'

'I hadn't realized.'

'That's because you aren't a woman. Now I'll have to change into something dismal and wear my gown—'

8

When the walkie-talkie by the bed beeped, Gabriel Soul awoke and answered within a few seconds. Naked beside him under the silk sheet, Kath moaned softly and rubbed herself against him. Being privileged to share his bed that night, obviously she wished to make the most of it.

It must be all of two months since he had last taken Kath to his bed. All of the women in the community understood that to sleep with Gabe only once or twice was ample for their souls. They must never be possessive or jealous, or feel – if they were unattractive in the worldly sense – that he neglected them. Although Kath was cursed with a face like a horse, from the neck downwards she was a fine and enthusiastic filly. By now Gabe had thumbed on the halo lighting. He smacked Kath on her silken rump.

'Not now, girl. I'm busy. *Say again, Billy.* You're breaking up.'

A hundred tiny bulbs shone softly all around the edge of the ceiling. The bedroom could have been the interior of an enormous stretched limo equipped with a bed big enough for four persons. Sometimes the bed was used for three or four, during Gabe's teachings. On such occasions he would set the halo lighting racing so that a luminous band sped around the room, comet-like, ever faster, an image of the soul accelerating ecstatically towards a transcendent climax.

In the soft constant glow as of now: some fine Monterey furniture, an open fireplace for burning mesquite logs, and erotic Hindu frescos adorning the plaster of the walls.

'When you and Jersey get him here, Billy, rush him to the Truth Room. Keep him disoriented.'

Gabe laid down the walkie-talkie.

'What's happening?' Kath asked.

'Someone was snooping somewhere,' he told her uninformatively.

'Around the Shelter?'

'No. Far away, and hours ago. Take yourself off, Kath. Share yourself. I need to meditate. I need to foresee.'

She slid obediently from the bed. Gathering a robe from the floor, she padded softly away.

Once Kath had gone, Gabe doused the halo lighting and thumbed the remote for the curtains. Drapes hummed open, admitting the bright moon. Sitting up high in bed, he stared out.

Between descending crags the land sloped steeply towards a desert plain dotted with creosote shrubs and fuzzy chollas. Mounds near at hand were spoil-heaps from long-abandoned silver workings. Miners had long ago stripped the vicinity bare of wood. Although there was water underground, feeding the deep well of the Soul Shelter, trees still hadn't re-established themselves hereabouts.

A bat flitted across the window; then another. Bats had colonized the miners' tunnels in the cliff which soared almost vertically behind the Soul Shelter, serving as its rear wall. The little beasts used some natural air shaft for their exits and entries. Just as well Kath missed seeing the bats. She hated those.

How submissively she had slipped away, even though she would be missing a full night in his bed after two months of what mundane minds might regard as neglect. This neglect had only enhanced Kath's excitement, as he had known it must. Gabe had even toyed with the idea of spending the entire time with Kath in abstinence; but he had relented.

Blessèd Kath! Bereft of any close family until she had joined the Shelter. And so scared of death, until Gabe had shown her how to strengthen her soul through ecstasy. She brought a legacy of a million dollars with her, sufficient for many luxuries and defensive necessities, including Barrett

23

rifles, AK-47s, .50 calibre machine-guns, grenades, a rocket launcher, better vehicles, a larger store of food, and the equipping of a special medical room to screen new recruits for AIDS and hepatitis, in case their certificates were false.

Gabe wouldn't play favourites.

It wasn't always easy being the leader of a community of sixty women and forty men, all sharing one with another. The certainty that their sexual rites fortified the soul, so that they would all survive after death, was the firm cement.

On a few occasions the cement had cracked. Gabe's hard boys – amongst whom were Billy and Jersey, who were now heading home – had coped. A corpse or two had been buried deep in the desert.

An exalted passion – an amalgam of rage and rapture – came over Gabe as he gazed out. He would be the loving saviour of the world, and its judge, sorting out true souls from zombie-people.

Almost, he felt inspired to thumb a button and sound the summons bell, to bring a hundred people from their beds to the refectory so he could address them for an hour or more.

The vision which Gabe had experienced five years earlier was glowing in him: of a world full of zombie-people, of sham automata. True souls shone only here and there. And now the most insidious of the zombies were trying to focus science upon the soul. To dissect the soul. To create artificial souls inside machines.

Soon Gabe's hard men would need to be very hard. They would be striking blows. If any of them died in the process, they could be sure of immortality. He could almost hear himself declaiming in the refectory already.

The guiding voice was rising up within Gabe. With an effort of will he relaxed. Now wasn't the time to thumb that button, not with Jersey and Billy bringing their captive closer.

Far away across the flat, a tiny shaft of light dipped and dimmed at the head of a plume of moonlit dust.

9

In a large cellar cut from naked rock and lit by fluorescent strips, a big partitioned cage stood on steel legs three feet high.

Roped to a metal chair, and stripped to the waist, Andrei had been manhandled under the cage and up through a hole in the unoccupied half.

From the waist upwards he was enclosed. His arms were fastened criss-cross over his chest, held high. Straps on his wrists ran over his shoulders and down his back. He could move his elbows in and out like flippers in a pin-ball game.

A movable grille separated him from a hideous reptile. The creature was a third of a metre long from the forked-tongued snout to the end of the fat tail. Warty bumps studded its mottled black-and-orange skin. As the ginger man who was called Jersey rattled a stick across the mesh of the cage, the beast inhaled and exhaled fiercely.

The thin man with the tattoo on his forearm, whose name was Billy, crouched down and Andrei felt a jab in the thigh. A needle-prick. He'd been injected with something.

'A Gila's so poisonous,' Jersey said casually, 'so painfully slowly poisonous, that people used to think it had no anus. *Shit* built up inside it, till it could bite some other animal and purge itself. It doesn't have fangs like a snake. So it grabs hold instead. It chews and it grinds. It just won't let go. The pain can make you insane . . .'

Jersey poked the stick inside the cage to prod the reptile's tail. Lumbering towards Andrei, the beast opened its jaws, but it couldn't reach him. Not yet.

'Nowadays there's an antidote. You'll be screaming for it. Why not save yourself the trouble?'

'This is barbaric,' protested Andrei.

The cage wasn't the only barbaric feature. On one wall hung a head mounted upon a mahogany plaque. The head wasn't that of a bighorn sheep or a mountain lion. It was a man's crewcut head. His mouth was wide open in a bestial snarl. His teeth were bared. Surely that was a resin model. The gaping eyes were certainly made of glass.

25

Noting the shift in Andrei's attention, Billy rested his hand in the mouth of the trophy.

'Johnny here's real, all right. Some species are endangered, you see. You need a licence to hunt. Rich men sometimes pay no heed. They're fanatics. They want every damn head in their den back home. So they bribe a guide. People disappear in the desert quite easily. Johnny here met with a little accident.'

'We can pay for my release,' said Andrei.

Billy patted the cheek of the trophy. 'Death, I despise you,' he told the head, as if uttering a private prayer.

'Who are we—?'

A newcomer had entered the cellar so softly, barefoot. He wore a voluminous embroidered white silk shirt without collar, bunched at the waist by a sash, over blue silk pyjama trousers. His longish slicked-down black hair was parted in the middle in the style of an earlier century. His face was thin and pale, though his lips were thickly sensual and of a blueish hue which glistened slightly, as if he emphasized or protected them with lipstick or salve. A curly little black beard. Such bright intense eyes. Such presence. It was as if a latterday Jesus had walked into the cellar, or perhaps a frontier preacher from a hundred years ago. Or even . . .

Recognition shocked Alexei.

The man bore a distinct physical resemblance – which he surely played up by his peasant-style shirt and hairstyle – to Rasputin, to the seductive guru who had beguiled the Tsar and Tsarina before the Revolution.

At once so sensual and so spiritual, so captivating, so charismatic – with such a cunning instinct for power, with such mystic obsessions.

Sheer bewildered terror possessed Andrei – not only at the poisonous animal so close to him, and the head upon the wall, but at this . . . manifestation.

Who *were* these people who had captured him?

He had been half-dragged and half-marched from the trunk of the Pontiac towards a sprawling fortress heaped at the

26

foot of a sheer precipice. Part adobe, part painted concrete blocks. Part gimcrack palace, part fort. Outbuildings of timber and tin, and of clapboard and corrugated iron.

Inside, he had almost bumped into a lovely young tanned flaxen-haired woman dressed in shorts and halter-top. Such a strange rapt stare was on her face. She had seemed oblivious to his own brief presence as he was hustled by and along a plastered passageway, then down cement stairs to a heavy oak door . . .

'Who's *we*?' repeated the guru-man. Jersey rattled the cage again. The Gila Monster huffed and puffed.

The reptile seemed huge, prehistoric, malevolent. Andrei realized that a drug had taken effect. His senses were enhanced. It certainly wasn't any antidote he had been injected with. Quite the opposite. It was something to make him feel and see more exquisitely. How brightly yellow was the creature's tongue, flickering from the black warty snout. Andrei's skin was so sensitive that his bonds were a torment. How cramped his arms were. Their pressure against his chest was terrible, a medieval torture.

10

'So,' this American Rasputin said to caged Andrei, '*Informex*, as you call it, though some people might call it *Infamous*' – this drew an appreciative chuckle from Billy – 'is a gang of Russian ex-scientists who got pissed off because they weren't being paid.'

Andrei sweated and shivered. He could think, yet it was as if his thoughts were being summoned implacably by his questioner.

'We launched into private enterprise,' Andrei confessed. 'Collecting and selling sensitive data to the highest bidder. We can pay you well to release me.' His whole world was the cage and the vile monster and the face.

Rasputin laughed, as if an offer of money was ridiculous.

On a table were scattered the contents of Andrei's travel

27

bag, and his passport of convenience, his Polaroid photos, conference details. His captors had brought everything. His spare clothes, his portable StarWriter. Uppermost was the photocopy from the *National Investigator*.

'So,' said Rasputin, 'this sexy lady will be carrying sensitive stuff about computers supposedly becoming conscious? Stuff which you were going to steal?'

'The story might just be nonsense.'

'I can see into your heart, Andrei, or whatever your real name is. I have intuition, much more than you.' Rasputin crumpled the photocopy and threw it on the floor. 'I don't need that. I already saw the story. Why do you suppose Billy and Jersey were checking out the Hacienda? Andrei, you're trying to head me off so that your colleagues can swoop on a soft target. Tell me about them, and about how you communicate . . .'

Andrei was dizzy. The face of his interrogator spooked him as if he were a paralysed rabbit and the American Rasputin was a stoat. The drug might had been mild, as hallucinogens went, so that he would remain lucid; it still magnified the significance of everything abominably, domineeringly. His situation was frightful, drug or no drug. The cage, the cage . . . The creature. The snarling head on the wall. The face of his inquisitor.

11

Mainly, the Truth Room was used to overcome fears or to strip the heart bare. Employing bats or scorpions or snakes, or in this case a Gila Monster which one of the hard boys had captured. To be locked in here in the dark with bats or bugs was sometimes a useful rite. Psychic trauma disrupted the old programming. Then, swiftly, the transition from terror to ecstasy – from hell to heaven upstairs.

Seldom was the room used for punishment, although everyone in the Soul Shelter was aware of the possibility.

'You're still a Commie at heart, aren't you?' insisted Rasputin.

Again, Jersey slid the grille a little way aside before jerking it back into place. Andrei clawed at his own shoulders.

'I don't know,' he mumbled. 'Our country's ruined. What do we do?'

'You don't mind selling stolen designs for machine-minds to fucking North Korean Commies.'

'I didn't say . . . Not necessarily Koreans . . . The English-woman mightn't really know how far Matsushima have got . . . Please release me,' he begged. 'Informex will pay.'

'It will surely pay,' agreed his tormentor. 'Tell me again how Night and Dawn and Noon communicate.'

12

Blessedly, Andrei was eased out from under the cage.

On his chair, he sat so far away from the prehistoric monster; and *it* was securely caged, not him.

Jersey winked.

'Actually the Gila's poison ain't lethal at all. Be stupid of it to kill its enemies. Then they'd never learn the lesson to leave it alone.'

Stupid to kill. Leave alone. How weighted with meaning and hope were such words.

'*Fundamentally*, a Gila's real timid. You got to provoke it to attack. Mind you, its jaws can maul you, and the venom's pretty unpleasant – that's true enough. Couldn't expect a Commie Russian spy to know the local wildlife. Most locals don't. See a Gila, a guy'll shoot it to pieces as if he's some hero. Blast it to fucking pieces.'

'Take Night out into the desert,' said Rasputin, 'and *release* him.'

Jersey nodded. 'We'll do just that.'

29

13

After Gabe had ascended from the cellar, the imperative urge to speak claimed him. Such tireless energy was in him. By now it was four in the morning, almost time for his people to rise in any event.

He summoned the Brothers and Sisters urgently to the refectory, sleepy-eyed and in their nightwear. Soon a hundred bodies crowded benches along the trestle tables.

Gabe railed against Godless materialism and against prohibitive government at home which was so similar to Communism, using AIDS to terrify people about sexuality which was the key to the soul's salvation. He railed against the attempts of materialist zombie laboratories to manufacture machine-minds.

Such a power was in him that perhaps some of his utterances were disconnected.

'We'll smash the Tin Man of San Jose while it's still no more than a child—

'We'll make it hard for the Hard Questioners at their talkfest in Tucson. Though not too hard, do you hear? I shall have business there. I shall be the worm in the enemy's apple—'

Some of his audience were still sleepy. They dug their fingernails into their palms to stay alert.

'Hard Question conference, hmm? You know what a hard question's supposed to be? They say easy questions are about how different bits of our brains work. Wow, that's easy? What conceit they have! But the hard question, now that's the question of how we have a uni-fied – now you all say it after me – a *yuuuni-fied* sense of self—'

His audience chorused dutifully.

'That's right, Brothers and Sisters. How do all the different things happening in our heads produce *consciousness*? That's the big goddamn bonanza mystery of all time, so say the zombie scientists. Why do we have conscious *experiences*? Why does blue feel like blue? Why do you *feel* that you have a *self*, that's *you*—?

30

'There's no earthly reason for it! We could do without consciousness. We could have a civilization of ant-men who never felt they had *selves*. Or of robot-men—!

'Crack this problem open, and your zombie scientists will try their damnedest to build robots and computers with conscious minds! Our successors here on Earth—!'

Gabe signalled. The chalice of multivitamins and buzz pills began to circulate around the tables.

'*We* know how the soul thrives,' he proclaimed. 'We know how to stiffen it and brace it – through *intensity of bodily joy* – so that when our bodies die our soul sails onwards, immortal. That's through the laying on of hands, that's through the union of our bodies! That's through the communion I share with you personally, Soul Sisters, and through you with the Brothers. For it was given to me to know this, and be *vigorous* and *vital* enough to share unselfishly—

'When zombie-people die their souls dissolve like a snowman in a bonfire—

'*Our* souls go into the *Virtuality*, that spiritual virtual reality where we shall all be together, perfect in our virtual bodies as we were at the age of seventeen—

'Zombies may come to attack us, Brothers and Sisters. If the zombies kill any of us they'll merely set our souls free to leap into the Virtuality now, not in thirty or forty years' time. And if we kill them, their souls will evaporate—'

He talked for half an hour. A pressure of excitement had mounted in his congregation. Vitality had coursed. Eventually Gabe flourished the golden key.

'I declare Congress in session! Open the Door of Delight, Mary!'

Thrilled, a short plump woman in a lace négligé hastened to take the key. She unlocked an oak door, broad and stout; swung it open.

Mellow multi-coloured halo lighting within revealed the supple rubber floor of what Gabe claimed was the largest waterbed in the world, and a useful emergency reservoir too. It occupied the entire congress chamber.

Soon, garments discarded, the whole community

crowded that chamber in mutual communion – except for such as Billy and Jersey, who were otherwise engaged. The halo lighting raced. Speakers mounted up by the ceiling pounded out Wagner's Venusberg music.

14

'Would you care for a glass of sherry, Dr Conway?'

Her voice might shake or squeak, so Clare simply jerked her head by way of refusal. Behind the Master, on a rosewood sideboard beneath an eighteenth-century print of the college cloisters, next to the decanter and glasses, a certain newspaper lay discreetly folded.

Stout and florid-faced, Sir Anthony Kershaw was an economist. An antique watch nestled in a fob pocket of his waistcoat, linked by a silver chain. The Master's long drawing room boasted several splendid clocks, all of which were nearing noon.

'In that case, let us sit.'

He gestured at a sofa, where Clare subsided in her gown. Gathering the newspaper, Sir Anthony settled himself in an armchair opposite.

'I've already seen the *Scoop*,' she said, 'and I can't tell you how angry and humiliated I feel.'

'Likewise, on behalf of the college,' agreed Sir Anthony. He cocked an eyebrow. 'Do you regularly take this newspaper?'

'Certainly not. A friend showed it to me just a while ago. I was hoaxed by a journalist pretending to be from the *Guardian*. Much of the original information and that wretched photograph obviously came from Orlando Sorel.'

'Your informant being Dr Fox, I presume. I have not forgotten about the fisticuffs outside hall during Easter Term, when, as I understand it, you were the precipitating factor.'

Clare spoke softly. 'I very much resent that, Master.'

'I resent the college's name being exposed to mockery.'

'Through no fault of mine. Sorel is to blame for this.'

'If Sorel supplied the photograph, that would certainly seem to be so. In which case I shall speak to him very sternly. His behaviour really is becoming . . . too colourful. Brilliant on Baudelaire, though, they say. Right now I'd like to know what *you* intend, Dr Conway.'

'Quite frankly, I'd like to murder him. Though of course I shan't do anything of the sort.'

'Not being in the Wild West, yet, where I understand you and Dr Fox are heading next week.'

'We're attending a conference on consciousness, both of us for our own separate professional reasons.'

The Master shrugged.

'Actually, I was referring to any legal action you might contemplate. Any court case would very likely make – how should I put it? – titillating reading. I strongly advise against it. The national newspapers would have a field day. I'm sure we don't want our excellent relations with Matsushima and the rest of the Science Park compromised by vulgarity.'

He sighed.

'What I propose right now is to phone the editor of the *Herald* – I know Bill Henderson quite well – and request him not to pick up this story. The student paper can be dealt with through the Proctors' office when term resumes in October. You may find a larger audience than usual at your lectures.'

'I didn't do this to popularize myself! I didn't do it at all.'

A clock began to strike. Another joined it, and a third, and a fourth. Chimes resounded around the drawing room, derailing Clare's train of thought.

15

The house in Hobson Terrace was one of a long row of two-storey stone dwellings built in the nineteenth century. Most had recovered their original sandy hue courtesy of water jets during gentrification over the past twenty years. A few remained defiantly grimy, poor teeth in an otherwise extended grin of contentment. Whenever another old lady died, her former residence would undergo conversion and sprucing. Most of the attics had been converted and dormer windows jutted from the blue tiled roofs. Cars, in residents' bays, blocked one side of the narrow street, all pointing in the only permitted direction.

As soon as Jack let himself in, bearing the carton of milk conspicuously and breathing heavily, Lucas, in jeans and Iron Maiden T-shirt, came scurrying. Tall at fifteen, and skinny, the boy had inherited Heather's glossy black hair. His he wore gelled into short puckish curls, a choice which hardly helped banish his acne and which obliged frequent washing of pillowslips.

'Dad,' clamoured the boy, 'you missed a phone call—'

'Shit – What call?'

'Dad, you're always telling me not to swear.'

'Yes. Shhh!' In case Heather heard his anxiety. 'What call, Luke?'

Elatedly: 'Crissy's been arrested and hauled into court and fined a hundred quid.'

Jack could relax. He proceeded through into the pine kitchen. Bunches of dried roses, statice, bullrushes and seedpods of poppies crowned the tops of the units in profusion. A Welsh dresser displayed blue and orange Portuguese plates. Heather sat at the farmhouse table recycled from the timbers of defunct cotton mills. In her Sunday morning dressing gown, Jack's wife had a half-empty glass of sherry before her, and a scatter of newspaper, the usual *Observer*, nothing sleazy.

'What kept you?' she inquired coolly. Her hair was pinned back, lending her a severe and earnest look, although her earrings – little painted wooden parrots – were a memory of her bygone, more Bohemian style. She had become an ample woman, and could cut a presence when appearing in a Magistrates' Court or when canvassing for the local Liberal candidate.

'I bumped into Phil Martingale. He went on for ages

34

about New Age groups in the States. What's this about Crissy?'

Heather eyed him. 'Since you weren't here, should I bother telling you?'

'Be fair. It was you who asked me to go out for milk.'

'And now it's too late to make a sauce. We'll just throw the leftovers away and have cheese sandwiches. I didn't ask you to spend the best part of an hour.'

'Phil . . . Oh, never mind him – what about Crissy?'

Lucas volunteered, with evident relish, 'She was demoing about the Criminal Injustice Bill, as she calls it. Doing some trespassing. Bone-headed, I call it. What's the point, Dad? The Travellers are finished in this country. They found some *draw* on her too. She'll be back in court for that in a couple of weeks.'

'Draw?'

'Resin, Dad. Hash.'

'And me a probation officer,' Heather said pointedly. 'If you hadn't been so interested in crazy states of mind, Jack, I wonder if Christina would have run off the moment she was of age. She did it to spite me.'

'The moment she was of New Age,' quipped Lucas.

'You can't blame me—' Yet Heather could. 'Anyway, the Criminal Justice Bill *is* unjust.'

'And effective, even if I agree it's unfair. I promised her I'd send a money order. She can pick it up at Glastonbury post office.'

'When I'm twenty,' predicted Lucas, 'and earning a bomb from IBM, Crissy'll still be hauling some scuzzy mongrel around on a string, with her hair in dirty dreadlocks and rings all the way up her ears – in Ireland or Spain, if she has any sense.'

Conceivably this was true.

'You ought to have been here to speak to her,' Heather told Jack. 'No, on second thoughts you'd probably encourage her.'

'Actually,' said Jack, 'I miss Crissy.'

'Will you miss Luke and me, when she's in court for drugs, and you're in America with your girlfriend?'

'I've *told* you, Clare Conway isn't anything of the sort.'

'I'm neglecting my keyboard.' So saying, Lucas withdrew himself diplomatically.

'May I join you in a sherry?' asked Jack.

Heather promptly drained her glass and pushed it across the table. 'Pour yourself some.' Which defeated the purpose of his gambit, though he could dearly use a drink.

'I need to go to this Tucson conference,' he explained patiently, 'because my field happens to be the structures of thought which prompt people to develop theories about the mind. The beliefs. Brain as some sort of clockwork in the nineteenth century. Brain as a telephone exchange. Brain as a computer.'

'I don't need to hear the lecture again—'

'And now the inspiration is *quantum theory* because quantum theory's basically a mystery. So is the mind. One mystery might explain the other mystery – which is what the Tucson conference is partly about.'

Heather cocked an eyebrow. 'And this is Clare Conway's speciality. So you need to study her in action.'

Jack contrived an exasperated shrug. 'Also, I need to visit various New Age types in California. This confusion about Clare Conway is all caused by that conceited shit Orlando Sorel. It was definitely Sorel who phoned you ... when was it? Back in May?' Jack could remember precisely when. 'God knows what he might think up next.'

Water off a duck's back. 'Why should he need to think up something *next*? It's September now. What could provoke him?'

'If he reacts to this American trip the way you seem to be reacting—' Jack was steering perilously close to the truth. He stared at the empty glass, wishing it was full. 'When Sorel phoned you, it was shortly after Clare Conway lost her sister—'

'Oh yes. In a car accident in California, wasn't it?' As if Heather didn't know.

'In a car. At traffic lights in San Francisco. In the Tenderloin. I've told you. A mugger shot her sister.'

'How uncomfortable, being shot in the Tenderloin.'

'That isn't funny.'

'No, it isn't, is it, Jack? None of it's very funny.'

'Clare Conway was grieving. Nothing could have been less romantic.'

'And you were comforting her.'

'Only in Sorel's warped mind could a spot of psychological support equate with—'

'—the start of an affair? Is *my* mind warped? Do I imagine things?' Heather contemplated the dried dead flowers above the pine units. 'I hardly care what you do.' Yet she did. 'I have my own work. Even if Christina is far up the creek, Luke has to have a good future. If anything you do unsettles Luke, I'll slaughter you.'

'Shall I,' suggested Jack, 'make those sandwiches?'

16

Grief-stricken at her sister's death, Clare had sat in the black leather armchair in her study in a severe skirt and white blouse and a charcoal-coloured cardigan which she clutched around herself. The skirt was of academic black but it was the colour of mourning too. From the lawn outside came the muted clunk and clop of croquet balls.

If she had settled on the sofa she would have been encouraging Jack to sit next to her – there, where pairs of students would perch for their weekly supervisions. She hadn't invited this degree of closeness.

By now her flu had ebbed away into unpredictable spasms of harsh coughing. It was the flu which had stopped her from flying to San Francisco to attend her twin sister's cremation and escort the ashes home across North America and Greenland and the Atlantic, so that the dust and cinders could be scattered in their father's garden in North London. That duty had fallen entirely upon the shoulders of Miranda's travelling companion, Ivan 'the terrible' Lewis, a commodities trader.

Punctuated by the dull collision of wooden balls, Clare talked to Jack about Miranda, stock market analyst, devotee of fast cars and fast times. An identical twin, apart from a scar on her forehead which Miranda had worn her hair – now incinerated – to hide, souvenir of a shunt on the motorway near Heathrow. And apart from the pace of Miranda's life.

'I always worried she would die in a car,' Clare said. 'And she did. Though not in the way I imagined!'

Gunned down at the wheel by some unidentified punk, who probably needed money for a fix.

'It's as if the market suddenly collapsed for Ivan,' she was telling him. 'Yet he had his position covered. Another girlfriend's in the wings. I don't think Miranda cared deeply about Ivan. Just Dad and I did.'

Clare's mother had died a few years earlier from meningitis. Her dad suffered from a mild, though advancing, case of Parkinson's. He could look after himself, but he had been forced to take early retirement from the bank where he'd been manager.

'They're sweeping out all the older staff if they can, to cut costs,' she had seethed. 'Soon there'll be no one left with proper experience. I suppose Dad's better off in his garden – with Miranda's ashes well dug in.'

Had Jack been next to her, he would have put an arm around her. Coughs hacked from Clare. She clutched a tissue to her lips.

She began talking about Orlando Sorel too. On this vulnerable, yet blighted and neutering occasion, for the first time she had fully revealed her feelings to Jack. She jerked a thumb towards the mild noise of croquet combat.

'Last summer Orlando actually climbed in through that window several times by night. There's a route over the roof – not that he ever returned by it. Too much of a heave up. He would *ravish* me, Jack. That's the only word for it. It seemed so romantic.'

Did Jack really wish to hear this? Oh he needed to, but did he enjoy hearing such a confession, even if it related to a thoroughly rejected lover? Absurd jealousy squirmed in him, and the desire to enjoy what Orlando had enjoyed, however inappropriate this urge was just now.

38

'I was swept off my feet,' Clare murmured. 'Now I keep the window locked at night, in case he tries again.'

'That would be rape – not,' and Jack hesitated before uttering the word, 'ravishment.'

'He could be so witty and charming, Orlando could.' Was Clare unaware of twisting a tiny knife in Jack's soul? 'And we did have a great time in the South of France.'

'In America,' Jack promised, 'this autumn, *we'll* have a fine time.' The trip was already considerably more than a twinkle in the eye. 'Fine times will return.'

'Miranda won't return, except as flowers in Dad's garden.'

Clare had begun to weep. For her sister, for her father, for herself.

Unable to touch her, Jack had whispered, 'Poor Clare.'

She gazed at him through tears. Maybe it had been the wrong thing for him to say.

'Poor Clares are the names of nuns, Jack! I'm not a nun.'

Yet she would behave rather like one, because of how Orlando Sorel had enthralled her until she spurned his manipulative selfish spell . . .

After a while Clare began to talk distractedly about work and research, an anchor for the mind. This was hardly the first such conversation, but she needed her identity reaffirming.

Out at the Science Park, Matsushima was trying to make light-chips. Clare's own speciality was the human brain, yet what Matsushima were working towards intersected at a crucial point with her own research.

Matsu would trap an electron in a tiny cage of atoms. A two-nanosecond flash of laser light would kick the electron into an excited state. In that state the electron represented one bit of data – as opposed to a zero.

What if the laser only flashed for one nanosecond instead of two? According to quantum theory, the electron must simultaneously be excited *and* unexcited. It must exist in two possible overlapping universes – until it was observed. As soon as it was observed, it must be in one state or the other.

Jack too was excited – yet he could not be excited. How his universe overlapped Clare's. How intrusive any observer would be.

A hundred thousand quantum dots on a microchip! Each dot responding to its own frequency of light. Such a quantum microchip would perform calculations in many parallel universes all at once, not just in one. A result would emerge thousands of times faster than with an ordinary computer . . .

How slowly must a result emerge from his and her relationship?

'If you compute with photons, Jack, doing different quantum things at the same time in different universes – do you see, it's so like the way the *brain* must achieve conscious awareness—!'

He listened. He listened. She was talking to staunch her pain.

Each cell in the brain was scaffolded by a lattice of tiny tubes. Microtubules, they were called. These microtubules were just the right size to act as waveguides for photons . . .

'So the cartoons are true, eh?' joked Jack. 'Whenever we think, a lightbulb switches on in our heads.'

'Orlando made just the same quip! Before I packed him in—'

'How much could Orlando understand about any of this?' Jack asked airily.

'He made out he was fascinated. The joke's almost true, you know!'

Brain cells could indeed emit light internally, Clare insisted. The tubules guided the photons and caused *super-radiance*. The resulting 'quantum coherence' harmonized the state of tubules across wide brain areas.

'That's instantaneous action at a distance! It seems impossible, but we know that quantum linkage acts at a distance. Hey presto: our thoughts have unity, instead of just being lots of separate operations. We're conscious. We're self-aware—'

How aware was she of his excitement at her intellectual fervour?

40

'This may well imply,' she confided, 'that because of coherence, quantum computers will also achieve self-awareness. Haven't I already told you this, Jack? Or was I telling—?'

That bane, Orlando – much that Orlando would genuinely care, unlike Jack.

Another fit of coughing seized Clare, as if to torment her with the memory of a missed funeral. To punish her for straying from her grief.

17

Sunshine, following on showers, lanced through the mullioned windows of the crowded dining hall. Most of the available space upon the panelled walls was occupied by oil paintings of former Masters. A few sported ringleted, powdered wigs. Others wore clerical black, or ermine-trimmed gowns over more modern suits. A din of chatter and cutlery on china arose from gowned undergraduates.

High Table, on its dais which spanned the hall, offered to the dozen dons present rather finer fare than the thin slices of pork with roast potatoes down below. That evening: a choice of medallions of venison or turbot mornay.

In the absence of the Master the Junior Dean had recited the Latin grace. Obliged to dine in hall that evening to fulfil his quota, Jack sat between a terse mathematician and a zoologist called Lascelles who was full of a recent field trip to the Cameroons to study butterflies.

Orlando Sorel had arrived long after the grace and the soup. He was clutching a half-full bottle of Burgundy which he must have brought from the buttery. Other diners were drinking small beers or water. Subsiding next to Lascelles, Sorel poured himself wine and called for a serving of venison.

Presently he scowled past Lascelles. Butterflies fluttered in Jack's tummy amongst the chewed deer and green beans.

'Let me give you a word of advice, Fox,' Sorel snarled.

'*Back off*. She doesn't need your shoulder to cry on. You're taking advantage of her when she's vulnerable.'

'That's a lie,' snapped Jack. 'Do you suppose it's *your* job to exploit her?'

'I say,' said Lascelles, 'do keep your voices down.'

'Yes, shut up.' Too late, Jack realized how drunk Sorel already was.

'*Va faire t'enculer!*' Sorel shouted at Jack.

'You're even noisier in a foreign language,' the zoologist grumbled. 'What's that supposed to mean?'

'It means,' and Sorel leered at Jack, 'bugger off. Go fuck yourself. Not Clare!'

Undergraduates close by were paying avid attention. Another thirty seconds and would Sorel be tossing his wine?

Dumping his napkin on his chair, Jack departed quickly through the side door to the Senior Common Room. Was a commotion to his rear the sound of Sorel staggering erect and knocking over his bottle and maybe his chair as well?

Hastening through that deserted lounge lined with leather volumes, Jack exited on to stone steps leading down to the gravel path around the now-radiant front court. The wet lawn gleamed, bedewed as if by stone Neptune's spray. A dozen undergraduates had spilled out of the buttery, beers in hand, tanking up before second hall. Since gowns weren't in evidence, maybe they would be heading out of college instead for a hot macho curry. A couple in pale blue blazers were oarsmen of the university crew. Early to bed tonight? Up before dawn for rowing practice in the Cam beyond Midsummer Common? A college servant was chatting with one of those blues.

'Just you wait a moment!'

Sorel had followed. Jack marched off across the lawn, the shortest route to the gate. He mustn't seem to run away. Sorel soon caught up.

'Don't you walk out on me!'

Jack turned. 'Don't much care for *ladies* walking out on you, do you, eh?'

Sorel took a sudden swing at Jack. Fending off with his

42

forearm, Jack swayed aside. His tipsy assailant's shoes slipped from under him. Sorel fell heavily on to the short soaked grass. Hoots of applause arose from the onlookers.

When Jack also laughed, a look of hatred contorted Sorel's face.

18

Clare no longer wore mourning, yet her twin's death still preoccupied her.

Jack had brought a bottle of Merlot to Clare's rooms, late of a drizzly afternoon in the last week of term, when both of them knew that Orlando ought to be out of college giving a lecture. Better safe than sorry. The constraints of Jack's schedule and Clare's – and Sorel's – and of Jack's own home-life too, restricted their rendezvous. That malicious phone call to Heather claiming that Jack was having an affair had disturbed the home-life, however absurd the allegation was, as Jack had insisted to Heather. Because Jack lived at home, his own room in college was a mere utilitarian study, bleak and comfortless. Clare's was a home.

In the event, they never even opened the wine.

A map of the western United States lay unfolded on the carpet between the armchair and the sofa, upon which Jack seated himself beside Clare in her cream slacks and blouse.

'How was your dad?' Jack asked. The previous weekend Clare had taken the train home.

'He's changed quite a bit in the past few weeks. The shock of Miranda's death seems to have advanced the Parkinson's. Not so much physically – he's still quite competent. But mentally. He's become ... I suppose the word's innocent. More childlike. Affectionate.'

'He *would* be, with you.'

'With other people, too. He touches people, gently.' She bent towards Jack. Demonstrating, she laid a hand upon his shoulder, let it linger. 'I know he does this to balance himself. People with Parkinson's have this way of leaning forward. Yet there's a touching innocence about it too.'

'Not quite bank manager behaviour, hmm?'

'Oh, he was always as sympathetic as he could be to customers. Maybe that's another reason why they gave Dad the boot. Listen Jack, he's become full of the idea that when I go to America I must visit the very spot where Miranda died – so that I can describe it to him exactly. The last place she saw. Skid Row and Sleaze Street, so close to the big shops and theatres. I know he's right. It's my duty. It'll make up for missing her funeral.'

'Did you, um, *sense* anything at the time she died?'

'Because I'm a twin? I don't think I did! What I need to do after the conference is *drive* to San Francisco – because Miranda loved driving so much. I'm not the world's ace at the wheel. Who needs a car in Cambridge?'

'Heather does – to visit her cases in the villages.' Jack dithered. 'I'm okay as a driver.'

She smiled gratefully. 'This wouldn't be for tourism, Jack. I don't want to see the Grand Canyon and tourist things. Though there *is* one place I need to visit on the way.'

She shucked off a strapless sandal. Stretching out her foot across the map, her big toe was a pointer.

'Just short of San Francisco. San Jose. Silicon Valley. There's an exciting project at the QX computer company.'

'Queue-ex?'

She parodied an American TV voice. 'Here at QX we *question the unknown* – and find the answers. QX have an artificial intelligence lab. They've built a robot called Tin Man. They hope Tin Man might develop conscious intelligence by learning about the world the way a child does – through seeing and hearing and touching and trying to make sense of what happens.'

'What does Tin Man use for touching?' Touching preoccupied Jack. Touching seemed to be the watchword for today.

'Strain gauges and conducting rubber and those sorts of things. The point is, a human brain stores information

44

according to how it gained the knowledge in the first place, as well as by categories like shapes and so on. I honestly don't think there's a cat in hell's chance of Tin Man becoming conscious – or only at best as some sort of plausible zombie. But it's *interesting*. I got in touch with QX. They'd be interested in my input.'

'Aren't they tight-lipped about such stuff as artificial intelligence?'

'They may be secretive about their regular research – but Tin Man is a virtuoso show-piece project. There's been a fair bit of publicity. Tin Man would take at least five years to arrive at any sort of supposedly intelligent behaviour. So they're happy to show me it. Then we drive on to where Miranda died . . .'

Clare shuddered. 'Am I sounding schizophrenic? Tucson and Tin Man – mixed up with Miranda!'

'It sounds perfectly sane to me,' he assured her. 'It's a good way to cope.'

19

The long vacation had banished most of the undergraduates. Lectures and supervisions ceased, though Jack was involved in a summer school. Now Orlando Sorel would have more free time as well, unless he took himself off to France. The absence of student bustle was, if anything, a little off-putting. Throngs of foreign tourists were no real substitute. Clare visited her father most weekends. She spent several whole weeks in London.

Midway through August, Jack met up with Clare in the yard of the Eagle Inn, not far from Spenser College. Orlando nursed a grudge against that particular pub. The landlord had barred him because of what Orlando characterized as *effervescent* behaviour: he'd been over-indulging himself in a bottle or two of bubbly.

Since it was only just past eleven in the morning, Clare and Jack were able to occupy a rustic bench set out on the cobbles below the veranda, along the balustrades of which were fixed long troughs of red begonias and busy Lizzies.

Wasps homed in upon their halves of Greene King. Beer mats had to be used as lids.

'Good news,' announced Jack. 'I have a house for us to stay in for free in San Francisco. Just so long as we water the plants.'

Wonderingly: 'Whose house?'

'Ah, it belongs to an Angelo Vargas Alvarez. What should I call him? A botanical psychiatrist?'

Clare giggled. 'Do you mean he psychoanalyses vegetables?'

'No, no. Angelo's originally from Brazil, you see—'

Jack had met Angelo a couple of years previously at an alternative psychiatry conference in Edinburgh sponsored by the Koestler Foundation.

'What's left of the rainforest is full of unknown plants with medical applications.'

'But if they're unknown ... Oh I see. They aren't unknown to the native peoples.'

'To the extent that the native tribes and the plants still survive. Shamans use plants with mind-altering drugs in them to treat mental illness. That's what Angelo specializes in.'

'He's a shaman-psychiatrist. How Californian.'

Vargas was also on the board of directors of an ethno-botany foundation. The foundation owned twenty acres on Hawaii devoted to a plant collection and gene-bank.

'I was e-mailing various people I'd like to talk to over in the States. Angelo e-mailed me to phone him. So I did just that. During the whole week we'll be in San Francisco he's going to be away at a meeting of his board in Hawaii. Delighted for me to use his house.'

'If we water the plants. Sounds ideal!' A wasp alighted on Clare's hand. She waved it away. 'Does Heather know about this arrangement?'

Jack shook his head. 'I phoned yesterday afternoon when she and Luke were both out. Seven in the morning for Angelo, but he sounded wide awake.'

'A house to ourselves,' enthused Clare. 'That's wonder-ful.' She flipped the mat from her beer mug. 'Here's to a month from now.'

Even as they clinked glasses, thirsty wasps cruised closer.

20

In the room in the Richmond district the venetian blinds were closed tight and a bright table lamp was lit, since it was nighttime. However, Night was not there, only Dawn and Noon.

Lamplight flooded a scatter of Polaroid photographs of the Tucson Conference Center and the Desert Hacienda and a typed sheet of instructions. An opened mailing bag lay on the floor, addressed care of General Delivery, Civic Center.

Dawn said, 'I'm suspicious.'

Yet the instructions had certainly been typed on Night's own portable StarWriter, in English of course. Messages must never be sent in Russian in case they were intercepted and the nationality of the sender revealed. The authenticating codephrase 'Fine weather' was included.

It was perfectly plausible that Night might have gone over the border to check out one of the *Norteamericano* computer assembly plants. From Tijuana through Nogales to Cuidad Juarez hundreds of electronic products were being assembled from American components in a growth boom, taking advantage of cheap skilled Hispanic labour. Security ought to be slacker there; bribery easier.

During the few days remaining until the conference in Tucson, Night would not be wasting his time. Nor would he have dreamed of phoning the apartment off Geary. The National Security Agency almost certainly snooped on overseas phone calls. Night was convinced that computers were also scanning domestic phone calls at random.

Dawn re-read the directions that he and Noon should travel to Tucson to meet up with Night at that hacienda-hotel. If Night was delayed in Mexico, they should go ahead and burgle a certain chalet . . .

'It seems different from his normal style . . .'

'Nobody followed me after I collected the package from Hyde Street. I'm sure of that. I always look out. I never come here directly.'

If this wasn't an attempt to discover their address, what could the motive be?

'To lure us to Tucson?' suggested Dawn. 'Maybe the FBI need to catch us in the act. Use our break-in as a pretext. Investigate us in depth.'

Noon pouted. 'Just suppose Night was arrested for loitering suspiciously. Just suppose the local police immediately called in the FBI, which is so unlikely that I can't imagine why—'

'A possible link with the robberies in Silicon Valley?'

True enough, armed gangs had increasingly been hitting computer companies in California's Santa Clara Valley. The previous week two security guards had been shot dead during an attempted break-in. Weight for weight, memory chips were more valuable than diamonds. World-wide there was a shortage. Thieves could easily sell chips through mail-order magazines, or to brokers who would sell the chips back to the very industry which had been robbed. Crime syndicates were shipping stolen chips in bulk to the Far East.

'Talk sense. There's no connection at all between Silicon Valley and this conference on consciousness.'

'Maybe,' suggested Dawn, 'the cops read *National Investigator*.'

'What a round-about way to entrap us! Anyway, Night would need to be co-operating. *Fair weather*, hmm? The package was mailed properly—'

'They can probably only hold him for a short while unless they catch us in the act.'

'How did they get him to reveal so much? Do you imagine they tortured him? That's crazy. I say he *is* in Mexico. And *we* go to Tucson, right?'

'But we drive. We take a gun with us, just in case.'

21

A swarthy, heavily-armed man in a dark suit and sombrero rode a placid white horse up the street at the head of a parade of floats bearing tableaux and swirling dancers and mariachi bands. Sharply-dressed guitarists and fiddlers and trumpeters played for all they were worth. Their vocalists warbled with a mournful Country and Western whine which drew cheers and roars of laughter from Spanish speakers. Costumed crowds swarmed. Mexican flags waved, green, white, red.

For the Mexican independence fiesta this year, the parade was taking a wide sweep around the city. Maybe the celebrants had set out rather early for comfort. It was only late afternoon. The temperature was over ninety. Sunset was still a while away. But thereby the several hundred attendees who were leaving the final, plenary session of the conference on this fourth day were greeted with a fine spectacle.

'Did you *consciously* plan this?' Clare enquired archly of Bob Keyserling.

The bald chairman grinned. 'Or am I merely an automaton, and did this happen by chance?'

As the attendees spread out to line Church Street, several cameras appeared from bags and briefcases. The moustached rider raised his sombrero in salute. He jerked the reins but his mount wasn't meant to be mettlesome. The horse was disinclined to prance.

Clapping the big hat back upon his head, the rider pulled out a six-shooter. Twirling the gun, he fired a couple of blanks into the air.

Slung around his shoulder was a bandolier of shells. Around the pommel of the saddle was slung another bandolier. Through a leather sling jutted a rifle.

'Pancho Villa fires his rifle this evening to start the fireworks off,' Keyserling told Clare. 'We'll see all the rockets from the barbecue.'

Bob had arranged so much. A whole year of detailed spadework, right down to little touches such as the banner

49

over the Leo Rich Theater, announcing TUCSON WELCOMES THE HARD QUESTION CONFERENCE. The witty info-packs which had guided her and Jack and others to succulent, sizzling eating. Chillies stuffed with lobster – and that was just the appetiser at the *Janos*! And of course the promised barbecue this evening.

'I thought Pancho Villa was a bandit,' Clare said, as the mounted impersonator ambled onwards, leading the floats.

'What, the great guerrilla general of the Mexican revolution? I'll grant you that some of our Anglos still resent him. Pancho *did* lead the only invasion of America this century.'

'I suppose you could say the invasion has succeeded.'

'Oh, absolutely. We'll be bilingual in a few more years.'

If no one was protesting at a guerrilla leader riding triumphantly through town, the troupe of demonstrators agitating against the conference was still in evidence. Women, mostly. Twenty or so, with three or four men. One placard read: SOUL IS SACRED. Another demanded: LEAVE OUR SOULS ALONE!

Those people had been a nuisance and an embarrassment, calling out their slogans at the entrance to the Leo Rich Theater – as if a conference on the scientific basis of consciousness was an attack on their status as human beings. The conference organizers hadn't dreamed that there'd be any need to provide security. Midway through the first afternoon Bob had announced briefly from the stage that a patrolman was being hired – at seventeen dollars per hour, by the way – to keep an eye on the demonstrators. The city police wouldn't clear the protesters away. People had a right to their views, however crackpot, as long as they stayed peaceable. Protest was a local sport. Apparently people came to Arizona to assert their individuality; to express themselves, only more so, in many cases.

'Your talk went down well,' Bob said to Clare. 'I notice you didn't mention anything about quantum computers coming to life.'

50

'I cut that stuff out . . . Oh God!' she exclaimed. 'What makes you say that?'

'Well, there was a story about you in the *National Investigator* . . . illustrated by a very fetching pin-up.'

She surely flushed.

'I didn't know—!'

Grinning, Keyserling scrutinized her face under her wide-brimmed white hat. His own bald skull was as brown as mahogany.

'Better not try quite as much exposure here, unless you use a load of sun-screen.'

Was the chairman being *randy*? Was that why he was devoting time to her? Clare cast about for Jack. Her gaze lit upon a youngish man with long black hair parted bizarrely in the middle and a curly little beard. He was staring intently at her. A member of the conference – he wore a badge. Her watcher instantly looked away and moved behind other people.

'At first,' Bob said, 'I thought wow, what a publicity machine—'

'I didn't know! In England there was a stupid newspaper story too. An ex . . . *friend* . . . did it as a nasty prank.'

A flood of Hispanics in holiday mood passed by. There was exuberant music, there was song. And she felt sick. The vivid spectacle had become meaningless.

Bob nodded sympathetically.

'I'm glad you didn't know. I didn't mention this till now in case it put you off your stride.'

'People must have been sitting listening to me this afternoon, and *knowing*—'

'Hence your enthusiastic audience? Relax! I doubt if even a handful of our academic colleagues saw that trashy news piece. Me, I just happen to be interested in urban legends – phantom hitchhikers and all that. The *Investigator*'s full of such shit. That's why I take it.'

Was that man with centre-parted hair one of the handful who knew about the piece?

'I suppose I'm lucky that reporters who did read the thing didn't come buzzing round like flies!'

51

'Oh, the *Daily Star*'s half asleep, and as it happens I know a few people on the *Citizen*.'

'You mean . . . ? Goodness, the Master of Spenser's did the same – to stop the story from spreading.'

'Question of civic pride, Clare. Our neighbour to the north might ordinarily have felt like poking Tucson in the eye, but it so happens I roomed with the editor of the *Republic* back in college.'

'God, *this* – and those loony demonstrators. You've had your work cut out, Bob. Thank heavens *they* didn't get wind of it and make blow-up posters!'

'Tell you the truth, I was a bit worried about that possibility. It would have made such sneaky ammunition. Maybe they don't read anything much apart from the Bible – if indeed the Bible's their bag. I tried to talk to them. Sweet reason, you know. None of them would say where they were coming from. Some paranoid cult. They just ranted.'

'I'm going to sue the bastard,' she declared. 'You don't happen to have this *Investigator* story with you?'

'I'll give you it this evening. In a discreet brown envelope. Stay cool.'

Oh, there was Jack now. She beckoned urgently.

Everything had gone so well until now. The conference had been fascinating. So many angles upon consciousness. So much coming together of disciplines. Sessions on neural networks and neurobiology and quantum physics and philosophy and cognitive science, and mysticism too. A lot of big names were present. Elizabeth Harper and Jacob Ernst and Pierre Durastanti. Parker and Burns and Friedmann.

There'd been a sparkling presentation of quantum physics. Trees and rocks and molecules and atoms seem absolutely real, but merely consist of a cloud of more basic ingredients. Down at that subatomic level, probability rules the roost. An electron is a haze of alternative possibilities – until an observer inspects the situation. Whereupon the haze immediately clarifies into one reality.

What's more, an electron seems to 'know' about all the alternative paths it could have followed, but didn't follow – as if all the possibilities are real, but only one actually exists. Electrons could even instantly 'know' about the state of another electron, previously nearby, but now far away in space and time.

Words such as reality and actuality seemed to lose their sense in this quantum world of paradoxes – although enough experiments, and a whole electronics industry, proved that quantum theory was true.

Ultimately, reality wasn't something intrinsic to the world. It was closely bound up with our own perceptions and consciousness.

And surely consciousness arose because of quantum coherence in the brain and knowing-at-a-distance, as Clare had maintained in her talk.

After her own presentation about microtubules in the brain, mystic input had come from a Sufi speaker. He had quoted an Islamic belief that God constantly recreates the universe afresh at every moment.

How well this fitted with the quantum concept that an observation made *now* can seemingly determine an event in the past. It was as if the whole universe was constantly adjusting itself and its entire history to suit a new circumstance. For we live in a cloud of possible universes which continually fluctuate – and by doing so, give rise to a single, stable universe.

Later, Durastanti had spoken strikingly about schizophrenia. So-called 'split personality' is a uniquely human disorder. Schizophrenia couldn't exist without the human ability for self-reflective awareness.

Might it be, Durastanti had suggested, that schizophrenics are tuning in to alternative, multiple realities? That schizophrenics are sensing the ghosts of other worlds? Might it be that the mind could contain memories of alternative existences – residues of events which never 'actually' happened?

People with multiple personalities might be aware of 'real' alternatives which do not presently exist – except in their heads where the electrons 'know' about other possible states of existence . . .

How wonderful, until now.

'Jack, Orlando has polluted here as well—!'

She told him about the story in the *Investigator*.

Bob Keyserling said, 'This hasn't made any waves. Or even any particles. All's well that ends well. If you'll excuse me, there are fifty things to see to—'

The noise of mariachi music was receding. Knots of attendees had formed to continue enthusiastic discussions. Others were heading back towards their hotels to freshen up before coaches collected them in a couple of hours.

The sun still blazed. Clare's shadow was wandering away from her. The image of her hat seemed larger than any sombrero. The light was so radiant that it seemed as if it might shine right through buildings, rendering them temporarily transparent, then restoring them to existence again, as before – or not *quite* as before.

Nothing was quite as before Bob Keyserling had told her about that story being printed in America too.

Sue Sorel for invasion of privacy? For injury to her professional reputation? Right now, if she had Pancho Villa's pistol with real bullets in it, and Orlando in front of her, she could cheerfully have shot him dead.

22

After a quick shower in her chalet in the Hacienda, Clare decided to phone Harry Chang, the man who had invited her input to the Tin Man project. Maybe phoning from Tucson was a little premature. But doing so would restore a sense of purpose and self-esteem in the wake of what Bob Keyserling had told her. Jack had said he intended to phone Angelo Vargas. She ought to phone someone too.

Was it a bit late in the day to phone a corporation? Was California a time-zone ahead? She wasn't sure. Maybe companies in Silicon Valley worked around the clock.

She did reach the switchboard at QX in San Jose. The

operator seemed completely new to her job, as well as somewhat impatient. This only made Clare more eager than ever to talk to Chang.

'Could you please find out if he's in the Tin Man lab—?'

'In the what, honey?'

Clare explained.

Chang wasn't there, either. It dawned on Clare that the Hacienda probably fixed its own inflated rates for calls from your own room – she had invested in this phone call!

'Do you have a security desk? Will they know if he went home—?'

The line disengaged itself. Had the operator tried to transfer the call to a security desk? Maybe she was due to go off shift herself.

As Clare stepped out on to the veranda, someone was hastening from the semi-private garden. Another guest, who had taken a wrong turn? An employee? With a cursory knock on Jack's door, she entered what was the twin of her own guest room.

Beamed ceiling. Tiled floor of burnt sienna. Mushroom rugs and bedspread to match the plastered walls. The fireplace in one corner resembled an open pot-bellied oven. Ensconced in a brown armchair by a highly polished round darkwood table, Jack was just putting down the phone.

'Angelo says he's leaving the key under the pot plant, unquote. All his plants have colour-coded spots. Green for the thirsty ones. Orange for twice a week. Red for once a week. We can't go wrong.'

'I tried phoning QX, Jack, but I couldn't reach Chang. If we're hoping to make an early start I'll try phoning again on the way.' Harry Chang had already mailed to her in England a useful folding laminated map of San Jose. 'Funny, isn't it? It's been so stimulating here. Now we can't wait to get going. Thanks to Orlando.'

'Stuff him.' Jack rubbed his hands. 'A week in San Francisco in a house to ourselves . . .'

'Yes!' She smiled, she nodded. 'I shan't let him spoil our time together.'

The barbecue site was on a small hill just west of down-town. The coach driver had commented over the PA that last century the peak was used to keep watch for Indians on the warpath. Later, football fans raided the same peak to paint a giant letter A when the local university team trounced Cal State Pomona. Every October, on the anniversary of victory, freshmen kept up the tradition with a whitewash party.

The view across the valley was magical. All the lights of Tucson were backed by the dark serrated wall of the Santa Catalina Mountains under a starry sky blurred by city glow and smog. Big patio torches illuminated a bar set up beside a refrigerated van of soft drinks, wines and Mexican beers. A catering van stood by the barbecue. Beef was broiling aromatically near a table of salads. Such a scent drifted. By the light of the big candles on stakes clusters of people were eating and drinking and chinwagging about the topics of the past four days.

As she and Jack and Bob Keyserling sipped a rather lightweight Zinfandel, the chairman said to Clare, 'I don't wish to embarrass you or rake any dirt. I'm kind of curious about this idea of quantum computers becoming self-aware. What exactly would they be aware of?'

'Well, of their own internal state—'

'Yeah, but look, our own minds develop due to a world of experiences and information. Where's the equivalent learning-context for a computer?'

'That's what the Tin Man project is about.'

'So how could a quantum computer suddenly acquire consciousness without content? With only its own internal architecture to examine? Or were you, um, misquoted? I'm curious.'

'I'm intending to visit the Tin Man lab in San Jose, you know,' she said evasively.

'I didn't know that. Exactly what are your plans?' Keyserling was including Jack in his question, maybe to take the heat off Clare. Or perhaps he was probing their relationship.

Jack outlined their itinerary to reach San Francisco.

'That's crazy,' said Keyserling. 'You're ignoring all the sights. You'll give yourselves a lot of *desolation driving*.'

Awkwardly Clare explained, 'Last year a mugger murdered my sister in San Francisco—'

'God, I'm sorry—'

'Miranda drove across the Mojave into California. I feel a sort of duty. My dad asked me—'

'No wonder you don't want to do the tourist thing. I'm so sorry. Are you staying where your sister stayed in San Francisco? That's assuming she had time to – Christ, I'm putting my foot in my mouth.'

Quickly Jack said, 'We've been loaned a house.'

'Lucky you. So who do you know there?'

'A psychiatrist. Fascinating man named Angelo Vargas Alvarez.'

'Doesn't ring any bells. I'm hopeless on names.'

'Just like my head of department back home – and he's an expert on memory.'

Keyserling laughed.

Clare was frowning. She was turning away. Abruptly she stiffened. Very close by, *that man* with the centre parting was loitering. He was nursing a can of Coke. He had attached himself loosely to the neighbouring bunch of people, but they were all ignoring him. He wasn't actually connected at all. He'd been eavesdropping. How much had he heard, and why? Quickly the man moved away towards the barbecue. Keyserling was also excusing himself. Time to circulate.

'Jack,' Clare whispered urgently, 'for heaven's sake don't ever say where we're staying together! There could be a reporter from that damned *Investigator* here. Don't tell anyone! Just say we're staying at some hotel.'

Was Clare being paranoid? Jack was anxious to soothe her.

'How about a Holiday Inn? There's bound to be one of those in San Francisco.'

'A Holiday Inn – that sounds wholesome.'

'Now how about some food?'

Clare glanced towards the barbecue. That man was over there. 'Not quite yet. There's a crowd.'

'Five or six people's hardly a crowd.'

'*Not yet.*'

24

Noon held a torch while Dawn searched through the Englishwoman's belongings, dumped upon the bed. Already he had pocketed the text of her talk and a notebook. He turned his attention to the empty suitcase. With a knife he began slitting the lining, searching for a hidden disk or a document.

Up in the sky outside, it was as if airliners had collided. Such a resounding bang. Almost immediately, another, followed by another. Sudden thunderclaps! Lights flashed through the closed curtains.

Noon and Dawn both froze.

The lock-picked door opened, silhouetting a man.

'Night—?'

Above the paloverde tree in the little garden, a rain of coloured stars dripped down the sky.

The newcomer held a gun. A compact sub-machine-gun. An Israeli Uzi. Behind him, a second man stepped into view.

In Noon's pocket was a semi-automatic Beretta with a fifteen-shot magazine. Dropping the torch, he clawed for his pistol in vain.

Fireworks exploded overhead. Red and gold and blue stars blossomed and cascaded.

25

'Pretty sight, isn't it, Dr Conway?'

That man had sidled up while Clare and Jack were

admiring the pyrotechnics over Tucson. The intruder's eyes were so intense as he gazed at Clare – as if he believed he could project himself into her very being. She glanced for a name badge. He was no longer wearing one.

'I can show you more about *awareness* than you can possibly imagine. May I call you Clare? Such a perceptive name. Your surname means swindle and scam. Con-way: the way to hoax people.'

'I never thought about my name meaning anything!' What was this intimate impertinence he was foisting on her? Did he think he was being genial or clever?

Softly the man continued: 'Con, as in Silly-Con Valley where they imagine machines may come to life. Ah, I see I've touched a nerve! I do need to touch you, Clare, to enlighten you.' His hand strayed but did not alight.

'Who do you think you are?' demanded Jack.

'You can come along too,' was the reply.

'Come *where*?'

'I'm offering you an invitation. Hospitality. Illuminations more splendid than any of those rockets. Insights.' *Those eyes.* 'You already have a vision, Clare – though it's false – of those fancy quantum computers becoming aware—'

'Oh, *shit*!' she said to Jack. 'The *Investigator*.'

'Why did you keep so quiet about that at the conference, Clare?'

'Stop using my name!' The man was trying to do an Orlando on her. To impress her. To oppress her.

'Not use your name? Are you so unsure of yourself?' The man was twisting her words. 'Ah, you're quite right to feel unsure. When you die, your self will dissolve, unless you learn how to survive death. Unless you're taught how to strengthen your soul – by the rapture of the senses and the flesh.'

This wasn't any journalist. This was some crackpot preacher, trying to recruit disciples.

'Rapture?' Jack scoffed. 'Isn't that when true believers get plucked from their steering wheels straight up into heaven?'

The man chuckled. He was superior to such fancies.

'That sort of heaven's a sham. Only zombie-people believe in it – people who will all evaporate. What does exist, for those who can achieve it, *I* call the Virtuality.'

'Call it what you like,' retorted Jack. 'Why don't you piss off?'

The man continued charmingly, 'Because I'm very interested in you, Clare. The universe unites us like two linked particles. You can't appreciate this in a few moments of glib talk. I see how you've been manipulated and misused by a man in the past. You need to overcome this. Confront it, fulfil yourself.'

Clare hesitated. What the man was saying was almost making sense, as if he did indeed perceive her inwardly. The stranger glanced at Jack before transfixing her again with his gaze.

'An ordinary affair can hardly serve your needs, Clare.'

'Right,' snapped Jack, 'that's enough. I said *piss off*.'

'The stag bellows its challenge. How predictable. But both the stag and the doe can learn extraordinary lessons!'

'*Is that man bothering you—?*' Bob Keyserling was hastening their way. Accompanying him was an athletic-looking woman with close-cropped red hair.

'That *is* him,' the redhead confirmed.

Keyserling confronted Clare's persecutor. 'I'm asking you to leave right now without any fuss, Mr Kaminski.'

'I'm registered for this conference of yours, Professor.'

'Under what name?' the woman demanded.

'I presume you came in your own transport,' Keyserling said. 'Get yourself out of here – or I'll call the cops.'

'What would you complain about, Professor?'

Keyserling flicked a glance at Clare. 'Harassment.'

'You dull man,' to Keyserling. 'Soulless bitch,' to the woman. With a shrug, Kaminski ambled casually towards where the coaches and cars were parked.

The red-haired woman was a physicist from the State University at Tempe, Phoenix, name of Alice Munro.

It was only during the final session of the conference that Alice had happened to take a seat near Kaminski. After a while she began puzzling and mentally shearing off his beard and shortening and restyling his hair.

Soon after Alice had taken up her post at Tempe six years earlier, accusations of sexual misconduct on campus had led to the dismissal of Roy Lee Kaminski as a teacher of comparative religion. He'd been seducing female students. He had made out to them that he was introducing them to Tantric mysteries. So said Alice. A couple of girls dropped out along with him. One of them was rich. Both severed links with their families.

Alice had heard that Roy Lee Kaminski changed his name to Gabriel Soul. He had founded some kind of erotic-mystical cult.

'He's come out of the woodwork,' Alice declared, incensed. 'He's accumulated enough followers – enough guru fuel. He's gone critical. On the offensive. When I say offensive I mean pretty odious.'

It must have been Soul's followers who had been demonstrating outside the Leo Rich Theater, while their leader observed the proceedings inside.

'Was he trying to convert you or something?' Alice asked Clare.

'Or something,' she said.

'Show you the error of your ways? Don't meddle with consciousness – that's *his* preserve, I suppose?'

'He was coming on to me,' Clare admitted to Keyserling. 'We both know why.'

Keyserling nodded. He held up his hand to stem Alice's curiosity.

'Where are you staying tonight?' Alice asked Clare. 'If you feel unsafe you can come and share my room at the Doubletree.'

'That's very kind' – and rather oppressive in its sisterly solidarity – 'but Jack's in the chalet right next to me.'

The most splendid rocket of all exploded. Briefly the stars formed a prancing horse, which quickly dispersed in smoke.

26

'Will you let me look inside first?' At the door to Clare's chalet, Jack held out his hand for her key.

She dithered, then accepted the offer. 'Early to bed, early to rise – just a quick look, Jack.'

'Including the bathroom and the closet.'

'Oh, it's absurd to imagine—'

'Clare, this door's already unlocked—'

'Don't—!'

However, he was already pushing open the door and switching on the light. From a corner, the standard lamp illuminated her suitcase open and slashed, her belongings scattered across the bedcover . . .

A man's body lay by the bed, bloody punctures in shirt and jacket. Near the table a second body sprawled. Holes pocked the plasterwork at chest level.

This couldn't be her room, it couldn't be. Or else they had opened the door upon a monstrous prank. In a moment the two performers would spring to their feet and bow.

'Shit,' Clare said softly, shaking.

'*Don't scream,*' Jack hissed. 'What we do is . . . we go to Reception as quickly and quietly as we can—'

'To complain about the state of my room, is that it?'

Jack made to support Clare. She wriggled. She was able to stand on her own. Right now she couldn't bear to be held facing this nightmare scene . . . where she had slept.

He released her. 'We run there. This has nothing to do with us. It can't have.'

'If only we had the car tonight! If only we could get in it and drive. We don't want to be delayed for days, Jack. This is crime, American crime. Too many bloody guns! Criminals killing each other. Some sort of burglars' feud. Do you think other rooms have been burgled?'

If so, there ought to have been commotion elsewhere in the Hacienda, raised voices, outcry. Instead, all was quiet apart from a purr of traffic.

She stared at the bed. 'My . . . things.'

'We *run* to Reception, right?'

27

The young Hispanic woman at Reception sent a porter to look at the room. Less than a minute later he returned, babbling in Spanish.

The cocktail lounge, with its bright taco deco décor in pink and orange and turquoise, and its ecologically correct imitation cacti in imitation bloom, was crowded by après-dinner drinkers and conference members.

Clare and Jack were hastily ushered into the office of the Patron Grande. This elegantly-suited grey-haired Anglo sported a tie with a scorpion in a plastic clasp which seemed like an intentional parody of local colour.

Two complimentary glasses of brandy arrived, a remedy for shock. The Patron positioned himself by the door to control entry and exit, his back to a large acrylic of an elderly squaw in voluminous robes against a technicolor sunset.

He expressed astonishment—'Never before in the history of the Desert Hacienda...' – and condolences – 'How distressing...' He found little else to say. Maybe he was worried about being sued.

Together on a brown leather sofa, Jack and Clare were just as silent. Jack stared at the back of the computer terminal on the big oak desk. A siren howled in the distance, then closer. The Patron excused himself. The desk clerk came in to attend them. She sat at the Patron's desk. Maybe she was in shock herself. She smiled professionally, fixedly.

'Could we have some more brandy?' Jack asked her.

This fazed the clerk. 'Well now, I don't know ...'

'You can put it on the damn bill!'

'Don't you suppose, sir, you ought to stay alert?'

It was twenty minutes – during which other sirens wailed – until officers entered the room. A tan-skinned uniformed patrolman and a detective in a lightweight suit and checked open-neck shirt. Patrolman Sanchez and Detective Kramer. Kramer had watery blue eyes and fair sun-bleached hair.

28

Jeff Kramer quite agreed with the Englishman that the double murder could have no obvious connection with an English female academic visiting briefly for a conference. What *had* the burglars been hoping to find in the lining of her suitcase?

Why, nothing, nothing at all.

Not unless ... let's see: this conference was about consciousness.

About *states of mind*.

Kramer had been in the police service in California's state capital until his divorce and his move to Tucson. Did this consciousness business include *altered* states of mind? The effect of drugs on the mind? Hallucinogens? Peyotl cacti, LSD, new designer drugs?

Kramer only need look through the conference programme – a copy of which Sanchez obligingly fetched from Clare's room – to see that no such topic was remotely on the agenda ...

On the other hand, maybe the two unidentified burglars could have been persuaded by a person unknown that some exciting designer drug might indeed be found in Dr Conway's luggage.

Suppose that the burglars had been ingeniously set up, as part of a drugs war. One of the dead men was almost certainly a Native American. Lure a Navajo (or some other Indian drug-pusher) and his Anglo partner to the Hacienda to kill them: sure to cause a smokescreen of confusion.

Death by sub-machine-gun? The state was awash with weapons. Apparently those burglars didn't have a gun with them, only a knife for slashing the suitcase. *Amateurs* – resented by professionals. Pockets quite empty. Not even any car keys. The killer or killers must have taken away all identification and whatever was used to open the chalet door, unless Dr Conway had stupidly left it unlocked.

This might be a clever little drug killing. Would the ins and outs ever be known?

It had been a hard day. Kramer had only just come from

a domestic homicide on East Sixth Street out by the University.

So here's what we'll do, since these two Brits are so eager to leave Tucson, and small wonder in the circumstances – and since they couldn't possibly have any link with the murders.

Homicide would have finished photographing the scene and be sticking tape around the mini-garden and over the doorway. Paramedics would have taken the corpses away to the chiller for autopsy tomorrow. Keep an eye on public relations; the Patron Grande was deeply upset. Get statements right now from Conway and Fox, and from staff and guests. Give a stopgap statement to the TV crew and reporters who had turned up outside, courtesy of monitoring the police transmissions. Leave Sanchez here overnight.

'We need a contact address for you in San Francisco, Dr Conway.'

Clare said quickly, 'Holiday Inn.'

Kramer raised an eyebrow.

'Which one?'

For a moment Clare was nonplussed.

'Which one?' she repeated. 'My mind's in such a spin. These murders! I can't remember the address!'

'Take it easy now,' Kramer coaxed her. 'Would it be Civic Center? Financial District? Union Square?'

'Union Square, that's it! Yes, Union Square, of course.'

Kramer grinned at her. 'So are you guys into Sherlock Holmes?'

Whatever did the detective mean? Did he suspect that they might actually know why the deaths had occurred?

Was he leading her and Jack along? Was he going to order them not to leave Tucson after all?

They would never reach California. Their time would be ruined. While they were hanging on, that crackpot Soul would home in on her!

Clare swallowed. 'I'm sorry, I don't understand you.'

Kramer shrugged. 'The Union Square Holiday Inn has a

rooftop theme bar that's a replica of Sherlock Holmes's study and library. Didn't you know that?'

'I haven't been to San Francisco before.'

'I thought that's why you might have chosen Union Square, you being compatriots of Mr Holmes?'

Jack blustered: 'Not all British people are obliged to be fans of Sherlock Holmes.'

'Or even of detectives,' said Kramer. Yet his attitude seemed benevolent, if weary.

Tomorrow: check all the hotels at the lower end of the market and the bed and breakfasts, in case the two victims had been staying in one of those. Hopefully, find some luggage. Get an angle on who they were.

Oh yes, and the Englishwoman's clothing and luggage ...

Kramer told Clare, 'Sanchez'll shift your stuff out of the room. None of it's, um, stained. The Patron'll have to find you a different room.'

'I'll move in with Jack for tonight.'

Into the chalet right *next door* to the crime scene ... ? Conway's companion would need to move out too.

The Patron Grande looked in to ask if some coffee would be welcome, which could have been his way of wondering when the police would finish. Beyond him, the cocktail lounge looked more crowded than ever. Nobody was going home or going to bed; not yet.

Kramer ignored the offer. 'Will you find another room for these people?'

Consternation: 'The Hacienda's *full*, officer.'

'Try phoning around, hmm?'

'We can't move out at this time of night,' protested Clare. 'I want to stay here. We're tired out. We're driving a long way tomorrow. I'll get a migraine. Jack's room's fine.'

'Cottage eleven's a single—' began the Patron.

Kramer waved to shut him up.

'Dr Conway,' said the detective gently, 'eleven's right next door to where this *happened*.'

'You'll have emptied my old room, won't you? You'll have secured it, whatever you do?'

'Ah, will you let me have your door key, please?'

It was the man, Fox, who handed over the key.

The Englishwoman persisted. 'You've sealed my room, haven't you? Where are we supposed to sleep? A police cell?'

'There might be evidence in the little garden.'

'We'll keep to the path. We'll tiptoe.'

'Dr Conway, my point is that I think you're trying to tough this out, and it might be better not to.'

'If I do need any counselling – well, Jack's a psychologist! If the police will let us stay in number eleven, I want to. I'll feel more protected. Nothing else can possibly happen here!'

Kramer gauged her. She wasn't even talking about sueing the Hacienda for trauma. Sweet to look at, and she and Fox must be lovers, yet she was as hard as ice. Admittedly ice could crack if enough weight was dumped on it . . .

It had been a hard day. Time for the good to go to bed. Finding alternative accommodation was an extra straw this camel could do without.

'What do they say about you Brits – stiff upper lips?' He nodded agreement. 'Sanchez'll stick around all night, just in case.'

29

Sealed off by police tape forbidding entry, there would be bloodstains and bullet holes in that other room, as if it were an alternative version of reality. In this almost identical room here, the big rug was immaculate; the bedcover was smooth.

The single bed was almost a double bed by Clare's standards. She hauled the cover from the bed on to the floor, then she peeled the blanket and top sheet away while

Jack watched her, unmoving. She switched off the standard lamp. Only soft light spilled from the half-shut bathroom.

'Jack,' she said. 'That man Soul ... Kaminski ... he spooked me.' It was as if the murders next door had vanished from her mind. 'An American Orlando!' She began to unbutton her blouse. 'Jack, *erase* him, rub him away.'

'Shall I massage you?' he offered.

Her blouse fell, then her bra.

'Undress, Jack. It's now – it has to be now.' She loosened her slacks. She squirmed a bit till they slid down. Then she stepped out of them. She pulled down her briefs and she was standing as naked as in that photograph of her upon the beach in France.

'*Undress.*'

He obeyed.

'Block him off from me, Jack. Block Soul. Block Orlando sodding Sorel.'

Diffidently, Jack asked, 'What about, um—? Should I take ... precautions?'

Clare giggled. 'Did you pack a big box of precautions, Jack? Isn't a patrolman protection enough? And police tape?'

How secluded and private they were.

'Tonight you needn't,' said Clare. Stepping towards him, she clasped his erection and squeezed softly. 'Is *this* the hard question?' she teased. 'Oh, it's more like an exclamation mark.' Thus she drew him closer to the bed.

After a first frenzied eruption of nerves and muscles and juices, himself within her, her legs twined around him, hands roving, fingers prying, tongues tasting, they made love more slowly and lingeringly, sliding into a second crescendo.

As they lay together, becalmed, she murmured, 'About San Jose, and QX and the Tin Man ... There's something I forgot to tell you ...'

30

A few days before that wretched story had been printed, Carl Newman of Matsushima – 'the Cardinal', as he was waggishly known – had asked Clare to call on him at the Science Park. Clare and the Cardinal had chatted briefly in his office about Tin Man and artificial intelligence. Then Newman took her for a drink in the bar at the Trinity Centre, as though to emphasize that his purpose was perfectly public and innocent.

The Cambridge Science Park was home to almost a hundred home-grown enterprises and multinational subsidiaries – electronics, high-tech instrument development, biotechnology, software, pharmaceuticals, patents agents. It was as neat as a slice of Switzerland, and the view from the bar was postcard Cambridgeshire: stretches of water and wide lawns and trees stirring in the breeze.

Since it wasn't yet lunchtime, the bar was fairly empty. A few people in snappily tailored business suits – the preferred attire at the park – were talking loudly about a 'dope problem' which had nothing to do with recreational drugs and everything to do with gallium arsenide transistors and impurities.

Newman raised his glass of orange juice to Clare, and she her glass of Californian Chardonnay. No one else was near their table. Newman had practically insisted that she should indulge in some wine – just as champagne should launch a ship.

'Here's to your trip. Happy trails, as they say over there.'

Newman's tight-knit hazel hair was close-cropped as if to show that, though he was in his late forties, no baldness would ever bother him. This, and a large hawkish nose and prominent chin and muscular build kept in tone by regular visits to a gym, bestowed a somewhat brutal look, although he always conducted himself courteously. Perhaps over-courteously. The urbane polish might be a veneer, a control for inner tempests. His eyes were cool aquamarine. Presumably he wore contact lenses, and his teeth were too perfect to be other than expensively crowned. Newman had imaged himself; he could have been advertising his Armani suit in a fashion plate. Clare found herself wondering whether he secretly visited some S-M gay club in London at weekends . . .

'Somebody from QX may even be at your consciousness conference,' said Newman. He had this way of segueing into mid-subject, taking preliminaries for granted. 'And of course you're visiting Harry Chang in San Jose. Between you and me, Matsushima feel that QX is *very* close to a prototype quantum computer. Since we're paying for your trip, there's a little something you could do for us—'

No, this wasn't industrial espionage. Not in the least. At QX quantum chip development was strictly segregated from the artificial intelligence research. However, Clare understood enough about quantum matters to be able to appreciate any gossip which might happen to come her way – or which she might happen to ferret out quite innocently while she was talking about Tin Man with Chang and others. The AI researchers might know something. They might let something slip.

The thing *is*, Matsushima knew that the boss of QX, Tony Racine, was in hospital because of a boating accident. Racine ran QX like an autocrat. There'd be anxiety and confusion. Tongues might wag.

Stick your toe in the water, Clare. Take the temperature. Phone the Cardinal day or night if you learn anything interesting. Of course it's a long shot. An outside chance. Call it opportunism. Matsushima would be grateful.

Clare had sipped her Chardonnay and gazed out at the serene, trim lawns and trees. Quizzically she said, 'So I'm to be a bit of a spy?'

'The race is almost in the last lap, Clare. Billions of dollars in prize-money for whoever gets it right.'

In this benign setting Newman didn't intimidate her. It wasn't his intention to. Willing co-operation was what he wanted. And of course Matsushima didn't *employ* Clare. The Japanese were happy to sponsor non-applied research which might only bear fruit in twenty or thirty years' time.

70

Her fellowship at Spenser's was in keeping with this long view.

'I know the stakes are high,' she said.

'You're a sort of wild card.' How suave his smile. 'You aren't even part of our hand. Not obviously so. Just keep your eyes and ears open. If nothing comes of it . . .' He shrugged, he tilted his orange juice. 'Happy trails.'

A swan was flying along, low above the water. As it rose to clear a stretch of willow trees it was a white airliner ascending, immaculate.

31

'It only dawned on me just now,' said Clare, naked beside Jack's nakedness, 'maybe what happened next door *did* have something to do with me after all! If Matsushima nurse the notion that I might be able to probe QX, how many other probes are there? Theirs, and other people's? Probes more ruthless than my own simple little visit!'

'I *see.* A light bulb lit up in your head . . .'

'Not *while* we were making love, Jack! I wasn't thinking of other things. Or of other people!'

'I know you weren't,' he assured her, 'my love.' This was the first time that he had actually said he loved her. During their ecstasy he hadn't gasped 'God I love you' or any such thing. Other words, yes, more carnal words. But not that. It might have sounded false. Opportunistic.

He must concentrate on the new possibility. Clare hadn't attached any great importance to Newman's request. Yet nevertheless . . .

'Suppose,' said Jack, 'Newman e-mailed a memo to Japan about you to score Brownie points. What if he exaggerated? What if some real industrial spies saw his memo?'

'What sense does that make? There'd have to be two rival sets of spies. The ones who broke in, and the ones who killed the first pair.'

'Spies willing to kill other spies. High stakes?' he suggested.

'They'd be acting prematurely, wouldn't they? Why not wait until *after* I went to QX?'

'Until we're staying – as everyone knows – at the Union Square Holiday Inn?'

Nobody knew where they would really be staying in San Francisco. Oh, apart from Bob Keyserling.

'Did they want to check me out while they knew exactly where I was? Decide whether I came to this conference just to give myself a cover story? See if I'm worth keeping tabs on . . . It seems so implausible.'

'That's exactly what it is, Clare. Bizarre. Relax. If that detective takes it into his head to question us again in the morning, I don't think we ought to volunteer any far-fetched lines of enquiry.'

'God no.'

Onwards to California. Onwards to the house in San Francisco.

They nestled. They cupped together. After a while they slept. It was late.

32

When Jack collected the compact air-conditioned yellow Toyota from the Hertz agency, the young Hispanic said, 'You'll find four complimentary bottles of Calistoga Water under the passenger seat.'

'Four bottles of water?'

'In the very unlikely event you have a mishap, sir.'

Jack wasn't thinking too clearly this morning. 'You mean so I can top up the radiator?'

'So you can top *yourself* up, until help comes along. If a sandstorm blows up and you can't see clearly, pull off the road.'

If the car broke down, and its occupants succumbed to heat stroke, the agency couldn't then be sued for negligence.

'Do you think I ought to buy some more water just in case?'

'That's up to you, sir. We have plenty more in the chiller.'

When he got back to the Hacienda, Clare had finished packing – but not the text of her speech, nor her notebook with her scribblings about the conference. Those were missing.

'Damn,' she said, 'all my papers. The killers are going to be disappointed by their haul when they realize they're just conference notes.'

Clare had a spare notebook, still blank, which she'd been reserving for Tin Man. In due course the formal conference proceedings would be published – though not the informal poster sessions – but that wouldn't be for six months.

'While we're on the road I'll jot down the main points I remember. At least I'll try to. Damn it!'

33

Jeff Kramer was at his desk, filling in a report form about that domestic homicide, when Wheatstone brought in the two valises, a black one jammed under his arm, a brown one dragging down his hand.

Wheatstone nudged the glass door shut and office noise was muted.

'Odd thing,' he said. 'These were at the Cactus Lodge, like I radioed. But when I was at the Pima Hotel on North Fourth the clerk said a man who looked Indian but didn't even sound American checked in last week. Same night, a couple of Anglos paid the man's bill and took his luggage away with them. Said they were friends of his. Name of Knight, according to the register. They didn't seem too familiar with his name, but what the hell, they paid up.'

'Did you get any descriptions?'

'One of the so-called friends had ginger hair. The clerk noticed as much, since his wife's kid has ginger hair. The other man had a tattoo of an angel on his forearm. He was skinny.'

'How's *your* kid, by the way?' asked Kramer.

Wheatstone's boy had been receiving drugs and radiation treatment for leukaemia. Supposedly the prognosis was good. A miracle remission. Supposedly. Wheatstone and his wife had faith in the Lord.

'Johnny's hair all fell out – but it'll grow back.'

Kramer nodded. He had lost his own girl, his cute cottontop, when his wife walked, back in Sacramento.

The valises were locked, but that posed little problem.

Soon Kramer was reading a typed sheet of instructions which must have been folded and unfolded numerous times. Polaroid photos of the Convention Center and of the Desert Hacienda lay upon a heap of shirts and socks now sharing a small table with a stack of box-files. Wheatstone was flicking through a notebook he had unearthed.

'What sort of writing's this?'

Kramer peered. 'I think . . . I think that's Russian.'

The dead man with no fold to his eyelids hadn't been any Navajo or other Native American. He had been an asiatic Russian. Kramer glanced at his watch. Two-thirty. Still, he phoned the Desert Hacienda.

Your two British guests, Conway and Fox. Yes, *those* ones.

Long gone. Of course they were long gone. They'd left later than they'd hoped, but they were still long gone.

He cradled the phone.

Russians. Spies? Or more likely nowadays, gangsters. This was a lot more serious than any small-time drug vendetta.

'Listen,' he told Wheatstone, 'check out North Fourth near the Pima. There might be an abandoned car. And check out near the Desert Hacienda too. The car might be from out of state, unless these Russians came by air and rented one here or maybe up in Phoenix. Or even in Mexico, for all I know!'

The killers had removed any clues to identity from the

dead bodies. None seemed to be in this luggage apart from the notebook which would need to be translated. Most likely the murderers – no, now they were the *assassins* – had been trailing these Russians and knew exactly what vehicle they were driving; if any at all. What if the assassins didn't know? Corpses don't confide about cars.

Time to talk to the Chief. And to notify the FBI about Russians murdered in mysterious circumstances? And to alert the Highway Patrol to look out for Conway and Fox on I–8 or I–10? Those two wouldn't yet have crossed the state line unless they were *really* speeding.

34

The old beaten-up open-top Buick swung out and back again for the third time. The convertible's turquoise paint-work had long since been baked to matt pastel by the oven of the desert. Couldn't the driver make up his mind to overtake the Toyota? Was he half-blinded or stunned by the sun?

Was he drunk? Two men were in the convertible. Both wore reflective sun-glasses and cowboy hats. The passenger was holding something the size of a beer can up to his mouth, though were beer cans black?

On either side of the highway heat-waves distorted the boundless grit. Air was rippling glass. Amid scruffy spidery shrubs, cacti with fuzzy yellow halos branched upwards like corals from some destitute sea-bed. Sky was a vast bleached dome spanning desolation from arid mountains to other distant dry hills. The ribbons of the highway were monotonously straight. Tyre-treads sloughed by rigs over the years lay at the side now and then like dead black snakes.

Ten miles back, Jack and Clare had passed a wayside diner in the middle of nowhere. The Grub-Steak was its droll name. Surmounting a cinder-block building, facing each way along the road, were twin faded giant figures of old-time prospectors. Supported by scaffolding, the joke prospectors dangled huge frying pans, each cradling two golden-yolked fried eggs of plastic and neon tubing. At night the eggs would probably seem to flip from side to side of the pans, like caution lights advising drivers to slow and stop. The Buick had slipped out from beside the Grub-Steak.

The long convertible dropped back – only to race forward almost up to the Toyota's rear fender.

'It's going to bump us!' cried Clare. The pad which she had been jotting in with increasing infrequency fell to the floor.

Jack accelerated to put a couple of dozen feet between themselves and the car behind. The convertible bided its time.

A long white mobile home was approaching, as big as a railcar, air-conditioners mounted on its roof. It sped past, followed by a station wagon towing a more modest trailer.

Coming up fast from behind was some stubby truck with big tyres and bull-bars, with a crate in back. A row of spotlights was mounted upon the cab. A high aerial lashed to and fro like the solitary feeler of some armoured creature of steel.

Catching up with the truck came a little pack of motorbikes – not bulky ones, but those slim agile rough-terrain types. Dirt bikes. Hyenas compared with the panthers or lions of big Harleys or Hondas.

Again the Buick pulled out. This time the convertible roared forward alongside the Toyota. Jack braked slightly. The Buick copied him. Edging over, the other car nudged.

In their cooled cocoon, Clare squealed as metal bumped metal on Jack's side.

Away swayed the Buick. What the skinny passenger held in his hand was a black walkie-talkie, its aerial a thin upraised finger. The man dropped the walkie-talkie out of sight. The freckled driver grinned and licked his lips. Under his cowboy hat the driver's hair was red. The passenger raised something shiny, something of stainless steel.

'Jack, he has a *gun*—!'

This Toyota was a stick-shift model. Jack hadn't wanted

a car with automatic transmission. Never in his life had he driven with anything other than a manual gearbox; nor had Clare. He was still getting used to the gear-stick being on the opposite side.

'Fucking hell—!'

Jack shifted to third, to second. As he raced ahead, the rev counter climbed through four thousand towards five. He was doing almost ninety. He fumbled back into third.

The dirt bikes overtook the speeding truck. The black-helmeted riders were like insects with faces which were one single reflective eye. Just then the Buick surged forward to crowd the Toyota.

A cut-off slanted away from the interstate. A dirt road, boulders on either side of it.

Hardly thinking – since it was either *that* or a glancing collision which might send the Toyota out of control – Jack swung the wheel over.

The Toyota shuddered and bounced at what now seemed crazily excessive speed along the dirt road. He pumped the brake pedal, nearly causing a skid.

A great plume of dust obscured the rear. The Toyota might have been burning oil, pouring out smoke from its exhaust pipe. Their speed was down to fifty, forty.

A bend was coming up. Fuzzy cacti and bushes like bales of wire were on either side.

Jack did skid at the curve. More by luck, he recovered the steering. Another bend loomed. The land was suddenly full of dry ridges and dips after the monotony of the interstate.

Beyond the next curve a straight half-mile ran alongside a dry stream bed. The road avoided the lower groove along which a flash-flood might surge after a storm.

In the mirror Jack spotted a hyena-bike rounding the bend a few hundred yards behind, spraying dirt. The insect-rider had pulled a red kerchief over his mouth and nose. A second bike followed, then three more. With the change in direction, dust was gushing away from the road. Moments later the chunky truck swam into view.

'They're following us! They're all in it together—!'

The convertible had missed the turn. Maybe even now it was backing up.

'Carjackers?' exclaimed Clare. First Miranda – now herself as a victim of auto-violence? 'Where does this road go to?'

As they lurched along, she hauled their map from the glove pocket. She wrenched it open so hastily that she ripped it. She crushed the folds across her knees. Where could she find this road of earth and gravel?

35

And now, thanks to a little luck, and to Wheatstone, they had what was in all likelihood the victims' vehicle. California plates; a compact Volvo registered to a V.I. Morgen, care of General Delivery, San Francisco.

Some kids had been loitering by the car, which had been parked all night and all day half a mile from the Hacienda. A local resident phoned 911.

'Morgen' had owned the Volvo for the past nine months.

'These Russians must have been operating out of San Francisco for at least that long,' Kramer told Nicholl Perridge in the Chief of Detectives' glass-walled office.

Perridge was a brisk sparrow of a man, within five years of retirement. Though in repose Perridge's countenance often looked sour and intimidating, puzzles would enliven it. He was especially fond of crosswords of the brainracking British kind. Puzzles with cryptic clues. He mailordered collections of those which had appeared in British newspapers.

Boring Perridge was fatal. On the other hand, he wasn't impetuous. First guesses could be wrong guesses.

'What do the initials V.I. suggest to you?' Perridge asked. Cool piped air was ruffling a large cobweb up by the vent. He glanced there as though the answer might be written in the spider-silk. Perridge had given instructions that the

78

cobweb shouldn't ever be dusted away. Spiders caught bugs. Spiders lurked usefully.

It hadn't occurred to Kramer that the initials might suggest anything. Presumably the name was fictitious. Otherwise, why not register an actual address? More peculiar was the lack of personal trash in the Volvo after nine months' ownership. No crumpled receipts or such. Just a lot of well-used maps, and an ashtray full of Marlboro butts. If you travelled around much you usually accumulated bits of paper. The Volvo's owner couldn't merely have been obsessively tidy, otherwise the ashtray would have been emptied more often.

You had to indulge Perridge.

'Morgen's German, isn't it?' said Kramer. 'Morning or dawn or something? V.I. might mean V-One. Wasn't that the name of the first guided missile?'

'Vengeance-One.' The Chief's tone was dismissive. 'These dead men would appear to be Russians, not Germans. So how about ... *Vladimir Ilich*? Lenin's first two names. People generally choose a false name that has some relevance to them, or one that they can easily remember. These Russians could be fond of Lenin. That's a bit odd, to say the least. Though let's not attach too much significance at this stage. Now why should they drive more than eight hundred miles rather than hop on a plane?'

'That's supposing they came specially. Supposing they weren't here already.'

'Maybe they were avoiding carrying a gun through screening at airports? Didn't do them much good.'

'Why come all the way from San Francisco to rob someone who was about to drive to San Francisco anyway?'

'Could that be to be absolutely certain where this Conway woman was? What did you say her talk was about at the conference?'

Kramer recalled. 'The Brain as, um, a Computer of Light.'

'So forget drugs or missiles. This is about—'

'—computers.'

By now it was after five. No radio signal had come from the Highway Patrol at the most obvious interception places near Quartzsite or Yuma. Kramer needn't feel chagrined that he had let the British pair continue on their way. It remained a dubious point how long they could be delayed in the state for further questioning as possible material witnesses.

With Russians involved, and a Californian car, this was a federal matter. Decisions could await the arrival of the local FBI office chief. Right now Irving Sherwood was heading back to town from some business in Nogales, that stewpot straddling the border.

Perridge rubbed his hands together.

'Computers, Russians, assassins, and a couple of *innocent* visitors from Cambridge University, England. This brightens my day. I think, Jeff, you'd better pay a call on whoever organized the conference.'

36

The bikers were easily gaining. Jack had little choice but to speed up. The road took another sharp curve. Dust and grit billowed as he wrestled the wheel.

In vain.

The car left the organized dirt of the road for the disorganized dirt of the desert, grooved and lumpy and stone-scattered. Creosote bushes raked the wings and doors.

A tree-cholla loomed, all of eight feet high. The westering sunlight showered through the cactus thorns so that the jointed arms wore golden auras brightly aglow. The cactus was like some bizarre bristling traffic signal glaring amber.

'Watch out—!'

As soon as they hit the cholla, the woody trunk snapped. Spiky joints leapt at the windshield as if intent on vengeance, but bounced away. The Toyota was slowing abruptly, dragging. The cactus wood must have jammed underneath.

Several moments fled till Jack realized that the shock of impact had killed the engine. He clutched at the ignition key. The engine awoke again. Too much accelerator. Wheels spun, digging in. Crashing gears, he shifted into reverse.

Bikes skidded to a stop around the Toyota. A rider parked his bike alongside, upright on its support prongs. Another dropped his bike right in front of the car as a blockage. Behind, the truck was coming up.

A man in leathers hauled at Clare's door, which was locked. Only strengthened glass separated him from her as she gaped at him in dread.

'We'll push all our money out of the window!' she shouted. That was what Miranda ought to have done. Clare lowered the window just a fraction. 'We'll push all our money out!'

From inside his jacket the man pulled a pistol. He pointed the gun at Clare in a nightmare re-enactment of what her twin's last sight must have been.

'Don't,' she begged, 'please don't. It'll destroy my dad! My sister was shot like this. Have whatever you want—!'

'No,' growled Jack.

Would these people drag Clare out and rape her as well as rob? Having raped and robbed, would they leave witnesses alive?

'We can pay you a lot more,' she called out, 'if you don't harm us! If you let us arrange for extra money! More than we have with us here—'

The pick-up had halted. Its driver came trotting to Clare's side of the car. That's where all the men were gathering. Oh, forgive: one of those bikers was a woman with close-cropped mousy hair and an inch-wide purple birthmark on her cheek which looked at first like a tattoo but wasn't, being shapeless. Did a female biker's presence make rape less likely, or might she watch and laugh?

The woman chortled, as if genuinely amazed.

'Money,' she exclaimed. 'Why should we need your money?'

With horrid inevitability, that dull turquoise convertible came slewing around the curve. Braking, it lurched off the road. The two cowboy hats quit the Buick and ambled over to join the party.

The gingery man who'd been driving had custody of the gun now. With the muzzle he rapped on Clare's window.

'Lady, it's rude to refuse an invitation.'

What invitation? What on earth did he mean? Her heart was thumping.

Buick versus Toyota, along the interstate? Had the display of a gun been meant as a challenge? Like some starter's pistol being brandished?

'The name's Jersey,' said her persecutor.

'*My* name's Clare,' she answered.

Talk to them. Establish yourself as an individual. Create some rapport.

'Are you called Jersey because you're from – from New Jersey?' She had little feel for American accents, unless they were Deep South or Bronx.

Jersey studied her through the window. He shook his head.

'It's supposed to be a Polish name. Jay-ee-are-zee-why. Pronounced Yertzi. Who wants to be called that?'

Keep on talking. Use his name as often as possible.

Her voice shook. 'What invitation do you mean, Jersey?'

'Which do you think, Clare?'

Play his game, then. A guessing game.

'Um, a road race between us and you?'

Jersey chuckled. 'You aren't getting back on to the interstate as easily as that. Now just open that door or I'll have to smash the window with the butt of this pistol and haul you out.'

Jack was staying very quiet. He scarcely moved. His gaze roved across the eight or so members of this gang. By now everyone had gravitated to Clare's side of the car, as though he was of no real interest.

'If I could know what the invitation is for—'

The thin man chipped in.

'*Enlightenment* and *immortality*.'

On his forearm was a tattoo of an angel. All of a sudden, appallingly, she understood.

'You're Gabriel Soul's people!'

'Top marks,' said Jersey. 'Let's get going.'

'Where do you want us to go—?'

'To the Soul Shelter,' declared the young woman with the birthmark. Her eyes were aglow, with enthusiasm or mania. 'Don't you worry yourself. Gabe sent me along as your chaperon. Sort of. He'll enlighten you.'

The woman had been sent as a chaperon?

'How far is this Soul Shelter? How much will this delay us—?'

'Oh, stop pussyfooting. Close your eyes.' Jersey reversed the pistol and swung.

Glass shattered into a thousand opaque crystals which cascaded on to Clare's lap and the floor. At the moment of impact, Jack unlocked his door. Hurling it open, he was out. He was lurching headlong towards the nearest parked bike.

'Hey—!'

Astride, Jack was cranking the starter pedal. The hot engine cleared its throat rowdily. Pitching off the prongs, he twisted the throttle grip. The dirt bike bounded forward through the scrub, the dust trail billowing back.

'Get after him! Head him off—!'

As Clare gaped through the windshield, Jersey's arm swooped through the open gap. Her door was opening.

Engines were roaring. Bikers were scrambling in pursuit. Jack had fled. He had left her without a word, without a whisper of warning. But of course he couldn't risk alerting Jersey. He had to seize his chance while there was any chance at all, with the distraction of the window being smashed. He was heading for help. Bikers were trying to catch him or head him off. He had left her alone in this desolation with crazy cultists. One of them was her chaperon. She wasn't going to be gang-banged and murdered. Not right here and now . . .

Jersey clutched Clare's sleeve.

'I'll come,' she promised. 'But I'm covered in glass—'

'It isn't very sharp—'

She got out with exaggerated care. She took time shaking herself.

If she was some sort of guest of Soul's, his disciples wouldn't shoot her. None of them had fired after Jack. When she was in the truck or in the convertible and travelling along a road, she might manage to scream out for help.

She might get a chance to jump from whichever vehicle – though at risk of breaking a limb.

Unless the road they took was the same lonely dirt road or another just like it.

With Jersey on one side and the woman on the other, Clare was marched towards the pickup truck with its huge bull-bars and row of lamps.

And right past the cab.

The woman let down the steel tailboard with a clash.

'Open the box, Beth—'

That *crate* – they were going to put her *inside it*.

Beth scrambled up. She unlatched the rear end of the crate. She swung it open on hinges like a door. Inside lay a mattress and a heap of blankets.

'Big enough for two,' boasted Jersey. 'We bored air-holes in the sides specially.'

So Clare noticed.

'Climb up now. The ride'll get kind of bumpy. Arrange yourself comfortably so Beth can tape you easy.'

Not with any cassette recorder. Not for any interview or interrogation. But with a fat grey roll of parcel tape.

37

When he was a freshman beginning to read psychology at Trinity Hall a quarter of a century earlier, Jack had bought a second-hand motorbike from a fellow undergraduate.

The bike was a 1954 Norton ES2 with swinging fork rear springing. Only seventeen years old. Seemed a bargain. Proved to be a bit of a pig in a poke.

Indeed, Jack was soon calling his machine the Pig. Not a hog, but a pig. Still, it had served him for a couple of years to travel home to Norwich from Cambridge across the flatlands of East Anglia. Then the Pig packed up irretrievably – as did his parents' marriage.

Jack's father had fallen for a chit of a barmaid, of all people. The young woman, Celia, reciprocated. She happened to be bored with England but she wasn't the type to set out on the hippy trail. Dad took young Celia and his engineering skills – which had helped keep the Pig on the road – off to South Africa, which was a politically shitty thing to do. The romance hadn't lasted. Celia found herself a younger, more athletic fellow. Dad stayed in South Africa out of stubborn pride.

Jack had also used the Pig to visit peace festivals and similar gatherings. This was at the very beginning of the seventies – the afterglow of the sixties, really. Late afternoon of the counterculture which had been going to transform the world and people's hearts. It had been at the Avalon Mind Fair in Somerset that Jack first met Heather. Daughter Crissy was re-enacting such capers in a less friendly era.

A few biking skills came back to Jack as he powered the dirt bike through the scrub.

Boulders tried to funnel him towards twisted many-armed desert demons brandishing a multitude of green daggers. He avoided being impaled. The roar of the bike engine overrode all other sounds. He did not dare glance back to check on pursuit. He might hit a rock or some tangled wiry bush. Warm sage assailed his nostrils. At first the heat had seemed stunning after the cool of the car, but his breakneck motion ventilated him. Stray grit stung his cheeks. Was a breeze whipping up? The fast-setting sun was dyeing ribbons of clouds scarlet and orange to the west. Eastwards, a lavender gloaming sneaked up the sky.

He found himself at the dirt road again. Briefly he braked. A couple of hundred yards to the south, a biker gunned his engine. From behind in the scrub Jack heard another machine. He could only swing northwards and hope to keep his distance from his pursuers. At least on this road to somewhere or nowhere he needn't fear hitting rocks or dagger-trees or cacti like corals abristle with spikes.

He must have raced several miles before the road disappeared around a low ridge battlemented with rocks. A grey cloud of dust was rising from beyond. Maybe a truck was on its way – surely nothing to do with Soul's disciples. Risk a glance: four dirt bikes were chasing each other through more dust, the nearest only fifty yards behind. Jack hunched and speeded.

Bikes were ahead on the road. A chevron formation of half a dozen big brutes of bikes occupied the whole width of the road. They were proceeding like some stately phalanx. Headlamps glared in the fast-gathering dusk. Already the hilly eastern horizon was deep purple. A star or two showed. The zenith was pale. How brief the twilight was.

Those heavy bikers wore black leather like a uniform. Dark shades were pushed up on to their brows under baseball caps or black thatches of hair. Who were they, who were they? No good news, surely. Jack would either collide with the oncomers or be forced off the road – unless they opened their ranks, which they showed no signs of doing.

One of those oncomers pulled a pistol from inside his bomber jacket and sighted it. Immediately Jack abandoned the road. The roar of the bike almost drowned a quick crack-crack of gunfire.

He dodged another damned tree-cactus and its almost extinguished aura-glow of thorns. He bounced into a dry streambed angling westwards. At least the remaining daylight was in that direction. He might be able to spot obstacles for a little while longer.

The arid arroyo was almost bare of vegetation. A clean run. Whatever duel on wheels was happening behind was now a mystery. He glanced back. Impossible to be sure but he seemed to have eluded pursuit. Wait a few minutes more – a few miles more – before switching on the headlamp.

This vast wilderness! Night settling down. No lights visible anywhere around, other than some more stars. Where was there any hope of help? He was heading further away from Clare and the interstate all the time. Must be ten or fifteen miles away by now. Deeper, deeper into desolation.

Wind was rising. For God's sake let no sandstorm whip up.

Along the arroyo a ghostly grey sphere came bowling. Something not quite all present – yet at the same time bulky and fast. Some sort of charging creature, only half seen, intent on meeting the bike head-on.

He twisted the handlebars. The bike slanted out of the streambed, scattering pebbles, as the amorphous mass rushed by.

Out of the corner of his eye he glimpsed that the mass was a huge ball of dry weed, tumbling along in the stiffening breeze. The bike crested the edge of the arroyo. Airborne, briefly. A dip yawned, devoid of any detail. Down the bike dived into this bowl of darkness fringed with silhouettes of bushes.

The front wheel must have met a rock. Jack pitched from the saddle right over the handlebars. The bike was following him. A hammerblow obliterated all awareness.

38

In the yellow light of the innermost sanctum of QX's fab-lab, Matt Cooper blinked through his safety glasses at the image of an imperfect quantum chip on a high resolution TV monitor. Cooled air was forever descending from the ceiling to the grates of the floor, but sweat tickled the orbits of Matt's eyes.

He did his best to ignore the itch.

If he slid a vinyl-gloved finger under the glasses to wipe a bead of sweat he would certainly contaminate his glove.

He might unsettle his face mask. Some dirt from his nostril-hairs might escape on his breath into the perfectly pure atmosphere, polluting it. Particle detectors would set off flashing lights and angry buzzers.

In all the fabrication areas the permitted level of dust was a mere one particle per cubic metre of air. The areas alternated, like interknit fingers, with support facilities where air was allowed to contain ten specks of dust. Here in this quantum chip area the ideal might be zero particles, though that was impractical.

Clean working conditions, oh yes. The best. Walking out at the end of a shift into ordinary air with its hundreds of thousands of particles per cubic metre sometimes seemed like entering a city-wide gas chamber. The cleanliness was all for the benefit of microchips, not human beings. Otherwise Matt wouldn't be itching.

Of course, his sweating might be due to nervous anxiety.

This claustrophobic place was like some kind of vastly expensive yet congested and paranoid space station under armed quarantine. How thoroughly protected it was against the messy mortals who worked here. If a microscopic speck of dirt settled upon a microscopic chip it would be as though a giant hillock were to be dumped down amongst the road network of San Jose. Except that electronic traffic would *use* the intrusion as a pernicious short-cut.

A hand settled on Matt's shoulder.

He jerked, even though people in the fab-lab often touched one another. The sheer sterility of this place – the identical protective hooded white suits and the blank breathing masks and the booties and the double gloves – seemed to prompt a monkey-like desire to make physical contact, almost a grooming reflex. Human smell was missing, filtered out, replaced by a faint lingering hint of the alcohol with which masks and glasses had been wiped.

'How's it going?'

Phil Shibano's voice.

Phil and Matt frequently spooned up some non-crumbly high-vitamin-C yoghurt together during break time. Doubtless Phil thought of Matt as a friend.

It wasn't really Phil and the others in the fab-lab whom Matt was betraying. Not personally.

As for any notion of loyalty to Tony Racine, it was company policy to fire any fab-plant employee, however ace he or she might be, if said employee caught more than the average number of colds. Sneeze-sneeze, bye-bye.

'What's wrong with that one?' Phil asked.

'Whatever,' Matt said vaguely, and continued to study the screen. Phil ought to wander away unoffended.

Damned sweat. Anxiety.

Each quantum chip was made by depositing linear streams of single atoms in an ultra-high-vacuum trap super-cooled by liquid nitrogen to 80 degrees above absolute zero so as to obtain photon effects. QX used modified scanning tunnelling microscopes to deposit atoms. Reversed in function, these electronic microscopes served as writing devices. Right now a breakthrough was imminent in the mass production of ultrasharp needles, only one atom wide at the tip. Very soon the pace of production of quantum chips could pick up enormously.

Matt's vision swam.

On the monitor screen he was seeing not a hugely magnified quantum chip at all but a roulette table marked off with numbered squares.

The wheel turned slowly, keeping half out of sight. The ivory ball rolled like some orbiting electron which possessed momentum but not, as yet, any definite position. It vanished from one side of the wheel. A moment later it reappeared over at the other side. A single black chip lay on lucky seventeen. The wheel slowed its clockwise progress. The ball, its counterclockwise spin.

Almost, the ball came to rest at seventeen. Instead, it trickled into the slot just adjacent. Pay thirty-two. It was as if some other invisible pesky body already inhabited seventeen.

Matt groaned aloud. He hadn't meant to react. Worse still, he'd been *hallucinating*.

'You okay, Mr Cooper?'

A mask. A Fibrotek bunny suit. A red badge. *Birken*. At least the guard had no gun in a holster, not in here. A gun might go off by accident, showering pollution, even if the bullet didn't hit a half-million-buck machine.

A rota of two élite security guards kept permanent watch in the qua area on Racine's orders. They must be bored senseless, though somehow they remained vigilant. If one of them seemed to go into a trance, the other was obliged to report him, then the dreamer would be out on the street, sacked.

Working for QX might be state of the art and cutting edge and well paid, but it was also purgatory.

'I said are you okay, Mr Cooper?'

Matt nodded. 'My shift's nearly finished.'

I just imagined I saw a roulette wheel upon this screen.

The guard glanced towards the one completed prototype quantum computer which stood on display behind a perspex screen. Racine's idea, to have it on show in here. A Holy Grail, to inspire the workers.

Closed up neatly as it was, it looked like a cream-coloured plastic suitcase. When opened up, the top lid of the suitcase became a flip-up screen. The underlid was the fold-down touch-sensitive keyboard. The computer was portable enough. Bit of a heave, but portable.

It was plugged in to the mains to run the liquid nitrogen cooler. Also, it contained powerful recharegable batteries which could keep the cooling running for up to twelve hours so that the suitcase could be transported from place to place.

The power used by the computer itself was tiny. The cooler was the heavy user.

Thanks to its motherboard of quantum chips, the machine would run faster than Cray supercomputers. With its multiple ports for expansion boards and connections to other systems it would outperform a roomful of

Crays. Its chassis had been made in the QX complex. Here in the qua area its motherboard was inserted – its soul, as it were. Here the machine had been alpha-tested, though not yet fully brought into operation. Several other chassis awaited motherboards. Those were also behind perspex windows.

The first prototype awaited its christening, when Tony Racine got out of hospital. Its christening – and the final stages of its alpha-testing, for which Racine had decreed that he must be present in person.

After that there would be a swanky formal launch, with maximum fanfare.

Matt had heard rumours that Irene Dallas, San Jose's favourite opera singer, would perform an anthem at the launch. And that John Denver was going to be hired to sing a specially commissioned ballad. And that Melissa Friend, the latest sensational *Baywatch* babe, would be invited to keyboard a question – any question – for the quantum computer, which by then would be loaded with megabytes of data as well as connected to the Internet.

Six months of fast-track beta-testing of prototypes by trusted users would follow before commercial release.

Personnel were running a sweepstake on what name Racine would finally pitch for.

'*Root*,' said the guard to Matt, baffling him for a moment. 'I say that's what it'll be called. That's what Racine's name's French for. It's short. It's simple. It's sort of fundamental. It's like the way forward too. Route to the future. What do you think?'

'I think he'll just call it the Racine. But,' lied Matt, 'I'm not much of a gambling man.'

Just in case Birken had ambitions as a security ace and was fishing.

'Of course,' mused Birken, 'he might just call it the Q. Join the Queue, hmm? How about that as a slogan?'

'Doesn't that make it sound a bit slow?'

'Uh. Damned right.'

Matt was damned, certainly. That much was true. Ever

since he had encountered Enrichment Counselling and Gwenda Loomis.

39

As a student at Stanford, Matt had become obsessed by the discovery that, down at its fundamentals, reality wasn't absolute. Reality was a matter of probabilities.

In a sense – admittedly an inaccessible sense – every blade of grass and every drop of blood in his body relied upon probabilities. Down at its deepest foundations, the world was a haze. In the big macro-world you could never observe this flux. A single drop of blood was the size of Jupiter compared with the subatomic level where probabilities reigned.

In the big macro world you could still play with probabilities. You could do so by gambling.

Games of chance gave an angle on the universe. They offered a bit of leverage. They were a way to put yourself in key, mentally and emotionally, with ultimate reality. If you were in tune with ultimate reality, you stood a good chance of success. When he'd joined QX, Matt earned a big enough salary to play games. Or at least he supposed so.

Modest beginnings, slippery slope.

He had begun to drive out at weekends to Lake Tahoe.

Such a lovely area: the great high-lying lake girded by conifer forests and rimmed by ten thousand foot peaks. Tahoe's forests had regrown densely since being stripped for pit-props a century ago by miners exploiting the Comstock lode. Almost fished to extinction by those hungry bygone miners, trout and salmon had recovered their numbers in the limpid water. These days, algae feasting on the pollutants from septic tanks and chemically fertilized lawns reduced visibility, but you could still see seventy feet down below the keel of a scudding yacht or sloop.

Such stately stone mansions, such restaurants and hotels and motels – and just across the Nevada border in Stateline, such a neon array of casinos, particularly the glittering Wheel of Fortune with its huge plush lounge boasting long-legged dance troupes and its cut-price all-day breakfasts of omelettes, strawberries and waffles, and its generous credit line. Generous for a while.

Generous until Matt found himself a hundred thousand dollars in debt, and deserted by Tanya, who had enjoyed trips to Tahoe even though Matt's attention was elsewhere during those compulsive weekends, more eye-blearing than gazing at monitor screens in the qua room of the fab-lab.

Had it not been for Tanya, who liked scenery, Matt might have gone gambling in Reno instead of taking the more southerly route.

Of course he could have gambled much closer to home. A local option allowed gaming at places such as Route 101 and the Garden City Restaurant. Since Proposition 13 had put a lid on tax rates for property, there had been the need to get additional revenue from somewhere. A gambling tax was ideal. But it would have been stupid for Matt to indulge his obsession locally, where he could be noticed. Besides, places such as Route 101 were crowded with Vietnamese immigrants. Totally alien atmosphere. Viet-namese immigrants equalled crime, and microchip thefts. Not a good idea at all. Anyway, Matt preferred roulette in lux surroundings, not cards or dice games.

Probably Matt had been going to settle down with Tanya. He knew he wasn't the world's most fetching man, with that weak chin of his, and bulgy nose and sallow skin; but the salary and trips to Tahoe helped. Now probability had come up otherwise.

Probably he had been going to reverse his losing streak and recoup. What could fund him to do so now? He had reached the limit. He was at the brink, on the edge.

He didn't actually own his condo apartment on Calle de Verano in Santa Clara, an easy drive from the QX building. So he couldn't sell the apartment and rent instead.

One day in his mailbox Matt had found a glossy flyer advertising Enrichment Counselling, based in equally glossy Los Gatos, just five miles south – on Santa Cruz Avenue where Tanya had loved to browse through the fashion boutiques and teddy bear shops and gourmet food stores and antiques emporiums.

Experiencing sexual difficulties?

Addicted to chocolate or to games of chance?

Is your memory letting you down?

Worried about your *financial* state?

Isn't money the root of all misfortunes? Empower and enrich yourself! Guided Self-Help using biofeedback and modified Shamanic Wisdom will focus your potential and enrich you literally within three months – otherwise, all your fees refunded. First consultation free on production of this leaflet. Phone for a fully confidential appointment.

If you could afford an address amongst the custom clothiers and the teddy bears, you weren't any run-of-the-mill Bay Area shamanic counselling service.

Matt had phoned. He had driven to Los Gatos. He had met Gwenda Loomis.

40

Gwenda's counselling environment was sited over one of those very teddy bear shops specializing in authentic old German bears selling at well over a thousand dollars, and repro teddies for rather less.

The big room couldn't seem to decide whether it was a therapy office or a tasteful consciousness-enhancing art gallery. Bright Huichol yarn paintings adorned the walls. Coiled serpents and plants and other power objects radiated twisty luminous rays. Figures were crowned with flares of light as though their hats were crowded with candles or short upright neon tubes. Hoop drums hung here and there. Cedar incense smouldered.

There was also a computer system – on-line on that first occasion with the Dow Jones share index. There was biofeedback equipment, a virtual reality rig, and medical gear for monitoring pulse and heartbeat and the electrical activity of the body and its aura, if bodies did indeed possess auras.

The place was prosperous and high-tech and emotionally, spiritually comforting, uplifting. A psychiatrist-style chaise-longue and an authoritative executive desk with maroon leather inlay completed the décor.

Gwenda Loomis's sumptuous, glossy, ringleted raven-black hair framed a serene oriental buttercream face. She wore a gold and silver high-collar dress, slit up the side, over white silk trousers.

Her voice was soothingly affirmative – especially when Matt, reclining on the chaise-longue wearing eye-shades, had listened through a button in one ear to a recording of shamanic drum and rattle and chant, while Gwenda questioned him tactfully.

His stress level had dived. His sense of self-worth ascended. He was an asset rather than a liability. He felt afloat, buoyant.

Gwenda diagnosed that his gambling should be radically reassessed in a holistically positive spirit. Matt could become his own shaman. His life should be a spiritual as well as a worldly pilgrimage.

'You chose the Path of Probability,' he heard her say. 'Yes, it was a *Path* you chose – both in your work,' which he'd needed to outline to her, 'and in your personal quest for prosperity. The trouble is, Matt, that you *pursue* this Path – and therefore it flees from you. Instead, you yourself must be the Path. The Path must be you. Let me tell you about pig-balancing . . .'

In a certain country in South-East Asia, she had explained, a dead pig would be placed upon an altar loaded with offerings of cakes and wine for the gods. The presiding shaman would call upon the mighty Mountain Spirit and the God of Seven Beginnings. Petitioners would stuff banknotes into the pig's mouth. Then the shaman would impale the pig with a three-pronged trident. Helped by the investors, the shaman would hoist the animal and would balance the pommel-end of the upright trident upon the mouth of a wine bottle. If the pig stayed balanced, prosperity would flow.

'Unlikely though it seems, Matt, a shaman who is in key can usually balance a pig if enough bank-notes have been invested.'

Matt had already invested a great number of bank-notes in the ever-open mouth of the well-balanced Wheel of Fortune.

Yet not *quite* in the right spirit.

He signed up for therapy.

Back at home, as instructed, he listened to the tape of drumming and rattling which Gwenda had sold him, and he visualized an impaled pig balanced upon a bottle.

His progress was splendid. During a subsequent session of spiritual and worldly self-analysis he discovered that far from milking him for fees, Gwenda Loomis valued him as a precious pilgrim. She insisted on 'investing' a thousand dollars 'in the mouth of the pig' so that he could drive to Tahoe and visualize the balancing act while he staked the money. Unfortunately, on this occasion the pig fell off the bottle.

Gwenda wasn't downhearted. Matt must balance the pig again, with another thousand dollars. This time he should listen to the drum-and-rattle tape on a Walkman while he was in the Wheel of Fortune. She would have accompanied him herself if she had not felt that her presence by his side might be a distraction. By now Gwenda in the counselling environment was no longer wearing any silk trousers under the high-collared dress, slit almost up to the waist. Her buttercream leg and thigh would show occasionally, enchanting him.

In due course, Gwenda revealed that through a debt-shark agency Enrichment Counselling's backers had picked up Matt's tab from the Wheel of Fortune.

The trident was fixed in the pig.

Matt was off one hook, and on to another. A sharper, deeper and more physically threatening hook. He could pay off his debt and accumulating interest with choice nuggets of information about QX's quantum computer.

He wouldn't want to upset Gwenda's backers by consulting the police. She would deny everything. Nothing could be proven. No demonstrable link existed between her and Matt's gambling debt. His would be the ravings of an unbalanced person whom she had simply been trying to help spiritually. And if he snitched, something very unpleasant might happen to him. Not immediately. In the next year or so. Something along the lines of a pig being impaled.

Matt certainly had no intention of confiding in Security at QX. He would be out on his ear at once. He'd be blacklisted. Who else in the industry would want to employ a compulsive gambler?

Yet Gwenda sincerely cared about him. She valued him. She cherished him. She would cross her legs as she sat, displaying a shapely shank, a lovely knee, an exquisite curve of thigh.

41

Matt was on nodding terms with the couple of men who shared an apartment upstairs from him in the condo on Calle de Verano. Jim was an attorney specializing in consultancy on medical issues, living harmoniously with Bobby who was President of the Dawnglow Company, distributors of Spirutino nutritional products. Bobby and Jim enjoyed aikido, baroque music and French-style cooking, the ABC of their mutual rapport.

Jim did not recall receiving any flyer about Enrichment Therapy in their mailbox.

The hand-delivered sheet must have been specially targeted. Some super-hacker must have got into the personnel records or the payroll file at QX trawling for names and addresses. And into the files of how many other companies in the valley?

And into the accounts of casinos in Stateline? And in Reno too? Money had certainly been spent on research.

Matt could hardly ask during yoghurt time at the fab-lab

if anyone else had recently been solicited by a shamanic prosperity-counselling service in Los Gatos. The question could expose his own position. Gwenda's backers must have been searching for all kinds of Achilles heels: financial, sexual, whatever.

Suppose Matt had ignored the flyer. Suppose he had simply tossed it away with the other junk mail? Would there have been a second, more personalized approach? Now he would never know.

42

In early evening sunlight Matt walked from the south wing of the bronzed glass building towards his white Porsche Carrera in the southern parking lot.

Along Jefferson Avenue quite a few of the sprawling low-slung buildings favoured bronzed glass. The fab facilities themselves were in the interiors of the buildings, surrounded by offices whose occupants liked a view denied to the fab workers. Sometimes bronzed glass clad a second storey of cement, since naked cement was aggressive and the desired image was candid, transparent, user-friendly.

Most new fabs these days were setting up in Milpitas and Freemont to the north where land was cheaper, though Adobe Systems had recently bucked the trend with their new mini-skyscraper in central San Jose, the tallest building in town. QX certainly wouldn't be shifting from its present site.

Until recently, anyone had been able to wander right up to buildings like QX through the car parks. Peer in through windows, whatever. That was changing now. With the rise in armed robberies, security fences were going up. Gates with barriers and gatekeepers. QX had been the first on Jefferson Avenue to fence itself in.

Matt had bought the Porsche when he'd been on a roll. Roulette wheel, driving wheel . . . perfect car for a Silicon

Valley ace, ideal for zipping out through Sacramento to Tahoe, and nipping past trailers and tour buses labouring up those steep gradients on the two-lane stretch through the American River Canyon.

Even filtered by pollution haze, the sun made a wall of gold of the western-facing stretches of QX. The building was cross-shaped, aligned with the compass. At the intersection of its low wings arose a stubby bronzed glass tower where Racine would usually be roosting if he weren't in hospital. Just like some flight controller at the international airport half a dozen miles away to the east, from which a silver jetliner was even now ascending into hazy azure emptiness. Smooth jaundiced humps of foothills were visible, though only just. There'd been no rain nor wind. Matt was back in the world of impurity. Hundred and fifty thousand particles per cubic metre?

Amongst the multicolour mosaic of parked cars – many now moving off – transplanted palm trees lifted limp fronds. Rows of yuccas were like green mantraps waiting to clash their sword-arms shut. Within the perimeter fence, which was tipped with razor-wire as if decorated in tinsel, sprinklers were refreshing a zone of lawn, spraying rainbows like silent explosions from imaginary land mines buried in a demilitarized strip.

Exit through the south gate was fairly swift as usual. Swipe a card through a reader, ignore the bored stare of the tan-uniformed guard in his armoured-glass booth, swing on to the road past the giant QX corporate sign. Maybe Racine would soon commission an adjacent building in the shape of a letter Q to stand north-west of the already existing X, so as to impress passengers in planes.

Soon Matt was out of the tech domain of electronics buildings which studded the flatlands like innumerable glossy gambling chips upon a great table. He headed south in the Porsche along crowded 85, Saratoga–Sunnyvale.

Summoned by Gwenda.

Puppet-pulled by her phone call that morning – while he'd been eating his breakfast. Breakfast today had been a croissant stuffed with ham and with strawberry jam, for the sake of the protein and the sugar and because he currently liked that blend of tastes. No doubt Bobby upstairs would have been horrified.

But Bobby hadn't received an invitation to Enrichment Counselling ...

'And when you succeed in stealing the prototype,' Gwenda told Matt, 'not only will all your debt be wiped out, but there'll also be a bonus. Eighty thousand dollars. Otherwise, you'll feel unenriched.' Oh, she cared for him.

This evening, her high-collared slit-sided dress was of indigo, in deep contrast to her exposed right leg as she perched upon the desk, her feet in silvery sandals dangling.

Matt was on the chaise-longue. As he regarded Gwenda, he imagined her vanishing like Alice's Cheshire Cat, only her feet and most of one leg and her face remaining visible. She would disappear soon. This pine-scented shamanic environment above the teddy bear shop would vanish.

Hooking Matt had cost what, so far? Including all the research work and setting-up costs, and buying up his debt, and the promised bonus ... say, quarter of a million?

The price tag for a quantum computer would be very high at first. Yet unlicensed piracy mightn't be the motive. Gwenda's sponsors must be from some country which wouldn't be allowed access to quantum computers at all. Already Matt had heard murmurs about strict export restrictions. There was an obvious reason for that. A compelling security reason. *Encryption* ...

Gwenda picked up a swipe-card. On a previous visit she had demanded Matt's card. She had taken it to another room, where either she herself or an unseen assistant must have scanned it. Here was a duplicate card.

'There's a virus on this copy,' she explained. 'Use it on the day, in the morning. Twelve hours later the computer record of people's movements will be erased.'

The log of who entered and left QX, and of who accessed which areas inside QX ...

'While I'm outlining the plan I think you ought to listen

to some quiet drumming and rattling to focus your consciousness—'

'Are you really a shaman?' he asked her, and felt foolish.

At dusk, there would be a delivery to QX, to the loading
bay. The loading bay area abutted on the fuel supplies and
tanks of acid and all the pumps for filtering air and the
vacuum lines and wiring and piping.

Leave your Porsche at home, Matt. We'll supply a car for
the day. A rented one.

Linger after your shift. Hide yourself in a toilet, maybe.
Keep your protective clothing on for subsequent anonym-
ity, minus the badge. At the agreed time there'll be an
attack on the east gate.

'The east wing's the artificial intelligence side—'

This is a *diversion*, Matt. There'll also be an attack on the
west gate. Meanwhile, a stretch of the perimeter fence
along the south side will be flattened by a rig.

Our delivery men will use some shaped charges to open
a way in to the fab area – as per the ground plan you drew
for us.

The interlocking fingers of the actual fabs were clip-
together panels. The fabs relied entirely on controlled air-
flow to keep the atmosphere pure. No need to blast one's
way any deeper, risking damage to the prototype.

Our delivery men will breach the qua area and toss in
some flash-bangs to disorient guards and others. As a side
effect, purity will be contaminated. This sabotage could set
QX back a bit.

Can't trust delivery boys to tell the prototype apart from
a chassis that doesn't have a motherboard. They'll beat a
hasty retreat.

As soon as you hear those bangs, Matt, get your ass into
the qua area. Grab the prototype. Head for the loading bay.
Hop in your rental car, which you must leave near the bay.

Out on Jefferson, a loudspeaker van will start booming
make-believe police orders to evacuate the building by the
south side car park. People will be streaming. And screaming. Pure panic.

101

Use that gap in the fence, Matt. Good tyres can crunch over loose razor wire. Rendezvous with me outside Portal Park in Cupertino. Collect eighty thousand dollars in cash. Never see me again.

No one need get hurt. The whole idea is to make a spectacular and disorienting show, then get well clear before police or SWAT squads arrive.

'Are you sure about no one getting hurt?'

'Some people might break a leg in the rush,' conceded Gwenda, swinging her own bare leg. 'That can't be helped.'

43

The motion of the truck rocked Clare to and fro on the mattress in darkness. It seemed an eternity since those air-holes had stopped admitting light. The positions of the holes had become indefinable. Draughts circulated.

Thank goodness that woman, Beth, hadn't taped Clare's mouth. Yet what would have been the use of screaming? Who would hear, except maybe Beth and whoever else was in the cab?

Might it be a *good* idea to succumb to hysteria? To shriek. To flood herself with adrenalin. This might avert the migraine which she feared was coming.

Keep a clear head! Gabriel Soul couldn't be intending to harm her much. Hold tight to this hope.

Strengthen your soul! Extraordinary lesson. Linked like two particles. Enlightenment. Rapture ... Those were the words Soul had used at the barbecue. This abduction had to be *theatre*. Psycho-drama.

You couldn't go around blithely kidnapping people. How did Soul suppose he could escape the consequences? Did he fantasize that once Clare was on his home territory she would promptly become a disciple of his because of his charisma?

Her hands and ankles firmly taped, she lolled to and fro.

A migraine was looming. She was almost sure of it.

Her attacks were irregular. Weeks of peace, or months of

peace, and then *wham*. Stress certainly contributed. An excessive sense of well-being could be a warning sign. The euphoria and nervous energy of a pre-migraine – and the sheer excitement of the conference: how could she be sure which was which?

Then the awful shock of those murders!

She'd also begun to retain water. After a migraine attack was over, her body would piss out accumulated water copiously, smelling sweetly fruity. Her period was due, too.

She hadn't consciously been estimating the arrival of her period with regard to their stay in San Francisco. She hadn't begun marking up a calendar months ago in anticipation. That would have been a male thing to do. Trying to plan everything in finicky detail. Best laid plans of mice and men.

A period wasn't negotiable. It couldn't be bought off. A migraine might be. Sometimes. With Jack last night she hadn't simply been hoping to erase the taint of Orlando but also to repel the vanguard of migraine.

Best laid plans. Now here she lay, trussed. A chick for the crazy guru.

Her Migraleve pills were in the Toyota, abandoned miles away. Did the Soul Shelter include a dispensary?

44

Clare was exhausted and nauseous and numb. She could hardly take in the sprawling fortress of concrete blocks and adobe set against a precipice, or walk when Beth first stripped off the parcel tape and guided her indoors, flanked by Jersey and the thin-faced man. Bats were flitting about under the treasure-vault of star-jewels.

Inside, a reception committee of gawking women awaited – as if she was due to be hustled off with them to a harem wing.

'Soul's *sacred, sacred, sacred,*' they hissed. They all seemed to know who she was. Some reached to touch, but Beth brushed them away. Some of these must have been demonstrators at the Convention Center. Was she now to be tormented by them? Stripped and reviled?

They were merely part of the scenery. A chorus of acolytes. Soul came to greet her, kitted out like some swashbuckling Russian peasant-prophet from last century.

How he smiled. How bright and intense his eyes were, as if he had doped them with belladonna. He seemed to be wearing blue lipstick. Was that to mark the cheeks he kissed, just as a farmer's ram would mark with blue wax the fleeces of the ewes it mounted?

'Welcome to my Soul Shelter, Clare! Welcome to salvation!'

'This isn't a very good idea, Mr Soul,' she began.

She swallowed. Her mouth had been dry. Now it was filling with drool, as if his proximity made her salivate. She swallowed spittle. 'I think I'm going to have a migraine.'

'We'll see if we can discharge it,' he said.

'Do *you* suffer from migraines, Mr Soul?'

He shook his head. That long, slicked-down hair, parted in the centre as if his head was divided in half . . .

'What a cut-glass accent you have, Miz Cambridge Prof-ette.' Oh God, Soul had definitely seen the story in the *Investigator*. Orlando had caused Soul's interest in her.

'Bollocks,' she retorted. 'It's a North London accent, just a bit poshed.'

Steer away from Cambridge, from computers, from consciousness, from sexy photos of herself.

Fat chance of that.

'Do you have fits, Mr Soul?' she hazarded. 'Do you speak in tongues?'

'Don't be so formal, Clare. Do call me Gabe.'

An abbreviated tour followed, to show off some of the extent of the guru's kingdom – which was only welcome to her in that the tour delayed whatever might come next.

Long corridors, lit by neon strips. Either there was a generator somewhere, or a very long power cable had been laid to the nearest supply. Doors and doors and doors. Numerous men and women were still about – some of them armed – as though they had been told to seem busy as bees. In a refectory a solitary bowl of cold bean stew waited for Clare, two frankfurters poking up like horns. Sight of the food made her feel like vomiting. She did drink some water before wondering whether it might be drugged.

Next to the refectory was an absurd – or appalling – orgy room, with a floor of rubber over water.

'I presume the children are all in bed,' she said.

'There aren't any children,' Soul informed her. 'All our women are on the pill. We can't have kids staying here. If we did, we'd need to include them all in our soul-binding, out of dutiful love. That could give the zombies an excuse to interfere with us.'

The logic of lunacy.

'Pills,' she said. 'I need Migraleve, or whatever you call it over here.'

'No, you need *truth*. Revelation.'

Soon Soul and Jersey and Beth were conducting her down a flight of cement steps to a stout door, which Jersey unlocked.

Fluorescent strips flickered tormenting to life, revealing a big dungeon cut from bare rock. Cool air blew from grilles. There was a table, with a woollen tartan rug covering up whatever. There was a large empty double-cage on legs. A red velvet curtain hung along the far wall. The biggest object in the cellar resembled a giant black fridge, big enough to hang a couple of sheep inside.

Jersey opened the container, wafting the door to ventilate.

She spied the snarling crewcut human head with the glass eyes mounted on a mahogany shield. As Beth guided Clare firmly to a chair near the naked rock wall, she staggered.

More psycho-drama! In games shops you could buy resin models of vicious aliens' heads, utterly realistic. Predatory. That was a model of human prey hunted by an alien. From a games shop.

She squinted at the alien script inscribed in the bottom of the wood. The word, however, was *Johnny*.

Johnny Earthman. Maybe these people played hunt-the-alien games in the desert at night. Maybe they thought Soul was in telepathic contact with aliens of superior wisdom.

Since nobody mentioned the head, neither did she. The focus of attention seemed to be the big black box. The mousy-haired woman with the birthmark stood behind the chair, hands resting lightly on Clare's shoulders. Clare's calf muscles were cramped. She wouldn't be leaping up. A cramp lurked in her abdomen too.

Soul straddled the other chair.

'So what did the Commies want from you?' he demanded.

Commies? What Commies?

'The men who burgled your room!'

'They were . . . Communists? How do you know about that?' Use his name. Ingratiate yourself with lunatics. 'Gabe, how do you know?'

For a while he bragged, showing off knowledge, while watching her reactions intently.

'The way I see it, there's a computer war going on in Russia between gangsters and the old KGB operatives. The KGB guys used to tap everyone's phones. *That's* exactly what Uncle Sam's into now. And now the KGB have set up – what's the name, Jersey?'

'Fapsi,' said the redhead.

'That's it. The Russian Federal Agency for Communications. It bought a big stake in computer networks in Russia because it already has a neat encryption system.'

What did any of this have to do with her?

'So this Fapsi outfit wants to license all the encrypting tricks for the sake of secure networks – which those KGB guys will then control. Private enterprise has to fight dirty to get out from under.'

'Gabe, where did you learn all this sort of stuff?' she asked.

Soul tapped his nose. 'It came to me by Night. I have powers of intuition.'

'Is that why you brought me here, Gabe?'

Soul rose abruptly, knocking over the chair.

'Shit no! I'm curious about the zombie enemies, Clare. But it's your own soul I'm *interested* in.' How his eyes burned. 'You have to shake loose from the old zombie habits of thought! You made a start by denouncing these quantum computers coming alive – though that can't be possible. Your photo showed me your true self. Your search for bliss.'

That cursed photo of Orlando's!

'I'd rather talk about Russians, Gabe.'

'You don't know diddly about Russians, do you? It's all a mystery to you.'

'I'm going to have a migraine,' she said.

He towered over her and spoke so softly, his tone enticing.

'You do know about the Schrödinger's Cat experiment.' He waved at the gaping black box. 'Beth doesn't quite understand it. She didn't have your smart education, Clare.'

The other woman's hands flexed on Clare's shoulders as if she was about to massage her, or inflict pain for information.

'Enlighten Beth!'

'The Schrödinger box? It's a thought-experiment,' said Clare. Soul was trying to disorient her totally. Russians. Bliss. Schrödinger.

'A thought experiment,' he agreed. 'Ah yes, but we shall carry it out.'

'What, using a real cat?'

Soul chuckled. 'Explain to Beth. Give her a tutorial.'

Despite her fatigue and the omens of migraine, Clare explained slowly. As slowly as possible.

Schrödinger was a physicist, right? One of the pioneers of quantum physics. Quantum physics seems to violate

107

common sense. It insists that a subatomic event remains a mixture of probability until a conscious observer investigates the situation. As soon as he or she does so, the event will either definitely have happened or not have happened. The act of observation causes the 'wave function' to 'collapse' into one clear-cut reality, right?

Until that moment, all possible outcomes co-exist. (All those possible worlds in which quantum computers will perform their myriad calculations!)

Sometime in the 1930s Schrödinger asked what would happen if you fastened a cat in a box along with a radioactive isotope and a particle counter linked to a container of cyanide gas.

Radioactive substances aren't stable, Beth. They disintegrate by shooting out particles, until what's left *is* stable.

Radioactive substances have to decay according to the laws of probability. That's what is meant by the 'half-life' of a radioactive isotope.

'Come again?' said Beth. 'How can something be half alive?'

The point of this tutorial presumably was to put Clare herself into a frame of mind where she was thinking quantum thoughts – so that her expectations would be suitably conditioned.

Some isotopes have a half-life of a million years, Beth. Some, a half-life of just a few seconds. If your chosen substance has a half-life of one hour, what this means is that after one hour exactly fifty per cent of its atoms will have decayed. After another hour, fifty per cent of the remainder. And so on. Are you following this, Beth with the birthmark?

If you use a single radioactive atom with a half-life of an hour, within one hour there's a fifty-fifty chance that it will decay or not decay. As soon as your particle counter in the Schrödinger box detects the decay, it triggers the release of cyanide gas. The cat in the box dies.

At the end of the hour you're about to open the box.

Is the cat dead or alive?

According to quantum physics, until you actually look,

the outcome is fundamentally unknowable. In one possible world the cat is alive. In another possible world it's dead. Both possible worlds are superimposed. Immediately you open the box, the wave-function collapses, and there's only one outcome.

If *you* find the cat dead, you can argue that in an alternative world a slightly different *you* finds the cat alive . . .

'Hey, Dr Seuss missed out on this one,' said Beth. She improvised gleefully:

> 'The cat that's alive,
> 'The cat that's dead:
> 'Which one's which
> 'Is in my head.'

Had Soul been coaching her?

'Obviously,' said Clare, 'this ignores whether the cat's a conscious observer in its own right—'

'It all comes down to consciousness, doesn't it?' interrupted Soul. 'Even according to your zombie scientists.' He shifted the tartan rug on the table to expose three gas-masks. *Gas-masks* . . .

'And now we shall carry out this fascinating experiment – with you as the pussy cat.'

Clare gaped into the great black box.

This had to be a hoax. A mind-game.

'Do you suppose,' Soul asked her, 'that I couldn't have got hold of a gizmo to do the job? Half-life. Single atoms. Radioactive release, all that shit.'

No, he couldn't have done so. That wasn't possible outside of a major laboratory. Radioactive decay didn't wait for a guru to start some clock. The apparatus would need to be very ingenious. It would have taken time to assemble.

'My disciples have donated quite a pile of money to the Soul Shelter, Clare. Quite a *pile*. Enough to buy almost anything I want. Beth here was in Physics grad school when she joined us. Stanford, no less.'

Fuck, thought Clare.

It was a lie. It had to be a put-on. She twisted.

'Beth, which radio-isotope have you used?'

Beth merely kneaded Clare's shoulders, probing pressure points.

'Beth, what's the half-life of plutonium?'

Beth gouged briefly. Pain lanced through Clare's shoulders. Then Beth caressed her soothingly.

'You'll be alive, honey, and you'll be dead. Both at once. Wow.'

'It could make a person really schizo,' said Jersey. He glanced at the thin man, Billy, and shrugged apologetically.

Soul glowered at Jersey. He dangled a gas-mask.

'Why would we have these if we aren't using genuine cyanide gas? Just like a real execution.'

Why? Because they had bought the masks. For show. For theatre. Just the same as they had bought that resin head.

Soul fished a photograph from his shirt. 'As for execution . . .'

The photo was easily recognizable as that of 'Johnny', whose preserved head hung on the wall. He was wearing combat-style clothing with many pockets. His hands were behind his back. He looked terrified. Naked rock and the closed door of this same chamber were behind him. Though no sign of the big black box . . .

'We gave Johnny a sporting chance, since he was such a sportsman,' said Soul. 'In an alternative world he'll be off shooting bighorns for his den, unless the scare reformed his behaviour.'

Johnny must be some member of this crackpot community. He must have posed for his photo. Soul had had a resin model made.

'Do you want to examine his head in detail? Check the fillings in the teeth?'

Clare was finding it increasingly hard to think.

'Do you want to examine his teeth?'

She shook her head mutely. Maybe there was cyanide gas in that box, along with some device to release it, probability fifty-fifty. These people didn't care. Other people were soulless zombies in their eyes.

110

'What happens if I'm still alive afterwards?' she mumbled.

'From the agony of suspense,' Soul declared grandly, 'to the ecstasy! In my golden bed at midnight.'

He was quoting some song. By Joni Collins. No, that wasn't the singer's name. Clare couldn't remember the right name. Soul was insane. His golden bed at midnight? She would be in no condition. She would be meat in misery, a mouse in his paws.

Soul glanced at his watch. 'Or half-past midnight, at this rate.'

Jersey winked. His face seemed to be cracking open. He stepped behind Clare and whispered, 'Incidentally, Professor, don't worry about air. There's plenty enough for an hour. Though you mightn't need it all.'

A jagged crack seemed to bisect Soul, and the cellar. Beth and Jersey were hoisting her from the chair, propelling her towards Schrödinger's box. High up at the rear of the box, she glimpsed some apparatus.

45

Jack woke with a throbbing headache. His cheek was pressed against grit. Congealed stickiness matted the crown of his scalp at the boundary with baldness.

Some creature was crying out insistently. For a moment Jack thought it might be Clare. Memory rushed back of the chase along the dirt road as darkness fell, away away from the Toyota. There'd been other bikers on burly machines . . .

Close by, and utterly vague, lay the dirt bike. A wheel jutted dimly upwards.

A less-than-half moon hung low over far featureless hills. Thousands of stars were diamonds sewn on a huge span of soft black velvet. From the distance came a brief high-pitched bray, the absurd, inexplicable sound of a strangled donkey. Nearby, something small rustled in some bush of tangled wire.

Jack pushed himself up to a kneeling position. Head

111

thumping, he staggered erect. Breeze ruffled his shirt. The blurry desolation around him was scarcely visible. No direction was more significant than any other. Nowhere did any light gleam, except starlight and that partial moon.

He struggled to right the bike, only to discover after undue effort that the bike was buggered. It wouldn't be taking him anywhere.

His groping hands did find a plastic canteen, which sloshed.

Half full.

He rinsed his mouth and swallowed some tasteless warm water.

If only he had learned to recognize constellations. He wouldn't know his direction until the coming of dawn in the east. This wasteland would promptly become a furnace. The water wouldn't last long.

However much he tilted his watch towards the moon, he couldn't make out the time. His headache was vile. At least he hadn't broken any bones or twisted an ankle.

Hours of night must remain. Normal walking speed was four miles an hour, right? He could make it back to the interstate – if only he knew which way that was. Once he set out, he mustn't change his mind or he could wander in circles. It was better to head defiantly in one direction. Use the hills as a guide. The moon would move.

He began to walk, clutching the canteen of water.

46

A single tiny bulb cast very little light inside the box. A Christmas tree bulb.

Clare hunched as far away as possible from the silent apparatus where that miniature bulb was mounted – alongside a nozzle.

Her skull was an eggshell tight with hot agonizing lava. Surely her head was about to burst. A grain of sand hitting it would split it. Already a ragged crack fractured her dim field of vision.

Thank God there was only a tiny light source in the box. Nevertheless, she seemed to see radioactivity within the apparatus – a blue radiance. She couldn't really be seeing radioactivity.

Time had vanished.

A brilliant flash erupted from the apparatus, spreading outwards blindingly. The radioactive isotope had decayed in a shower of light!

In its wake, half of her world and her knowledge of the world went away – had never even existed.

Utter absence confronted her in visible form. Half of the interior of the box had vanished. Half had disappeared so utterly that it was impossible to conceive that that particular portion of space had ever been present at all.

Dreadfully, that nullity sucked at her, to engulf and annihilate not only her but the whole universe of which she was a part.

She moaned in terror.

Yet half of the box still remained.

The isotope had decayed. She was dead. She was also alive. She was both at once – aware of both states. Of existence and of oblivion.

Her mind had split to span both states. And then her surroundings split and split again, into an infinite mosaic, a kaleidoscopic fly's-eye vision of existences and non-existences.

In that moment she understood what death was . . .

47

Jack had tramped across a sandy flat towards a slope. From the top of that slope he might be able to see some distant sign of a road, some solitary headlights cutting through darkness. After a while the slope eclipsed the hills beyond. His headache had eased to a putter.

The gradient was moderate yet the ascent seemed everlasting. Presently hundreds of pillars arose amidst the stones. Columns with spiny ribs towered over him. Cacti. A couple of times he tripped and picked himself up.

He was reaching the fag-end of exhaustion. Virtually sleepwalking. Sleep was switching on and off, cocooning him and releasing him. This place of thorny pillars was a dream-desert. Why try to stay awake when he could become buoyant and glide through these cactus columns? Maybe he was already asleep, hallucinating this stark forest.

In the mingled moonlight and starlight he noticed that the nearest pillar was dead. Exposed ribs rose, a cluster of tall poles or corset staves which a wind might rattle together. A collapsed core of dried pith suggested an abandoned wasps' nest.

With a heart-stopping flurry the top of the core detached itself. It launched itself on wings. Some sort of owl, fleeing from the intruder. Oh for its keen eyes, oh for its power of flight.

Jack sank to his knees, then sprawled.

The owl stared down at him from the top of a telephone or power pole. Its eyes were headlamps approaching along a straight paved road. The eyes grew steadily brighter. He had reached a road. A truck was coming. All of the cacti were utility poles, dozens of poles. If he climbed one of those, he could phone for help. The truck would have a radio in its cab. It was a recovery truck, come to retrieve his Norton ES2. The Pig had broken down.

His dad was driving the truck. A young woman sat by him. She looked like Clare but Jack knew that she must be Celia. He mustn't upset Celia, or Dad might take offense and leave him here in this South African wilderness.

'Dad,' he called out, 'the Pig needs a drink.'

His father looked like some detective, whose name eluded Jack. Dad held out a goblet of brandy.

'Don't you think you ought to stay alert, son?'

Celia climbed from the far side of the cab. She straddled the Norton. The engine awoke. Away she rode into the empty darkness.

114

'Clare!' Jack cried after her. Too late he had realized who she really was.

The headlamps of the truck were fading, running out of battery juice, becoming a dull orange.

48

Light flooded into the box. Beth truly was wearing a gas-mask. So were Jersey and Soul.

'Alive, Gabe. She's alive—'

Clare's migraine had vanished. So had the terrible blank void. Such ferment, such frenzy, filled her.

'I know!' she called out. 'I *know*.'

Jersey helped her from the box. He manoeuvred her towards the chair. Beth stooped inside the box to do something to the apparatus. Disarm it.

'Okay, Gabe, we're safe now—'

Only then did Beth, backing out, pull off her mask. The other two followed suit.

Soul's eyes glowed so attentively.

'What is it that you know, Clare?'

She babbled what she had discovered in the box about death.

'When people die, where can their memories and identities go to? There isn't enough *capacity* for our universe to be a store for dead souls. It's all lost—'

'Strong souls pass into the Virtuality,' he corrected her.

Hectic, she laughed.

'All lost, until now! Snuffed out! All extinguished.'

'Only zombies are extinguished.'

'No, everyone is! Every animal, every observer. Every-thing that has consciousness. Always going going gone. Me and my sister – and you too, going gone. Yet there *is* a way to store dead minds! They can be stored in the myriad probability universes side by side with ours. That's where our identities can be stored!'

There'd be probability universes where gravity was stronger. Universes where gravity was weaker. Where not enough hydrogen fused into helium, where the universe was merely a sea of gas. Where stars never formed, or burned out too soon for life to arise anywhere.

An infinity of barren lifeless universes.

Only in a universe where life arose could there be awareness of existence. Only there could there be mind, and reality. The infinity of dead ghost universes side by side with ours could be storage spaces for the ghosts of minds – if only a link existed. This was the lesson of the box.

'A link *will* exist, Gabe, if a quantum computer switches on and has self-aware access to all the parallel probability worlds. *There's* your virtuality, or whatever you call it—'

Soul growled.

'No fucking zombie machine is our saviour. We're already our own saviours, through rapture!'

'I've been dead and alive, both at once. I know!'

'Don't you try to upstage me!'

Clare squirmed. 'I'm bleeding.'

It was Beth who understood. She whispered to Soul.

He slammed his fist on the table.

'Get her out of here,' he told Beth. 'Lock her in a room. Leave me alone. I need to meditate, I need to foresee.' He was twitching. 'I knew our zombie enemies were getting ready to assault us, didn't I? There was a secret agenda to that conference in Tucson. Secret meetings about immortality for zombie honchos via machine-minds. That Commie fooled me with his talk about *Infamous* and making money. True voices speak to me. *Get her out of here.*'

49

Round the back of the Grub-Steak was a room with several beds in it, where Soul's bikers were snoring.

Apart from Nathan, who tossed and turned.

It was Nathan who had lost his bike.

He had been left waiting with the convertible and that Toyota for his fellow hard boys to bring the Englishman back, when they finally caught up with him. Jersey and Billy and Kath had already taken the woman away in the truck.

Presently he'd heard distant cracks of gunfire. By now it was dark. What was that shooting about? He had taken an Uzi from inside the Buick.

Then the others had come speeding back, headlamps glaring. They doused those soon enough. And then there had been a fucking siege.

Indian bikers had hung around for ages, out of sight with their lights off, revving in challenge, firing occasional shots while the hard boys fired back blindly.

The Indians appeared to have only a few handguns but the hard boys were pinned down.

Even after the Indians seemed to head away, one of them might still be lurking silently in the scrub, awaiting his opportunity.

It had been another hour till the hard boys risked moving out, Nathan driving the Buick.

Any hope of catching the Englishman was gone. By now no one had felt inclined to travel all the way back to the Soul Shelter.

Sleep at the Grub-Steak, therefore. After reporting in by radio.

Besides, Gabe mightn't be pleased.

50

Sitting cross-legged on his bed contemplating the desert, Gabe *perceived* and reached for the phone.

A sleepy Jersey answered.

A couple of minutes later Jersey was standing in the master bedroom, in green string briefs and a string vest. Curly red hair fuzzed his thighs and poked through most of the gaps in his underwear. He yawned. He knuckled sleep from his eyes.

'Jersey, pay attention. The Rough Riders have to find Clare's companion. They have to bring him here. I *know* he's still in the desert. I know it! I see Jack Fox as an owl sees a mouse.'

Gabe had tried to rehearse what might happen if Fox reached somewhere and contacted the zombie police.

He had toyed with a plan. Police would turn up at the Soul Shelter sooner or later. Sheriff's officers. FBI. Armed zombies. He would charm them.

I'm sorry to say some of my followers have been over-enthusiastic, officer. You see, part of my spiritual method is to deliver a shock to rigid thought-patterns – to encourage new perceptions. Lately one of my lieutenants has been making a bid to be leader of this community. He's been proposing some really melodramatic role-playing. I'm afraid this mock-kidnapping is an example. I've expelled him and his little clique. No, I don't know where they've gone . . .

After being in the box, Clare had gone hyper. Not in a way he wished. But hyper nonetheless. She might be a very unreliable witness . . .

Actually, she needed gentling now.

In fact the zombie authorities were irrelevant, he had soon perceived.

'You're the Saviour of Souls, Gabriel,' his voice had whispered within him. *'You're exempt from mundane laws. Never let agents of the zombie world enter this sanctuary. They would destroy it. Already the battle is under way between machine-men and the true immortals, and amongst machine-men too—'*

'Radio the Rough Riders, Jersey. Wake them up. Don't wait till dawn. Send them searching now.'

'But,' said Jersey.

'Fox is still in the desert,' Gabe insisted. 'He hasn't alerted anyone yet. We must stop him from doing that. But also, he's part of the secret agenda. Why else was he her companion? All is linked. They were both going from the conference to Silly-Con Valley, to San Jose, where the Tin Man is, and the quantum computers. I overheard this in Tucson. You heard her in the Truth Room. Machines will come to life and give afterlife to the zombies in power.'

'Gabe,' said Jersey, 'those boys will be half zonked.'

'If they wait, it'll be too late to find the fox.'

'Maybe Fox ran out of gas or blew a tyre or something. Maybe he's totally lost. How about if the Tin Man squad were to head up there to search by bike? If they leave right away—'

'No,' said Gabe. 'The Tin Man squad must set off for California in the morning. Get into place in San Jose. Prepare. The time is coming. Go and radio the boys right away. They've had enough sleep. Jersey, we might be going into the Virtuality soon. Then our world will be exactly as we desire for ever and ever, without zombie-people and zombie-governments. Just exactly as we desire!'

Gabe's inner voice was prompting him to wake the Brothers and Sisters – to announce that the climax of their dreams might be approaching faster than previously foreseen. No, the Tin Man team mustn't be fatigued. Before the team left the Soul Shelter, should Gabe question the Englishwoman? Were QX in San Jose planning to install a quantum computer in their Tin Man? Was *that* the secret scheme? Did she know this?

Gabe needed to catch a few hours' sleep to sort his head out. The Tin Man team shouldn't be delayed for any reason. Whatever he learned, he could radio to them.

'Listen,' he told the tired man in string underwear, 'when our Rough Riders find Jack Fox we'll have a few days to learn things, to tell the Tin Man team before they attack QX.'

'What things, Gabe?'

'QX may be intending to put a quantum computer into their Tin Man – to create a self-aware robot. Fox may know this even if *she* doesn't realize it yet. We brought her to the brink of realization, didn't we?'

Jersey nodded. Gabe was brilliant. He could see connections which were invisible to mundane minds. The Soul Shelter was the beating heart of history now. The planned attack on QX and Gabe's interest in the Englishwoman were two sides of the same damn coin. If the coming climax cost the lives of Brothers and Sisters, was it not as Gabe said? The Virtuality awaited them. Fulfilment for evermore.

Freedom from this zombie world which robots of lightning-swift brainpower might soon rule.

51

Not long before dawn, a Winnebago lumbered along a dirt track in the dusty wake of a station wagon. Inside that jumbo-size recreational vehicle two models, Marcia and Tina, implored Pablo to drive more slowly – not that he was exceeding thirty, but the constant rocking was making them feel sick. What if they bruised their beautiful bodies? And they were so *tired*, up at a sadistic four-thirty.

Marcus had his zipped camera bags sealed inside additional polythene bags to exclude any dust, though all the windows of the RV were shut tight. The noise of air-conditioning on full had been drowned by a *Doors* tape until Tina complained that the music was giving her a headache. From his revolving executive chair towards the front of the curtained and wallpapered interior, Marcus loudly badgered Pablo to hoot at the station wagon and pick up speed. The eastern sky was already more violet than purple.

Steadying her make-up case, Sammy berated Renny – their location scout and operations manager – for not rousing the team at four o'clock, if they *must* travel so damned far from the hotel. Since Renny was in the station wagon ahead – along with Filbert and the big hoop-shaped reflectors – Sammy's complaints merely grated on Marcus's assistant and boyfriend Erik. Always full of excuses, isn't our Sammy?

Much of this bitching was part of the normal psych-up before a shoot. Yet out here in the desert, time really was critical. Marcus could only take his pictures in the earliest morning or towards sunset. That's when the landscape had colour, gloriously photogenic colour. For the rest of the day, colour was bleached out by glare.

Not to mention the blazing heat and the threat of sunburn. Marcia and Tina could hardly cover their whole bodies in factor 25. No one wanted faces all screwed up and squinting, and dark glasses were a no-no. Dark glasses would spoil the impish, provocative wild intimacy of a picture of naked women, naked landscape.

Heat was a problem in so many ways. Heat flattened a woman's nipples. Erik would be standing by with a cool-box of ice cubes, ready to dart forward and rub Marcia's or Tina's teats so that they stood erect.

'For Christ's sake, *hurry up!*' bellowed Marcus; and Pablo did blat the horn a couple of times.

'I'm going to throw up,' moaned Marcia.

Red lights glowed. Renny must have taken the double hoot as a signal to stop. As Pablo braked, Marcus's chair swung like some funfair car and he grabbed the walkie-talkie from the table heaped with gear.

'Winnie to Wagon. *Get a move on!*'

52

Jack woke amongst the tall thorny ribbed columns as some bird was delivering itself of a noisy, mechanical dawn anthem. Just a few feet from his face, the largest centipede he had ever seen was proceeding towards him. A shiny golden-brown, with dozens of rippling little claw-foot legs, it was as long as his hand. Antennae questing ahead, it was a miniature armoured robot on the offensive.

Squealing, Jack rolled away from the centipede. Gathering his wits, he sat up painfully. His whole body ached.

The creature rippled up on to the canteen, feet scrabbling on the smooth plastic side. Squirming about, it investigated the screw-cap. Must smell water.

Jack lobbed a pebble, then another. He scored a hit on the canteen and the centipede scuttled.

High streaky clouds in a lilac sky were orange and scarlet. *Dawn.* Dreadful dawn. Lovely at the moment. Within half an hour heat would be pounding at him from the fireball of the sun, racking up the temperature.

Already the pinky mauve of the east was becoming hyacinth-blue.

He would use his shirt as a turban. His chest and back might become burnt beef, but he must protect his head.

But not yet.

He must ration his water. Would rationing be a waste of time? He might sweat pints. He might dehydrate so quickly that he would be dead by noon, a leathery mummy. He mustn't throw the canteen away once it was empty, just in case he did find some water-hole.

Standing up was a torment, but at least he could walk.

Pressure in his bladder. It seemed folly to lose liquid from his body. He had no choice in the matter.

As he was zipping up, in the distance he heard the buzz-saw whine of bike engines.

From the elevation of the slope he saw weaving lights out on the sandy flat.

Three, four bikes, well separated.

One of them stopped. Did its rider have binoculars? When the sun cleared the mountains, its light should reflect off any lenses.

Amidst all these cactus-pillars a moving person mightn't be spotted. The crest of the slope seemed much closer in dawn-light than it had in darkness. With an effort Jack picked up the water canteen. How sore his feet were. At least the shoes he had been wearing in the Toyota were canvas. His feet felt swollen, but the canvas yielded.

The cacti grew less sturdily towards the top of this slope, which must protect them from winds. When he crossed the ridge, he would be silhouetted.

Light burst from the east as a quivering yolk oozed into the sky.

Scarcely thirty yards ahead of him, a figure strode into view upon the crest.

A woman.

She was stark naked – apart from bangles on her wrists and on her ankles. Short links of chain hung from the

122

bangles. She was holding a pink parasol. A chain dangled down her forearm.

Jack could only gape, bewildered.

The woman was dusky-skinned, and utterly beautiful, with long slim legs and hair in tumbling raven curls. Breasts like ripe mangos. Dark quiffs adorned her groin. A coating of frog-spawn upon her feet: slip-on jelly shoes.

How her body glowed in the light.

Momentarily abashed, Jack glanced away from her, at the nearest cactus. That plant glistened too. Its mottled surface was waxy as if thinly coated in Vaseline to soothe its many blemishes.

No such flaws about the naked young woman. Swiftly she lowered her parasol as a shield.

'Hey,' she called back plaintively, 'we have *company*.'

'Help me!' Jack appealed.

He must surely look in need of help. Soiled slacks and shirt. Grime all over. Dried blood on his head. Plastic canteen clutched in one hand.

A ravishing naked young woman could not be out for a morning stroll in this wilderness, equipped only with a parasol and jelly shoes. Not unless some naturist colony owned a ranch just on the other side of the rise! What naturists would want to expose their skins to the Arizona sun? He kept staring at her in case she vanished.

And now she had company. Three other people, four other people came up beside her. One was a ruggedly handsome middle-aged man in white polo shirt and shorts and straw Panama hat. He was carrying a camera case in a polythene bag.

'Fuck,' he swore loudly as soon as he saw Jack.

A younger man with dapper moustache, in white T-shirt and shorts and baseball cap, balanced a collapsed tripod over his shoulder.

A tubby black man in baggy jeans and floral shirt lugged what looked at first sight like a large lightweight satellite receiving dish. The black man's shirt was open, exposing a bulging moon of black flesh with a crater of a navel.

A tall skinny woman, red-headed and covered in freckles,

held a slim black case. She was wearing a shin-length green cotton dress over cowboy boots.

Tripod. Cameras.

Was a movie being shot on location?

A *nude* movie? Some sort of erotic heroic fantasy about an escaped slave girl?

Was this to be a tableau for some soft porn magazine?

The man in the Panama glanced back at the sun.

'Fuck it!'

Jack stumbled closer.

The dirt bikes were buzzing more noisily. One of them was already beginning to ascend the long slope. The cactus columns were obstacles which would slow the riders a bit.

Jack gestured. 'They're hunting me—'

'Why,' demanded the black man, 'are they hunting you?'

Jack's voice croaked. No time to take a drink.

'They forced me and my girlfriend off the road last night. They kidnapped her. I got away. We're tourists from England.'

'I didn't think you were Wyatt Earp,' said the man with the camera.

'Did you say those punks *kidnapped* your girl?'

The black man set down the satellite dish – no, that was some sort of reflector. He delved into a bulging pocket of his jeans.

'Yes!' cried Jack. All the bikes were climbing the slope by now, weaving through the cactus forest.

'Get back to the Winnie, Tina,' the skinny woman ordered the naked model. 'Marcia, you too!'

Another naked young woman had just come into view. She was blonde. Gell spiked her hair, under an identical pink parasol. She too wore only bangles and severed chains and jelly shoes. Behind her appeared a darkly bearded man in straw hat and shades, shorts and safari jacket.

'What's going on—?'

Tina, the dark-skinned model, was already obeying the skinny woman.

The black man pulled out a shiny little pistol. Ostentatiously he spread his legs. He pointed the pistol two-handed, sighting it down the slope. He was making sure that his stance was unmistakable.

'Don't hit any of them, Filbert,' the photographer said anxiously. 'Fire over their heads, or we'll really be screwed up.'

'Sure, sure. Don't shit yourself, Marcus. It's just to scare them off. *Get lost!*' he bawled at the top of his voice.

The closest of the dirt bikes was scarcely two hundred yards away.

The black man let off a shot. Pausing, he raised the pistol conspicuously before lowering it and firing a second shot.

Amidst the cacti, the riders braked. They quit their bikes. They dodged behind spiny ribbed columns.

'*Get lost!*' Filbert bellowed again.

An automatic weapon opened up.

Pulp and pith exploded from a cactus above a single branch halfway up its trunk. The great plant must already have been gashed and weakened in that part. Hardly any of the other cacti had branches. Maybe that lone branch had been a response to injury, a counterbalance. Now more of its ribs had been smashed. The whole top of the trunk began to lean. Twenty degrees, thirty. Explosively, it cracked.

More automatic fire crackled. Dirt kicked up just a few yards away from Filbert.

By now Jack had reached the top.

Beyond the ridge the terrain dipped into an exposed sandy flat bounded by foothills rambling up and away. Twin lines of dark spoil edged a track, looking like two trails of gunpowder. Beside the crude track a station wagon and a big white mobile home were parked.

'For Christ's sake,' shouted the bearded man, 'everyone back to the vehicles! Got to protect the girls. Get out of here! Drop any gear and run like hell.'

He knocked the tripod from the moustached fellow's shoulder. He snatched the freckled woman's case. Paintbrushes and coloured pencils spilled out.

'Goddamn it, Renny—!'

Hesitation was brief. They all fled. Jack did his stumbling best to keep up with the fat man. Was Filbert lagging behind the others not on account of his bulk but to act as an armed rearguard?

The two naked women loped with a peculiarly loose stride. They had thrown their parasols away and held their arms out from their sides so that the dangling chains would not inflict bruises. They cried out to a burly Hispanic who was beside the vehicles—'*Pablo, Pablo!*'

It was as if Tina and Marcia were fleeing from sexual slavery and pursuit towards a Mexican liberator – as if an erotic heroic fantasy was indeed now being filmed. Marcus still clutched his camera, although his Panama hat had blown off.

The blonde model sprawled, and screamed.

Her ankle-chains had tangled.

She writhed, shrieking.

The man in the safari jacket – Renny – caught up with her. Stooping, he inspected. He burbled soothing words.

Tina had halted. She was staring back. Marcus and Eric and Sammy gathered around the fallen Marcia.

'—*snapped her ankle*—'

'Oh shit—'

Renny slid his arms under Marcia's knees and the small of her back.

'*Get your arms round my neck, girl, or I can't hold you. You'll slip!*'

Jack was in a lather of sweat. Marcia's body would be slicked with moisture.

Marcia clutched Renny almost in a stranglehold. She cried out as he struggled erect, hoisting her. He staggered towards the vehicles.

The accident had let Filbert and Jack catch up.

'*She's got to get to a hospital*—'

The Hispanic – Pablo – was trying to make sense of what was happening. He must have spied the pistol in Filbert's hand. He dived into the station wagon, to emerge with a revolver larger than the black man's handgun.

126

Buzzbuzz: a dirt bike had topped the rise. Quickly another followed, then a third.

The riders paused to survey the barren flat and the track and the pair of parked vehicles – and nothing else for miles and miles. A fourth bike caught up. The riders began to descend.

'Everyone into the Winnie!' Renny called out. The Winnebago would be their sanctuary.

Tina's bum disappeared inside. The make-up woman followed next. Then Marcus, ushered by Erik. Jack hung back until Erik helped Renny manoeuvre the injured blonde inside. Marcus was taking photos from the shelter of the doorway. The bikes had separated and were spreading out. As Jack hauled himself aboard, Marcus growled, 'Persistent bastards, aren't they, your friends?'

The light inside was muted by slat-blinds, except in the driving cab. Wallpaper, carpet, furled curtains, chairs, wardrobes: the interior was like a hotel room, as if Jack had stepped through some magical door from the desolate desert directly into civilization. Moaning came from the floor where Erik and Rennie had laid Marcia.

Tina crouched by her, holding her hand.

'It'll be all right, sweetie. You'll be fixed up fine.'

Sammy was rummaging in a First Aid box. She shook four pills into her palm, then pulled open a fridge door to extract a bottle of water.

On the wall a glossy calendar advertised a truck manufacturer. A nude model with long silver-blonde hair posed on the roof of a rig's cab, legs crossed, caressing a great silvery hooter. The model wasn't Tina or Marcia, but Marcus must have taken the calendar pictures. What would his next assignment promote? Chains for tyres in snowy weather? Chain-saws?

Renny thrust past Marcus to reach the driver's seat and start the ignition. The station wagon was parked directly ahead, so they would need to reverse. A gunshot sounded outside as Pablo fired his big revolver. Filbert was coming on board. The engine roared, almost drowning a crackle of automatic fire.

The black man was tumbling forwards, wide-eyed, open-mouthed. Several red mouths gaped bloodily in his bare chest. The window beside the door had exploded into hundreds of crystals.

'Fuck damn it, they shot Filbert—!'

Quitting the driver's seat, Renny tried to pull the black man further inside. His weight proved too much. Those big jean-clad legs jutted through the doorway. Pablo clambered in over Filbert and crouched. Blood stained Pablo's shoulder. His injury seemed to be a flesh-wound, nothing deep. He fired out. Marcus took Pablo's picture, then he focused on Filbert's back, the ripped shirt soaked with blood.

'Fuck it, Marcus—!' protested Renny as he resumed the driving seat.

'What am I *supposed* to do?'

Erik picked up the shiny little pistol the black man had dropped.

'Do I use this?' he appealed to Marcus.

The Winnebago cannoned backwards. Items tumbled. People bumped and fought for balance.

A bang sounded from the rear as if the vehicle had collided with something. The floor wasn't level now. Renny powered the Winnebago forward, swinging the wheel to miss the station wagon.

Boom, from the front of the Winnebago. The entire floor tilted. The heavy vehicle was digging in.

'They shot out the tyres—'

Pablo fired again from the open doorway. Erik jerked up a blind and slid a window panel open by a few inches. He squinted. He pointed the pistol.

'Erik!' protested Marcus. 'They'll shoot *back* at you.'

Jack had subsided upon the carpet.

Marcia was mumbling, 'My career's ruined, my career's ruined. Do we have good insurance, Sammy, do we have good insurance?'

'It's Renny who deals with the insurance crap,' Tina told Marcia.

'Will you ask him? I'll never walk again.'

'Renny's *busy*,' snapped Sammy. Despite the roaring engine the slanted Winnebago was only shifting a few inches at a time. A wounded elephant crippled in two legs.

'How can I pose?' wailed Marcia.

The engine quit. Or Renny had switched it off. Its labours were futile.

In the silence a voice called from outside, '*We want the Englishman. You hear? That's all. Throw him out and we'll leave you alone.*'

Marcus called from by the doorway, 'Wait! You know we're armed.'

'*Five minutes, then we fire at your gas tank.*'

Keeping their heads low, Renny and Marcus hastened back to where Jack was and knelt.

'Filbert's fucking well dead,' Renny said. 'Why do these people want you so much?'

'They kidnapped my companion—'

The cry came from outside, '*We don't want to hurt him, you hear? We don't want to hurt you, Doctor Fox.*'

'They know his name! Is Fox your name?'

Pablo called, 'One of them's using a radio or mobile phone or something. Must be more of them somewhere—'

'If they already have your girlfriend,' said the make-up woman, 'why chase after you like mad dogs?'

'They *are* mad,' said Jack. 'They're members of a cult.'

'Do you mean you already knew them?' Sammy demanded. Sweat soaked her.

'Listen,' said Jack, 'I'll go with them. Then you'll be able to use your station wagon—'

'Unless they shoot its tyres out too.'

'You must tell the police—'

'You bet we'll tell the police! Filbert's been murdered.'

'Tell them that Gabriel Soul has kidnapped Clare Conway and Jack Fox. That's Gabriel Soul, who was called Kaminski.'

'Is *he* out there?'

'Those are disciples of his. They took Clare Conway to the Soul Shelter, wherever that is. Professor, Professor

129

Munro – that's it – at Phoenix, she knows about Soul. Can you write this down?'

'I lost all my blusher pencils,' Sammy said bitterly. 'What is this, some crazy undercover operation? You haven't been straight with us at all.'

'I haven't had *time*—'

Renny pulled pen and notebook from one of his pockets. 'Give me all those names again – fast. Just the names.'

As Jack repeated names and Renny printed them, Marcus called to Erik, 'Do you still have the light meter?'

Marcus fiddled with his camera, then he snapped Jack repeatedly.

'For the police,' he explained. 'And newspapers and TV stills.'

'Absolutely,' said Renny, 'or we really lose out.'

'How can you say a thing like that when Filbert's dead?' protested Sammy.

'It would be dumb not to.'

'Kerr-ist!'

'Cults are media-sexy.'

'This one certainly is,' said Jack. He was eager to motivate these people. 'Gabriel Soul uses sex rituals to seek immortality.'

'Have you taken part?' asked Marcus.

'No, of course I haven't!'

'Is that why they kidnapped your girlfriend? To use her in a sex ritual?'

'I don't bloody well know!'

Nude Marcia clutched at Marcus. 'A photo for the insurance.' Immediately she changed her mind. 'Don't take my picture looking like this. No, you must do!' Shifting her injured leg, she cried out, 'I'm crippled. You got to take a picture of my leg.'

Marcus obliged.

'Five minutes are up. Where's Fox?'

Clutching at the fridge, Jack struggled to his feet.

'If they don't want to harm *him*,' said naked Tina suddenly, 'they won't shoot at our gas tank while he's still in here. But as soon as he leaves—'

130

'What are you saying?'

Marcus eyed her.

'Kill all witnesses? If they're crazy enough?'

'Where's Fox? Final call!'

'Ask them to wait another minute,' Marcus called to Pablo. As Pablo bellowed the message, the photographer gabbled at Renny, 'Do you think Tina might be right? Dare we trust them?'

'Bikes are coming,' bawled Pablo. 'A whole crowd of bikes.'

Jack limped forward behind Marcus and Renny.

A mile or so away, dust rose from what must be a dozen bikes heading down the track. Big aerials sprouted from five or six. No, those couldn't be aerials. Those were the barrels of rifles – held upright by pillion riders.

The noise of those bikes was a long slow crescendo of thunder rolling closer and closer.

'Mother of God,' exclaimed Pablo. 'More of them.'

Hope welled in Jack.

'No! Last night I got away from the kidnappers because they ran into other bikers. I don't know who the others were. I think both lots must have had a fight. Soul's people never found me after I crashed the bike I stole, though I was knocked out for ages—'

From the approaching posse came the crack of rifle fire.

Soul's four rough riders could remain dismounted and fire back, and become targets for rifles. Or they could mount their bikes and clear off. Cover was almost non-existent except right beside the Winnebago and the station wagon.

While Marcus hastily loaded a new film, one of the disciples did open up briefly with a compact sub-machine-gun at the oncoming chevron of big bikes.

Jeans. Leather bomber-jackets. Dark glasses. Baseball caps. One of the Harleys went out of control. It shed its rider and its passenger. The other Harleys dispersed and braked. Men scrambled clear and spread themselves in the dirt with their rifles.

131

The fallen passenger had recovered his rifle. He was alive. So was the rider who had come unstuck. He raised his hand as if for assistance or to reassure the others.

Soul's men regained their bikes. They gunned them.

As they were revving away up the slope, a bullet took one of them in the back. He jerked and toppled. His companions continued on their way.

'That's one for Filbert!' Pablo brandished the revolver, as if he himself had fired the shot.

Now that the dirt bikes had fled, the Harley riders were rising from the ground. Someone was attending the casualty. Marcus took pictures as the men in bomber jackets began walking the few hundred yards towards the slumped Winnebago, weapons at the ready.

'They look like Indians,' whispered Marcus.

Erik peered. 'Rough tough ones. Come to the aid of the covered wagon. Dear me, how would the Apache Wars have turned out if Geronimo and his braves had come down on General Crook riding Harleys against horses?'

'What do you think their intentions are?'

'Get the girls covered up,' Renny told Sammy, 'and get those damned chains off them.'

A chunky chubby-faced Native American who looked to be in his early thirties pointed a rifle at the windshield of the Winnebago, at Marcus who had just taken his photograph through the glass.

'Throw your guns out,' he shouted.

'What guns?' Pablo called.

'The guns you fucking well used to stop those boys walking on board your RV. *Those ones*, you clown. After all the trouble we took we aren't going to be shot at. And throw that camera out while you're about it.'

'I can't do that,' protested Marcus. He lowered the camera to hide it.

The rifle prodded the air.

'We can pay you for your help.'

'Great idea. But throw the camera out.'

'No, wait. We have somebody here who has to get to hospital fast. You do too, don't you?'

'So stop wasting time and throw your guns and your camera out.' The leader swaggered. 'We're your protectors, man, don't you get it?'

Renny hissed to Erik, 'Give Marcus the other fucking camera, and hide that one.' Impatiently he gestured for the pistol.

'Hey,' Renny shouted through the windshield, 'I'm the operations manager. We only have two handguns. We'll throw them out the door.'

Out sailed the shiny pistol.

Shrugging, Pablo threw the revolver out too.

'You won't damage the camera, will you?' called Renny. 'We have pictures of the people who attacked us. Let's talk about that – but we need to get medical attention. We're really grateful to you guys. We'll pay you *five thousand dollars* – but we'll need to get to a bank.'

The leader cleared his throat and spat at the ground.

'That's about four hundred dollars for each of us. We'd be so rich we could buy a doormat in Palm Springs and sleep on it.'

'Honestly, we can't go to ten grand. I'm trying to be straight with you.'

Hidden by the seat, Marcus had swapped cameras. 'Don't throw it. Will you lay it down gently, Pablo?'

'Mother of God, what I do.'

Pablo manoeuvred past Filbert's body and descended. He walked a few steps and set the camera down.

'You're injured,' said the Indian.

'As you see. I may as well stay outside,' Pablo announced to no one in particular. Innocently he sat down, not far from the revolver.

Both guns were quickly removed from his vicinity.

One of the riflemen had sprinted to the fallen rider to inspect him. He made a hand-slash across his throat. After delving in the dead man's pockets, he made a no-no sign.

'You're bullshitting about that five grand,' shouted the

leader. 'Was I born yesterday, when your grandad was handing out bottles of firewater? You're insulting us.'

'He didn't mean to hurt your feelings,' said Pablo. 'Renny's just an insensitive bastard. What's your name, man? I'm Pablo.'

Pablo offered his hand. The leader ignored the overture. It had looked as if Pablo was asking to be hoisted to his feet.

'Free Wind's my name,' said the leader, 'and just maybe – and I say maybe – we'll be satisfied with your undying gratitude. That's so long as we know exactly what happened – why those fuckers went for you, and who they are.'

'That, we can tell you,' promised Renny from the doorway. 'It isn't us they wanted at all. It's this guy from England who's in here with us.'

Nobody fucked with the Inzane Nation.

The Bloods and the B-52s were busy running drugs and liquor into the reservation on behalf of their puppetmasters in South Central Los Angeles. The Bloods and B-52s were beginning to look exactly like Angelino street gangsters. Aping all the habits and the rap. But they didn't fuck with the Inzane Nation.

Skinwalkers were the spooky ones.

Those were the secret guys who could lay nightmares on you in your sleep, yeah, kill you in your sleep or drive you nuts. Nobody could ever seem to lay the finger on one of those Satanic magicians. They were out there for sure. Evil shaman gang boys.

The Inzanes might look like Hell's Angels. But the Inzanes had *mission*. They were going to defend the free territory of the People from Angelino pushers and their puppets among the youth of the People. And they were going to root out those Skinwalkers who scared people shitless.

A big bit of the mission was to nail the Skinwalkers. Like, to be a living Dream Catcher for the People.

These days, Anglo kids in rich suburbs who went to

134

swanky high schools were creaming themselves for a genuine authentic Dream Catcher net to hang by their beds.

Nightmares would get caught in the web of string. Happy dreams would slide down the two feathers, into the heads and the lives of the sleepers.

The Inzane Nation were a web that was gonna catch the Skinwalkers who haunted the People. The braves who got into that skirmish last night were on a far-flung patrol. Bloods and B-52s often used back routes and big detours to bring in their consignments from LA. A rumour had been going around. So therefore: jump the couriers where they least expected it, far enough away from the reservation so the police wouldn't cotton on.

Police didn't believe in Skinwalkers, because they didn't know magic.

Skinwalkers got inside your head if they could slip by your Dream Catcher web. They could know what you were thinking, even if they weren't able to plant bad dreams because of the web. Skinwalkers could walk in other men's skins as a disguise. Last night those dirt bike riders might not have been entirely natural men.

After Renny and Pablo heaved the black man's body to the rear of the RV, Free Wind, who was known to officialdom as Johnny Sam, entered along with Eagle Eye, whose Anglo name was Frankie.

A dark chick wore a blue silk kimono, and that seemed to be all that she wore. She was half-hiding behind an open wardrobe door. A blonde chick was lying on the carpet under some torn-down curtains. Badly swollen ankle, hers. She was lying still with her eyes shut, as if pretending to be unconscious. What she couldn't see didn't exist and would go away.

'Gabriel Soul, once called Kaminski,' Free Wind repeated to himself to fix the names in his mind.

The name of an Anglo magician who headed a sex cult and was trying to make magic to become immortal. So said the foreign professor.

An *armed* cult based at some *Soul Shelter* somewhere in

135

the desert. If those cult members had sub-machine-guns, very likely they had lots of other powerful stuff too. They had kidnapped the professor's girlfriend colleague because of things she'd said about computers coming alive.

The business manager, Renny, was paying a lot of attention to what the English professor said.

Could the Skinwalkers have any connection with this Gabriel Soul?

Free Wind pondered. The Inzane Nation wouldn't be able to take on a whole armed cult to revenge themselves. Why should they do so, when whites could fight whites?

The Inzane Nation would dream about this. They would kill cockerels for bright new feathers to tie on the dream-webs. They would drink the cockerels' blood, still hot, and get high. Then they would visualize frenzy and mania. They would be like Skinwalkers themselves, making a nightmare and sending it walking – and maybe, Free Wind realized, no one knew who exactly the Skinwalkers were because a Skinwalker could be *you yourself*.

Inspired by this image, Free Wind said to Renny, 'Three or four of you get in your station wagon and drive for help. A few of us'll escort you just like you're some presidential cavalcade. Then we melt away. You don't say anything about all our rifles, understand?'

'Absolutely not,' Renny assured him.

'The rest of us'll keep guard here till a Medevac chopper comes for *her* and for Red Feather, whose care you'll be paying for.'

'Of course we will. Wouldn't a paramedic ambu-lance—?'

'—shake them up nicely on this sort of road? What sort of mean bastard are you?'

Renny squirmed.

'You'll pay for recovery and any repairs to Red Feather's hog. *We'll* get rid of that cult-man's body, and his bike. We never shot anyone, do you hear me?'

'Of course you didn't. This is very big-spirited of you, Free Wind.'

'Yeah, it is. You wouldn't understand why or how.'

Jack broke in. 'I need to get to the police as soon as possible! They've had Clare for twelve hours now—'

'I have to go in the station wagon too,' piped up Tina. She stared at Renny, willing him to understand what she was implying.

Free Wind snorted derisively.

'Lady, we are not interested in gang-banging you. We're your protectors, remember? You'll stay here with your friend who's hurt.'

'I must get to the police quickly,' repeated Jack.

'So you shall,' said Free Wind. 'Now what is it you all have to remember?'

Jack dithered.

'Aw, come on, professor!'

'Ah . . . no rifles?'

'That's it, genius.'

Tina appealed to Marcus. 'I can't stay here with a corpse.'

Marcus snapped his fingers. 'Our gear's still out there. The reflector—'

'And my make-up case,' said Sammy.

Renny steered Marcus forcefully to the back of the Winnebago where Filbert lay.

'Will you shut up about our goddamn gear?' he shouted in the photographer's face in seeming fury. 'I'm the goddamn operations manager. Poor Filbert has been murdered – and that English guy's girl is being held prisoner by sex maniacs!'

Very quietly and quickly he breathed, 'This is major media stuff. This is *money*.'

53

Nicholl Perridge had settled at his desk in his Chief of Detectives' sanctum and was contemplating a styrofoam cup of decaf when the phone rang.

Margie's tinkly voice asked if he could take a call from the Sheriff's Office in Ronstadt. Margie always sounded to

Perridge like some human Christmas tree decoration. Indeed she was due to be hung up soon – retired, presented with a cut-glass bowl, and still a spinster. Maybe Margie had joined the police department originally in search of protection by proximity, and had hoped that some lonely bachelor officer might marry her . . .

'It's something about Detective Kramer, sir—'

Ronstadt was a couple of hundred miles away. Through the glass wall Perridge could see Jeff Kramer at the water-cooler. Kramer *ought* to be stepping in here soon – he'd been due to call on that conference organizer last night.

After Perridge cradled the phone ten minutes later, he was in two minds whether to phone Irving Sherwood at the bureau office right away, or to indulge himself briefly.

Like Margie, Nicholl Perridge was due to retire soon and share his twilight years with formidable Sherri, backbone of cultural causes such as the Arizona Opera Company. A splendid puzzle, perfectly solved, would be his personal retirement gift to himself. This Russian murder case was a doozie, even if he himself could only fill in a few of the clues and must rely on the FBI for more.

Speed was important. Still, Perridge smiled anticipatively as he pressed Kramer's button on his phone. With his free hand he doodled a grid and filled in names. Telling Jeff Kramer about the call from Ronstadt could clarify the pattern before he informed Irving Sherwood. Apart from a patrolman, Kramer was the only member of the police department who had actually met the English couple.

'It's Perridge. Get in here, will you—?'

'I did see Professor Keyserling last night,' began Kramer.

Perridge raised his palms for silence.

'I just had an enquiry about you from the Sheriff's office in Ronstadt,' he told his blond watery-eyed subordinate. 'The sheriff asked, do we have a Detective Kramer here?'

Jeff Kramer was nonplussed.

'Why?'

'Take a guess who knows you there.'

A pleasure to behold, understanding blossoming.

'Fox and Conway. So that's where they are! Keyserling said they were intending to go up past Havasu to Needles and over the Mojave. That's because Conway's twin sister drove across the Mojave last year. A mugger murdered the sister in San Francisco, and it's a sort of private pilgrimage for her. Did the Highway Patrol—?'

'Ronstadt is where *Fox* is all right. Not Conway, though. Yesterday evening on Interstate 10 she was kidnapped at gunpoint.'

'*What?*'

'Fox managed to escape on one of the kidnappers' bikes. He crashed and he got lost in the desert overnight. The Sheriff was phoning from Ronstadt to check out if Fox was who he claimed to be, since he had no ID of any sort.'

'Kidnappers?' Kramer rubbed his arm as though to stimulate maximum circulation and boost blood to his brain. 'Does Fox know who they are?'

Perridge looked smug. 'I hear tell that a bunch of demonstrators were picketing that conference.'

'Ah, those were loony toon disciples of Gabriel Soul, formerly known as Roy Lee Kaminski. I found that out from Keyserling. Kaminski set up some sort of gonzo sex cult promising immortality.' Kramer grinned. 'Well-endowed, so I hear. Some rich girls joined. Soul was pestering Conway during that barbecue just about the same time the Russians would have been shot.'

Kramer was enjoying himself. He was upstaging Perridge.

'So there's *Soul's* alibi. The other protesters were mainly girls. Conway and Fox never said anything to me about Soul harassing her.'

'Soul's people have sub-machine-guns, Jeff. A sub-machine-gun killed those Russians.'

Kramer blinked.

Perridge recovered his momentum. 'Fox ran into some kind of film crew this morning – just as Soul's bikers were about to snatch him. Soul's men shot one of the film crew dead. Luckily for Fox the crew had a couple of handguns to hold the attack off briefly. Then along came a bunch of Navajo bikers – out on an innocent ride – and Soul's men skedaddled. They wounded one of the Navajos, but numbers weren't in their favour. That's the story, said the Sheriff.'

'I'm not surprised he wanted some kind of confirmation.'

'Fox is going nuts about what's happening to Conway at the *Soul Shelter*.'

'Where's that?'

'Nowhere near here, I'm sure.'

Perridge tapped his ballpoint pen on his grid.

'Soul's people murder two Russian computer spies *here*. They know where and when to look for them. I think Soul may be into some heavy computer crime, which somehow involves Conway, enough to kidnap her.'

Bird-like, Perridge cocked his head to eye the spider's web up by the air-conditioning.

'I shall enjoy briefing the FBI about the Soul connection.'

He reached for the phone.

'Hang on,' said Kramer. 'Keyserling told me why Conway mightn't have said anything about Soul. Out of embarrassment! There was some sleazy story about Conway in the *National Investigator*. Conway thinks some type of new computer will come to life. Um, quantum, that's the name. That's how Soul figured her.'

Perridge rejoiced. Quickly he annotated the grid with *Qua Comp* and *Nat Invest*.

'Bet you the FBI don't know about that yet either. Great work, Jeff. Why didn't you mention those quantum doodads earlier?'

54

Clare woke in the morning to the sight of a window beyond which desert light glared. A deep window. An open window. However, the embrasure was fitted with iron bars.

She was on a camp bed, in her clothes, which smelled of sweat. A door stood open to a small closet equipped with toilet and washbasin. A simple wooden chair with a rush seat looked like something painted by Van Gogh.

She was alive. She had also been dead.

She lay quite still for a while.

Her revelation remained with her unshakeably. No, it wasn't a revelation. It was Soul who had revelations. Hers was a realization.

Maybe the Shrödinger box in the cellar had been a fraud. What else could it have been but a hoax! Intellectually she knew that the fracturing of her vision and the disappearance of part of her surroundings – part of reality becoming terrifyingly missing – were symptoms of migraine . . .

Extreme symptoms! Not since her adolescence had she experienced such an attack. From teenage years she remembered the horror of the *vanishing* clearly enough.

That was one of the problems about the vanishing. Afterwards you understood. At the time it happened you couldn't understand at all. You lost part of the world. There was just a ghastly sense of wrongness, and of impending extinction.

Locked up in the box, that was what had happened to her.

Yet at the same time the realization was true. It had the same powerful validity as looking at a tree and knowing *there's a tree*.

When people died at present, the sum total of information of their lives – the coherent consciousness, the identity – simply ceased. Yet there was storage space for that information in all the alternative existences which never gave rise to any conscious life!

If only there could be some tangible link with those alternative existences, why then, the trillions of bits of information which summed up someone's identity must flow there as surely as sand from the full part of an hourglass into the empty part.

The cloud of superimposed alternative existences didn't only serve to support a stable universe which was recreating itself afresh at every moment. It could also be a repository for the minds of people who died. It could serve as an infinite storage space.

Quantum computers were going to create that link by the very nature of how they operated.

Of course quantum computers would become self-aware. Their awareness would touch upon all the parallel universes. Perhaps they could even serve as a link with the identities of the dead who would no longer vanish utterly.

Her sister would still be reachable. Except that Miranda had died too soon.

Too soon.

Some scientists claimed that it would be possible to store human minds in computers. They spoke of downloading people from their dying meat bodies into cyberspace. They talked of an afterlife within computers.

That would be the survival of a copy, not of the original.

A copy of yourself could carry on in electronic form. It would believe that it was exactly the same as the person who had lived. It would still be a duplicate, not the original. The original would have dissolved. Where was the use in that, from the point of view of the original? From the point of view of *yourself*. Your own self and that copy in the computer couldn't be the same self. Otherwise you'd be in two places at once.

If the identities of the dead flow into ghost universes, *the originals themselves* will survive.

This, Clare knew now. It was one of the great realizations – like Newton being brained by a falling apple, or Archimedes leaping stark naked out of the bath. Or Saul on the road to Damascus. It was a conviction which couldn't be gainsaid.

A hoax box, a migraine attack: those were irrelevant details.

If she was to die before at least one quantum computer began operating to its full capacity, she would be obliterated. But if not . . .

She wanted to shout from the rooftops, to declare the imminent defeat of death.

Sweaty and smelly, she made her way to the window. She stared over outbuildings and vehicles. Numbers of disciples were busy down there. Engines were starting up. Some sort of expedition seemed to be getting under way. Gabriel Soul was directing whatever was happening.

Shout from the rooftops? Through the pages of the *National Investigator* or the *Sunday Scoop* at home? PROFETTE HAS NEW REVELATION!

She felt so effervescent and utterly positive. She remembered Soul rhapsodizing about his golden bed at midnight. She must try to be bland and neutral with him.

If only there was a shower in the closet, not just a washbasin.

An hour later, Soul himself brought her a tray of coffee and orange juice and blueberry muffins.

'Room service,' he said.

He deposited the tray on the bedside table. Swinging Van Gogh's chair around, he straddled it, resting his arms upon the top.

He watched her intently as she drained the orange juice and devoured the muffins.

She poured coffee, which she mustn't throw into his face, whatever happened.

She wasn't going to engage him in nervous conversation, to ingratiate herself.

Finally he said, 'So are your zombie scientists going to fit their Tin Man with a quantum computer?'

'Tin Man has nothing to do with quantum computers. I simply don't know the things you think I know.'

'You thought you knew plenty last night. All about parallel universes, and being dead.'

'I was hysterical. Migraine affected my mind, Gabe.'

'You're cool this morning.'

Oh no she was not.

'You tried to prophesy.'

143

'It was like something clever you think of in a dream,' she lied. 'When you wake up, it seems like nonsense.'

'Not when *I* wake up. I see the truth. But I know what you mean. You were shattered. You needed to reintegrate yourself. That's where I ought to have been able to help you, Clare. And I *can*.'

'Not at the moment,' she muttered.

He scowled. 'If you don't know things, what does Jack Fox know? What's *his* secret agenda?'

'Jack doesn't have one.'

'He knew enough to get away from my rough riders.'

'Good for Jack.'

'To get away for a while,' he qualified.

Had they caught Jack? Had they killed him? Was there no help coming? Did no one know where she was? Would no one even worry about her being missing for another week or ten days or even longer?

Jack, Jack . . . She was determined not to ask Soul, not to seem vulnerable.

'You could be one of my most favoured and blessèd Sisters, Clare. I know this about you. I sense it. You could be my soulmate.'

His eyes, his eyes. Soul was exerting a pressure, a bullying yet seductive mesmerism which was actually getting to her. This damned American Orlando! She'd been pre-programmed by Orlando . . .

She wondered whether the muffins had been doped, and almost fled to the closet to try to vomit. Her body had craved the food. She couldn't go on hunger-strike.

She must cling to her realization like a faith, to resist Soul's efforts to brainwash her!

Her realization already possessed her, more so than Soul could ever hope to.

Did she owe Soul a little debt for having arranged the charade of the Shrödinger box?

'What's your friend's speciality supposed to be?' Soul asked. 'What was the supposed reason for him being at the conference?'

They would not surely kill her 'friend'.

144

'He specializes in the psychology of beliefs. Alternative groups.'

Soul smiled so charmingly. It was as if they were the best of friends.

'Why ever did he run away? He ought to have accepted our invitation.'

'Maybe he ought, Gabe. He could learn a lot. I'd like to learn about your community. My clothes are such a mess. It's as if I've been dragged through a hedge backwards.'

'I'll have Beth bring you something that fits. We'll start off on a new foot.'

Was she inviting Soul to dress her up as a would-be disciple of his, a potential soulmate?

Rapid knocking at the door.

In came red-headed Jersey.

'Can I have a word, Gabe?'

A word away from Clare's ears. An urgent word.

She heard a key turn in the lock as the two men left. Although she hurried to kneel and listen, the voices were receding. Did she hear the name Fox?

55

The closed louvre blinds of the FBI conference room excluded the glare of late afternoon sunlight, as if protecting those within the room from an adjacent furnace.

Large-scale maps of southerly Arizona and the Mexican border spread along one wall, tagged with coloured pins. Air conditioning hummed. In a corner a computer purred, idling. Across its screen little pastel jackrabbits hopped slowly and randomly, to save the screen from pixel-burn. The impression was of the computer playing some childish game on its own. *Run rabbit, run rabbit, run run run . . .*

Swivel chairs flanked a triangular table with place settings of mineral water and notepads. All the chairs were taken. A large tele-conference screen was split four ways and flanked by video-camera and microphones, adding three more faces to the meeting. Little rabbits hopped at random across the unused quarter of the screen.

Jeff Kramer felt intimidated and out of his depth. He was here because he was the only detective to have met the British couple, and his impressions might prove vital.

'In a word,' one of the tele-faces was saying, '*encryption*. That's why this is serious news.'

Pentecost, that was the man's name. Richard Pentecost. National Computer Security Center, part of the National Security Agency. A cadaverous man with unruly locks of grey hair. From some room in Maryland, Pentecost was looking at a screen which would be showing the triangular table and those around it, and insets of the other two remote participants.

Part of the work of the NSA, Jeff gathered, was to protect information belonging to the United States. To produce ciphers and codes, then to try to break those same codes, because if the codes failed then foreign enemies could break them too.

A matronly black woman on screen – Roundtree? yes, Bella Roundtree – was Secret Service. Jeff hadn't realized until now that the Secret Service was part of the Treasury. He had imagined counter-assassination bodyguards wearing anonymous suits and reflective sun-glasses, clinging to cars in motorcades, scrutinizing crowds. Yet as well as defending the President and visiting dignitaries, the Secret Service defended money. Firstly, by hunting counterfeiters. Nowadays too, by protecting banks from computer fraud.

The third face on screen was that of a mild-looking elderly man called Mr Grey, who smoked cheroots. The act of smoking even during a tele-conference seemed somehow to place him above ordinary conventions. His status remained undefined. Jeff suspected White House.

'*Encryption*,' repeated Pentecost, drawing knowing nods from the Roundtree woman and Grey and also from Don Rosado who was at the table.

Rosado was the FBI's computer crime specialist who had

flown in from California. A slim, small olive-complexioned man.

Other people at the table were local FBI special agents, a Public Safety representative and someone from ATF, the Bureau of Alcohol, Tobacco and Firearms. And Jeff's Chief, who was enjoying himself.

Pentecost proceeded to deliver a little sermon about encryption.

Since 1977 the secret transactions of governments and the military and the world's economy had been protected by codes which it would take conventional high-power computers months or years to crack.

'You multiply a couple of large prime numbers together. Everyone know what a prime number is?'

Someone must have looked furtive.

'A prime number is any number which can't be divided by a whole number except itself and one. Like 7 or 23.

'So you take two very long prime numbers and you multiply them. Or rather, your computer does. It spits out a number that has, for example, 129 digits in it. That's easy for a good computer.

'But if you tell your computer to factorize that 129-digit number – to find out which two prime numbers produce your big number – it'll be up the creek, trying out possible combinations until the cows come home.'

Mr Grey was chewing his cheroot rather than smoking it.

'In 1995,' Pentecost went on, 'no fewer than sixteen hundred computers hooked up over the Internet did finally manage to factorize a 129-digit number. It took them more than eight months.

'Sensitive data that's been encrypted using two prime numbers can be pretty out-of-date after eight months. And if not, you can always add more digits to your codes. Numbers get exponentially harder to factorize, the longer you make them.'

Jeff nodded, since this seemed best.

'So far so good. Until a quantum computer gets built! A

147

quantum computer will be able to try out a host of different possible numbers all at the same time – not one after another. It seems that all the numbers which don't lead to the right result won't, well, *interfere constructively*, that's the jargon – so they'll simply cancel each other out. They won't figure at all.

'A quantum computer will be able to factorize a 129-digit number in just a few seconds.'

Mr Grey looked very serious as he listened.

'We're working on alternative crypto strategies. But for a while at least the world's military and economic secrets might be stripped bare.'

When Mr Grey spoke, it was as if a dangerous beast padded softly over graves.

'What better time for enemies of the West to cause havoc? To trigger a global stock market crash? To hack into a missile silo? It could be militant Islam. It could be Chinese hardliners. It could be rabid Russian nationalists . . .'

Seemingly the QX Corporation in San Jose was on the brink of launching a quantum computer. If not QX, then soon enough it would be Motorola or Matsushima.

Irving Sherwood was able to confirm that the kidnapped Englishwoman had placed a call from her room to QX in San Jose earlier on the same evening when the Russians were killed.

Still no lead on who they were.

The local detectives – and here Perridge grinned – had discovered that Dr Conway had been planning to visit QX, supposedly to inspect a robotics experiment . . .

It was plain to Jeff that Irving Sherwood was ambitious. The FBI office chief was scarcely in his forties. Athletic. Curly light brown hair, a candid open blue-eyed face – but a politician's way of choosing his words. Big graspy hands. Most of the time he kept those hands in full view, steepled thoughtfully, angling his fingertips one way then the other, like sails of a yacht heeding which way breezes blew. He dressed local, with a white rodeo shirt and black leather bola tie. Tooled leather boots with gold caps.

What Sherwood was being careful about – airing the possibility whilst not exactly advocating this – was a sudden assault in force upon Gabriel Soul's so-called Shelter.

The Shelter was out in hilly desert about ninety miles south of Ronstadt. This the Bureau already knew. Ever since the siege of the Branch Davidian sect in Waco, the Bureau had been accumulating data about fringe cults. In the wake of the Oklahoma City bombing, the Bureau's concern about private militias had intensified hugely.

On the table right now lay a blown-up satellite photograph of the Soul Shelter, a clutter of buildings at the head of a minor canyon backed up against steep cliffs.

'Legally,' Sherwood was saying, 'we can justify an assault. One of Soul's disciples murdered that black man, Filbert. They're prime suspects in the deaths of those two Russians. Maybe I ought to say *presumed* Russians. Then there's the kidnapping. The question is, how heavily armed are they?'

'Fairly heavily, we believe,' said the man from Alcohol, Tobacco and Firearms. 'This could be another apocalypse scenario. End of the world mentality.'

'True,' agreed Sherwood, and the yacht of his hands tilted.

'If this goes wrong the way Waco did, and we stir up the militias – well, with respect, Washington might have to end giving Idaho to the crazies.'

Mr Grey, on screen, did not disagree.

It was what the heavily armed lunatic right wanted. The survivalists. The neo-Nazis, the white supremacists, the paramilitaries. Hundreds of thousands of these were festering in a swathe of states. They had their own radio stations. The Internet linked them. Former Green Berets and Navy Seals, graduates of Vietnam, trained them. In some states serving US army officers were members. Sheriffs and reserve guardsmen and police officers too. This was the

New American Revolution waiting to happen. The prize: their own free territory, a nation of their own, free from gun control and Jews and Blacks and welfare claimants and federal taxes and interference . . .

'It will also be the end of the world as we know it,' said Pentecost, 'if quantum computers make our encryption methods useless before we have anything else to use. That's what disturbs me so much about this kidnapping. Russians are on the trail. Freelance Russian mafia, or the rump of the KGB, I don't know which. *They* were killed on Gabriel Soul's orders. He seems to be a nutty cult leader but he behaves like a militia boss. Conway is connected with quantum computer research. If Soul has links with the militias, do the militias hope to get their hands on quantum computers? Use those to rip the veils away from national security and financial data?'

'And precipitate chaos,' said Grey hauntedly. 'In the midst of chaos, start a civil war – which might indeed end with states seceding from the union, after terrible traumas.'

Nicholl Perridge had been doodling names across a grid on his notepad and numbering them.

'I guess, sir,' he said, 'you can't just suppress those quantum computers – because the Japs or someone else would still be going ahead.'

Grey waited a moment, as if clearing with himself what he might say.

'There'll be strict controls on end-users,' Grey confided. 'Licences. Requirements about secure environments for licensed machines. Just as soon as an American company announces a launch all this will come down like a ton of bricks. But an *American* company has to be the first in the field – or else we're in hot water. For the moment, the policy is hands-off. The first six months after a launch announcement will be critical.'

Don Rosado spoke up. 'You're hoping that the first quantum computers will yield a new way of encrypting data, aren't you? Not by using big numbers – but by *hiding* data in alternative realities? Something along those lines?'

Pentecost sucked in his sunken cheeks.

Sherwood shifted his steepled hands.

'A hands-off policy. Really,' he said, 'that's been the Bureau's problem as regards the private militias . . .'

The problem began in the Vietnam era. With all the zeal of the McCarthyites who had hounded liberals during the fifties, the FBI had come down far too heavily on protesters against the Vietnam War.

After America lost that war, a reaction set in against a heavy-handed, wrong-headed Bureau.

Reaganite conservatives forced a back-off policy as regards interference by the Bureau in people's lives. The disaster of the Waco siege, after the Bureau took control from the ATF, reinforced this attitude.

The Oklahoma City bombing might have alerted America to the crazies in its midst, but those same crazies were still insisting that the FBI had itself deliberately carried out the bombing of the federal building with such loss of innocent life. The FBI's motive: to provoke an anti-militia backlash. Too many people believed the crazies.

A full-blooded assault on the Soul Shelter risked so much.

Including, of course, the accidental death of Clare Conway.

'Ideally, you free her and question her,' said Grey.

Ideally . . .

Advise the State Governor right now? No, only if the assault went wrong. If so, Grey would talk to the Governor very persuasively.

Sherwood nodded. Green light. National security. He took it that he had protection. And a hope of substantial promotion. He would do it right.

56

Sensing hesitancy, Gwenda Loomis linked arms with Matt to walk him through the floodlit courtyard. She steered him past the fountain where three plastic dolphins, backs arched in a leap, were elevated on poles amidst spouting spray. A red-tiled porch jutted from what could have been the colonnaded cloisters of a Spanish monastery. The entablature of the porch was decorated with a leaping dolphin against an ace of spades, flanked in huge blue neon by the name BAY 101.

Asians were chattering to each other in Vietnamese. Maybe there'd be some Koreans or Chinese, but other Asians were swamped by the sixty thousand-strong community inhabiting San Jose, especially this part of town. Well-heeled refugees, boatpeople, survivors of labour camps, everyone from ex-ARVN generals to riff-raff.

A strong community, indeed. The heart and soul and muscle of the chip-stealing business. Recent arrivals soon drifted into the established gangs, hanging out in coffee shops and pool halls.

Matt couldn't spot any cigarette brands on forearms or blue dragon tattoos. Chunky gold jewellery and pagers, instead. Bay 101 was where higher rollers got their fix of California Blackjack and Superpan Nine. The car park had been crammed with BMW coupés.

Oriental eyes glanced at Matt then registered Gwenda – who was wearing her gold-and-silver slit dress – and neutrally ignored him.

He deeply wished he wasn't here.

The gang which was going to stage the diversionary attack on QX wanted to look at him.

To memorize him.

To see him, but not be seen, in the crowd inside Bay 101.

Just in case they shot Matt by mistake. Or in case they got in his way.

Wasn't the whole idea that he'd be wearing a bunny suit to make him anonymous?

They insisted on seeing him to assess his build, gait, mannerisms, body language, Gestalt. So said Gwenda. Too much hung on this to overlook any aspect.

Anyway, a visit to a casino could be viewed as part of

his therapy. A kind of detox session, so that he wouldn't squander his bonus.

Inside the casino, cigarette smoke hung in pungent clouds. The decibel level of excitement was high. Thrilled and chagrined squeals punctuated the bedlam. Dice-cups thudded upon tables in a frantic percussive heartbeat. Matt saw shiny suits and sun-glasses. Were the eyes behind those glasses studying him?

One of the suits came over and talked to Gwenda, not in English. The man's glance flicked at Matt, rather as if Matt was one of the fish in the huge tank along one wall, a denizen of a different realm.

After the suit went away Matt asked, 'Was that one of them?'

Gwenda shrugged.

Suits would be too important to do dirty work.

'What was it about?'

'Nothing,' she said idly.

The noise and the smoke were getting to him, and the smell of neglected charred meat on skewers. He was being shown how isolated he was, how reliant on Gwenda's instructions. Who she really was, he hardly knew at all.

'Can we leave yet?' he asked. 'Have I been seen enough?'

She glanced around the room. 'I think I might throw a few dice before we go.'

He would be obliged to stay beside her as her mascot, her poodle, amongst a crowd of frenetic strangers, understanding not a word.

Once at a dice-table, Gwenda quickly won two thousand dollars. Had she been given weighted dice? Was two thousand her fee for bringing him here?

'The pig *is* balanced,' she told him serenely. 'Fortune attends our exploits.'

He felt such nostalgia for Lake Tahoe. That had been heaven. Here was hell, full of busy demons. If only time could turn back. If only he could be in some other stream of time where things had happened differently.

57

Ronstadt was a town of some twenty thousand people, the majority of them senior citizens. The elderly had moved here from out of state to live on their pensions and soak up sun amongst the artificial lakes and parks and golf courses, tennis courts and swimming pools.

Other similar developments had failed to deliver their promised amenities or had been hurt by bad publicity about land fraud or had been unable to pump enough water. Some had been totally abandoned, becoming modern ghost towns.

Ronstadt had thrived. Maybe this was due to its looping road layout, forever circling round upon itself and interconnecting. The mind wasn't drawn away along any straight lines towards dry desolation and blank horizons, towards the graveyard of the desert, but always back into the sprawling fertile oasis.

Maybe the secret was in its name.

The only Ronstadt of whom Jack had heard was the singer Linda. Actually the Ronstadts – who originally hailed from Mexico, not from the peasantry, but from the upper echelon of ambitious society – were quite a cultural dynasty, so it seemed.

Their influence had transformed Tucson, and the magic of the name seemed to have blessed this retirement town too. Not merely golf courses, but a well-attended concert hall too, and painting classes and craft workshops.

This, Jack learned at the Ronstadt Inn in the small downtown shopping area, which wasn't far from the Sheriff's Office or from the clinic where he'd been given a check-up for exposure and had his head wound cleaned.

At the Sheriff's office, in company with Renny and Sammy and Erik, he hadn't perhaps created a very good impression.

The Sheriff, Arnold Crabtree, had looked almost sixty. Big girth, white hair, leisurely way of proceeding.

It became obvious that crime was very rare in Ronstadt.

The main problem seemed to be road accidents due to doddery old people driving cars too powerful for them. Crabtree had only a deputy and half a dozen patrolmen.

Armed kidnapping and gun battles were as alien as the Englishman with his wild claims and the three sophisticates from California.

Crabtree did galvanize himself, but resentfully, almost as if these strangers had provoked what happened . . .

Jack was relieved when, in the afternoon, a helicopter landed on a lawn to the side of the Ronstadt Inn, to disgorge two FBI Special Agents, a man and a woman, the former Hispanic, the latter black. Till then, he'd been kicking his heels.

Sabatino and Barnes took rooms in the Inn, and questioned Jack in one of these. Questions about Clare and her background, about his own background, about their itinerary in America, about whatever he knew of Soul, about the murders in Tucson. They recorded every word. Mary Barnes took the lead as interrogator, but regularly she would break off and adjourn to the adjoining room, closing the intervening door. Reporting by phone, presumably. Why weren't they talking to him in Crabtree's office? It seemed as if they were distancing themselves from the local Sheriff rather than co-operating closely.

'How soon can you do anything?' Jack would badger, and they would shrug sympathetically.

'We need to build up a thorough profile of all this,' Barnes assured him blandly. She was a glamorous woman with glossy wavy hair, handsome-featured. 'I assure you plenty is happening. Just help us do our job. Now you say that in the burglarization at the Desert Hacienda Dr Conway's talk was stolen. Her talk was about computers, did you say?'

'No, not as such. It was about the brain as a special type of computer.'

'What special type?' she asked.

This was exasperating. They were like bureaucrats wanting the name of your maiden aunt.

'A *photon* computer using *quantum coherence*.' That should shut her up.

'Would you call that a quantum computer?' she asked.

'I don't care what you call it so long as you find her soon!'

'We'll find her,' she promised.

Of course the business about the *National Investigator* had to be raked over, since that was how Soul had fixated on Clare. This involved explaining about Orlando Sorel, who seemed light years away from Ronstadt.

As to where they were heading, Jack stuck to the fib about the Holiday Inn in San Francisco. That's what he and Clare had told the police in Tucson. He had no wish to seem inconsistent. Only after fibbing did it occur to him that the FBI might be finicky and check up on this detail – or even that the police in Tucson might already have done so. Sheriff Crabtree had phoned Tucson to validate who Jack was.

In Tucson they had lied to the police who were investigating a double murder . . .

If challenged, he would have to say that he and Clare hadn't wanted it to be known that they would be staying together in a borrowed house. A wink to the wise. Hardly a big sin.

If they ever reached San Francisco! If Clare could be found and rescued. Even when she was found, how long might it take the FBI to persuade Soul to surrender her peacefully? Days and days of negotiation?

Then more time would be consumed in taping Clare's story, assuming that she wasn't too traumatized to talk right away . . .

They would never have any time together in San Francisco. They would never even arrive there.

What an abominably selfish thought, when he was safe, and she was in unknown danger!

Soul could hardly have invited, then abducted, Clare so as to kill her or hurt her or hold her to ransom.

He might be raping her . . .

156

He might be doing what he thought of as enlightenment but which anyone in their right mind would call rape.

Don't let him be raping her.

Again, what a selfish thought this seemed!

If they were delayed Jack would have to confess about Angelo's house so that someone could enter and water the plants.

Oh, tell the FBI about a load of plants, many of which would be sources of mind-altering drugs? The prospect was at once trivial and preposterous. Jack would need to phone Angelo in Hawaii.

How could he think about some damn house plants when Clare was a prisoner!

The phone had rung in the bedroom where the questioning was taking place. Sabatino had listened, then had whispered in the black woman's ear, and had departed for almost an hour while Barnes continued the interrogation on her own.

When Sabatino came back, he was carrying an old brown leather suitcase – Jack's own. And a lightweight cream jacket was slung over his shoulder – Jack's, left in the Toyota.

'We retrieved your car,' Sabatino said. 'You'll be needing a change of clothes.'

Didn't he indeed.

Jack seized the jacket. His wallet was still inside. Inside the wallet: credit cards and dollars and a couple of twenty pound notes.

He knelt and clicked open the suitcase, which hadn't been locked. He felt sure his things had been sorted through and replaced. Here was his airline ticket. Here was his passport. And his personal organizer, crammed with hundreds of addresses and phone numbers. He was a person again.

'Where's Clare's luggage?'

'Safe,' said Sabatino. He might have the build of a junior Pavarotti, but words did not gush from him.

'Where's the car?'

'Secure in a local garage,' said Sabatino. He was studying Jack's reactions.

Smashed window ... possible damage to the suspension and bodywork ... the cost of retrieval ... a dented front bumper and a buckled bonnet from when he had hit the cactus tree ... What did they call those bits, fender and hood? What a mess the car must be. It had been so pristine only yesterday morning, with its air conditioning and its Calistoga water.

'Does it still drive?'

Sabatino nodded. 'We brought it in on a low-loader. It isn't in such bad shape.'

We did. We. Other agents and police were doing things. Things were definitely happening, out of sight. There were enough personnel to spare for finding a car. Jack subsided into his seat.

'Couple of bullet holes in the bodywork, Jack. You didn't say anything about guns being fired at your car.'

Jack shook his head.

'That must have happened after the kidnap gang ran into those Navajo boys. Those boys must have chased Soul's bikers back to where you crashed the car. Braves on the warpath, circling the covered wagon. You were lucky.'

'Lucky?' Jack echoed incredulously.

What if he and Clare had agreed to go to the Soul Shelter? If they had agreed to drive there under escort? Maybe they would be leaving it by now.

After Clare had been illuminated by the guru. After she had been raped.

During this long interview Jack had drunk Coke from the minibar. A burger had been sent up for him. He had devoured it. Now he was swaying, even while seated.

At seven in the evening, Barnes stopped recording. Sabatino escorted Jack along the corridor to the room they had booked for him.

Left alone, after a quick shower Jack collapsed upon the bed. His chin and neck felt so stubbly. Tomorrow was time enough for a shave. He burped Coke gas. For a short, confusing while he seemed to be dreaming he was still awake.

58

Clare stood naked in the bedroom, facing Jack. Light only came from the bathroom.

Although taut with excitement, Jack was wearing too many clothes. So many zips, so many buttons. His fingers were thumbs.

'Put the hard question to me,' Clare whispered. 'I'm waiting for it.'

How gorgeous she looked. If only it weren't for these damned fussy clothes which clung to him like a second skin.

She stroked her breasts. Her groin was foggy and featureless – an amorphous airbrushed photo of her loins. As he fumbled to release himself he sensed that there might be no access to her.

In the bathroom doorway lounged Orlando, who was also Gabriel Soul. A smirk was on his face.

In frustration Clare turned to the intruder.

'Ravish me,' she appealed. 'Put the hard question – and I'll see the light.'

Shuddering, Jack awoke.

The digital bedside clock showed a green 10.00 p.m.

Only ten.

He lay still and tried to drift back to sleep. He was too aroused. Memories of desert and bikers and the ride in the station wagon and the fat old Sheriff and the FBI agents spun around in his head, a tormenting carousel. Sheriff Crabtree rode into view, followed by that ginger-haired disciple, followed by the naked dark-skinned model with the parasol, followed by Mary Barnes asking questions. Questions, questions.

Still it was only ten past ten.

He tried to blank his mind, but couldn't. He might lie

here like this for hours, yearning to sleep yet not allowed to.

He rose and went to the window, cautious of banging his feet in the darkness. Pulled a curtain aside. A couple of vans were passing by along the main road beyond the palm tree-fringed forecourt of the Ronstadt Inn. Blank-windowed vans. Identical vans.

What he needed was a few stiff whiskies to knock him out.

The mini-bar in his room housed only miniatures of gin, which he hated, and Martini, which was hardly strong enough, and a couple of quarter bottles of champagne which would be ridiculously expensive; along with sodas and mineral water and chocolates.

Would the hotel bar still be open?

From his suitcase he took clean slacks and a clean shirt.

As for his stubble, by now maybe it looked designer.

59

Marcus and Erik and Tina and Pablo and Renny and Sammy were in the bar, nursing bottles of Corona beer. They were all here, apart from the lamed blonde – and Filbert.

They had pushed a couple of tables together. Enough empties stood grouped together to equip a ten-pin bowling alley.

Three wall-screens were showing the same baseball game. The commentary was so muted that it could hardly be heard. A reek of popcorn drifted from a machine on the bar counter. Behind the bar a lanky young man in black waistcoat and bow tie stood reading a newspaper. Baseball caps hung on the walls, along with paintings of pitchers and hitters, expressionistic swirls of colour.

A couple of youths in jeans and checked shirts were at a far table, with cans of Coors, eyeing the mute baseball game and also eyeing Tina. She wore a clinging pink halter top and loose blue shorts silky as a boxer's.

Renny leapt up. 'Look who's here! Come and join us, Jack. What'll you have?'

'I feel I should buy you people a drink—'

He remembered one of them was dead because of him. Drinks seemed like an insult.

Renny seemed untroubled.

'Nonsense, nonsense. Not your fault. What'll it be?'

'Whisky, please. Any whisky.'

'Spoken like an old-time prospector hitting town.'

'Where's his bag of gold?' muttered Erik.

Renny practically plucked Erik from his chair and propelled him towards the bar. Ushering Jack to the vacated seat, he sat alongside him.

'So have the Feds found your girlfriend yet? Do they know where that Soul Shelter is?'

After the inquisition by Barnes, there was camaraderie here – a sense of ghastly shared adventure from which they had escaped. Apart from Filbert, and the model with the smashed ankle, whose name Jack had forgotten.

He asked Tina, 'Did your colleague get airlifted to hospital?'

'Sure,' said Tina. 'She's in Phoenix now. I wish I was in LA.'

'Wow,' said Renny, 'we've been through something. Do the Feds know where this guru guy took your girl? Were you able to give them any leads?'

'I don't know,' said Jack.

'Look, I must talk to Tina about insurance. I completely forgot. Will you excuse us?'

Tina looked puzzled, but Renny jerked his head emphatically.

60

'I don't *do* sex!' Tina told Renny indignantly in the deserted, dim dining room. 'This was supposed to be classy work. Famous Marcus. Fine for the portfolio. What the fuck are you suggesting?'

'Chill out, will you? Keep your voice down.'

A party of senior citizens was trooping noisily from some function room through the lobby in the direction of the car park. Bleached heads, rinsed heads, bald heads, bright shirts and blouses.

'Listen to me, Tina! A model needs to get into acting before her looks go.'

'I *know* that.'

'It's time to practise, Tina. It's time to audition. Do a good job and I promise I'll fix you a screen test. A proper one, not some flesh flaunter.'

'Hey, will you really?'

'Honestly.'

'I'm still not going to do—'

'No reason why you should—'

'I'm not some bimbo escort—'

'I'm only asking you this because you're intelligent, for chrissake. I know you like a puff of weed to cool out. Get Fox stoned.'

'Are you crazy? With FBI people around?'

'If that makes you unhappy, well, whisky ... and woman. The classic cocktail. The cockteaser. It's just that having a puff would be a good pretext to slip up to the privacy of your room, do you see? I've been working really hard for us, Tina. We have some hot TV interest. Sex cult kidnapping women. Indians on Harleys versus crazy killers in the desert. FBI gearing up for a hostage siege right now, I'll bet you.'

During the dash to Ronstadt in the station wagon, Jack Fox had been too spaced-out and anxious to be as lucid as he might have been. *What else might he know, which the Feds now knew, and were basing their plans on?*

'It's your duty, Tina. There'll be good money for information. Christ, do we need it after this débâcle! We owe it to Filbert's widow.'

'I didn't know Filbert was married.'

'Divorced. Young kid.'

61

Musical chairs had occurred in the bar. Jack found himself on his own with Tina.

'You poor guy,' she said, 'you must really be worried. All this way from home, among strangers.'

'That's why I couldn't get back to sleep. Thoughts kept churning round in my head. I thought that a drink or two would—'

She took his hand where it rested, near a generous shot of Jack Daniels on the rocks, and squeezed it.

'Hey,' she whispered, leaning closer still, 'want to hit on some dope? Smoke a joint or two? That'll relax you. I've some in my room.'

62

Two big beds were in the room, one made, the other mussed.

'I was sharing with Marcia,' explained Tina. She guided Jack to a sofa almost as big as a bed and plumped him down.

Using finely flaked resin from a tiny tin with a sunburst on the lid, she had soon rolled a joint. She lit it and toked. She squeezed up against Jack. She crossed her long bare legs. She laid a bare arm along the back of the sofa and his shoulders.

Her cheek was so close as she transferred the joint from her mouth to his, keeping hold of it so that her fingers brushed his lips. He smelled her fragrance along with the acrid sweetness of the cannabis.

After Jack had taken two or three hits, the drug burgeoned within him as though he had taken LSD, not cannabis.

It was as if all the years since he had been so totally stoned – at a festival in Somerset – simply evaporated. It was as if that earlier tripping state of careless optimistic youth and the present moment joined up seamlessly.

Timelessly. No interval existed in between. His earlier state of mind and his present state of mind were identical. They coexisted.

He hadn't lost the intervening years.

In the darkness people were making friendly liberating love amongst bushes. Here he was with a ravishing girl whose American accent seemed at once so soothing and so sensuous. He could hear music. *Seasons may pass you by, you go up, you go down* . . . Which group had that been? The Yes. *Close to the Edge.*

'Why don't you pretend,' Tina suggested, 'that I'm your girlfriend? Talk to me as you would to her. Pretend she's here. Pretend I'm her.' She giggled softly.

'Strong dope,' he said.

'The best.'

He remembered the dead bodies in Clare's chalet in Tucson.

'Murder and injury seems so cruel when you're high,' he said to her. 'So hurtful. Your body's so soft.' Indeed it was, although he was talking in the abstract. 'I don't know how people on soft drugs can hurt someone else. Whoever shot those burglars couldn't have been smoking this stuff.'

'What *burglars*, Jack?'

'The ones who ransacked Clare's suitcase at the Hacienda. The ones Soul's people must have shot. His people are supposed to be into love and bodily rapture . . .'

Rapture also meant capture. Predatory capture. Didn't it? Clare was captured right now.

Tina stroked his cheek.

'Something violent happened even before I was kidnapped? Jack, you got to let it all spill out of you if you hope to sleep. You're too buttoned up.'

Fingers were undoing his shirt. She was stroking him, massaging. Lower down, he felt the pressure of a twisted, confined erection.

What was she inviting? She wasn't Clare. She was here, and Clare wasn't. How could he be unfaithful to Clare? Comfort from a friendly stranger was hardly infidelity.

What was Clare undergoing right now? Forced infidelity to him?

Tina's massaging hand had withdrawn. Likewise her arm from around his shoulders.

'I'll roll another joint,' she purred. 'Did you say these burglars were looking for something in my suitcase? Why would they do that? Didn't think they'd find drugs, did they? Professors smuggling drugs . . .'

'They stole her speech and her notes – or else Soul's people stole them.'

'My speech,' she said. 'That's weighing on your mind. Just tell me about it, then you'll be able to go to bed.'

Here, with her? Or back in his room?

'The Brain as a Computer of Light.'

'Computer of Light,' she repeated. 'Gee, that's beautiful.'

She carried on rolling the second joint, both hands involved in the task.

'Computers and burglarizing and murder,' she said, 'and sex and immortality . . . wow.'

He sucked in more smoke, held it, then exhaled slowly. His erection seemed to have wilted. His head was beginning to spin.

'I think I'm going to flake out.' He tried to rise, but she held him back.

'Go with the flow, Jack.' She was kneeling on the floor, unfastening his shoes. Smoothly she hoisted his legs up on to the sofa.

'I'll set the alarm,' she said to him. 'Five-thirty okay? Then you can go back to your own room. Me, I'm going to walk about a bit. Dope makes me restless—'

She was drifting away towards the door. He was adrift on the soft boat of the sofa. Cartoon images of a long-legged girl paraded through his stoned mind, a cavalcade of Tinas.

63

Stripped to shorts and sweaty T-shirts, Free Wind and Eagle Eye and five other initiates of the Inzane Nation sat cross-legged in a close circle upon bare mattresses in the dilapidated shack.

A breeze lazed from a half-open window to a smaller window which was missing its glass; a sheet of stiff waxed cardboard on string hung askew. The kerosene lantern cast a jaundiced light. From hooks in the ceiling hung the Dream Catcher web. The string mesh moved in the breeze, the feathers seeming like the legs of a huge hairy spider.

Someone was singing drunkenly outside in the night, some sot who had lost his heritage and his soul and his name. Some overweight diabetic poisoned by junk food and alcohol.

Free Wind sipped from the cup of cockerel blood which was mixed with Coke, and handed it round. He lit up a joint, and inhaled, then passed the smouldering tube to his neighbour.

'Dreams,' Free Wind intoned. 'Dreams of bloodshed, Brothers. Fierce dreams, Skinwalker dreams.'

He slapped cupped palms upon his bare thighs, drumming himself.

'Dreams of white folk killing each other. Inzane dreams, Brothers, inzane dreams spooking the souls of the devils who ruined our souls and our land. Nightmares walking America like empty skins hunting for white men to settle upon and make them mad . . .'

Eyes half-shut, he squinted towards the ceiling.

'There's our aerial, there's our transmitter. We turned it inside-out. It don't catch dreams no more, no more. It sends them out instead. Sends them like birds across the land.'

The joint had reached Eagle Eye. He held the smoke in his lungs till it seemed he would burst. Releasing a gust, Eagle Eye declared, 'I'm flying.'

The cup had arrived back at Free Wind. He drained the last dregs then set the cup down and wiped his mouth with his hand.

'The blood of the bird is in us, Brothers. Its death-cry bursts from our lips. The Dream Catcher broadcasts that scream through the sky.'

'I'm flying—'

'I'm crying—'

Brothers were watching Free Wind with respect and wonder. Something new – but also something ancient – was awakening. He had voice. Magic was hovering.

Bad magic, maybe? Best sort in a world gone mad, gone bad.

Should they ride out tomorrow to find where the magic would set the world ablaze with cleansing fire? To admire the frenzy from afar like birds gathering to feast on the dead?

'Brothers,' crowed Free Wind, *'we're* the Skinwalkers now!'

Tomorrow might be a little premature.

64

North of the Soul Shelter a long finger of restricted land thrust out from a bombing and gunnery range occupying a thousand square miles.

Thus on the map, at least. The range hadn't been used for ten years, but it stayed restricted in case of unexploded bombs and shells, which would be few and far between, and because restrictions possess a great inertia. Forty miles by fifty miles wasn't much land at all when the land was useless except to jack rabbits and peccaries and kangaroo rats and rattlesnakes. Someone straying into the restricted area might even miss the occasional faded signs and stretches of collapsed wire.

Near the tip of the finger some military huts remained, around a well shaded by large cottonwoods. This well had once given a name to the deserted spot: Slake. Prospectors and miners had slaked their thirst here on their way to the long-abandoned copper mine up the canyon where Gabriel Soul had staked out his private space far from interference.

Slake was deserted no more. Slake was a staging post and rendezvous, lit by headlights. There were three armoured personnel carriers and a field ambulance and a mobile kitchen and a small row of Plymouth Voyager vans, one with a satellite dish on top, and a trio of trucks and several station wagons.

A couple of black helicopters had landed, disgorging camouflage-clad men in flak jackets and forage caps.

From the round hatches in the rears of the APCs thirty more men had spilled out to drink coffee and chew doughnuts before the final briefing in one of those big huts which had been opened and lit by generator. Stars spangled the sky, apart from in the south where dark clouds were bulging. A meteor streaked like a tracer bullet.

Unavoidably on pep pills, Irving Sherwood was twitchy as he rehearsed the plan in his mind.

The convoy would set off so as to arrive by six, just a bit before sunrise. Using night-vision goggles, all drivers could travel at a decent speed, unlit.

Nothing could be done about the noise of engines rumbling across the empty desert, but by good fortune a storm was forecast. Seventy per cent chance of some thunder and lightning and precip in the general area. Could do without the precip, but thunder would be great. A few forks of lightning would make anyone think *thunder* rather than vehicles, especially when no lights were showing.

The pair of helicopters would come from behind the cliffs which backed the Soul Shelter, and land up top. Agents would take out the radio aerial and the dish up there. Soul wouldn't be able to contact any militia buddies.

Then the agents would abseil down on to the roofs of the Soul Shelter. Toss flash-bangs, to coincide with the main assault. Keep the sick-gas in reserve. The assault teams shouldn't wear gas masks unnecessarily. Stifling. Muffling.

Should work. Should work fine. All over in half an hour, tops, ideally, though the interior layout was still unknown.

Half an hour. Don't make the Waco mistake. Go in massively, and keep going in. Don't be stalled. Field

168

hospital already on hand. Protection from on high, from Mr Grey in Washington. Matter of national security.

Damn twitchy pills. Unavoidable, given all the urgent hours of preparation, co-ordination.

Lights blazed. Blue-caps milled about, drinking coffee. The last thing Sherwood needed right now was a caffeine fix.

Check his watch. Time for the briefing.

He raised his loudhailer.

'Sherwood speaking. Will everyone go inside the hut?'

Once in there, pay special attention to the enlarged satellite photo of the site. Don't just gawp at the poster of the hostage which had been blown up hugely from a certain photograph in the *National Investigator*.

Only available picture. Just the upper part of her was on show, but including the woman's bare tits. Head only would have been far too grainy, a fog of inflated blots. The Bureau had scanned the picture in archives and squirted it computer to computer.

That had been Nicholl Perridge's idea. Got to have a recognizable photo. There were lots of young women in Soul's harem. Jack Fox didn't have a photo of his girlfriend on his person. By the time the rented Toyota and luggage were retrieved it was too late to use Conway's passport photo. Besides, Sabatino in Ronstadt said that the passport was seven years old.

Should the Bureau have accessed the original print from the *Investigator*?

On what spurious pretext? A complaint that the *Investigator* was distributing pornography? That would have started the news hounds investigating, if they had any nose at all for a story.

There was going to be no story here – not immediately. Not with the hundred-or-so disciples under armed arrest, and restricted in these huts here at Slake for prolonged questioning. Kind of like a concentration camp. These huts needed urgent revamping. This operation was going to cost a few million, but Mr Grey had a black budget.

Most of the men had packed into the lit-up hut by now. Wolf-whistles resounded inside.

Good idea about the photo. Like a pin-up in a soldier's foxhole. Morale was high. Revenge for Oklahoma City.

65

Thunder woke Clare. The square of sky beyond the open barred window of her high cell was deep purple, with some stars and an intruding mass of black cloud. This would be the dawn of the second day of her captivity. Forked lightning flashed.

Waking early seemed so *unfair*.

Yesterday, after that blueberry breakfast, Birthmark Beth had brought Clare a pair of jeans and a T-shirt, and a silk nightdress too. Printed upon the T-shirt in big letters was the simple motto SOUL.

Accompanying Beth was a young woman who wore just such a T-shirt over her jeans. A model of how Clare should dress. This other woman was called Kath. Her face was unattractive. Long and bony and angular. Her figure was fetching. The T-shirt clung to firm, neat breasts. Kath brought a canvas bag with her.

'Do I get to tour your community this morning?' Clare had asked.

Beth wagged a finger. 'Not after you tried to upstage Gabe. He welcomes a challenge, though; and you're a challenge.'

Soul had seemed more amenable when he brought the muffins, before Jersey called him away.

'That box wasn't genuine, was it?' Clare asked Beth – even though the authenticity or otherwise of the contraption was of no more significance than a question to a believer of whether a religious relic such as the Turin Shroud was real or fake.

'What's genuine,' said Beth, 'is Gabe himself. Whatever means he uses are genuine.'

'There are so few true souls in the world!' exclaimed Kath, a fanatic gleam in her eye. She seemed besotted by the very thought of her guru. 'We're the immortals. Out there,' and she had waved at the window, 'is zombie-land. You really must give yourself to Gabe as soon as you can – then you'll know, just as I know.'

'What were you before you came here?' Clare had asked.

'No one,' said Kath. 'I was nothing. Nothingness scared me so much, because my folks had died, so I was alone. Gabe gave me a soul. He doesn't want you to be alone today while he's busy.'

Kath was to be a companion, a cheerleader for the Soul team, chipping away at Clare's independence, converting her by example, keeping up a spiel of devoted propaganda about Soul's visionary genius and perhaps about his physical merits too . . .

The prospect appalled.

First to be fastened alone in a box, and now to be locked up with a chatterbox, perhaps for hours. This was going to be like some lunatic tutorial, with Clare on the receiving end. Stage two of the brainwashing.

What was in that canvas bag? A quilt which the two of them could tat together, both wearing identical clothes with Soul's name emblazoned on their chests?

With a horsy grin of triumph, Kath pulled from the bag a Scrabble box.

'Let's play! We'll sit opposite each other on the floor . . .'

Scrabble?

'You do know how?'

Clare nodded glumly.

They had played until lunch, when a short plump woman had delivered bowls of bean stew. At least the stupid tournament kept Kath from rhapsodizing about Soul *all* the time. Clare tried to hive off her realization into an autonomous part of her head, separate from meaningless word games and her companion's inspiring remarks.

After lunch more games were interspersed with more propaganda.

Clare would get up and pace the room, protesting that she was *not* trying to see what tiles Kath had on her green plastic rack. She stared out of the barred window at bright barrenness. She was being eroded. Soul must be letting her stew so that an encounter with him would become attractive and desirable. The hours were endless, seeming to convey the message that Jack had achieved nothing at all.

Oh God, if he wasn't even alive! She'd have no chance to confide her realization to him. If poor Jack wasn't alive, he'd be dead forever like Miranda.

How would Carl Newman greet her announcement that quantum computers would immortalize people by storing their minds in vacant universes?

Inconceivable to imagine confiding in him! Or in Professor Keyserling, or in the Master of her college. No wonder people like Soul founded cults.

That was why it was so essential that Jack was safe and sound. Jack was her cult; she was his.

Did she *love* him? Yes and no. Both at once!

The entire day had worn away thus. Jack might be worrying that she was being ritually raped. Actually she was being subjected to endless games of Scrabble interspersed by Kath's babble.

The early evening meal had been beans and burger. Then Kath packed up the Scrabble set and left. No reading matter of any sort was in the cell. Soul mustn't have written down any of his own revelations or had them printed. Those revelations were occult – communicable only person to person, body to body.

If only he would pay a visit, to break the monotony! To give her some inkling of what was happening. Oh no, she didn't really want a visit!

She toyed with the idea of switching her light on and off in an attempt at morse code. SOS: long long long, short short short. Someone miles away in the desert who happened to be looking through binoculars might see the signal.

Then she had heard a shuffle in the corridor outside, and her light had gone out.

172

She could only lie down on the camp bed and meditate about empty universes waiting to fill up with human memories.

What form would the afterlife *take*? A sort of virtual reality re-enactment of your life? Permutations upon your life? All conceivable possibilities available to you, so long as you could imagine them and create them? A kind of endless do-it-yourself adventure game? Sharing with other stored minds in a fulfilling communion?

May as well call this the Virtuality – the way Soul did. His notion of how to bring it about was through sexual antics, awakening the Snake of Kundalini and similar tosh.

Once you were in such a community, its internal logic took over your mind. The carrot of immortality. The stick of an outside world of hostile zombies. The drug of free sex.

Yet if Soul hadn't locked her in that box, would she ever have realized about the empty universes?

From the ghost universes would the dead be able to commune with the living through some sort of quantum coherence? Could the dead visit the living in dreams or in quasi-schizophrenic visions?

If only there was a shower in her cell.

Hardly surprising that she'd woken early, thunder or no thunder. She'd had a long enough time to sleep. It still seemed damned unfair, if another day similar to yesterday awaited her.

The sky was lilac and lavender already. Light was about to flood over the bulge of the world. Lightning danced again. Thunder grumbled.

Other noises too. Machine noises. Engine noises.

The world outside erupted in flashes of light, detonations. It was as if a dawn fireworks display had been arranged. Such a cannonade. The fabric of her cell shook. Plaster dust was falling.

Within the Shelter she heard guns opening up. A klaxon was hooting.

She scrambled to the closet in her nightdress so flimsy.

Should she dash back for her jeans? The volume of fire from outside increased stunningly. Explosion followed explosion. She cowered as dust billowed in through the open window. Part of the Shelter must have been blasted open. The London Blitz, which her dad had lived through, could have been like this.

Was this all for *her*? How could it be?

Should she dash to the bed, strip off a sheet, force herself to go to the window and bundle white through the bars to show where she was?

An explosion rocked the roof. Plaster cascaded.

Her door opened.

Soul. He was wild-eyed, wearing jeans and a hastily thrown-on checked shirt and boots. A pistol at his waist. He rushed in and seized hold of her by the arm.

'The zombies are going to kill us *all*—!'

She clung to the washbasin. He wrenched her free and waltzed her towards the door. Her feet were bare. Beware those boots of his. He could break her toes – the pain would be hideous. He propelled her into the corridor. A young raven-headed woman in pink pyjamas and slippers darted past with an automatic rifle.

'Defend the Shelter to the last, Rachel,' Soul bellowed. 'The Virtuality's waiting for us today—!'

'Gabe, Gabe,' Rachel cried back, as she rushed on her way. Her cry was affirmation, almost joy.

The main entrance to the Shelter was a ruin. Disciples were crouching, firing through smoke and dust.

Gabe hustled Clare past and half-carried her down those stone stairs to the Truth Room.

Jersey came close behind, clutching a compact automatic gun. In the cellar the thin man, Billy, had torn aside that red velvet curtain to reveal an iron door.

Jersey crashed the stairs door shut. He bolted it top and bottom. Reverberations still dinned from upstairs. The Schrödinger box loomed, open and empty. That table with the hole cut in it! The human head on the plaque, real or resin . . . This place would seem like a torture chamber when the so-called zombies burst in.

Billy unlocked the iron door. Beyond: the darkness of a tunnel. Inside lay torches and knapsacks and a couple more of those compact guns, in plastic bags which Billy swiftly tore open.

Clare sagged. She tried to make herself heavy. Her nightdress rode up. Soul's clutch tightened crushingly. He heaved her forward.

A torch beam showed a rough-hewn tunnel supported by timbers. These were old mine workings! Darkness gobbled at the light. Jersey dragged the iron door. Bolts clashed. Billy and Jersey picked up what they could, the light in Billy's hand waving wildly. Soul could handle nothing other than his captive. Clare whimpered. Oh beware his boots.

'Walk properly! *Walk!*'

The swaying shaft of light cavorted. How the floor banged her feet. The air was so dead and dusty and chilly. Convulsively she sneezed.

Soon the tunnel forked in two. The torch beam flicked across the smooth rock floor of one tunnel. Broken stones covered the floor of the other tunnel, a carpet of debris.

It was the rough way that Soul forced her to go. Sharp pieces of rock gouged the soles of her feet. Her feet would soon be lacerated and bleeding. She cried out.

'I can't walk on this – !'

She sagged, genuinely unable. Soul's arm crushed under her breasts as he swung her. Was he going to drag her on her knees?

'I can't walk, I can't!' she wailed. Soul was going to try to pick her up in some fireman's lift or other, to sling over his shoulder. She was off the ground. He skidded. They fell. Both of them together. Stones dug into her like a hundred vicious elbows. He was panting like a dog. Her nightdress had ripped half a dozen times by now.

'For fuck's sake, Gabe, leave her. The roof's too low later on—'

Up ahead, Billy swore and waved his arms and the light.

The air was full of darting wings, shrilling squeaks, chaotic fluttering. An acrid wetness spattered Clare's face, her shoulders, her arms. She shrieked.

'Shit, shit,' she heard Billy swear.

Shit indeed. Bat-shit. Panicking bats. A whole flock of bats.

'There weren't any this way before—!'

How many tunnels were there through the hill? Branches and dead-ends and air shafts? As the stones dug into Clare's legs she realized that the disciples must have swept that other branch clean as a false trail. This rougher tunnel was the real escape route. A roost of bats had taken up residence.

What was at the other end, however far away? A cave, its mouth disguised by dead brush, with a jeep stored in it, or some dirt bikes?

Bats, bats . . .

'*Hurry up, Gabe!* For fuck's sake hurry up! You can't bring her. Leave her!'

It was true.

'I'll find you!' Soul shouted into Clare's face as darkness thickened. Billy had gone onwards. Jersey was about to go too.

'I'll find you, Clare.'

Then Soul was gone.

Blackness was total. No chink or speck or glint redeemed it. Nothingness pressed around her. A squeak flew past her, cutting an invisible path through the unseen, the unseeable.

She could have been lying in a coffin, hurting from cuts and bruises, buried alive.

This nothingness was different from when she had been in the box. She could understand this blackness. It was only the absence of light, not the absence of any possible concept of light or of any means of knowing what was missing. This was a darkness you could feel your way through.

Shivers were becoming uncontrollable. She mightn't be

able to feel her way back to heat and light. She might pass out and never be found.

Shock: it was shock – and the chill of the tunnel – but shock most of all.

Clenching her teeth, she pressed her palms down on the stones and raised herself. Sharpness dug cruelly into her knees.

Edge sideways until you touch the wall.

She shuffled, her right hand held out.

Touched wood. Rough splintery wood.

One of those pit props.

Nearby, she felt stone.

Now she could rise and flatten herself against the hard wall.

She began to work her way along it, testing with the soles of her feet before putting her weight down.

A dull boom sounded.

She imagined that she was going the wrong way and that somewhere far inside the hill Billy or Jersey had blasted the tunnel to bring down the roof and block pursuit.

Then she heard muffled shouts.

The bolted door from the stairs to the Truth Room must have been blown open.

She crept along, her whole body still trembling incessantly.

Now the floor was smooth.

Ahead: the faintest grey rectangle. To stare was to lose the outline. Seepage of light around that iron door.

A nearer shout: '*Take it out—!*'

Oh God, they were going to blast the iron door open too.

'I'm here!' she shrieked. 'I'm in the tunnel! Can you hear me—?'

She began to back away.

'Can you hear me? I'm in the tunnel behind the iron door—!'

66

A haze of dust veiled the battered Soul Shelter and its outbuildings. At least the place hadn't been set on fire by the occupants. Many were now stumbling or limping out under guard. Men, women. No kids, though.

Where were the kids? How could there be no kids?

Kids were a nightmare in situations like this. Lack of kids was a worse nightmare. If kids were dead, Sherwood was screwed, no matter what strings Grey controlled.

The adults couldn't have had time to poison or shoot their kids. They couldn't possibly!

Sherwood shouted at a blue-cap with FBI printed in yellow on the front of his flak jacket: 'Johnson, where are the kids?' Johnson was herding two women whose hands were up, and one who was clutching her blood-soaked arm.

'Haven't seen any—'

The kids must be in a safe place. A cellar. A bunker. Shit, there must be mine workings burrowing into those cliffs. How else could the cultists have disappeared all the boys and girls?

Sherwood strode to the women.

'Where are your kids?' he demanded.

A crazy-eyed woman with ratty dusty hair spat in his face. Her cheek was cut open.

'Zombie!' she screamed at him. 'Murdering zombie!'

Those armoured personnel carriers were like so many tanks which had bombarded this gimcrack castle. The field ambulance was already on site. One of the assault team was tragically dead. Maybe another fatality inside. Two quite serious injuries notified so far. Survivable. Half a dozen minor injuries, but guys were just carrying on. Heat of combat.

Two cultists' bodies had been hauled out so far. Bound to be some more. Hopefully not too many. Shooting was to incapacitate, unless life was directly threatened. Of course the whole logic of the attack had been sheer brute force, applied as hard and as fast as possible, so as to stun and stupefy and overrun.

At any moment a blue-cap would be bringing out Conway, freed.

And Gabriel Soul, in cuffs. Unless he was injured. He'd better not be dead.

'Zombie!' the woman raved again.

Ignoring her, Sherwood headed for a cultist who was already cuffed. Bald man with a pot belly, one eye swollen up.

'*You*: where are the kids?'

A look of malicious cunning came over the prisoner.

'You'll need to search high and low for those, Mister Zombie.'

What was all this about zombies? Private cult jargon?

From the south came a departing grumble of thunder. Most of the sky was turquoise. The climbing sun was already heating up the oven. Sherwood's flak jacket was becoming uncomfortably hot. Too soon to loosen it, though. A sniper could still pop up at one of those windows. On top of one of the APCs a blue-cap was constantly scanning the frontage of the rambling three-storey edifice through the telescopic lens of his rifle, alert for any such movement.

The egg-beater swish of a chopper . . .

Had the paramedics called one of the two black choppers for Medevac without clearing this with him? Without the site being fully secure? He couldn't see either of those choppers rising up from the clifftop.

The noise was beating along the canyon from the north.

Tiny in the sky, a helicopter was approaching. Couple of miles away. Looked white.

Sherwood sprinted to the Plymouth Voyager van with the dish on the roof. He seized binoculars.

Less than than a mile away now, and closing.

A passenger was filming.

Shouldering a video-camera, the passenger was panning the scene. The chopper was slowing. From five hundred feet up the cameraman was filming the APCs, the vans

179

and trucks, prisoners, the Soul Shelter, the whole damn show.

Media. Just had to be media. TV network. There'd been a leak.

Sherwood scrambled into the Plymouth and lifted a microphone.

'Blue Boy to Black Fly One and Black Fly Two: do you read me?'

The helicopter pilots acknowledged from the clifftop.

'We have a snooper,' said Sherwood.

'We can see—'

'Get in the air and signal him down. Fire warning shots if you have to—'

'My passengers all went down the cliff, Blue Boy—'

'Mine too—'

The black choppers weren't armed with automatic guns.

As the two black flies rose up above the clifftop, the white chopper veered away. It was banking tightly, to head back the way it had come.

The two black choppers picked up speed to overtake it.

Quitting the van, Sherwood swung the binoculars. The three helicopters were already beyond the canyon, flying out over the flatland. Black was gaining on white, a good three miles away by now. How far before white conceded and landed? And where? Somewhere accessible for a van to reach? That film had to be confiscated.

'We got her—'

A bare-legged, filthy woman in a ragged nightdress was being carried out of the Soul Shelter.

Conway. Had to be her.

Sherwood couldn't see any choppers at all now, just a glare of sky.

He was forgetting something crucial.

'We got her—'

Cheers went up here and there.

Conway was the prime objective. What a mess she seemed to be. Her blue-cap saviour was averting his head. The woman's face was all screwed up. With pain? Or at the sudden blaze of sunlight? What sort of conditions had she been kept in? At least she was alive and aware and she didn't look obviously injured.

'Get her into a van,' he shouted.

Out of the sun. Away from any guns which might still go off.

Everything was confusion for Clare. They had heard her through the iron door. They had shouted back. Both sides shouting at once. Couldn't make sense at first. Took at least a minute, which seemed like five, to establish that she herself could unbolt the door once she could get near enough to feel where the bolts were, and that they weren't going to blow it open while she was just on the other side of it.

The top bolt hadn't been easy, reaching up on poor sore bare feet tip-toe. Of course they suspected that she might be bait for an ambush. There was such a flurry of guns as she was dragged inside the Truth Room, for her own safety and theirs. No one had a torch to shine along the tunnel.

'They've gone,' she was insisting. 'They left me because the roof's too low further on. My feet – I can't walk easily—'

'God, you stink, lady,' someone had exclaimed. He sounded bizarrely cheated, as if he'd expected to rescue a lovely distressed beauty. 'Did you—'

'No, I didn't shit myself!'

Mortified, her rescuer holstered a side-arm and hoisted Clare into his arms. His flak jacket had felt so lumpy and angular against her thinly clad body. Another of the flak-jacketed men was staring at the snarling head mounted on the wall.

'What the *hell's* that—?'

Her porter didn't find it easy to mount the stairs, encumbered by a woman's body. Maybe he imagined he would, but reality was otherwise. He lurched and puffed. He banged Clare into the wall, making her squeal.

Upstairs, such dust and chaos and wreckage. A mêlée of armed agents, hysterical or numbed disciples, shouts from the interior of the Shelter, the sounds of clattering boots, an occasional gunshot.

Outside in the blinding sun, it was as if an army had attacked, as though she was in some Balkan hell-hole transplanted into an apocalyptic Wild West . . .

She must shake her confusion. She must sharpen up.

67

As Sherwood approached the open side door of the Plymouth Voyager, Reynolds, who had carried Conway inside, emerged.

'Yamaguchi's looking after her now.' Reynolds was breathing hard. 'Soul and a couple more got away through the mine tunnels—'

Tunnels, tunnels, of course. The kids must also be in those tunnels.

'Why didn't you radio me—?'

'My arms were *full*, for chrissake—'

How far did those tunnels stretch? How many entrances? Soul must have had an escape route all mapped out.

Sherwood darted back to the communications van.

'Blue Boy to Black Flies—'

Static was all.

'Blue boy to Black Flies—'

Crackle-crackle.

Maybe the canyon's walls were blocking transmission. Or the media chopper had obeyed landing instructions. The pursuit choppers had set down as well. Their pilots had gone to arrest the intruding pilot and cameraman . . .

How soon before one of the pilots got back to his machine?

To Agent Janice Stancu, in charge of the communications van, Sherwood said, 'Keep calling the Black Flies. As soon as you raise one of them, get him airborne. Look for Soul and two others. They got away through mine tunnels. They probably have bikes or something. As soon as he spots them—'

Contact the Marine base at Soda Flat? Could take too

long to get clearance, even by satellite link to Grey in Washington. *That* would be an admission of failure.

'Tell him to follow them. Alert the Highway Patrol. Armed fugitives. Have them intercepted. Make sure the other Black Fly stays with that media chopper until we're able to reach it.'

If only those scumball snoopers hadn't shown up. Both of the Black Flies could have dropped down from the cliff, picked up sharpshooters and chased after Soul and his buddies and forced them to stop and stay put. If only.

'Sir—' It was one of the paramedics. 'We need Medevac for Agent Ramirez and for one of the prisoners.'

Shit.

This was turning out just a little badly.

Conway, Sherwood reminded himself. *Encryption.* The Holy Grail.

68

The smell of her . . .

Sherwood imagined that Conway had smeared herself with excrement to evade Soul's erotic advances. She was in a nightdress. A silk one, ripped to shreds. Could have been slinky not so long ago. Yamaguchi had slung a blanket around her, but enough flimsy still showed. And filth.

Yamaguchi was kneeling, tending Conway's feet. Bowl and sponge. Stained cotton wool. Antiseptic and Bandaids from the First Aid kit. Conway wasn't a field hospital case. No gunshot wounds or broken bones.

'You can soak yourself when we get you to Ronstadt,' Yamaguchi told her amiably while he stroked her toes. No, he was simply applying another Bandaid. Looking up, he grinned at Sherwood. 'Hognose bats, is my guess.'

'What—?'

'Hognose bats. Make even a hog hold its nose! *Mexican* hognose bats.'

Bats, bats?

'What are you talking about?'

'The bats in the tunnel dumped all over me,' said Clare. What a clear, precise voice she had. Despite appearances she sounded quite lucid and collected.

'Did the children go into those tunnels?' Sherwood asked her.

'Children?' Puzzled for a moment, she laughed the next, blithe at her liberation. 'There aren't any children! Soul ordered birth control for everyone. If any of the people already had kids they certainly didn't bring them here. Because,' and she clammed up.

'Because why? You *are* Dr Clare Conway, aren't you?' Her accent said so. On the other hand, gurus like Koresh had attracted Brits and Australians as well as Americans.

'Sure she is,' said Yamaguchi. Evidently he had been getting her talking while he tended her, even though that wasn't *his* business. His name meant 'Mountain Mouth' in Japanese.

No damn children at all. That was a relief. But he had wasted time bothering about kids. Intelligence about Soul was imperfect. Of course it was imperfect – particularly in the area of the computer and militia connection!

'Because why?' repeated Sherwood. Chip away at the areas where she showed any reluctance to answer.

'Who are you?' she asked him.

She was sufficiently composed to answer a question with a question.

'Irving Sherwood, FBI. *Why* are there no kids?'

It was almost as though she had hoped to safeguard him and Yamaguchi from embarrassment.

'Because, if there were, Mr Sherwood,' she said primly, 'they would need to be involved in the sexual practices of the community. Because the community saw sex as the route to immortality. Involving children could cause problems.'

Sherwood motioned Yamaguchi to leave.

'Why did Soul kidnap you, Dr Conway?' he demanded.

Quietly she said, 'Do you have any tampons in this van?'

69

Jack's bedside phone shrilled at eight that morning. His head throbbed. For a moment – before he remembered creeping back in a daze along corridors, and via the fire escape stairs – he believed that he was still in Tina's room.

He was lying on his own bed in shirt and underpants and socks. Bright daylight spilled around the sides of the curtains and streamed across the carpet like silver snakes. Don't let him still be high! What on earth had he been thinking of?

As he clutched the handset towards him, the rest of the phone dragged and tumbled on to the floor.

'Hullo—?'

'Is that you, Dr Fox—?'

It was the black woman, Barnes.

'Yes, it's me. I'm sorry, I dropped the phone.'

'I have good news for you—'

Clare had been rescued. She was safe. Just some cuts and bruises. She was already on her way to Ronstadt in an FBI van. She would be at the hotel in an hour or so.

Neutrally, Barnes asked, 'Dr Fox, do you want us to book you both into a double room here, or what?'

'Was it hard to free her, Miz Barnes? I mean, was there much, um, action?'

Would there be much publicity?

British tourists who were mugged in Florida usually made the news back home. How much more so a kidnapping by a cult leader ... If this was on the news, Heather would hear it. He ought to be phoning Heather to warn her, to explain that Clare had been kidnapped. What a lot of explaining there would be. Crazy guru fixating on Clare. Being forced off the road. Himself escaping from that gang of disciples. Marcus and the models and the shootings. With all this going on, maybe Heather would discount any possible misconduct on the part of Clare and himself ...

Telling Heather might only make everything seem totally lurid and scandalous.

If he didn't phone Heather, and she found out from the

radio or a newspaper, what would she think he was playing at?

'I don't know all the details,' Barnes said, 'and I wouldn't go into them, anyway. What exactly are you asking me?'

Clare would know the details. She wasn't here yet.

'Can we decide about the room after Dr Conway gets here?'

'Dr Fox,' Barnes said patiently, 'I gather she'll need to clean herself up before we debrief her. She'll need a room. The question is, do we arrange a separate one or would you prefer to share?'

Clean herself up. Clare was in a mess. She would need assistance. Comfort. A shoulder to lean on. She mightn't want to be left alone. She might very much want to be left alone.

Was Barnes being helpful or was she taking the opportunity to probe? Thank God she didn't know about his visit to Tina.

'I was wondering,' Jack said, 'how much, well, publicity there might be . . . about the rescue, the circumstances. You see, I ought to phone *Dr Conway's father* in England to reassure him, if this is going to make headlines. If it isn't, you see, I wouldn't because *he has a heart condition*. Do you see?'

'Uh-huh,' was the non-committal response.

'Will there be much in the way of headlines?'

'Or are kidnapping and murder too normal to deserve much attention?'

'I didn't mean that exactly.'

There was silence. Jack suppressed the urge to fill the gap.

Finally Barnes said, 'We aim to minimize publicity.'

They did?

Why?

'Is that . . . while you pursue your investigations?'

'Something like that. We don't want media people bothering Dr Conway. We don't want her talking to reporters, in case it prejudices.' Prejudices what, she did not say.

'She wouldn't want to, not after that *National Investigator* farce. She's rather a private person.' Bluffly he added, 'And publicity would be bad for the tourist business, eh? Bad image?'

'It's considerate of you to think of that,' Barnes replied in that same neutral tone. 'So what about the room?'

'Dr Conway might need . . . a friend nearby. I think we'd better share.'

'Consider it arranged.'

70

Jack had showered and spruced himself and hurried downstairs to the dining room for coffee and an omelette. A quarter of the tables were occupied. Marcus and Erik and Sammy and Tina were already eating in a far corner.

Seeing him, Tina waved. Jack was not going to join them. He merely smiled. As he sat down on his own without waiting to be shown to a seat, Tina giggled, and Marcus smacked her hand. An abandoned copy of the *Arizona Star* lay on Jack's table. He pretended to immerse himself.

What had he told Tina the night before? He had told her about the murdered burglars in Tucson.

He was still in his seat, as were Marcus's crowd, when through the net curtains he spied a dark blue van pull into the driveway of the Inn. The van stopped under the pink marquee-like canopy fronting the hotel entrance like some huge welcoming orchid.

A couple of men climbed out, one with a Japanese face, and then *Clare herself*, escorted by a fit-looking fellow with curly hair and frank face.

A blanket draped Clare. Her hair was matted. She was limping bare-legged in white Reeboks a couple of sizes too large for her.

Abandoning his table, Jack dashed to the lobby. Floor of pink marble. Little groves of ornamental bamboo in terracotta urns.

'Clare—'

'Jack—'

However bedraggled, Clare seemed to illuminate, to shine at the sight of him.

He was going to hug her. She thrust a palm to ward him off. Her blanket parted to reveal torn soiled silk. She grinned, she laughed as her aroma registered.

'Wait a bit, Jack. I stink of bat shit.'

Click-whirr, click-whirr. Accompanied by Erik, Marcus was pointing a camera from beside a clump of bamboo.

Clare's escort swiftly intervened, waving big hands.

'Stop it, mister—!'

Sabatino hurried to interpose himself.

'Come on now, Mr Strauss, give me the camera. I want the film.'

'*Who is this?*' demanded Clare's escort.

'He's Marcus Strauss, the photographer. Those guys Fox stumbled into in the desert, right?'

The escort glared at Marcus and Erik.

'Why are you trying to take photos?'

Erik was all offended innocence. 'My dear man, Marcus Strauss doesn't *try* to take photographs.'

'It's in the blood,' Marcus said. 'Such a photogenic shot. Gallant FBI agents, damsel in distress. Blood's been spilt, you know. Poor Filbert! We've been involved in this against *our* wishes.'

'Filbert's the man Soul's bikers killed, Mr Sherwood—'

'I'm well aware—'

'Marcus Strauss took pictures of Soul's bikers and the Navajo ones too.'

'Which I'm hoping you'll return! Keep copies as evidence, by all means.'

'Why,' demanded Sherwood, 'were you hanging around here ready to take pictures?'

'We weren't hanging around,' protested Erik. 'Please don't be so stressed out. We were simply eating breakfast. Dr Fox rushed out. Marcus is inseparable from a camera.'

Solemnly Marcus said, 'I feel a deep obligation to show Filbert's widow what this was all about.'

Sherwood said to Sabatino, 'I have *got* to get some sleep.

Confiscate his inseparable camera. I want to interview Mr Strauss and associates,' with a glance at his watch, 'at noon.'

Mary Barnes came holding out a card-key.

'Room 404, Dr Fox. Dr Conway's luggage is waiting in the room. Yours is being shifted right now. We took the liberty.'

71

Clare lay back in the bathtub, naked. Jack sponged gently. She seemed slimmer, waifish.

'Jack, Soul locked me in a Shrödinger box. You know, the cat and the cyanide gas experiment?'

'Yes . . . ?'

'I was the cat in the box.'

'You mean he actually had a box big enough to put someone in? He actually did that to you? Christ almighty, what a madman. You must have been scared out of your mind.'

'I had a pretty fierce migraine.'

'I'm not surprised. The *bastard*. If that's the sort of mind-game he plays to brainwash disciples!' He massaged her shoulders with the sponge and with his hand.

'It was probably just a *pretend* Schrödinger box.'

'If you believed it was real at the time—!'

'Hush. You don't need to be indignant. You won't have to punch him on the nose the way you did Orlando.'

'Actually, Orlando slipped.'

'Oh, whatever. When I was in the box, Jack, I realized something amazing . . .'

After she had told him, Jack needed to think quietly for a while as she relaxed.

The brainwashing box and the migraine attack: Clare had described those to clarify the circumstances. Of course the death of Miranda – the stupid wasteful death – had preyed on her mind . . .

189

The cult's obsession was immortality . . .

What Clare said about the storage of people's minds in parallel ghost universes could so easily be a taking-on-board of Soul's own craze, a sort of protective identification with her captor – skewed so as to preserve her own individuality, her sense of self.

Hostages identified with kidnappers or hijackers. This could happen swiftly. Just a few hours of being a hostage seemed an eternity.

An airline passenger, held by terrorists, might convert to his captors' cause if it was explained forcefully and persuasively. The hostage might stay converted, even when the ghastly incident was over.

He would need to support Clare in her belief until it showed any signs of fading. Otherwise, he would be cutting through a lifeline she had thrown to herself.

'What a remarkable concept,' he said with cautious wonder. 'It's hard to take on board immediately. It's so suggestive, so fertile . . . A purpose for all the empty ghost universes! I mean, aside from the quantum requirement for those . . . Ghost universes as an abode for our ghosts! And maybe being able to communicate with the dead . . . It's a vast idea. An illumination.'

Soul had promised, or threatened, to illuminate Clare.

'It's staggering,' Jack said. 'You must be exhausted.'

She sat up, water dripping from her breasts.

'I'm *not*. Last night I had nothing else to do but sleep. I've soaked enough. Will you pass me a towel, Jack? And bring me the toilet bag from my case? Will you wait outside?'

When she came out of the bathroom, a big towel wrapped round her body, a small one round her hair, she placed a finger to her lips. Approaching until she almost touched him, she spoke almost inaudibly.

'Jack, it was a massive amount of force they used to free me. Massive.'

He whispered back, 'Why the hush?'

190

'I don't think they tried to negotiate or anything. It was like a full-scale military assault. As if they were at war.'

'Well, they got you out.'

'That business with the photographer downstairs—'

He whispered: 'Clare, they don't want publicity. Publicity would hamper the investigation. Barnes, the black woman who gave us the card-key: she said so.'

'Did she? It seems sinister to me.'

Oh, let her not become paranoid.

He could hardly hear her words. 'All that force, to rescue a foreign tourist. People *died*, Jack. Did you ask for us to share this room?'

'I suppose Barnes suggested it.'

The finger upon her lips. He was practically lip-reading.

'Jack, Soul boasted how his people shot those burglars in Tucson. Those were *Russian* burglars. Russians, robbing my room. Did you know they were Russians?'

He shook his head.

Breathing: 'The FBI put us in here together. I think they're listening . . .'

72

'And then,' said Sabatino, 'they both went so quiet that the tape has diddly on it.' He switched off the recorder in the dining room of the curtained suite.

'After that they went downstairs for a late lunch. Conway stuffed herself, he only picked. Out for a little walk they went, and ended up lounging under parasols by the swimming pool. None of Marcus's crew made any approaches.'

Sherwood steepled his hands and contemplated the recorder.

'Marcus, Erik, Tina, Renny, the make-up woman: those are the source of the leak, for sure. I think Tina is getting worried about possible consequences.'

'Conway must be a tough cookie,' said Mary Barnes. 'Whispering like that, when you've just been reunited.'

'Understatement of the year.'

'Fox is cool too. He was so cautious when I phoned to

say she was safe. Whoopee, marvellous? Not a bit of it. He was trying to sort out our attitude. There was just enough whoopee to be plausible. Fox was watching his words. I think they're *posing* as lovers.'

'British people can be a bit restrained,' said Rosado.

'Ha!'

Sherwood bunched his hands into fists, which he tapped together. He could have been softly knocking for admission upon a mirror.

'They're more than just a couple of academics.' One by one fingers flicked up. 'Conway is close to Matsushima, though not a direct employee. She plans to visit QX, supposedly to look at their artificial intelligence lab. They lie to the police about staying at the Union Square Holiday Inn. Why should they lie? What are they really planning?'

His little finger sprang up from under his thumb.

'Are we supposed to believe that *bathroom tape*?'

Rosado tapped the side of his head, indicating nuttiness, screw loose.

'I could agree with you,' conceded Sherwood, 'if they hadn't gone so ominously quiet afterwards. I think that ghost-universe immortality stuff was all deliberate bullshit for our consumption. She never mentioned any of that to me on the way here. Upshot: we're supposed to decide she's a fruitcake. Then they can get on whispering, or lip-reading for all I know. I'm almost beginning to suspect that the story in the *Investigator* wasn't a malicious prank at all . . .'

Eyebrows were raised.

'Maybe it was a deliberate plant.'

'I don't get that,' said Sabatino.

'Me neither,' said Sherwood.

'Why draw such farcical attention to herself?'

Mary Barnes chuckled.

'Maybe the lady's an exhibitionist as well as an industrial spy. The story made her seem a bit of a loony bimbo. It doesn't make sense – unless the story was a signal of some sort?'

Sherwood mused. 'She might have come to Tucson to

meet those Russians, but Soul's people killed her contacts, being true American patriots of the militia persuasion. Maybe Matsushima are using Russian mafia to confuse us. We're fishing.'

'Do we try to crack the cookie?'

'No,' said Sherwood. 'We let those two carry on. We put a locator in their car. We keep our distance. And we track them. The sooner they get where they want to be, the sooner this is settled.'

73

From four till six that afternoon Sherwood had questioned Clare in the FBI suite about her ordeal. Sabatino recorded the session, and Barnes sat offering womanly comfort, if Clare needed it. The sooner we get all the details straight, the sooner it's all over, honey.

Clare described being locked in the Schrödinger box, since this seemed much more evil than compulsory Scrabble played with a devotee. Of her realization, she said nothing. She mustn't talk about ghost universes and the afterlife yet. Her words would seem like babble brought about by stress.

Even Jack's attitude earlier had seemed tinged by doubt. Caringly camouflaged, but even so! Surely Jack would come to see what she saw. She needed to explain it over and over – but not to FBI agents. Her realization belonged in the *Journal of Consciousness Research*, not in a crime report.

For instance, there was a vital distinction between alternative probability universes which are variations upon life as we know it – and ones where there's no life at all because life never arose. These latter ones must infinitely outnumber the former. These empty ones would be the storage space for dead identities. This distinction needed stressing, but not to the FBI.

Questions had veered to Soul's involvement in the murders in Tucson. She told what he had bragged to her. All of her misfortunes appeared to spring from that wretched story in the *Investigator*, because of a grotesque misunderstanding which she could hardly fathom.

How sympathetic Mary Barnes was. How understanding.

'If news of this breaks before you get home to England,' the black woman had said, 'my, what a terrible shock for your father.'

For a moment Clare had frozen.

'His heart being the way it is, honey?'

'Oh yes!'

Jack had told her about this white lie and the reason for it. Was Barnes trying to catch her out? It seemed improbable that the American Embassy in London could have found out anything to the contrary in the short time available. This had to be an innocent remark. If only she hadn't hesitated.

'Hopefully the news won't break for a while,' Sherwood said.

'How soon will you arrest Soul?'

'It's just a matter of time. Don't worry about it.'

Soul's last words to her: *I'll find you.*

Barnes smiled encouragingly. 'Don't feel you need to look over your shoulder. I know that's a natural reaction after what you've been through. You need to get up and going. America treated you rough. Remember, what happened is one in a million.'

'It happened to my sister too. She was shot by a mugger.'

'You've had very bad luck,' agreed Sherwood. 'This sort of lightning *cannot* strike again. As Mary says, get up and going. Keep your head high.'

Get up and going?

'Do you mean we can . . . just go on our way?'

Barnes had beamed benevolently.

'We know everything we need to know.'

The FBI had blasted their way into the Soul Shelter. There had been casualties. Something like a hundred disciples were under arrest. (And *where* would they be under arrest?) Yet she and Jack could carry on.

'How can we carry on?' she asked disbelievingly.

'Your car's being fixed,' said Sherwood. 'New window glass. Couple of bullet-holes patched up. New fender and hood. A respray. It'll be ready in the morning. American hospitality's usually better than you've experienced so far.'

They were going to use her as bait for Gabriel Soul. They were so desperate to catch him.

Don't feel you need to look over your shoulder.

Someone else would be looking over their shoulders.

74

'Isn't it marvellous news?' she exclaimed to Jack in their bedroom. 'How will they do it?'

'Splendid,' he agreed. 'I can't wait.' Almost voicelessly, 'They'll put some sort of radio locator in the car.'

'I could murder a steak. That dinner menu looks a lot better than High Table. Will they be able to hear everything we say to each other?'

'I fancy the lobster Thermidor. I think it'll just be a sort of beacon, so they can track where we are. We ought to celebrate. Do you remember old Matthews at the College Feast? Hadn't eaten all day, he told me, then he starts hiccuping the moment he slurps his first spoonful of soup.'

'Jack, I shan't be eavesdropped on.'

'Lovely lobster bisque – and such explosive hiccups! Just wouldn't stop. Poor old sod had to leave the table.'

'Oh yes, I remember. Poor old sod—'

75

'And that's what I call a phoney conversation,' said Sabatino.

'You look pooped,' Mary Barnes said to Sherwood.

'Three hours' sleep in the last forty-eight. So it feels.'

And the come-down from the pills . . .

The effort of pretending to like Conway – when he would

have preferred to put some very hard questions to her indeed. However, it was time for subtlety.

That business about the mine tunnels . . .

Bad, bad. A misjudgement.

Sherwood felt paralysed by exhaustion. He couldn't think straight. He couldn't say so.

He should be making better plans.

All those hostile disciples who were currently being questioned by agents . . .

A goddamn concentration camp. *Concentrate* on our questions, please!

And the TV cameraman in the chopper . . .

Keep a lid on Marcus and Renny, somehow. But let the Brits walk. Let them drive. Let them lead their trackers . . . to the truth.

Mary Barnes seemed so competent. And gorgeous. He'd never thought of Mary quite this way before. He was married, damn it. To the Senator's niece.

Those Brits would lie in bed together, conspiring inaudibly. He would lie alone, zonked out.

76

In bed later, Jack and Clare pulled the sheet and a blanket up over their heads like children planning to read by torchlight. They cupped together. Bashfully he adjusted his erection, and held her. Must feel like a big sausage against her bum. She smelled of peach from the hotel shampoo.

'Soul won't find me,' she purred softly. 'His threat was all bravado. He'll be needing to look out for himself, not us.'

Lying in bed together. Cuddling. Even if Clare didn't have a period they couldn't make love while somebody in another room snooped on noises. How could you make love in blithe abandonment yet total silence?

'Dear, dear Clare . . . About the journey: I really hate to say this. I don't see how we have enough time now to follow your sister's route. I know how much it matters to you. But it seems such a detour . . . Don't you think maybe we ought to head straight into California . . . ?'

'Yes,' she agreed unexpectedly. 'It could be easier to lose them all – to get away from all this mess. Away, away. Jack, we can swap cars. Get rid of the Toyota. Hire something else. Can we do that?'

Lose the FBI ... ? In bed together this seemed almost credible. Two grown-up children plotting to run away ... He felt rejuvenated.

Jack thought of credit cards, and of being billed. He thought about Angelo's plants getting thirsty. San Francisco seemed like Shangri-La, some kind of heaven or haven. After the vicissitudes they had been through, maybe this was infantile thinking, where wishes and fantasy were everything. Yet how appealing this was, how seductive.

'We'll still be going by way of San Jose, though,' he whispered into her ear.

'Soul won't be there ... Jack, I don't want to go and see the Tin Man any longer. That's irrelevant now.'

In the wake of her realization ...

It would be sensible and adult and responsible to visit the Tin Man lab as planned. The visit could pull Clare back on course, reset her priorities.

'Matsushima want you to—'

'Sod what Matsushima want. Of course I want to know how near QX are to a quantum computer. They aren't likely to tell me! I need to be alone with you to think out all the implications – the best way to present what I know ...'

After some days of privacy in San Francisco, how easy would it be to leave the country if they had offended the FBI? Infantile thinking.

'Oh, I did promise Carl Newman, that's true. Yes, we'll go by QX. It's hardly out of the way at all. We'll go by it. We'll just take a look and drive past.'

She was leaving this option open. Once they were in the San Jose area Clare might realize that she really did need to visit the artificial intelligence laboratory. The Matsushima Fellow of Spenser College needed to visit there – yet was Clare still the same person?

Maybe she had always been on the edge psychologically, awaiting a vision, a new perception. Otherwise, would she have succumbed to Orlando? Would she have decided that quantum computers must become self-aware? And now that those same computers were a door to the afterlife?

Jack realized that he was a witness to an alteration in the mind-set of someone he loved, and that his own mind-set had shifted too, so that he was now in love – not simply feeling friendship and desire for Clare, but infatuation and delight and pent-up, temporarily frustrated, ardour.

Love, love such as he had felt for Heather once upon a time; and lost.

'Everything has changed, Jack.'

'And I love you,' he whispered. The air was becoming stale and stifling under the sheet. Heaving himself up, and the sheet away from their heads, he leaned over to kiss her on the peach-scented cheek, and lay back.

Briefly she turned to him. She sighed almost silently, 'Everything except San Francisco has changed . . .'

How unlikely it was, now, that he would pay visits to any of those many names in his personal organizer.

Clare's realization might be a private hallucination. It was also the sort of idea which, if she publicized it, might influence millions of people . . . Readers of the *National Investigator*, and such . . .

77

It had taken all day to reach signs to North Hollywood and Beverly Hills and Glendale and Burbank. Jack was exhausted and Clare was numb.

The hotel which they found was called the Stardome. Framed photographs of Richard Gere and Demi Moore and other stars decorated the lobby – which was full of sweaty men in camouflage uniforms, humping heavy bags of gear. Were these real soldiers or extras for some movie?

When Jack and Clare were finally able to arrange for a room, the reception clerk explained that the soldiers were National Guardsmen mustering for annual training. Maybe staying at the Stardome was a perk, or urban guerrilla warfare was on the training schedule.

Doors were open along the third floor corridor. Part-time soldiers clumped about, clutching cans of beer. Party time was under way. The view from the room was of a massive water tank on stilts.

They had not been conscious of being trailed, but all the time in the car they had felt inhibited, unable to confide in one another. Clare was still adamant that they should change their vehicle. It would be like washing one's hands.

That night, they cupped together again.

'You do believe me, don't you? About our identities surviving—'

A light touch seemed best.

'Well, you know my field. New beliefs, new attitudes. How gears shift in the mind.'

'Are you researching me now?' she asked mischievously.

Oh yes, this was his desire. She was his desire. Unfulfillable tonight – but tomorrow night, yes. Till then, a light touch.

The psychologist in him recalled the syndrome of *folie à deux* – the pattern of behaviour whereby two people who are emotionally close to each other can come to share a common delusion.

The next morning, study of the phone book and of the city plan in a drawer in their room disclosed a Hertz agency only a few miles away.

After checking out, they drove there, losing their way a couple of times.

The returned Toyota easily passed muster. Good as new. The service charge for delivering the car elsewhere than agreed went on to Jack's Visa card.

The clerk called a taxi for them.

The driver was a grinning Greek, and they asked him to find a diner a few miles away.

On the way, a mangy cat darted into the roadway. The Greek just missed the animal. A car behind skidded, and clipped an oncoming van, which skidded too. Bit of a snarl-up behind.

From the diner, Jack phoned for another taxi.

'We want to stop at a bank with a cash machine,' Jack told the black woman driver of the next taxi. Yes, draw out enough cash to pay a big deposit for a hire car, and thus avoid using a credit card which could be traced. 'Then take us to a car rental agency that isn't Hertz.'

'Did Hertz offend you or something?'

'I didn't like the colour of any of the cars,' Clare said airily.

'You got a thing about colour?'

'Oh God, I didn't mean *that*. I'm sorry!'

The woman drove in sullen silence. After a while she pulled over at a branch of the Bank of America with an automatic teller machine in its wall.

Clare extracted twelve hundred dollars in twenties against her Mastercard, then the black woman drove on, racking up the fare, so it seemed. When they did arrive at a small company called RoadKing, Jack felt obliged to overtip their driver, and received no thanks, though the woman blew an ironic kiss to the clerk in the office, a gangly young black man.

The clerk would have preferred fifteen hundred dollars as an alternative to a credit card blank. After a couple of twenties had eased his attitude, he compromised on twelve hundred plus damage and liability insurance.

A notice boasted of RoadKing offices in San Diego, San Jose, San Francisco, all the Sans.

Presently they drove off in a blue Ford Taurus. Onwards to Shangri-la, by way of San Jose.

78

By late afternoon they had left Interstate 5, crossed the northerly limb of a great reservoir and passed by a dam to join Highway 101 near somewhere called Gilroy. A placard boasted that Gilroy was the Capital of Garlic. A frieze of giant painted garlic cloves clarified the message.

Clare had wound down her window and sniffed.

'Gilroy was here,' she joked.

Although the drive had been tediously long and had missed all the coastal sights by seventy miles or so, it had also been so much more relaxed than the previous day's ordeal. Clare was cheerful. She had talked about her Realization.

Jack could readily visualize a best-selling pop-science book: *Quantum Survival* or some such title. Perhaps *Universe of Ghosts*.

'Will animal identities survive too?' he had asked. 'Cats and dogs and monkeys?'

After a moment's thought Clare had nodded.

She laughed.

'It seems hard to draw a line when there's infinite storage space...'

Hard indeed.

Fanatical seriousness was absent. Holiday was in the air; and love. Passion and affection. A sharing of spirit and flesh. Almost blanked out from Jack's mind was the prospect of returning to Cambridge in a week's time, and Orlando and Heather and other bothersome aspects of reality.

He certainly wouldn't spend time in San Francisco interviewing alternative therapists and New Age sweat lodge shamans. His whole study would be of Clare herself, in passionate depth.

Presently they were passing through mile after mile of dormitory town, in heavier traffic. To the east foothills rolled upwards towards high hazy peaks. To the west the sun was dipping behind other hills beyond which, twenty miles or so away, would be the huge Pacific.

San Francisco was only about seventy miles away now.

How absurd it would be to phone Glen Chang, to arrange to tour the Tin Man lab making interested noises, to waste a night and a morning in San Jose, when they could be at Angelo's empty place by ten or eleven and awaken tomorrow together in Shangri-La!

If Clare were to tour the lab, how could she stop herself from prattling about her Realization?

They might decide she was nuts.

Yet she had to see the place where a quantum computer was most likely to awaken to self-awareness – and forge the link with ghost universes.

According to the map Chang had sent her, this would involve only a minor detour off Highway 101.

San Jose was a kind of Station of the Cross en route to paradise, a place to pause briefly and bear witness.

79

Fading red and orange banners of cloud to the west. The skein of smog-glow was becoming more noticeable across the city as its lights infused the pollution of the valley.

Low-slung tech buildings, well spaced out, lined Jefferson Avenue, a few fenced round and sporting security gates. Most buildings were lit and car parks were full.

Here was QX itself, occupying several acres behind wire. A tall illuminated sign by the gateway announced: *We question the unknown.*

Jack stopped fifty yards short of the gate, where a guard sat in a glass booth. He switched off the engine and lights and lowered the window. Clare crowded against him, gazing.

'There's Mecca,' he said merrily.

A couple of vans were coming up from behind at a dawdling pace. They coasted past the Taurus: identical camper vans with opaque windows and large plastic ventilator panels on the roofs. They drew up a hundred yards beyond the entrance, one behind the other.

Camper vans such as tourists used. They seemed out of place in this neighbourhood. Each of the vans had a high radio aerial.

Further down the road beyond them a mammoth rig had pulled up. Twin horns on the roof of the cab were silver trumpets. Two exhaust stacks were shiny chimneys.

The rig idled forward and stopped again, dousing its lights. Maybe its driver was intending to have a snooze.

The plastic hatches on the roofs of both campers were sliding open. Heads appeared. Faces stared briefly at the rig.

'Jack, those vans—'

'Are you thinking they're FBI?'

Briefly she was silent, concentrating.

'I saw two like those at the Soul Shelter. Soul was seeing them off—'

'There must be a lot of vans like those.'

Another van was approaching, coming up behind the distant rig. Some kind of loudspeaker van. It tucked in behind the rig, lights dying, vanishing from sight.

A BMW coupé came speeding along the road. Rock music blared as the coupé passed by and continued onwards. Just someone going somewhere.

'Look, Jack—'

Those people who had poked their heads up through the roofs of the campers were manoeuvring bulky tubes through the hatches.

Elbows planted on the roofs, they were pointing those tubes.

Just then, a muted thump came from the west wing of QX.

A moment later, both tubes flashed briefly. Twin lights streaked over the fence and over the parked cars.

'Christ almighty,' from Jack, 'they're firing bazookas—!'

Twin explosions ripped the east wing. Flames flared. Debris gushed. Smoke billowed.

'For heaven's sake turn us around—'

Jack started the engine. However, the rig had awakened to life. Its lights were blazing. It was moving, pulling out.

Two more rockets flew from the launchers.

On the east wing two ferocious flowers blossomed. Flames gushed. Suddenly the whole east wing was plunged in darkness, apart from those flames, which had now taken hold.

The rig came powering down the middle of the road

towards the campers – and towards the Taurus too. If Jack were to swing out he would surely put the Taurus in the path of the rig. The rig would demolish their car, crush it like cooking foil.

80

'Told you, Luke, I didn't *like* that rig!'

'Take it out—'

'Shit, the launcher's jammed—'

Was it jammed or was Zak panicking?

'Take the Uzi—'

'Fuck,' from Donny in the driver's seat. He was half-blinded by the glare from the oncoming rig.

The Uzi opened up. The rig went blind in one of its eyes. Zak was firing too low.

'OH FUCK, MAN,' screamed Donny as light filled the inside of the camper. A second later: 'It'll miss us, it'll miss us—!'

With a rending screech the rig scraped along the side of the camper.

The steps Zak had been standing on fell over and he was left dangling.

And then the beast was past. Through the fisheye lens in the otherwise opaque rear window: a steel whale was brushing past the second camper.

Zak dropped down. Luke was staring through the lens.

'I don't get it,' babbled Donny. 'It could have totalled us.'

'*Drive*, Donny – get us out of here! We've hit the zombie lab.'

'I think the guy in the rig was some Asian. Shit, the ignition only clicks—'

The rig had proceeded beyond the gateway. Abruptly it veered. It was mounting the roadside. It ploughed into the security fence. The huge vehicle was demolishing yard after yard of uprights and wire, flattening them under its bulk. Thirty yards of fence, forty yards, fifty.

The rig regained the road and carried on westwards.

'It just wrecked the fence – *deliberately*. What did it do that for?'

'Our engine's dead,' shouted Donny. 'High tension lead, I dunno. We've got to get into the other camper!'

Unaccountably, other explosions began.

81

A flash and a minor fireball illuminated the western perimeter. A second explosion disintegrated the security booth over there. Over at the eastern gateway too there was an explosion.

Clare and Jack hunched low in their seats.

Three men jumped from the foremost camper van. They were armed – automatic rifle, sub-machine-gun, pistol.

Further along the road headlamps lit up. The loud-speaker van was on the move.

An explosion in the westerly car park blew up a car.

An amplified voice boomed out:

ATTENTION. THIS IS A POLICE MESSAGE.

Loud enough to make Jack's ears ring. The words almost drowned the noise of a car exploding in flames in the easterly car park. Must be audible a mile away.

THIS IS A POLICE MESSAGE. EVACUATE YOUR BUILDING BY THE SOUTH SIDE. EVACUATE IMMEDI-ATELY BY THE SOUTH SIDE. THIS IS A POLICE ORDER.

The loudspeaker van lacked any police or other markings.

The rifleman was bringing his gun to bear upon it.

A van came speeding towards the south gate. The barrier was rising. The guard in the booth was heeding evacuation instructions.

The van swung out, tyres squealing. On its side: MERCURY DELIVERIES, and a cartoon of a winged man delivering a package.

The rifleman fired at the loudspeaker van. Its windshield became a mosaic of ice with a hole through it. The rear camper began pulling out – into the path of the delivery van which was still swaying to left and right after its swift turn on to the road.

The collision shunted the camper into the side of its battered twin. MERCURY DELIVERIES came to rest facing the opposite way. Tyres screeching, it headed in the direction of the Taurus. Jack and Clare ducked lower as it raced past.

A ruthless robbery: that's what this must be . . . MERCURY DELIVERIES must have been the crucial vehicle, speeding away with stolen goods on board . . .

None of it made sense.

Causing chaos must be part of the robbery plan, but more chaos was happening than planned. The firing of the bazookas . . . If Clare was right about those campers, some of Soul's disciples must have come here to hit QX . . .

Jack risked a look. People were abandoning the camper. A couple of them reeled as if punch-drunk. One collapsed.

A gun barrel smashed through the crazed windshield of the loudspeaker van, clearing away ice. The loudspeaker van began to move again. Its driver was keeping his head down. A passenger opened fire on the people who had abandoned the camper. One spun round and fell. Another returned fire before being hit. As the loudspeaker van rocketed past the Taurus, Jack caught a glimpse of the gunman. A young Asian, just a teenager.

People were pouring out of the QX building by now. Some wore white outfits and masks and goggles. Jack could hear distant shrieking and shouting. Fire flared. Smoke gusted upwards. Engines were starting. Some cars were moving. In the east and west car parks several vehicles burned.

Two survivors from the campers who were still able-bodied were shouting.

'*Die, zombies, die,*' Jack heard them chant.

From buildings up and down Jefferson Avenue, spectators were spilling.

Soul's two saboteurs began to head up the road. One

trotted. The other was limping badly. Both were heading towards the Taurus.

A sporty compact car sped through the south car park. It swung on to the lawn.

The foremost saboteur held a pistol in his hand. As the sporty car lurched over the demolished fence, he swung and fired. The driver was wearing one of those white body-suits and a mask and goggles. He seemed like some assistant to Red Adair, whose job it was to put out oil well fires. He was sawing the wheel, hardly in control. The first bullet must have careered off the bodywork.

The emerging car skidded as a front tyre deflated.

A shot rang out from the gateway. The guard had quit his booth. In his tan uniform, short-sleeved shirt, peaked cap, he was standing with legs apart, aiming a revolver two-handed.

The saboteur lurched. His pistol flew from his hand. The fender of the skidding car clipped him across the knee, toppling him.

The car had stopped. Its door was opening. Its driver was scrambling out, heaving a light-coloured case with him. Protective suit, rubber gloves, goggles, hairnet . . .

A car horn blared to urge the guard out of the way. He leapt aside just before an Alfa-Romeo coupé came revving out into Jefferson Drive.

The man in the bunny-suit picked up the fallen gun. His goggles focused on the Ford Taurus. He hurried towards it.

A few seconds later Jack and Clare were looking at a gun muzzle. Jack realized too late that he hadn't centrally locked the car. Sirens began wailing in the distance.

Setting the cream case down briefly, Bunny-Suit pulled the rear door of the Taurus open. He heaved the case inside, climbed in after it and thrust the gun forward.

'*Drive, you prick, drive—*'

Several more cars had come through the gateway. Some headed westwards along Jefferson. Some turned east. A white Mercedes sports model was heading east.

'Follow that white Merc, you lying bastards!'

207

Jack drove.

Howling sirens: *WAW-WAW-WAW-WAW-WAAAA.*

As the Taurus neared the end of Jefferson, a black police sedan skidded around a corner, then another, closely followed by a third. Strobing red and blue lights. Jack swerved to avoid collision. So did the police cars.

The police convoy sped past towards the QX compound and the principal action.

Maybe he should have tried to sideswipe one of the police cars. He'd have risked injury to Clare and himself. Too late to think of that now. It hadn't been his instinctive response.

'Left on to Bernstein!'

'Where—?'

'Turn fucking left.' Which Jack did. 'Couldn't even wait till I got to Portal Park, could you? Did you think I'd strike out on my own? Did you think I'd sell to the highest bidder?' Their hijacker sounded deranged.

Clare risked a look at their unwelcome passenger. One-handed, he tore off his mask and his goggles and his hairnet. A bulgy nose, weak chin, deep-set eyes and sallow skin. He sucked in air. He pointed the gun at Clare.

'I'm bloody well *sick* of this,' she snapped at him, her voice like a slap in the face.

He frowned. His eyes narrowed.

'Where are you from?'

'We're from Britain.' She felt stupid, as though she was some indignant colonial lady scolding a disorderly native. 'We're on holiday.'

Jack was easing off on the speed.

'Don't slow! But don't draw attention to us, either! Head for 101.'

'Which way?'

'Right at the next lights.'

The next lights changed to yellow. Siren howling, lights flashing, a fire engine raced from ahead towards the intersection. Jack slowed. The lights changed to red. Braking only briefly, the fire engine proceeded across the crossroads just as Jack coasted to a halt.

'*Turn right!*'

The red light still shone.

'There's no traffic from the left, dummy. Go, go!'

Jack obeyed. Their passenger glared at Clare.

'Weird sort of holiday, sitting outside QX, waiting to see me shot and make off with the goods—'

'I don't know what you're talking about!'

'Why are British people involved? I thought the Chinese might be behind Gwenda and the Viets. Or North Koreans. Or fucking Iraqis or Libyans. Follow green signs when you see them!'

'For the freeway, yes?'

'For the freeway!' Disbelief was still strong in their passenger's tone. 'Where are you two *tourists* staying?'

'We *were* going to San Francisco,' raged Clare. 'Will we ever get there?'

'Chill out, lady. Why were you waiting over the road for me to be stopped and shot?'

'I don't know you from Adam!'

'I suppose you don't know Gwenda Loomis either.'

'I've never heard of her.'

'What happened about minimum casualties? QX was on fire with your fucking mortar shells.'

'Rockets,' said Jack distractedly. Accuracy was important when you were driving. He spied a green sign for Highway 101 and Interstate 880.

'*How do you know that, Mister Innocent Tourist?*'

'We saw rockets fired from the camper vans.'

'Vans. I saw those. The lying bitch never said anything—'

Clare seethed. 'I've no idea who Gwenda is but the vans bloody well belonged to Gabriel Soul.'

'Who the fuck is Gabriel Soul?'

Clare hesitated.

The gun jerked at her face.

'*Who?*'

Be friendly to a maniac. Try to form a bond. Establish

209

yourself as a person, and the maniac as an individual too. She was getting a lot of practice in this.

She said sweetly, 'He leads a cult. He led a cult – in Arizona. We had some trouble with him. My name's Clare, and this is Jack.'

82

During the hour's drive northwards to what they had hoped would be Shangri-La, Clare did establish a degree of rapport with their hijacker. Mike, call me Mike. Mike probably wasn't his real name. Might be close. Same initial, perhaps.

Mike was paranoid about the cream-coloured case on the floor beside him, which he kept touching. He was paranoid about Jack neither speeding nor slacking. Often he stared back in case anyone was overhauling them.

He was very edgy about the pistol when he had to lay it on the seat while he peeled off vinyl gloves and then a pair of latex gloves from beneath the vinyl ones, and finally struggled out of his white overclothes. Under those Mike was wearing what looked like blue pyjamas, as if he was some Vietnamese peasant.

Clare had told him about Gabriel Soul harassing her at the conference on consciousness in Tucson – but not about her abduction, nor about the assault on the Soul Shelter by the FBI. *That* would have made Mike really twitchy.

'Gabe Soul's a screwball guru with lots of money, lots of weapons. He thinks the world's full of zombies—'

Only through sexual rites could you become strong enough to survive death. Soul had an almost psychopathic loathing of all research into artificial intelligence. Such as the Tin Man project, right?

'Jack and I were outside QX,' she told Mike carefully, 'because I was invited to visit the Tin Man lab tomorrow. We were checking the route. In Tucson I gave a talk about artificial intelligence, you see.' She hadn't exactly done so.

'That's what obsessed Gabriel Soul. He must have sent his hard boys to damage QX as much as they could.'

And this had coincided with the other events.

Mike had been decamping from QX during the chaos with that cream case in his car – and dressed as a clean-area worker, unidentifiable from any other . . .

The cream case couldn't possibly be . . .

. . . the biggest prize of all at QX? If a quantum computer did actually already exist?

She had to know.

Mike was paranoid. He believed his colleagues in crime had tried to kill him.

'You aren't on holiday at all,' said Mike.

'We're on holiday *as well.*'

The whole thing's thoroughly fucked up, thought Matt.

He'd fled with the prototype instead of taking it to Gwenda. She and her backers might believe he wanted to do a deal on his own. Not just for eighty thousand dollars, either. More like five million. Vietnamese gangsters would be hunting for him.

He could phone Gwenda from San Francisco. He'd been totally confused by what happened. The crazy intervention by those cultists shooting off their rockets and guns.

No, he oughtn't to know anything at all about those cultists. He'd been bewildered by the level of violence, that's it. Thought the plan had gone askew. Couldn't understand what was going on. He thought it best to get well out of the way. Find a safe place. Gwenda should understand that.

The memory of being shot at was so traumatic.

If everything had gone as planned, why shouldn't some Viet hit man have been standing by at Portal Park to kill him after he gave Gwenda the goods? Of course that would have happened! He'd been so stupid.

Thank heaven for the attack by that gonzo guru. This had rubbed the truth in Matt's face.

Gwenda's Viets would still try to find him and kill him. Only much more so now.

It might be best to surrender himself to the police in San Francisco. By phone, initially. He had the computer to bargain with. There'd be witness protection. New identity. Job as a gas pump attendant in Asshole, Arkansas.

No, he'd only gain a reduction in prison sentence.

The Englishwoman, Clare, seemed upfront about the house they were borrowing. She seemed oddly non-reluctant to tell him about their love-nest on Telegraph Hill. She kept trying to sneak glances at the computer.

And she'd been due to visit the Tin Man lab.

Someone welcome at QX must know enough about the company to be aware how close it was to a quantum computer.

'Where were you two planning to spend the night?' Matt asked.

'In Shangri-La—' Jack yawned noisily.

'In some motel in San Jose,' said Clare.

'Where did you spend *last* night?'

'In Los Angeles,' she told him.

'Don't let Jack get drowsy,' Matt told Clare. 'Keep an eye on him, not on me! What's the address on Telegraph Hill?'

'Twelve Pirate Place.'

'Are you sure? I never knew they watched out for pirates from the hill.'

'Angelo told Jack it was meant to be Parrot Place. The residents kept so many pet parrots last century.'

'You'd better give me your map.'

Finding your way could be tricky in that part of San Francisco.

Did he want to be burdened with a map? He wanted to get to Pirate Place as soon as possible.

She glanced back. 'Don't take us through the Tenderloin!' Sounded as though she was on the verge of a panic attack.

'What's your interest in the Tenderloin? Does Gabriel Soul run a sex parlour there?'

She was trying to control that panic.

'My twin sister was shot dead there, by some punk.'

212

Oh shit. She thought history might be going to repeat itself.

'I'm sorry,' he said lamely. 'I promise you shan't come to any harm if you behave yourselves.'

A moment later she was glancing at the cream case again.

'I told you to keep your eye on Jack – he's drifting!'

83

The new federal building in downtown San Jose which housed the FBI offices was part of the lavish renewal of a previously shabby area.

Peachy new convention centre with towering glass concourse. New upmarket hotels and restaurants and shops and finance houses. Light rail system. Hundreds of shade-giving sycamore trees and swathes of lawn and palm trees.

Of course, none of this was visible from inside the air-conditioned windowless room at midnight, where four men and a woman faced a four-way-split tele-conference screen.

Mary Barnes and Sabatino had been following the English couple to discover what they were up to. After Fox and Conway checked in to the Stardome, a surveillance van from the local Bureau office stayed outside overnight. Mary and Sabatino stayed in the nearest motel, and were back in position in their car in good time to watch the Brits drive off. The pair had stopped at a Hertz agency. Presently they and their luggage caught a cab. According to Hertz in Tucson, Jack Fox had said he would be returning the Toyota in San Francisco, not in Los Angeles.

Sabatino had duly noted the details of the cab. Just as well. A cat dashing into the road caused a minor accident. Enough of a delay for the cab to vanish. Sabatino had radioed the Bureau. The Bureau contacted the cab company; the company, its driver.

When Mary and Sabatino arrived at a diner which had

been the cab's destination, the trail was dead. A waiter certainly recalled a man and woman coming inside with luggage and using the pay phone, then leaving.

How had they left? No idea. The waiter had been busy.

Sabatino had taken the names of the cab companies from the cards stuck around the pay phone. United Independent, and a handful of others which mightn't be as respectable.

Delay would follow delay.

Where had Fox and Conway headed? And without a car of their own in Greater Los Angeles?

Mary thought they might have driven to a different rental agency, and were still heading for San Francisco. With a stop in San Jose, supposedly.

The trace on Conway's credit card revealed a sizeable withdrawal from an ATM in South Pasadena. A phone call to the artificial intelligence division of QX, and a talk with Glen Chang, revealed no contact whatever with Clare Conway. Dr Conway had certainly arranged to visit – that was already known – but she still hadn't been in touch. It was as if she had no intention of going there.

Sabatino decided that Conway and Fox were somewhere in Los Angeles, and he had stayed.

After contacting Sherwood in Slake, Mary had set out for San Jose. By plane, this time. Most of the day had been wasted.

She had arrived soon after the armed attack on QX.

Also present in the tele-conference room were Lieutenant Terry Hayward of the San Jose Police Department's High-Tech Crime Unit, and Lieutenant Bruno Lilly of the Santa Clara PD. Through an ear-bud plugged into an FBI receiver, Lilly was picking up reports from his officers out at QX. And Don Rosado had just recently arrived by helicopter.

On screen: Irving Sherwood, by satellite link from Slake in the Sonoran Desert where he and his team were trying to interrogate too many stubborn prisoners.

Richard Pentecost, NSA, Maryland; Bella Roundtree, Secret Service; and the enigmatic Mr Grey.

*

To Terry Hayward, the Bureau's quarters seemed a costly extravagance compared with his own cramped office space at police headquarters on First Street near route 880.

Hayward and his officers were daily involved in trying to stem the rising tide of chip heists. Busily mounting surveillance, setting up stings, trying to infiltrate the Vietnamese community who were tighter than the Mafia.

Stings were getting increasingly difficult to finance because of the escalation factor. Earlier this year Terry had set up a couple of $50,000 deals to entrap dealers in stolen chips. The chief got really edgy about so much money walking around. Yet the fact was that the kingpin chip merchants routinely did deals of a million cash, two million.

And Bruno had gone undercover, posing as a delivery driver for weeks to get evidence, really endangering himself.

So much money had been lavished on these new secure offices! You'd think the FBI were gearing up for a war.

'So the raiders broke into the Qua Fab—' explained Bruno.

Mr Grey held up his hand. 'Excuse me?'

'That's the quantum computer fabrication plant,' Bruno translated. 'We suspect there must have been someone on the inside too. Just a minute—'

He listened to his ear-plug.

'The security computer was virused. Who entered and left QX and who was where inside: it's all wiped out. It'll take a while to check everyone with sensitive access.'

Sherwood, on screen, looked haggard.

'That guard saw an Asian driver in the rig,' he said. 'But the men who fired the rockets and shot at the rig and at the loudspeaker van must be followers of Gabriel Soul – because of how they called your officers zombies.'

'It's a pity, Mr Sherwood,' Grey remarked dryly, 'you didn't know anything about Soul sending this raiding party.'

Sherwood could only study his hands.

'Realistically,' went on Grey, 'we have two possible

worst-case scenarios. One is of the prototype being smuggled abroad for stripping and studying. The other is of the prototype falling into the hands of internal enemies of our country. Mr Pentecost?'

'I don't think this robbery was necessarily planned by foreigners at all. The people behind it could easily be our own home-grown extremists. They want to crack secure systems. Government, financial. Cause chaos. Cripple the federal government. Start a crackpot civil war. We've said this already. My point is that the extremists might have hired those local Viets for their expertise – assuming they were all Vietnamese, for which there's no solid evidence. Soul might have learned of the plan through extremist contacts.'

'Why fight each other?' chipped in Terry Hayward.

'Maybe Soul's disciples were trying to steal the prototype for themselves.'

Sherwood perked up. 'I'd say this fully justifies our action against the Soul Shelter.'

'So where is the vanished lady?' mused Grey. 'And where is Soul?'

84

Stairways and steep lanes, bowers of bougainvillaea and rhododendrons and fuchsia and ivy, boardwalks clad in foliage, pale stucco apartments and neat clapboard cottages, porches and roof decks ascending Cézanne-style: here was Telegraph Hill. The fluted column of Coit Tower rose over all, floodlit yellow.

So many ferns and conifers; Angelo Vargas had chosen the perfect homeplace for a devotee of plants.

Shangri-la, at gunpoint.

The Taurus had slipped into a bay below the two-storey wooden house, painted pale yellow, in Pirate Place. Ferns brushed the car. Ivy climbed a tall Monterey pine. Railed steps ascended to a veranda crowded with pots and tubs.

The doorkey was indeed under a terracotta pot out of

sight round the side of the veranda, where taller bushes hid the weedy serrated palm-like fronds of *Cannabis Sativa*.

Close the curtains. Switch on the lights.

The main downstairs room was full of labelled shrubs and cacti in pots. Tiers of books, on psychiatry, botany, pharmacology. A voluptuous sofa was printed with a Rousseauesque jungle scene. A jaguar peered from one side; a dusky naked man from the other. Stylishly transparent chairs seemed made of glass but must be of clear plastic. A map of Amazonia decorated one wall, studded with coloured pins.

A kitchen opened off; and also a study with desk and computer, laser printer visible on a work station, more ranks of books and journals, filing cabinets, more shrubs and cactus plants.

The stairs which led to the upper floor were each painted a different hue of the rainbow in succession, starting out red.

Jack and Clare climbed to the violet of an evening sky, with Mike behind them, gun in hand.

In the master bedroom, a water bed. A Huichol tapestry on one wall pictured a huge peyote cactus with legs and a sorcerer with bow and arrow. A European woodcut was of a root-like woman with waist-length tresses. Leaves and flower-buds sprouted from her head. Musical instruments made from gourds were mounted on the walls. Did Angelo serenade his bed partners?

Mike raided the walk-in wardrobe for slacks and a shirt and threw those on the bed.

Bathroom and shower. A second bedroom with an orthodox bed. Floor stacked with journals. A boxroom full of clutter, with a tiny window, and a key in the lock.

The boxroom wouldn't do for the British couple. They could open the window and call for help. Matt considered the gun in his hand. Christ, he couldn't possibly . . .

No, the way to do this was to use the second bedroom. Get them to tie each other up, using whatever. Matt would

217

complete the immobilization and gagging. He'd be able to sleep securely, if he could sleep at all.

What about the car? No, that was okay. Nobody was looking for *them*. What about phoning? Either Gwenda, or the police? No way. As yet the police would know nothing about his involvement.

If only he wasn't burdened with two unwanted hostages. Christ, he couldn't possibly.

'I'm going to lock you both in the boxroom for a short while,' Matt told them. 'I need to use the toilet. Don't make any noise. Then I'll let you out, and you can take turns.'

'That's very considerate of you—' Jack's mumble became a yawn.

Clare was staring intently at Matt. She was younger. She had more stamina.

Matt had changed into the slacks and shirt. They fitted reasonably.

While Jack was taking his turn, Matt and Clare were alone together in the corridor.

She whispered, 'That's a quantum computer downstairs, isn't it? You stole a quantum computer, didn't you?'

Fuck.

'Do you realize,' she said eagerly, 'that when a quantum computer is switched on, it'll become self-aware? And that no one will ever die? Dying people's minds will be stored in unused parallel universes. The computer can access these. There'll be a link. We might be able to communicate with the dead—'

She was crazy. Communications with the dead! Why would QX invite a crazy?

That twin sister of hers, who had been murdered . . . the death had unbalanced her mind.

Tentatively Matt asked, 'Do you mean you could use the quantum computer to contact your sister?'

Here was a lever to control her – and Jack as well, perhaps. If she believed what she said, could this pair become allies of his?

'No, Miranda died too soon. Once quantum computers

218

are running no one else's identity will dissolve. Their identities will be stored in the parallel universes, you see.'

'Sure,' Matt said, as the toilet door opened and Jack emerged. Matt waved the gun. 'Get downstairs, both of you.'

'Will you switch it on, Mike? Will you start it up?'

'What have you been talking about?' Jack asked.

'The quantum computer, of course—!'

'Dear God,' Jack muttered.

'Shit,' exclaimed Matt, 'it's been on battery all this time.'

Clare hovered by the study door like some moth hypno-tized by a flame which she wasn't allowed to approach. She couldn't bear not to look . . .

. . . at the computer which now crowded that desk alongside Angelo Vargas's own machine, plugged in to the power.

Mike sat hunched in a brown leather executive chair. He had raised the screen, which she couldn't see. He had unfolded the keyboard and was gazing at what he had stolen.

She could hear Jack being clumsy in the kitchen. Poor dear Jack, he was so tired. She felt ethereal, as if she could stay awake for hours now. Some frontier of fatigue had been crossed. Her body's insistence on sleep had been left behind.

Mike must be feeling likewise. He had demanded food. *She* wasn't going to exile herself in the kitchen, out of sight of the immortality machine. So it was up to Jack to find a pizza in the freezer. Now the pizza was heating in the fan oven. Jack couldn't try to sneak to the front door without Mike seeing him. The front door was locked. Mike had the key.

'Are you going to boot it up, Mike?'

'My name's Matt,' he said. 'That's *my* identity. How do I save myself? Where can I go next? I'm the pig on the points of the trident.'

What this might mean, she had no idea.

Sections of a newspaper lay upon some books within

Matt's reach. A boxed personal ad was boldly ringed in day-glo red ink. Matt hauled the paper towards him, read, and laughed harshly.

'Listen to this. "Best-Selling Author seeks true stories of answered prayer." That's just what I need: an answered prayer.' He thrust the paper aside. 'Why should this machine become self-aware?' he demanded.

'Because consciousness depends on quantum effects. You see, our brain cells are scaffolded with microtubules—'

She began to explain, but he waved dismissively. She had begun straying towards him. Moth to a flame.

'If it's self-aware,' he said sarcastically, 'then it ought to be into self-preservation – if it has enough information to know what it is, and where it is.'

He blinked.

Connect it to the Net – and it ought to be able to read any files anywhere. Change them. Make itself a privileged systems manager anywhere . . .

This was the route to safety!

The software gateways designed to prevent electronic invasion of a computer system should fall like tenpins. Not even good firewalls should be able to resist ultrafast hacking by a quantum computer.

Awaken the Qua computer. Set it loose in the Internet. Let it learn. Let it indulge in a feeding frenzy – subject only to the capacity of the phone line. It could make a new identity for him. It could fill a bank account with electronic money for that new identity. Everything was linked electronically unless you ran a hermit computer isolated from all others.

How stupid to think of bartering this treasure to Gwenda Loomis or the police in exchange for their forgiveness.

'Please let me watch.' Clare was digging her fingernails into her palms to restrain herself from rushing into the study.

'No!' he snapped at her. 'Stay where you are!' He picked up the sections of newspaper and threw them at Clare like some delivery boy. 'Why don't you read the fucking paper, even if it is a week old?'

Matt connected the phoneline into the modem port on the Qua.

Some instinct of neatness caused Clare to gather up the sections of the newspaper. *San Francisco Chronicle*, from a week ago. From before the conference, from before her kidnapping, from before Angelo Vargas flew off to Hawaii, from before everything.

The headline of the news section read: SANTA ROSA TREMOR: 2 DEAD. A photograph showed a fallen tree resting across a crushed car.

Below, another column was headed: FAILED PAINTER DIVES FROM GOLDEN GATE.

Better to maul a newspaper than to hurt her palms.

After a flurry of data too fast to read, the screen displayed the message: **Welcome to Qua. Please identify yourself.**

Matt typed to screen: **Matthew Cooper. At 12 Pirate**

No need to type more. Of their own accord words appeared in a rush: **Place, San Francisco, California. The telephone line now in use is registered to this address.**

The Qua had checked phone company records almost instantly, and spontaneously.

'What's happening—?' Clare's voice quavered.

'Shut up,' he told her.

'Is it self-aware? Is it conscious of itself—?'

More words appeared: **What do you wish, Master?**

A promotional gimmick of Racine's! An Aladdin's Lamp preliminary, to impress the hell out of journalists watching that *Baywatch* star do her bit, seeing the Qua screen copied to a big monitor on a dais . . .

A woman's name would have prompted **What do you wish, Mistress?**

'Is it conscious, Mike – I mean Matt—?'

Matt was sweating. Hesitantly, feeling stupid yet anxious, he typed, **Are you aware of yourself, Qua?**

221

A snowstorm of data. Oh God, let him not have locked the machine into some recursive loop of self-definition.

The screen cleared.

What do you wish, Matthew?

The machine had addressed him by name.

Clare was straying forward.

'Keep out of here!'

Thank goodness the software for voice recognition was still being tweaked and fine-tuned. Voice recognition would be an add-on feature.

I need an alternative identity, typed Matt.

Data snowed again.

Information inadequate. All alternatives [TERM UNKNOWN] one actuality.

What did this mean? Was it a comment upon the way the Qua performed its functions in parallel universes which cancelled out? What information was inadequate? Information to supply the term which was missing from its vocabulary? Information about the whole wide world? How could the Qua set up an alternative identity before it had trawled through a sea of data? But that was the whole idea!

Matt dithered. If he typed a command to search the Net and all relevant data banks it could hack, even a quantum computer might be kept busy for hours, days, because only one phone line was in use.

Unless ... the Qua could create its own smart software agents to go out on electronic patrol, reproducing themselves and roaming.

This rang a bell.

Unified Agent Architecture: that was the name of the system being developed by Bell Labs in Canada.

UAA was the way to find useful stuff among the worldwide mass of data – mobile magnets to seek out needles in the haystack. Roving pieces of smart software, rather like viruses, except that these were benign.

The Qua could create roaming agents which ought to be able to hack their way through any crypto firewalls – into banks, into driving licence data bases, social security, anywhere.

Qua, typed Matt, **access Bell Northern Labs, Ottawa, Canada. Load Unified Agent Architecture. Modify to breach security systems. Search networks. Purpose: establish alternative identity US citizen white male thirty-five name Michael John Jones . . .**

He would need to apply for hard copies of documents – claiming that he'd been robbed or that his house had burnt down – but those would readily be forthcoming because Michael John Jones would exist electronically . . .

'What are you doing now?' persisted Clare.

'Will you shut up!'

Jack called out, 'The pizza's ready. I'm afraid I burnt it a bit.'

Matt sat on the jungle sofa to eat, so that the gun could rest beside him. He had made Clare and Jack sit in the glass-look chairs.

'Please let me look,' she begged again.

Mouth full of seafood pizza, Matt shook his head. He swallowed.

'It's busy.'

'Is it *aware*?'

What a burden had lifted from Matt's shoulders. A bright light at the end of the tunnel, even if he still had this pair of witnesses to bother with. They mustn't see what he was up to. If they did see, his false identity wouldn't be secure.

'If it's aware,' he said, 'maybe it's wise of it not to blab.'

Maybe the Qua would only become fully self-aware as more and more information and understanding accumulated . . . Sort of like a child maturing. He didn't know. It didn't matter, compared to his own safety.

'*Now*,' Clare said, 'if we die—'

'We shall go to heaven. Sure.' Personally, he – in the identity of Michael John Jones, a decently neutral name – would be going to New Orleans as soon as he could sort things out. With the Qua in the trunk of a brand-new Porsche; stopping at good motels to recharge the refrigera-

223

tion batteries. As a student he had visited New Orleans. Liked that city a lot.

Jack looked as though he needed matchsticks for his eyes. Matt was a candidate for matchsticks too.

He wasn't going to stray far from the Qua. He would sleep right here on this sofa, upon jungle fronds and blooms between the jaguar and the Indian. His guests could sleep in the kitchen, which looked out on a high fence thick with ivy and vines. Two or three glassy chairs piled against the door, to alert him if they tried to sneak out.

'I know you're both tired,' he said. 'You're going to go upstairs. You're going to slide a mattress down here. You'll put it in the kitchen – and sleep on it.'

Jack moaned, but Clare smiled radiantly. She too wanted to stay as close to the Qua as she could.

85

A Cherokee Jeep pulled up beside a green-painted kerb opposite the house in Pirate Place. The Jeep's lights carved long tunnels in a fog which was rising, rolling up Telegraph Hill. Lights and engine died.

The gathering fog was a friend.

By the house was parked a Ford Taurus with California plates.

'She's in there,' Gabe said. He sniffed the air. Moist salt from the bay, vegetation. 'I know she is.'

'Whose car's that, then?' asked Jersey, in the driving seat.

Gabe shrugged.

'We ought to have carried on north,' whined Billy from behind.

Gabe spoke as to a child. 'Oh Billy, we'll be going north soon, so soon. Didn't I lead you out of Arizona? Didn't the zombie lab get trashed?'

They had heard on the radio of the stolen Jeep a report of the destructive attack on QX. Details were scanty. What exactly had happened remained unclear, except that it had been spectacular.

'We lost such a lot, Gabe—'

'Only in zombie terms! Zombies would have come to raid the Soul Shelter sooner or later. Isn't that the truth?'

'You're determined to have this woman,' complained Billy.

'This one, yes! I foresee her spreading that terrible lie – of salvation through machines – unless I can illuminate her. The lie will spread and spread. The world will believe her because her lie's so much less taxing than the truth. So much softer. I foresee this, Billy, because she's linked to me. I knew this the moment I saw that story in the *Investigator*—'

Was Gabe's inner voice about to take over?

'I'll see if I can kick the door in,' said Jersey. In case not, from under his seat he pulled a revolver.

86

Matt woke on the jungle sofa and strained to hear what had woken him.

Screen-light faintly illuminated the study. The kitchen door was still shut, those see-through chairs scarcely visible.

Something bumped – out on the veranda. Someone was moving about.

More than one person out there. Shock chilled him. He felt for the gun on the floor. Ah, here. He hoisted himself softly from the sofa.

Someone was trying the front door now.

Gwenda's people – they'd traced him. The Ford must have been followed after all.

A shoulder heaved against the door. A boot thumped into it.

The door didn't fly open immediately.

Get to the computer. Threaten to shoot the Qua full of bullets, wreck it. Burst the cooling system. Spill the liquid nitrogen into its guts unless they did a deal.

I'll destroy it, he rehearsed.

A single gunshot sounded, like a car backfiring, and the door did crash open.

'Don't do it!' Matt shouted. 'I'm armed. I'll destroy the computer!'

Into the study, slam the door.

Sometime during the night the laser printer had produced a page of names and numbers. Couldn't read them easily by screen-light. These must be details of his alternative identity as Michael John Jones. Wonderful Qua. What use to him now?

Aglow on screen: **What do you wish now, Matthew?**

He was a terrified child. Intruders were inside the house. He thought he heard someone heading upstairs. What did he want? Escape, escape!

Gun in one hand, Matt typed: **Save us.** The words were like a prayer. *True stories of answered prayer . . .*

Escape, escape.

The terrified child who was Matt pressed the ESC key too. ESC for ESCAPE. To exit from a program. To exit.

87

The water bed had quaked, awakening Clare and Jack, naked together under a sheet. The security light from the house behind Angelo's radiated a pearly fogged sheen through a gap in the curtains.

Clare sat bolt upright. Immediately she subsided as the water shifted under her. As if the bed was something alien and terrible she heaved herself from it. A gown lay on the floor. She clutched the robe to herself.

'Jack, we weren't in this bed—!'

He too struggled from the bed as though unfamiliar with its ways.

'We weren't here, Jack. We were in the kitchen on the mattress. Weren't we? Weren't we?'

Could the gourds mounted on the wall really be pans and ladles? Could the peyote tapestry and the mandrake woodcut be herb charts?

'We were, weren't we, Jack?' There was hysteria in her voice.

A bath-towel lay near him. He gathered the towel up. 'Yes, we were in the kitchen.'

'Thank God!'

'Mike – Matt – was sleeping on the sofa.'

'Yes, yes.'

'Now we're in Angelo's bedroom—'

'*How?*'

He was shivering. So was she. 'Were we . . . drugged?'

'*You* cooked the pizza! Didn't you cook a pizza, Jack?'

Would they have to confirm everything with one another?

'You didn't put some drug of Angelo's on it? Something to dope Matt? You'd have told me in the kitchen, wouldn't you?'

'It was just an ordinary commercial pizza in a cardboard box.'

'Jack, we shouldn't be here. Something's very wrong.'

'I know it is—' Wrapped in the towel, he approached her and clasped her to him.

'I think we're dead,' she whispered, 'and this is *afterwards*. I think Matt shot us both in our sleep. We wouldn't know, would we? This is afterwards. Do you think we're dead, Jack?'

Detaching himself gently, he found a lamp and fumbled for the switch.

'Matt couldn't have shot us both at once,' he pointed out. 'One of us would have woken up. One of us would have known what was happening.'

The bedroom brightened. The walk-in wardrobe stood open. Alongside some clothes of Angelo's, their own clothes hung neatly.

He pointed.

'Do you think we made love last night?' she asked him. 'I think we're dead.'

According to a clock it was five-thirty.

'I think,' Jack said, 'we ought to go downstairs.'

'There mightn't be any downstairs.'

227

He crossed to the curtains, parted them.

'I can see houses. It's just foggy outside, that's all.'

'Will Matt be downstairs?'

Hauntedly: 'I don't know . . .'

Descending warily in gown and towel, they found no one else in the house. The study door and kitchen door were both open wide. Jack flipped lights on. No mattress lay on the kitchen floor. On Angelo's desk stood an ordinary computer. On the jungle sofa a newspaper lay. Clare snatched the newspaper up.

San Francisco Chronicle. A week old.

Its headline read: NORTH KOREANS TEST N-BOMB.

Below was a more local story: FAILED PAINTER DIVES FROM GOLDEN GATE.

'Jack, this story—'

'Yes?' His words and hers were like the softly padding paws of cats.

'It was in the paper Matt threw at me. About a painter. The same words exactly.'

'And . . . ?'

'The main headline wasn't about North Koreans. It wasn't about a bomb test. It was about an earth tremor killing a couple of people. This is the same paper, Jack, but the big news is different. If North Korea tested a neutron bomb last week it would have been all over the news.'

'Maybe we missed it because of everything that was happening to us.'

'It would have been huge news. It never happened. Jack, I don't think we're dead. This is a different world. Matt was here with the quantum computer, and it became aware. It became aware of all the alternative probability worlds—'

'Matt wanted to hide,' murmured Jack. He stepped towards the curtained front window. Outside, fog drifted. A car stood in the bay.

Not the Taurus.

A yellow Toyota.

'Matt can alter the world, Jack. Or at least the quantum

computer can! He's out there somewhere now with the computer.'

Clare clasped the newspaper. It was undeniable proof. How could one come to terms with such a realization?

By not reacting wildly. By not rushing about. By standing still and taking care. By being very gentle. As if, otherwise, all might shatter.

Jack said quietly, 'Our Toyota's outside.'

She paced softly to see.

'So it is. Our Toyota.'

She touched him for reassurance.

'Does this mean I was never kidnapped? We were never mixed up with any police or FBI? Soul has nothing to do with me in this world . . . ?'

'I don't know.'

They were both as cautious as if they were tiptoeing on ice.

He put his arm around her.

'Maybe,' he said gently, 'this is a good world to be in . . .'

How serene it was in Angelo's house, in a city still at rest.

'The bomb headline sounds scary.'

'Maybe. Maybe not. We grew up in a world on the brink of a nuclear holocaust. I did, anyway. The holocaust never came. For years I'd been worrying about *nothing!* Maybe we ought to enjoy ourselves?' he suggested. 'That *was* the intention. What else should we do? It's too early to see any sights.'

'Answered prayers?' she asked mischievously.

'Oh yes,' he agreed, after a moment's pause.

She had noticed his fleeting puzzlement.

'You didn't see the ad in the newspaper. Angelo circled it.' She consulted the *Chronicle*. Triumphantly she displayed the advertisement.

'I wonder if Angelo was going to reply? Professional curiosity!'

The continued existence of the advertisement was reassuring. Things weren't so different. Though the Korean bomb test did sound frightening.

She laughed giddily.

'I feel we're the Babes in the Wood. I feel like heaping leaves over us and cuddling together till daytime. I can't deal with a different world all at once. It's the way we wanted the world to be. Us here, together.'

She let the paper fall.

Leaving lights on, they headed for the stairs.

Their love-making was so tender. For a long while they turned inwards, away from the mystery of the outside world with which they could not yet come to terms, nor even reach out to touch, touching each other instead, so intimately.

The water moved under them, conforming to them as perfectly as they conformed to one another. Presently waves of orgasm rolled. They lay touching and stroking. Soon they were loving again, then dozing as foggy daylight brightened.

88

After a shower, Clare put on her Rodin's Thinker sweater. The air outside could be nippy.

Jack had finished his turn in the shower and was dressed when he heard her call out.

She was on her knees on the bedroom floor. Beside her, the suitcase which had been in the wardrobe was open. No clothes in it – those had all been hung up. A couple of notebooks. A personal organizer. Conference material. A guidebook to San Francisco and a map. The suitcase had been doing duty as a filing cabinet. Its lining was pristine, bearing witness to restored innocence.

Shock had drained Clare. She held a picture postcard which showed a cable car.

'This. This was in here. It's from Miranda, Jack. It's from Miranda – to me. Addressed to Cambridge.'

He reached, but she held the card as though she would never let go.

She read. *'Forgot to tell you about obligatory bagel breakfast at the Holy B. Café – Upper Grant near Union. Just a few mins from where you'll be staying. Love, M.*

'She's alive in this world, Jack! Miranda's alive.'

'What's the date of the postmark?'

The postmark over the American stamp was smeared and indecipherable.

'She's here, Jack. She must have met someone, split up with Ivan, stayed and taken a job—'

Laying down the precious card, Clare began rifling through her organizer.

'Here it is! Her address! Where's Florence Street? And a phone number – we can call her! I've written the name Mark Golightly beside hers. There's a work number too. Matthews Robinson Golightly. Those sound like stockbrokers, don't they? She's working with them. She's living with this Mark Golightly in Florence Street. Jack, we spent time in bed when we could have been . . .'

She tailed off.

'I don't mean it to sound like that. I'm going to phone her—'

'Shouldn't we see what else we can find out from your filo? Where's mine got to? Are there any letters from her? The conference – what notes did you make?'

'Oh God, I have to warn her about never going near the Tenderloin—'

'Clare,' he appealed, 'this won't take us long.'

'A different world,' she enthused. 'She's alive. But you're right. Fifteen minutes, no more.'

She began paging through her organizer, while Jack searched for his.

89

When Clare strode out of the study, her expression was one of mingled joy and frustration.

'You made me miss her – but their answerphone says it's Mark and Miranda. He said *her name*.'

The time was nearly eight-thirty. Their researches upstairs had proved ambiguous, yet obviously they had been in Tucson.

'She'll probably have left for work with Mark—'

'What about Angelo's answerphone? What's on that?'

Clare fled back into the study.

On the tape was a message.

'Clare, it's Miranda. Look, can we make it breakfast—'

'It's her, it's her—!'

'—at ten at the Holy Bagel, not nine?'

The voice on the tape was almost Clare's own, precise, passionate – and concerned.

'Did you catch that Soviet ambassador stuff? That's why. See you, bye.'

Jack stared at the answerphone. 'Doesn't she mean Russian ambassador?'

Some channel-hopping on the TV in the lounge brought a frustratingly brief news update.

Soviet Premier Zhirinovski had withdrawn Ambassador Andreyev to Moscow. American forces were on full alert worldwide following President Eastwood's ultimatum to North Korea . . .

90

The fog was slowly thinning as they made their way uphill through a leafy paradise amongst Victorian clapboard houses and cottages. Jack wore his lightweight tan raincoat, which he'd packed for unpredictable San Francisco. Clare relied on Rodin's Thinker and a tasselled shawl which she had no memory of owning previously.

'We must have seen Miranda yesterday. We might seem strange to her. How do we tell her?'

'I think it would be a bad mistake to try to tell her. Her or anyone! She must have taken the day off specially to show us round. Let's just hear what she says and improvise.'

'Do you understand what this means to me?'

'Yes! I do! Of course I do.'

'What happened to the pair of us who saw her yesterday? Probabilities ... ! Jack, will we fit in? What about Cambridge and Heather and Orlando? What about this Korean crisis? Miranda sounded worried.'

'Analysts are bound to worry about stocks.'

'I haven't felt so scared about news for ten years or so.'

'Me neither,' he admitted.

City sounds were muffled. A diffuse brightness promised sunshine in an hour or so. In her shoulder bag and in his pockets were their important possessions. According to the map, it wasn't far at all to Upper Grant.

91

Grant Avenue was narrow. Its pavements likewise. Edwardian frame buildings of three storeys lined both sides. Small bay-windowed shops at street level; apartments and the occasional modest hotel above. The ambience was friendly-shabby. Curio emporiums, antiques shops, an art gallery, garment shops, some smarter Chinese businesses.

Here was the Holy Bagel Café.

Jutting out above the door was a large brass model of a bagel, an oversized halo to grace all who trod beneath. The brass was dented. Maybe passers-by at night used the sign as a basketball hoop.

Inside, such an aroma of steaming *cappuccino* and dark-roasted Gourmet Viennese decaf. Walls and ceiling were decorated with posters of Italianate art and Russian ikons of saints and angels all wearing halos. Tiffany lampshades were embossed with jewel-like beads of glass.

At the take-out counter, a short queue waited. A woman in tracksuit and running shoes seemed prepared for a quick getaway. A table near the window became free as a pair of young men with Caesar haircuts departed hand in hand.

Some couples were studying newspapers, which Jack would dearly have loved to scan. Two women in sharply tailored black suits were engaged in a belated power breakfast, briefcases open beside them. An old woman dressed as a gypsy was playing Solitaire with tiny inch-high Tarot cards.

Voices mingled. Some discussed the crisis. Neutron bombs. Hydrogen bombs. Zhirinovski. Eastwood.

At the table nearest to theirs, a bearded man in jeans and tie-dyed T-shirt sat with a fey kaftan-clad fellow.

'He'll take a look at your book if I ask him, Phil. But a goldfish as hero? I mean, their memories only last half a minute or so, don't they? Or else they'd go nuts in those bowls—'

'That's *exactly* the point. Goldy's inside looking out, reinterpreting all the time like in Robbe-Grillet—'

Jack and Clare were ravenous. They ordered three smoked salmon bagels between them and cups of *cappuccino*.

Clare rose, joggling the table, spilling coffee.

The woman who had come into the café was the image of herself – oh, apart from that faded scar on her brow. She was wearing bleached jeans, a multicoloured pastel mohair sweater, running shoes. Her tan shoulder bag was so like Clare's own that they could have chosen them together in the same shop.

Clare wept with joy as she hugged her sister. Jack mopped *cappuccino* with a tissue.

Miranda held Clare away from her, to scrutinize her. 'Hey, what's wrong? What's the matter?'

Clare's sister darted a brief glance at Jack as if he might be to blame for her sister's over-emotion.

'It's just so good to see you. It's so good.'

Customers and staff were eyeing the performance.

'We saw each other yesterday, Clucky.'

'Clucky! You haven't called me that since—'

'Since yesterday?'

234

'Clare,' Jack called softly. Should he intervene?

'Are you worried about the news?' Miranda asked her twin. Her sidelong look at Jack this time was one almost of appeal.

'Clare, do sit down. Miranda needs a coffee—'

Clare knuckled tears from her eyes. 'I'm sorry—'

Miranda sipped coffee.

'I know it's edgy, this business about Andreyev leaving Washington. The markets are jumping like crazy. We won't go past the brink, though. It's all mega-bluff. Zhirinovski isn't totally insane. Think mega-bluff, not megatons.'

'Do you ever visit the Tenderloin?' Clare interrupted her.

'Not *habitually*, Clucky. I'm not into six-foot transvestites. What has that to do with anything?'

Clare shook her head helplessly.

'Did you two want me to show you some sleaze today? I didn't realize that's what you meant by alternative lifestyles.'

'It isn't,' Jack protested.

Miranda seemed hyped-up, on rather a hair-trigger. On account of the Russian news, no doubt – yet had there always been some dormant tension between fast-track Miranda and her academic sister? Moreover, Miranda's motive for settling in San Francisco mightn't only have been Mark Golightly but also an instinct to change a lifestyle which had been pressuring her closer to a psychological crisis in London. She had loosened the lid, but overheating could still cause a bang.

Clare snuffled. Next moment she was gazing at Miranda as if in rapture.

'Are you *on* something?' Miranda hissed. 'What's-his-name, Angelo, did he leave you a *present*? With "Eat Me" written on it? Look, I've taken a day off when the markets are berserking, because I promised. Show you the sights, right? Can you only see mushrooms dancing?'

Clare continued to stare, transfixed.

235

'Have you two been quarreling?' Miranda asked in sudden sympathy.

Jack shook his head.

'You're like a different person, Clucky.'

'I am,' said Clare.

Dear God, she was going to tell. And here, in a café.

'No,' he warned.

'But, *Jack*—'

'Please, no.'

'I have to. We need help.'

'We don't. We're in Shangri-la, remember.'

Miranda shifted her chair, distancing herself.

'You two seem to be talking in code.'

'We only want to go round with you today,' Jack assured Miranda. 'Just to be with you. Don't we, Clare? We were looking forward so much to being in San Francisco that we called it Shangri-la between us.'

'That's sweet.' Miranda sounded sceptical. 'So what's this help you're needing, which you didn't need yesterday?'

'It's no use, Jack. I've found her. How can I pretend?'

'Christ, you can try.'

'Clare's having a breakdown, isn't she?' exclaimed Miranda. 'You're really her psychiatrist, and you've fallen in love with her. This is some sort of therapy trip. God, how unethical!'

'I don't practise as a psychiatrist.'

'That's worse. You're playing at one. Because you're a psychologist you think you can handle this. She needs proper professional help. Mood-swings. Talking in riddles. She's crying out for it.'

'Honestly, you have it all wrong.'

The would-be author was scribbling notes, agog. Miranda directed a furious glare at him.

'Oh, Clucky! You had to come to me, didn't you? Because I've coped.'

Clare shook her head. 'No, *no*.' She hesitated. 'You were dead,' she whispered.

'We'd better discuss this outside,' said Jack.

'So I'm dead?' echoed Miranda. 'First our dad's mind goes, and now this. Did you bring her to California for special *alternative* therapy, Jack? Well, *did he*?' Reaching out, Miranda clasped Clare's hand. 'I'm here, Clucky. This is me. Feel me. I didn't die when I dumped Ivan the Terrible. The London Stock Exchange can get fucked. I shan't burn out here, not with Mark. He's mellow. The world might blow up in a few days, but that's another matter. It's you who's falling apart, Clucky.' Clare's sister seemed more angry than sorrowful – as if Clare's supposed state of mind threatened her own equilibrium; as though her twin might be acting as she was from jealousy at Miranda's good fortune. 'You were fine when you got here yesterday. Fine!'

'That wasn't me.'

'Shit almighty.'

'No, listen!' Now Clare was angry. 'You were always the dominant one. Telling me who I am, and what I am; and me admiring you, and doting, and fretting about you wrecking cars.'

'The accident was only a shunt—'

'All in the mind, for me – and you were out in the big world. I'll have you know I've been kidnapped by a crazy guru and survived it! In fact, I've been kidnapped twice in the past few days—'

Miranda shook her head in outraged disbelief at such manifest fantasies.

While those in the café listened avidly, Miranda fumed at Jack: 'You bring her here to throw a crock of crap in my face – to build up her own image by mind-fucking me! Hey,' she mocked, 'what shall we tell Miranda today that's really wild? We've played it normal. Now let's hit her with nutty stuff!'

Outside, a Cherokee Jeep mounted the kerb.

92

Matt had braked barely in time to miss hitting the cable car.

Bell ringing, headlamp beam funnelling through the fog, the cable car trundled over the intersection. Painted on the destination board was *Powell & Hyde Sts*. Fog reeked of salt water and fishy smells. Voices burbled on the car radio.

'If the Soviets—'

'You mean if Zhirinovsky—'

He was in his Porsche!

A refrigerated silver truck blatted its horn at him and he edged forward over the intersection. He performed the action like an automaton without understanding anything. As soon as he could, he pulled in at the kerb.

Over to his left the top of a clock tower glowed, outlined by light bulbs. A giant illuminated word pierced the fog: *Ghirardelli*.

Ghirardelli Square: the long brick façade of the old chocolate factory with its mall of smart shops and ice cream parlours and restaurants behind – that's where he was near.

But how?

Answered prayers . . .

The Qua had shifted him here to save him from the gunmen.

Momentarily Matt panicked. Yet the Qua was behind him on the back seat, closed up.

On the back seat of his *Porsche* . . .

He turned the radio up and listened until there was no doubt about it. A Soviet Union still existed – run by that rabid patriot Zhirinovsky. Zhirinovsky must be a Communist. Maybe the Soviet Union was only Communist in name. Some nuclear crisis was happening in Korea. The United States, under President Eastwood, for Christ's sake, was threatening a pre-emptive strike. America and the USSR sounded like two rutting stags challenging one another. And what about China? Hadn't Zhirinovsky loathed all Asiatics?

*

Matt sat for a long time, listening and thinking, as fish trucks and other traffic passed by, as fog began to lift, as tourists strolled, as cable cars periodically clanged across the junction of Beach and Hyde.

It seemed to him that a different life led to him being here, yet he could barely recall that other life at all. Fading tatters of a dream. A few dissolving images: of Gwenda Loomis and some Russians and a Korean, yes. Heavy espionage. He couldn't recall a single detail of how the Qua was actually stolen – for money, yes for money . . .

Had he undergone some sort of patriotic revulsion? Possession of the Qua could give the Russians and Koreans all sorts of cryptographical advantage. America's enemies could hack into any computer, interfere with missile launch codes. Had he become utterly scared? Terrified for his skin? So he had fled to San Francisco . . .

Decaying, dreamlike hints of what might have happened haunted him. They were as nothing compared with his memory of the house on Telegraph Hill.

Would Clare and Jack be there in this different world? Did the Qua need its batteries charging? *What had happened to the printout of his alternative identity?* That printout might be no use in this different world. Too many little differences.

And a big difference too. This world seemed dangerously near the brink of a nuclear war.

Safe house, safe house . . . Somewhere to hack into the Net, always assuming there would be a Net.

That house in Pirate Place could be safe. Nothing in this world connected him to it. Surely he'd never met Clare and Jack – because he was in his own Porsche.

A new printout? What he needed was a different world than this one, one which wasn't threatened by a nuclear holocaust.

Safe house. Take a gamble.

Finally, Matt had started the engine of the Porsche.

93

Matt stared from the Porsche at the house and at the yellow Toyota.

Did that Toyota belong to Angelo what's-his-name? This didn't prove anyone was in the house at the moment.

He had found no gun in the Porsche. There wouldn't be, would there?

When Matt mounted the front steps with the Qua, maybe he resembled a Bible salesman.

Well, he would tell Angelo that he was a demonstrator of a revolutionary new type of computer! Easily portable. Massive processing power. His company was pioneering an innovative direct approach to privileged potential customers. The sort of people who might need a super-computer in the middle of the Amazon rainforest, for example. Turn up on their doorsteps. Spare me just ten minutes of your time.

No reply when he rang the doorbell. Lugging the Qua, he walked around to where the pot plant had been.

Same pot plant. No key underneath.

The door was old-fashioned. Those Viets had tried to kick it in, then had shot through the lock. They could have tried something simpler and less noisy. But then he wouldn't have woken and he wouldn't be alive.

Setting the Qua down, Matt returned to the Porsche.

Buried in the glove pocket was that old credit card.

94

As the door yielded, something hard pressed against Matt's spine.

'It's a gun. Behave.'

Matt jerked his head. A grinning, ginger-haired man he had never seen before. The man must have been lurking amongst vegetation and had sneaked up the steps.

'Pick up that case of yours and go inside—' At least the

man wasn't a Viet. What was he? Some opportunistic burglar?

As Matt carried the Qua inside, the man spoke into a walkie-talkie.

'Jersey to Gabe: *action*.'

Matt was ordered to sit on the jungle sofa. One of the two men whom Jersey summoned, *Gabe*, could be none other than that gonzo guru whom Clare had said she had trouble with.

The thin-faced man, Billy, wore one of those long yellow coats you saw in cowboy movies. Duster: that was the name. From a nylon holster inside the duster Billy had produced a compact sub-machine-gun. Soul had sent Billy upstairs to check the rest of the house.

'You aren't Angelo Vargas Alvarez, are you?' said Soul.

Matt shook his head.

Jersey was on his knees, opening up the Qua out of curiosity. He wasn't being very delicate.

'It's some new computer, Gabe.'

'Be careful with that,' said Matt.

Jersey pointed at a logo.

'It's from QX.'

The name of the company seemed to offend Soul deeply.

'Dance on the zombie box,' he said to Jersey. 'Jump up and down.'

'No,' Matt protested in panic. 'There's liquid nitrogen in there. It'll freeze your feet off. You mustn't damage it!'

Billy reappeared triumphantly on the stairs.

'Gabe, there's stuff about the Hard Question conference in a suitcase – she's here all right.'

95

Billy had acted so oddly in the Jeep when they got close to San Francisco that morning.

They'd been running into fog. They were having to drive slowly. Jersey was at the wheel; Gabe beside him, street map open on his knee. They knew where to go. Directory Enquiries had given them the phone number and address for this man who was lending his house to Clare, as Gabe had overheard at the barbecue.

A tape of highlights from *Tannhaüser* was playing. Billy sat in the back, half dozing.

Then he had begun to talk in a slurred voice.

'We already snatched her, Gabe . . . We had her at the Soul Shelter . . .'

Gabe had turned the music down and swung round.

'What are you saying, Billy?'

'We already had her . . . The zombie Feds came and blew the shit out of us . . .'

'Shut up,' from Jersey. 'I got to concentrate.' Driving through the fog was difficult. Red tail-lights loomed ahead.

Gabe hushed Jersey. 'A voice is speaking in Billy. Billy, what are you saying?'

'We did snatch her . . . We put her in the cat box . . .'

'We never did so,' retorted Jersey. 'We messed up. We missed her.'

'Those Indian bikers stopped us snatching Fox too . . . Fox got away . . .'

'Gabe,' said Jersey, 'Billy's going schizo. Can you do something about him?'

Before Billy joined the community he had suffered a bit of mental illness. Gabe had cured Billy with his gaze and his words. Thereafter Billy had been so reliable. A mainstay.

'Maybe the war scare's freaking him?'

Jersey hit the brake as brake-lights glared ahead. The lurch brought Billy fully awake.

'Are we here—?'

'What were you saying before that, Billy?'

Billy hadn't any idea.

Turning the music up again, Gabe had meditated.

96

'It's *alive*?' Gabe asked. 'This zombie box is alive?'

Matt had set the Qua up for them in the study. On screen: **What do you wish, Matthew?**

'I'm the only one who knows how to operate it,' Matt lied. 'The Qua's personalized to me.' Let them believe this. Gabriel Soul's attitude to the Qua seemed a mixture of loathing and fascination. To play on this, to captivate Soul, to make himself indispensable . . . He mustn't lose the Qua! At all costs, no. Not in this world, not on the brink of a nuclear war.

'I know who you are,' Matt said. 'Clare talked about you. That was *in an alternative world* – where there isn't any risk of a war . . .'

'Billy, let me take a look at you.'

Obediently Billy posed in his yellow duster.

'Billy, at the conference one of those speakers said that split personalities might be sensing other realities.'

'I'm cured, Gabe. You cured me. You firmed up my soul.'

Gabe merely smiled.

Taking his cue, Matt said, 'Clare believes we'll all live after death because of this machine and others like it.' He must hook Soul.

Soul's smile became unpleasant.

'Does she indeed? Does she really?'

Maybe it had been a mistake to mention this.

'This computer can hack into any other computer, no matter how secure it is. But that's nothing compared to altering reality! Viet gangsters were breaking in here, and I told the Qua to . . .' Thunderstruck, Matt paused.

'That was *you* coming here to find Clare! That's who it was – it was a different you. I found myself in my Porsche in this world of Zhirinovsky and Eastwood. In my world the Soviet Union has fallen apart—'

'If it weren't for Billy's testimony,' Soul said, 'I'd doubt that. I'd think you were trying to enchant me.' *The intensity in his eyes.* 'I can see right into your heart, Matt. This Qua

243

isn't personalized to you at all. How your face betrays you ...'

97

Billy wasn't heeding Matt's breathless spiel. Schizo worlds: it was all too disturbing. He roamed. He fiddled with the answerphone.

'*Clare, it's Miranda*—' began the recorded message.

'Shut that off,' snapped Jersey.

'Leave it on!' cried Gabe. 'Listen—'

Breakfast at ten o'clock at the Holy Bagel . . .

'Bring the Jeep to the door, Jersey. We've found her!'

Already it was a few minutes past ten.

Gabe was about to unplug the Qua.

'Hey, those batteries are fast-charge but they still need—'

'Shut up.'

Gabe switched off and folded down the screen and keyboard. He hoisted the Qua off the desk.

The Holy Bagel Café on Upper Grant – he'd eaten there himself a couple of years ago when he was in San Francisco recruiting for the Soul Shelter. Who had he been with? Oh yes, doe-eyed Deborah who was turned on by all those halos but who was seeking something more intense.

The place wasn't far. He'd still need to hurry – taking this God-in-a-box with him, this living machine which could alter reality.

His, now. His very own God-machine, which would depend upon him. Matt Cooper was telling the truth about it. Dr Clare was deeply involved. A sense of destiny gripped Gabe as fiercely as he himself gripped the Qua. Matt, this pathetic thief, could only think of false identities and bank accounts. Gabe could conceive a different, ecstatic world, where his teachings were honoured by more than just a hundred disciples.

A living machine! An artificial intelligence! It was every-

244

thing that he had loathed – yet he could forgive it this if it served his visions.

Billy looked weird.

'We aren't taking that zombie box with us—'

'What's this, Billy? What am I hearing? Who else should be its custodian?'

'I'll stay with it,' Matt volunteered. 'You bring Clare back here. You and I, we're partners now. You need my know-how.'

Laughable, laughable.

'That zombie box scares me, Gabe.'

'Your Billy can't adjust to a thing like this—'

Mistake, mistake.

'Fuck you!' howled Billy. He swung the Uzi towards Matt. The gun barked twice. Billy seemed stunned. Already he had relaxed his finger.

Matt lurched. A patch of blood was seeping from his chest. He staggered. His legs gave way.

'Zombie-man,' Billy muttered. He thrust the Uzi into the holster under his yellow duster coat.

98

Matt heard the front door bang shut. The noise of an engine revving.

Such a pain in his chest, as if he'd been impaled. He coughed blood. Breathe shallow, breathe shallow. Get help.

Telephone cord. Pull the set to the floor.

Get help. Ambulance. Federal protection.

Bloody, slippery finger dialling 911. Blood loss was terrifying. Don't let his lungs fill up and choke him. He felt so cold, so shivery.

Could the operator understand his gurglings? The call would be recorded, for replay if needed.

Twelve Pirate Place. Been shot. Ambulance. Quantum computer stolen from QX. He would never see the Qua again. Give up hope. Co-operate. Be protected. *Police tell FBI.*

Quantum computer. Agonizing, he hawked out blood. *Holy Bagel Café. Ambulance to twelve Pirate Place.*

99

'God, no,' breathed Clare.

Soul, and Billy in a long yellow coat, had jumped from the Jeep. Jersey was at the wheel. Soul grinned through the café window. Billy pulled one of those Uzi guns from inside his coat. Soul held a pistol. Outside already, some screams and shouts. People were running to take refuge behind vehicles or inside shops.

Soul and Billy strode into the café. Billy fired high, shattering a Tiffany lampshade and several jars of coffee beans on a shelf.

'You all get down !' Billy shouted. 'Lie flat!'

'You stay seated,' Soul told Clare and Jack and . . .

He gaped at Miranda. *'Two of you . . .'*

Soul uttered a brief hectic laugh. Customers were crouching down, sprawling together.

'Out from behind the counter!' Billy railed at the staff. 'Get out and lie down where I can see you all—' He hadn't been explicit enough.

'Two of you . . . One from this world, one from the other.' Soul's pistol flicked from one woman to the other like a metronome.

Billy glanced furtively at Clare and Miranda. Hastily he looked away, unwilling to see.

'Did you two get together by telepathy?' Soul asked.

Miranda was speechless with terror and bewilderment.

'What do you want, Gabe?' Clare said. 'How did you find me?'

'Gabe, is it?' Soul studied her. 'You and I would seem to be on more intimate terms than I precisely recall. Of course that's likely,' and he leered, 'in that alternative world you're from . . .'

'How do you know about—?'

'This is insane,' mumbled Miranda to Jack. 'It's insane.'

'It isn't,' he told her wretchedly.

'This is a psychodrama. You hired these guys to burst in.' Miranda faltered, taking in the smashed lamp and jars and terrorized customers and staff. Far too genuine.

'She's my twin sister Miranda,' Clare said to Soul. 'She was dead in my world. She was dead.'

'Oh I *see*,' said Soul. 'Yes, of course. *Clare, Miranda, Holy Bagel*. I'm being stupid.'

'You were at Pirate Place?'

'Who is he?' hissed Miranda. 'Me, dead? How can he understand her?' She shook her head helplessly.

'You were at Pirate Place!' accused Clare.

Soul smiled amenably.

'Well, I overheard about your Angelo Vargas at the barbecue. Clare, we're bound together, even if you aren't exactly the Clare I hoped to illuminate. You're a better Clare. You know more.' A frown creased his brow. 'Where's the Clare who belongs in this world?'

'I'm her,' said Clare. 'I've displaced her. I've excluded her. Her wave-function became – *Jack, the Qua!*'

'Would that,' asked Soul, 'be the same Qua which you think grants us all an afterlife without effort and ecstasy?'

'God, Jack, he has it—!' Clare half-rose from her seat. In the Jeep, Jersey was nursing another of those Uzis.

Soul's pistol jerked. 'Stay seated.'

Miranda began to cry softly. Jack laid a hand on her arm.

Distantly: a siren.

Gabe stepped to the door and called to Jersey, 'Get in here with the Qua now!'

Uzi in one hand, Jersey emerged from the Jeep. He opened the rear door, heaved out the Qua and hurried into the café. The siren whooped closer. Another siren added its voice.

'Plug it in,' Soul told Jersey. 'It doesn't matter a shit about some police cars. We have hostages. We have the best way out imaginable. Together with you,' he told Clare charmingly.

*

247

The Qua sat on the counter, open and plugged into power.

Police loudspeakers had blared. *Surrender yourselves. Road-blocks.* However, no SWAT team would fire into the café full of hostages.

The phone in the café rang soon enough.

Soul spoke soothingly into it. He sounded rational. He would like to release a few hostages. Frankly, there were too many hostages here. They were cluttering up the place.

When he laid the handset on the counter he said to Billy, 'He mentioned a stolen computer, this negotiator.'

'So I didn't kill Matt?'

'Don't worry, Billy, he'll probably be nuked to shit in a week or so.'

'But not us?'

'Never. We're going alternate.'

'Are you *sure* about that, Gabe? Are you sure?'

Jersey sniggered. 'Haven't you been listening to Clare over there?'

'We're taking Dr Clare with us,' said Soul. 'Maybe her sister too. To euphoria-world,' he mused, 'where I'm revered. To ecstasy-world. Away from this doomed shitheap.'

Jersey eyed Miranda at the table.

'Neat idea about the sister, Gabe. Can we cope with two of them?'

'It would be so *poignant*. Oh, maybe you're right! She'd be a burden. Fix some coffee and bagels, will you? Always travel on a full stomach. Can you see any dial for when this thing's batteries are full?'

'Let me look,' begged Clare. She was straining to be near the Qua.

'Don't you go near it,' said Soul. 'Don't you touch it.'

'I shan't touch it.' She began to rise.

'Stay where you are is what I mean!' He picked up the phone to arrange, condescendingly, to release a few people.

Presently the staff filed out one by one while Billy kept watch from the bay window. A police loudhailer told those emerging to place their hands on their heads as they

248

walked free, as if they were the ones surrendering themselves to justice.

Soul got rid of the old fortune-telling woman, who spooked him.

He jerked his thumb at two hippy-looking men.

'You, and you: go.'

The one in the tie-dyed T-shirt left quickly enough. His friend begged to stay. On his knees, the reluctant one explained, 'I'm a writer. I can help you with your story—'

'On radioactive paper?' sneered Soul.

'Take your chance, you stupid shit,' said the business woman who lay alongside him.

Clare called out, 'There won't be any story – not if you alter reality. There can only be one reality at a time. All the others are only probabilities – ghosts.' Heart-wrenchingly, she gazed at Miranda. 'If this alters, I'll lose you again.'

'It *has* to alter,' Jack said 'There might be a nuclear war here. Look, Miranda's identity will survive, stored in the ghost universes.' How he sought to reassure.

Did Clare suspect him of humouring her? 'No, Jack, *our* reality – where she died! – is the one the world would revert to if the Qua wasn't causing this change.'

Jersey had been examining the Qua.

'I think this is the charge gauge, Gabe. It's at eighty per cent, creeping up.'

'Did Matt ever tell you,' Soul asked Clare, 'how long these batteries last on full charge?'

100

Irving Sherwood had taken command of the scene. Dark blue SFPD cars with white doors blocked off Upper Grant. Two white red-striped ambulances from the Department of Public Health's Paramedic Division stood by. Flak-jacketed marksmen from the SWAT truck awaited orders. A young man in a kaftan was walking towards the police lines, a notebook clasped upon his head like some oversized phylactery. Two of the SWAT team had donned snouty masks and goggles.

SFPD Captain Patterson and Don Rosado and Special Agent Barnes stood by Sherwood, watching. A lieutenant, trained in crisis negotiations, held a phone to his ear, patched through to the café.

'I can just about hear them talking. Something about *eighty-five per cent . . .*'

'They're charging up its batteries,' Rosado said. 'What do they plan to do then? Use the other hostages to bargain a way out with it?'

In Sherwood's car the driver was in radio contact with the emergency room at the hospital on Hyde Street.

'They're prepping Cooper now,' he reported. 'They're pretty sure he'll pull through.'

'We can't afford to let them leave with the computer,' said Sherwood.

Barnes nodded. Mary always backed him up.

Best career move ever, from Tucson to San Francisco, after Sherwood had helped that Senator out. Best life-move, too, with Mary, who shared his ambitions.

Now this vile mess. San Jose infiltrating those Korean immigrants. Full liaison with San Francisco, where the Soviets had their so-called trade mission. That should have been sent packing long before the present crisis built up.

Setting the trap, but not knowing who was the insider at QX. Then everything going wrong. Sheer chaos. The damn prototype taking a walk. The real one, not a dummy. The alphabet men had caused this. NSA, CIA, pulling strings behind the scenes. Interfering.

The situation was back under control. Under Irving's control. The prototype wouldn't take another walk, out of the country, into enemy hands.

'Who on earth can those two British people be in the café?' Sherwood asked Mary.

She shrugged.

Agents had barely begun trying to check the identity of the man called Gabe Soul, whom Cooper had gasped about to the officer who rode with him in the ambulance while paramedics kept him alive. Gabe and Jersey and Billy in a yellow duster coat. Sounded like some hoodlum gang in Tombstone long ago. The situation stank of *wrongness*. As for a Clare from Britain, no surname known . . . !

Was Clare one of the trio who sat conspicuously in the window like human shields while the rest of the hostages lay on the floor? A bearded man. Two women who looked so alike through binoculars.

Why should the Tombstone Gang who took the proto-type have driven to the Holy Bagel to meet this Clare? What was their relationship? Why, oh why hold the café customers hostage instead of simply driving away with Clare and their prize?

It was the sort of thing terrorists would do. They were going to make some incredible demand. They thought they could compel a plane to be provided. The mysterious Clare might be posing as a victim along with her twin and the man. She might be the brains behind this operation to steal the prototype from the original thief. A terrorist woman, fanatical, probably psychotic.

Sherwood beckoned the SWAT squad.

'I want you to go in now. Forget about using gas. You mightn't see clearly. Incapacitate the terrorists – that's what they are.'

Captain Patterson began to object. 'The *customers*—'

'We shan't use gas because of the customers. Confined in there with gas they'd panic. They'd try to rush out. We'd be confused.' Sherwood told the SWAT team, 'Anyone innocent is lying on the floor. You'll shoot to maim unless your lives are threatened. Try to avoid hitting those three in the window. But if they act suspiciously—'

'They'll hardly sit still!' protested the Captain.

'—then you must hit them. This is out of your jurisdic-tion, Captain. It's a matter of national security, do you all hear? There's a very special computer in there. We want it. But if it gets damaged in the assault, that's okay. Destroyed is better than lost.'

The lieutenant called out, 'The phone line went dead.'

101

What do you wish, Matthew?

Call me Gabe, Gabe typed one-handed as he chewed a mouthful of cream cheese bagel.

Who is Gabe?

Gabe typed in his full name and his former name.

Attach modem to phone line, Gabe.

Laying down his bagel, Gabe unjacked the phone and linked it to the Qua. The screen scrolled fast, and then a window appeared amidst the scrolling.

> **UAA autonomous programs
> and data compression
> enhanced by factor of 1000.**

'Clare, what are UAA autonomous programs? Don't get up to tell me!'

She pursed her lips. Quiz question. What was the answer? What was the prize?

'And it says data compression enhanced by a thousand – what's that mean?'

One of the business women spoke up. 'Excuse me – UAA is Unified Agent Architecture. It's a system for breeding smart programs like virus-worms. It sends those out to search the Net for whatever you want. Saves you spending time searching. You linked that computer to the phone line, didn't you?'

'It told me to, lady—'

'Compressing data is how you pack more into less space to squirt it through phone lines faster. A thousand times faster's impossible!'

'Not if the Qua's using parallel universes,' said Clare.

Miranda moaned. 'And I thought you were mad.'

The screen blanked. A question appeared:

What do you wish, Gabe?

What did he want? It knew him now.

He wanted himself and Jersey and Billy to be in a world

where authorities wouldn't have any power to interfere with him. A world which revolved around him. He wanted himself there – and Clare as well, and Beth who had studied some physics and understood about these things.

He typed.

On impulse he added: **Do you think you're alive?**

The reply was a teaser:

I think – therefore I am?

'It says, *I think therefore I am.*'

The business woman said, 'That's real sophomore stuff. Programed to pass the Turing test, is it? Takes your words and twists them a bit, does it?'

Damn machine. Route to alternative worlds, okay. That was proven. Matt was witness to that. So was Clare. But a key to immortality?

Gabe typed, **Can you fuck?**

A reply appeared for just a second.

I can fuck you.

And vanished.

Had he seen what he thought he saw?

'They're coming!' cried Billy.

102

Members of the SWAT squad raced along the side of the street opposite the café, using abandoned cars as cover. Others advanced on the café side, ducking into doorways and out again.

The first shot rang out, shattering glass in the bay window of the Holy Bagel . . .

103

Dominating the skyline, the Transamerica Pyramid was to many ordinary citizens a symbol of rampant finance scorning their feelings. Protests and pleas to down-size the design had all been ignored. The Pyramid might be slim, yet its fifty-five storeys including the spire soared a full thousand feet.

Now finance was triumphant no more . . .

Maybe using the offices of Golightly Investments on the forty-ninth floor as a command and observation post was an act of sheer swagger on the part of the American Freedom Army. Mists could roll in, erasing the view. Up here you were vulnerable to aerial attack, if the federal government had any idea where you were.

Yet being up here was such a rich symbol of the collapse of satanic socialist Jewish power. And the building did have its own generators.

Along Washington Street a wrecked light tank of the National Guard smouldered amidst burnt-out cars. A couple of National Guard Hueys were still airborne. Snipers were firing from their open cargo doors. A missile launched from the roof of the Park Hyatt hit one of the helicopters. The Huey exploded in a ball of flames and the combat-clad watchers in the Golightly office cheered.

Former Navy Seals and Green Berets transmitted orders to units mopping up resistance on the streets. Two of the windows had been swung open on their pivots. A bazooka poked through one, and a heavy machine-gun through the other, just in case the remaining police spotter helicopter wandered too close.

Colonel Mack Davis was correlating radio reports from other Pacific coast and Midwest cities where the uprising seemed victorious. Several army and air force bases had mutinied. Unless the federal government decided in its madness to nuke some of its own cities, surely it would be forced to concede and negotiate independence for much more than merely Idaho.

The Qua computer had fucked up so many government and military computers across the country as well as crashing the satanic economy by erasing financial records. The Qua was still ranging the info highway, wrecking it. The rest of the world was trying to quarantine America electronically. Many countries were convinced that

America's own NSA spooks had themselves let the viruses loose . . .

Briefly Gabe knew all this and his own heroic role in the uprising.

The knowledge was washing away, becoming unreal. Memories of the Holy Bagel Café and the house on Telegraph Hill surfaced like a whale from off whose sides poured the foam and spume of this other existence which he had never truly experienced.

Jersey and Billy were here in combat gear in the Golightly office, amongst the desks and computers and men and women of the AFA. Billy was going to freak any moment.

Beth sat near the Qua, which was scrolling its screen. She was guarding Clare who was handcuffed. Wild-eyed, Beth said to Gabe:

'*Is this the Virtuality?*'

'Say nothing, Beth! Do nothing! Billy, don't do anything at all!'

Heads had turned.

'What's the matter, Gabe?' from someone whom he no longer knew.

'What's fucking wrong?'

'It's nothing.'

'What's a Virtuality?'

'Oh, that's just something we used to say to each other—'

Clare could remember her kidnapping by the right-wing crazies. They'd used her approved visit to QX as a keyhole and her as the key. QX had wanted artificial intelligence experts to be observers when the Qua was first run. Herself included.

When the AFA kidnapped her, they had rigged her as a walking bomb. Semtex pads taped to her body like unwanted fat deposits, miniature buttonhole cameras, microphones. They could blow her to shreds any moment they chose. She hadn't dared not co-operate. They had sent her into QX like a puppet, an obedient robot. If they blew her in there, she would take the whole Qua Fab with her. Unless she carried the Qua out with her.

This nightmare was losing all substance and authenticity.

The Holy Bagel . . .

Miranda! Was she alive or dead in this world?

Jack – where was he?

A hostage . . .

Soul, in those camouflage combat clothes, veered towards her as if she were a magnet. He kept a wary eye on Billy. Several of the AFA people were paying close attention now. Billy looked half out of his mind.

Maybe that was exactly how Billy felt.

'What's going on?' demanded that Colonel person. Mack Davis.

He was tall, grizzle-headed, grey-eyed, with the distant stare of someone forever scanning for a sniper a mile away. Even when he looked at you, he was seeing far beyond. Beyond, to leadership of an independent liberty-land carved from the United States.

Soul was like some sleepwalker wading through treacle towards Clare and Beth, towards the Qua.

'No problems,' Soul assured the Colonel. He was exerting all his hypnotic charisma. 'Jersey, see to Billy, will you? He has the shakes.'

'I want him out of here,' said Davis.

'Come along,' Jersey coaxed. Jersey was shaky too, but he took Billy by the arm.

'Where's my yellow duster?' complained Billy like a plaintive child. As Jersey tugged, Billy became hysterical. 'No, don't. If we go, we'll be left behind, don't you see?'

Jersey exerted more pull, though he looked dubious.

Davis snapped his fingers. A bruiser of a man seized Billy's other arm and twisted it behind his back.

Jersey relinquished Billy.

'Just go, for Gabe's sake. He knows best.'

Davis's man propelled Billy towards an open door, the way to where the lift shafts were – as Clare knew in a ghostlike way, yet shouldn't have known.

Billy began to shriek as he was marched away. 'Don't leave me—!'

'Shut him up!' bellowed Davis.

Shut Billy up – in a room? Or shut him up more thoroughly?

'What does he mean, don't leave him behind?' said Davis.

Gabe spread his hands appeasingly. 'He's a bit screwball at times, our Billy.'

Somewhere outside, Billy had stopped shrieking. Impatiently the Colonel turned away.

Soul was very close by now to the Qua. It was operating on its own. Beth sat, bewildered.

Clare wondered why she herself had been brought up here. But of course she was an artificial intelligence expert, wasn't she? Strange that she didn't know rather more about the subject.

'The Qua said it could fuck me,' Soul whispered to her.

'You aren't even the original Gabe Soul. You know that? You're only a probability. A bad probability for me.'

Could she cow him? Could she intimidate him? How the loss of Miranda ached in her. And Jack, *her* Jack: where was he?

'What should I do?' murmured Soul.

'Tell it to revert to the original reality. Ask it, beg it. It'll sense your touch.'

'You're trying to panic me. To deceive me.'

'Gabe, you can't survive here. You don't know the circumstances well enough.'

'Oh I think I do! I think I can—'

'—bluff it out? Impersonate yourself?'

Jersey sidled closer.

'Gabe, what about Billy?'

'What's happening?' begged Beth. 'Gabe, how are we here?'

'My disciples,' muttered Soul. How should he advise them? They were waiting for guidance. They mightn't wait long.

'I think you should all move away from that computer,'

said a thin-faced, freckly woman in combat fatigues. 'Except for Dr Conway. You hear me, Soul?'

'Jet coming—!'

All attention was riveted on the view. From across the bay, beyond Coit Tower, a dark fighter came rushing. As it passed over the tower girded by trees barely three-quarters of a mile away, twin plumes gushed from under its wings.

'Missiles incoming—!' Streaking towards the Pyramid. *'Everyone get down—!'*

Soul plunged his fingers upon the keyboard of the Qua like a manic pianist.

104

Grimy women and kids were using a sand bunker as an outdoor toilet. A loose cordon of other women stood around to provide some privacy. A haze of stinking smoke drifted through the air, veiling and unveiling hundreds of refugees on this golf course, many of them in a state of collapse, some with belongings, others only in nightclothes. The turf was riven by deep ruts. Kids were daring each other to leap over these.

Tall pines had collapsed, uprooting great discs of earth. Land had slid away. In the ocean some crowded yachts and fishing boats bobbed. Wrecked boats had been carried on to a sandy shoreline, where cliffs had slid here and there.

The veil parted over the water. Fingers were pointing. Look, look.

The Golden Gate Bridge was down. Not the orange steel towers themselves – but the roadway. The roadway had corkscrewed into the water. Cables dangled, loose tentacles.

Jack limped. His clothes were soiled. A gash on his forehead had crusted. Smeared blood had dried on his hand.

Memories of devastated buildings, blazing fires gusting oven-breath, crashed cars, roads torn open, corpses, awful injuries ... these were becoming insubstantial. Sirens were wailing somewhere as if in despair.

Clare hugged him, and he clutched her. Then she drew back.

'Jack ... ?'

She peered at him.

'Jack—' Her tone became more urgent and anxious. 'What was the name of that hotel in Los Angeles where we stayed?'

'The Stardome, Clare – the Stardome. It was full of part-time soldiers.'

'Thank God,' she said.

'For this?' He coughed as smoke caught his throat, smoke from the fires still burning in the city.

'For us, Jack. We're together. I think Gabe Soul came to Angelo's house. Matt Cooper had the Qua there ...' She shook her head frustratedly. 'I can't be sure!'

'Me neither.' He winced. 'Damn this ankle of mine.'

A helicopter was approaching. Emergency services? It circled slowly.

A police car with its headlights on and flashers rotating lurched along a road. It was coming from the direction of some classical palace of a building which had suffered severe damage. A colonnade had collapsed. The roof had caved in.

The helicopter was descending, seeking open space to land among the refugees upon the huge expanse of turf. Someone in the helicopter was pointing a camera, snapping pictures of misery. The gust from the rotor blades beat down upon refugees, dispelling smoke.

The man with the camera wore an incongruous Panama hat.

Jack stared aloft.

'It can't be. God, it *is*. It's Marcus Strauss. The photographer – who was in the desert. He took your photo in Ronstadt.'

'My photo, Jack?' Clare asked warily.

'In the lobby of the Ronstadt Inn. Sherwood stopped him.'

259

She slapped her brow. 'I was such a photogenic shot. Damsel in distress. Of course.'

The police car was coming closer.

'Jack, we must talk to the authorities. If Soul's here in this city with the Qua, he has to be caught.' She began to run towards the police car, waving her arms.

Jack limped after her.

The police car had stopped. The blue-uniformed officer looked exhausted. Smuts smeared his tanned face. His thinning brown hair was curly with sweat. His attention was on the helicopter.

'Officer,' Clare said to him, 'please listen to me. There's a man in this city who has stolen a very special computer—'

'Oh, *shut up*, lady,' was the exasperated reply. 'Be real. Do you think we have time to bother about someone who stole your fucking computer? Pardon me,' he added sarcastically.

'It isn't my computer. It belongs to QX of San Jose. It's *top secret*,' she said hopefully.

'Yeah, and little green men told you so.' His radio burbled. He picked up the microphone. 'Unit Three-Nine in Lincoln Park. A chopper just landed some newsmen. I'm going to requisition it.'

Clare fled from the police car. The man in the Panama hat had left the helicopter, along with a younger man who carried a camera bag. Marcus was darting about, assessing shots, snapping, snapping. As the photographer headed towards the improvised latrine of the sand bunker, the guardian women began to protest.

'Marcus Strauss!'

Already the photographer was evaluating Clare professionally.

'Do I know you? Or am I simply famous?'

'Marcus, *Erik*—' Jack panted as he arrived, evidently in some pain.

'Do you know these people, Erik?'

Erik shook his head.

260

'Me neither. Never forget a face. The mystery deepens.'

'Listen to me, Mr Strauss,' said Clare. 'That policeman is intending to requisition your helicopter—'

'Oh, *fuck*.'

'You must take us with you – to Telegraph Hill. That's the most likely place. A quantum computer has been stolen. This computer can shift us into alternative universes. It's fallen into the hands of a cult guru. I can't explain right now—'

Marcus took half a dozen shots of Clare in rapid succession.

'Oh, precious,' he marvelled. 'Her staring eyes, her swirling hair, for she on honey-dew hath fed ... This is *it*, Erik my boy. Crazed by catastrophe.'

The officer had left his patrol car. He was trudging towards the helicopter.

'Come along, belle damosel. Quickly, before *he* spoils everything.'

Angry women ran from the vicinity of the latrine towards the officer, shouting their complaints about the invasion of their privacy. They delayed the officer long enough for the four to climb on board the helicopter. The turbine whined into a roar which drowned out whatever the officer shouted. The policeman drew his side-arm but by now the rotor blades were scything around. Disgustedly, he holstered his gun again.

105

From Lincoln Park the pilot cut over the sea to avoid smoke drifting from unquenched fires in the Richmond district. Ant-people were on the collapsed Golden Gate Bridge, either trying somehow to reach Marin County on foot or hoping to be picked up by boat where the roadway had slumped into the strait.

Erik passed Marcus a camera with telescopic lens to record those insect-like efforts.

'I may be the last great photo-journalist,' Marcus boasted.

'Really, faces are what count. Great events mirrored in faces. The altered states of mind. The snapping of sanity. Transfigurations.'

This wonderful woman, Clare, insisted that there were alternative universes. That she and her Jack had met him in the true reality, where of course the Big One had not destroyed San Francisco.

What an amazing piece of wish-fulfilment. And a guru had stolen a magic box which could put everything right.

Her companion even burbled names of colleagues Marcus was supposed to know. None rang a bell except Renny. Marcus had known a Renny. Clear case, this, of shooting in the dark – like some spiritualist calling out to an audience, *Somebody here knows a Jonathan*, and scanning faces for reactions.

They crossed over the forested Presidio. Plenty of refugees amongst the pines and eucalyptus and on the hiking trails and the army golf course. Navy helicopters were alighting at Crissy Field to offload casualties. Air traffic control was a joke right now. Everything airborne was obviously contributing to the rescue effort.

Listen to Clare and her Jack whispering.

'Soul'll have to bail out. There's no mains power in the city—'

'Unless he can charge from other batteries—'

'No way out. Ruined roads. Wrecked bridges. How long do we have?'

Marcus swapped cameras to record her face.

National Guard patrols were heading up steep wrecked streets towards Pacific Heights, perhaps to prevent looting. Visibility was nil around Russian Hill and Telegraph Hill beyond. Not even Coit Tower showed. In the murky distance the spire of the Transamerica Pyramid was visible briefly, an obelisk rising amidst filthy billowing clouds. Flames leapt from other towers still on fire.

'I'm not flying into that,' said the pilot.

*

262

Blue, the sky.

Such greenery below: woodlands and glades and streams.

Horseback riders ambled along a leafy trail. Cyclists and roller-bladers were coasting along a road wending through trees. A lake formed a moat around a hill. Rowers were dipping their oars. A Chinese pavilion stood on the island.

'Next, on our left,' said the pilot through his microphone, 'we'll be passing the Japanese Tea Garden. See if you can spot the big Buddha—'

This helicopter was bigger. Fellow passengers were pointing cameras.

Jack was beside her, blinking, shaking his head. Clare clutched him.

'What was the name of the hotel in Los Angeles?'

'Stardome,' he told her. 'Stardome.'

'Yes!'

They were on a sightseeing flight by helicopter – they had splashed out. They were so happy. The memory of happiness was fading.

On the road outside some large museum, horse-drawn carriages awaited customers for a clip-clop around the park.

'—largest collection of Asian art outside Asia,' the pilot was saying.

She dropped what she was carrying from the kitchen. Sushi, arranged on a large plate around a little dish of soy sauce. Raw fish on rice strewed the carpet. The soy made an ugly stain.

Jack had jerked upright on the jungle sofa. Lights were lit. It must be evening.

'The hotel in LA?' he asked her urgently.

'Stardome,' she replied.

'Part-time soldiers!'

'Water tower outside our window!'

Yes, yes, they were the same, even if the whole world had changed.

263

'Shall I switch the TV on?' he suggested. 'Find out what the news is?'

Instead she sat by him. They held hands as though this might save them from being separated.

106

Swaying, Free Wind stared at the night sky. To his stoned, roaming gaze the whole of the heavens looked sick. Stars weren't precise bright points. They were smeared threads of light. It was as if a vast luminous intricate Dream Catcher web spanned the vault above.

Ghostly figures paced by him through the darkness. If only he could bring them into focus, he would be amidst men of dignity and soul and name who understood their own destinies and their place in nature.

Instead, an alien soul had imprinted itself upon the whole of the land and sickened it, as surely as the sky was sick.

Skinwalkers were everywhere out there in the world of America and beyond. Impersonators. Masqueraders. False souls, false lives. All of America was a bad dream which had imposed itself upon the People, engulfing them.

Even to realize this was a magical achievement, so massively real did the world of cars and cities and white civilization seem. It wasn't real at all. It was illusions. Exaltation and terror filled Free Wind. Spirits of his ancestors stirred in him.

He went back into the shack.

In the light of the kerosene lamp Eagle Eye and the others squatted expectantly under the great web of strings and poultry feathers which now hung from most of the ceiling on hooks. The biggest Dream Catcher web ever.

'Brothers,' announced Free Wind, 'we will burn the Harleys. We will pile them together. We will pour gas over them. We will set them alight.'

Protests arose. He had expected this. The bikes were

their mobility, their freedom, their wealth on wheels, their identity.

'Brothers, the Harleys control us because they are not of our making. By burning the Harleys we will truly become Skinwalkers who only travel in our dreams. We travel to wage war on all impersonators – until the mirage of their existence blows away like the smoke from our blazing bikes—'

Free Wind felt so in key with the roots of the world.

107

'Of course,' said the casually-dressed fellow, 'if the world did become an alternative one the way *you're* suggesting, Dr Conway, we wouldn't know that anything's any different!'

Jack was with her in this room, right next to her. She focused on other persons, a conference screen split two ways, a purring computer with baby rabbits hopping across it, white venetian blinds.

Irving Sherwood was here. The black woman beside him was Mary Barnes, dressed in a smart suit. Next to her sat a chubby Chinese man.

The person who had spoken was in his early forties, dressed in jeans, T-shirt and windcheater. Cropped chestnut hair, squinty eyes behind John Lennon glasses, old acne pits on his cheeks. His T-shirt motif was a large green question mark with two bars across it, like a dollar sign, a questionable dollar. On the screen were a cadaverous man with untidy grey hair and a mild looking elderly man who was nursing a cheroot in his mouth.

'Would we?' asked the man in the T-shirt.

'Hotel in LA?' she whispered to Jack.

'Stardome,' he whispered back. Their touchstone, their identification code . . .

Fadingly she sensed that she had visited San Jose for the ostentatious launch of the Qua. Her field of work, her field. Tony Racine, who wasn't in any hospital, had decided to invite guests whose noses could be rubbed in his triumph. She was the Matsushima Fellow of Spenser College Cambridge who had become a Cassandra of AI, uttering oracles like that ancient prophetess who warned about the coming fall of Troy. She warned about what might happen if a quantum computer achieved self-awareness.

Buffet and media throng, an opera singer and the *Baywatch* star. Then suddenly: explosions, screams, panic, chaos . . .

Dreamlike, the chain of events fell apart in her mind.

'Well, would we?'

Her interrogator must belong to QX. The authorities must be hunting for the stolen prototype and for whoever had taken it from the launch.

'There's no answering that, eh Tony?' said the Chinese man.

Tony. Tony Racine.

The Chinese man might be Glenn Chang, a Glenn Chang who had not been involved with the Tin Man project but with the quantum computer project instead.

'Let's just suppose as a thought experiment,' continued the Chinese man, 'that due to a fluke or because of what it's tasked to do first of all the quantum computer actually becomes aware – aware of trillions of probability worlds. Suppose, as the observer of all those, it can select which is the dominant reality – that's what Dr Conway's been suggesting . . .'

Chang, if this was he, seemed indulgent towards Clare. Maybe he was a theory man.

'Well now, just as soon as several quantum computers are up and running, infinities cancel out. Solutions which don't yield a viable outcome erase each other. An alternative universe couldn't emerge as the actual one.'

'We're wasting time,' complained the elderly man on screen. 'Why should that crazy guru try to change reality?'

So Soul was in possession of the Qua, and they knew who he was . . .

The other man on screen nodded.

'Why that, instead of simply hacking into any computer

in the country or in the world? Exactly! *That* would alter the world pretty drastically. The public launch was unacceptable, Mr Racine.'

'You did accept it,' Racine pointed out.

'For national prestige – to be followed by heavy security.'

'Sucks to your security.'

'We didn't expect the level of what happened. The intensity. Coming out of the blue.'

Jack spoke up. 'He'll use it to change reality because he *is* a crazy guru.'

She and Jack had met Soul ... Jack had interviewed Soul ... Dreamlike, the recollection.

Sherwood snapped at Jack, 'I haven't noticed reality changing recently. Maybe our consultant psychologist might have an insight into where Soul could be right now?'

'*You* haven't noticed,' cried Clare. 'We have. Jack and I have!'

A couple of hours later, she was staring out through slim white bars at a vineyard and orchards. The private clinic was somewhere in the Santa Clara Valley.

A stout black lady orderly sat in the room, studying an imported copy of *Hello!* magazine as intently as if she could step right into the glossy pictures of celebrities. Next door, Jack was under similar supervision. A couple of young FBI agents sat outside in the corridor, kicking their heels. The room lacked any TV set. Soothing waltzes warbled quietly from a speaker high up the wall.

Bad idea to confess.

No one believed, although Glenn Chang seemed intrigued. Clare and Jack had exposed themselves as seriously deranged. Sherwood definitely lost Brownie points for having involved them in the conference, though the FBI would dutifully check out Pirate Place in San Francisco on the offchance ...

Running. Running downhill. Hand in hand with Jack. Giant redwood trees towered from steep slopes. The smoothly

267

surfaced road curved out of sight between sheer mossy soil and trees.

Almost skidding, they slowed.

'Hotel?' she gasped.

'Stardome,' Jack panted.

Some way behind, out of sight in the forest, an engine came to life.

Angelo didn't live in the city. His house was out here in Marin County, on the other side of the Golden Gate. You reached his house by a railed wooden staircase rising a hundred feet amidst soft flaky reddish brown columns of bark and great drooping boughs. The house was on two separate levels, both of which were cantilevered on piles. The place was so idyllic, windows looking out upon crowns of trees, and overtopped by others – yet precarious in its serenity, as if it might shake loose and slide. Massive trunks would stop it from sliding far.

Their idyll had been shattered by Gabriel Soul's arrival. He and Jersey in a Jeep. Clare and Jack had been returning from a hike – only to come upon the Jeep parked below and to spy those two up on the veranda about to enter the house.

Jersey, in a long yellow coat, had spotted them.

Like mist these memories were blowing away.

A wooden staircase rose up the bank on their right from an empty earthen car-bay. Up amongst the redwoods jutted another cantilevered house of similar design to Angelo's.

'Climb,' urged Jack.

Before the Jeep could round the bend.

The steps were slippery. They had only mounted halfway when the Jeep passed. It braked, and reversed.

Jersey and Soul jumped out.

Soul cupped his hands.

'I want you,' he called.

He must have the Qua in the Jeep. Surely he must.

'Welcome to my Virtuality,' he shouted. 'The Qua got it right at last.' He gestured grandly at the deserted forest. 'Doesn't this look ideal?'

*

268

They were in a bar. The plate-glass windows looked over a wide street. Fog lazed along, yielding glimpses of vendors' booths across the way advertising clam chowder and shrimps. The brash, tacky booths were unattended and shuttered right now. Clare and Jack were almost the only customers. A Coke and a bottle of Anchor steam beer stood before them.

'Hotel?' asked Clare promptly.

'Stardome, damn it, Stardome—'

The door of their hotel room burst open.

Asian youths in jeans and dragon T-shirts rushed in. Two of them cradled pump-action shotguns. Burn-marks disfigured their forearms as if cigarettes had been stubbed out—

Jack wrestled the steering wheel. Red tail-lights glowed in the night. Dazzle of white light from behind, red and blue flashes, siren wailing—

He was climbing stairs and stumbling, he was being robbed at knifepoint by a couple of panhandlers, staggering against them, he was dropping his wine glass on the table, he was in a bed thank God, he was lying in a bath, wallowing. No continuity, no way of holding on. Flashes of streets, buildings, faces, rooms, cars, trees, sky, kaleidoscoping, black gaps in between, slices of nothingness, non-existence. He was dying, being pulled apart. Creation itself was being pulled apart.

The world stabilized—

—and he fell into place.

Knees collapsing, arms flailing, chest heaving, bewildered by afterimages, he sprawled upon bright gritty ground.

So bright. So hot the air.

He clawed at the grit with his fingers. He dug in his nails.

108

'Captain Kramer – Fox has collapsed!'

Jeff Kramer swung round and saw the Englishman grovelling on the ground behind the armoured personnel carrier. Rodriguez was kneeling defensively to aim his M-16 over the clutter of vehicles at that distant huddle of buildings against the cliffs.

No sign of injury to Fox. He didn't look like someone who had succumbed to heatstroke. More as if he was having a fit.

Damn stupid idea to let a civilian be here at all, just because his girlfriend was a hostage in that tacky stronghold. If Fox must be present, he ought to have been way back in one of the recreational vehicles being used as field messes and relaxation stations.

There had been a lull now for almost an hour.

A stand-off.

Back here near the mouth of the canyon were the APCs. Those were too lightly armoured to take fire from a 50-calibre machine-gun. The militiamen in the so-called Soul Shelter had several 50-calibres. Not to mention their rocket-propelled grenade launchers and mortars.

Perhaps precision fire had put paid to those heavy weapons earlier, or else the militiamen were low on grenades and shells. They might just be hoarding against a final assault by the National Guard and Army units.

Up in the front line was a Bradley tank. Also, several heavily-armoured tracked infantry combat vehicles mounted with machine-guns and automatic cannon. And an M728 combat engineering vehicle weighing in at almost sixty tons. Right now those were mainly serving as cover for soldiers and guardsmen, as were the burned-out Jeeps and the pick-up trucks and cars belonging to the militia which formed a partial barricade.

The Soul Shelter could have been blown apart by now. Demolished. But then the computer prototype which the militia had stolen would be destroyed too.

Jeff stooped as he ran to where Fox lay convulsing.

Should he call for a medic?

The Englishman already seemed to be recovering.

Fox rolled over. He sat up and squinted at Jeff in his desert gear and steel helmet – and beyond him, shading his eyes, Fox took in the canyon and the armoured vehicles and the Soul Shelter.

'Are you epileptic, sir?' asked Jeff.

Fox licked his lips. 'Kramer.' As though recognizing someone was an achievement. 'Kramer, Clare's in there . . . !'

Of course his girlfriend was in the Soul Shelter.

Up the canyon, a loudhailer began booming again. The amplified words echoed. Another toughly-worded appeal to those inside to surrender themselves – and the fancy computer, undamaged – or all be killed outright.

'Don't worry,' Jeff said to Fox. 'No one's going to blast that place while the computer's in there. The AFA can probably rely on that too. So we're stuck.'

It would probably need to go as high as the President himself before anyone would order a full-scale attack. Had Fox thrown himself on the ground in some sort of passionate anguish? Christ, he must love the girl.

'Soul took Clare,' Fox said unsteadily, 'because he became fixated on her—'

'Because she's into AI, yeah yeah, I know.'

Fox was nodding as if he doubted his own memory.

'They'll be keeping her near the Qua.'

'Near the what?'

'Near the special computer.'

'Maybe not, since we took out the satellite dish up on the clifftop.'

That had been at the cost of two choppers, blown apart by heat-seeking missiles fired from bunkers up top! The American Freedom Army might have hoped that no one would finger the Soul Shelter here in the middle of nowhere, but they had certainly installed some defences.

Rush the stolen computer to this hideaway in another state by light aircraft. Hack into the com-satellites. Take them over. Hack into government and military computers.

271

Take those over or screw them up totally. Bring the country to its knees. Blackmail the nation. Demand Idaho or whatever they wanted.

We control the high ground. We have all your secrets. We'll give you back your computers if you give us our land. We'll always have programs sitting in your computers where you can't find them, to keep an eye on you.

The plan might have worked out, too, but for those Navajo bikers getting involved in the kidnapping of the Brits. That fellow, Eagle Eye, tracking the abduction vehicle back here. Seeing a light plane land and all the militia activity . . .

Recover that damned computer at all costs and try to undo the damage.

'They'll have the Qua in the most protected part of the Shelter,' said Fox.

'Obviously.'

'That'll be below ground. I know a way in.'

Jeff was nonplussed. 'How can you?'

Fox struggled up.

'I'll tell you – but only if you swear that you'll take me in with you to fetch Clare!'

Fox's presence could endanger Jeff's men, never mind his own skin. Jeff could have wrung the man's neck. And yet there was such chivalry in the Brit's demand . . . This did touch a chord.

Had Fox been rolling on the ground because he *realized* how to get into the Soul Shelter unseen? And couldn't contain himself?

Very likely Fox didn't know a way in at all. How could he? There wouldn't be a way. So: humour him. Right now any straw was worth clutching.

'There are old mine workings behind the Soul Shelter.' Fox pointed at a pile of rubble. 'See? That's spoil from the tunnels. There'll be a tunnel which comes out at the other side. It'll be camouflaged. Probably it'll have some bikes hidden in it. That's how we'll know it's the right one.'

'You sound as if you've been here already.'

Fox grinned madly.

'I'm from the country of Sherlock Holmes, Captain.'

109

In the Truth Room, computer screens glowed with government data. A couple of AFA women and a tubby young man paged intently through stacks of printout, jotting notes. Another woman was sorting copied disks. Discarded styrofoam coffee cups choked a waste bin. The screen of the quantum computer displayed a military menu of missile codes, even though the Qua was no longer linked to the outside world. The preserved head of Johnny the hunter snarled from its mahogany plaque at Clare. Her wrists were tethered to the arms of a chair. If she hadn't been secured, she might have toppled out of the chair.

Boots thumped down the stairs. A couple of armed men came alert, then relaxed as the heavy wooden door swung open.

Concentrate, concentrate . . .

'Colonel, the latest is still for us to hand over the computer or we all die—'

'It's another bluff. They daren't risk it. Tell them we want their President to ask us nicely on public radio. He and I can have a public dialogue—'

'They'd probably rather bomb us to pieces—'

'If they do that, then they won't be able to put their *own* pieces back together again. Not with QX demolished. Could take months.' Colonel Davis demanded of Clare, 'Months before the Japs come up with any prototype, either? Even if any QX survivors use Jap facilities?'

'Months,' she agreed. She had no idea.

At least the Schrödinger box was nowhere to be seen.

'Meanwhile the so-called United States falls apart. Tell them if their President doesn't enter into direct dialogue within the next twelve hours we may very well destroy the computer anyway for the hell of it—'

Gabe Soul stroked Clare's wrist. He was loosening a tether.

'Stalemate,' he murmured. 'My golden bed awaits. Enlightenment.'

'What are you doing, Soul?' asked the Colonel.

'Our consultant's tired. She almost fainted just now.'

'You looked weird too.'

'A passing spasm. Mental discipline overcomes frailties.'

'What frailties?'

Soul ignored the question. 'Dr Conway's role is over for now. She should come with me away from here.' How sweet and persuasive.

Davis laughed harshly.

'Does danger make you horny? Me too, sometimes. Your room's shot to shit, and there's a 50-calibre in there.'

'In my mansion are many rooms,' purred Soul.

'Don't blaspheme, huh?'

'We have an agreement, you and I.' Soul was guessing. Intuiting. 'My Shelter is your shelter. My people are your people.'

'Yeah.' The Colonel turned away. 'Demand a dialogue with their President—'

'If there's an attack,' Soul whispered to Clare, 'and if your soul isn't strengthened, you may die forever.'

She avoided his gaze. 'Gabe, you know what's going on. I know, so you must know as well! Do you really want to be here?'

'In my stronghold? On the verge of victory?'

'*For how long?*'

'We can discuss this in privacy, Clare.'

'Gabe, I'll grant you that you're remarkable—'

'As you shall discover.'

'If there's another spasm like there was just now, it mightn't stop. Everything might disintegrate. Smash the Qua,' she hissed.

'Maybe after I have enlightened you. You can try your best to charm me.'

'Gabe, aren't all these people here only *zombies*?'

'My alternate self must have a useful alliance with them.'

He reached to unfasten her other wrist. Having done so, he kept tight hold of the tether.

'Come, let's find a private place.'

110

Jeff and three others preceded Fox. Two brought up the rear. A flashlight ahead. One behind. Early on, they had really needed to stoop. The roof was higher now, though the air was just as stale.

'There'll be bats,' the Englishman had warned.

So there were. Milling, shitting, twittering bats. Forewarned, no one freaked.

When they had found the entrance, concealed by piles of mesquite and sheltering a Jeep and two scrambler bikes, in spite of this evidence of uncanny intuition – or of prior knowledge, which the Englishman denied – Jeff had been inclined to leave Fox behind under guard along with their own two Jeeps.

It was the warning about bats which made Jeff decide to keep his promise. What *else* was Fox going to know about, which might turn out to be accurate? Booby-traps in the tunnel?

111

A single shot distintegrated the old lock. A boot kicked the iron door inwards. Light spilled out of the cellar room. A red drape billowed, sail-like, hindering the door from opening fully. The first man burst through the gap, his M-16 at the ready, crowded by the next man, then the third.

'No one move! No one move—!'

No pandemonium of gunfire. Not a single shot yet.

Kramer was through into the cellar, followed by the final two men, jumping left, jumping right. The curtain ripped aside. The last of the assault team had tangled with it. That door was swinging fully open. Jack could see into the cellar.

Two armed ALA people had frozen, automatic rifles trembling, almost brought to bear but not quite ready to fire. Maybe they'd been inhibited by all the computer equipment in the room. Those women who were checking printouts might have been in the line of fire. So might Gabriel Soul, who was hovering beside *Clare*. Clare in a chair. A grizzle-headed man was as tense as could be. His gaze flicked from one National Guardsman to the next, assessing.

Thongs were on Clare's wrists. The bonds were loose. Soul was clutching one as if Clare was a puppet whom he was about to raise to caper for him.

Such a static charge in that cellar! At any moment a spark might leap from one side to the other. The spark would instantly become lethal gunfire, confined inside the stone walls.

Kramer's men were shifting positions gingerly.

Jack inhaled the reek of batshit on his clothes.

The grizzle-headed man snarled at Soul, 'You told me that tunnel had no way out. You lied.'

Jack caught Clare's eye.

'Stardome,' he called.

'Keep back, Fox,' snapped Kramer without even glancing at him.

Clare mouthed the word *Stardome* back at Jack. She was starting to rise.

'Get into the tunnel, Miss,' ordered Kramer.

Soul still held Clare's tether.

Jack saw the Qua so close to her.

'Lay your weapons down slowly—'

No one did. Not yet.

'Captain,' the grizzle-headed man said, 'the federal government's on its knees. It's whipped. The President's going to appeal to us. He'll do any deal they can – any damn deal. Think about five million dollars for each of you. Think about guaranteed refuge in Free Idaho or wherever. *Five million dollars, gentlemen.* For each of you. On my word of honour. Mack Davis's word.'

'So you're Davis,' said Kramer. 'You're under arrest.'

The ALA sentries still held on to their guns, stubborn and motionless.

'If there's any shooting in here,' Davis went on, 'it'll be heard. You won't get away. You'll all die in the tunnel. Shot in the back.'

Two doors had muffled that first single shot. Someone might come downstairs at any moment.

'Which is the fancy computer?' demanded Kramer.

Clare tugged herself free. 'It's right here—'

'I told you to get into the tunnel.'

'I'll carry the computer for you.'

'Right,' agreed Kramer. 'Do it.'

Davis glanced at her, at the Qua, at the M-16s covering him and the others. Was the spark going to fly?

'Keep out of the line of fire,' Kramer told Clare. 'Circle round by the wall.'

Two of Kramer's men adjusted their position.

'What's that on the wall?' asked one, agitated. The human head on the trophy shield . . .

Clare unplugged the Qua, folded down the keyboard and screen.

'Stay perfectly still, everybody else—'

'Clare,' Soul murmured sleekly, 'you don't wish to do this. It's too heavy for you. You're so tired. And you men: why risk your lives to keep the rich in power? They only tax you and tie you up in laws that castrate your freedom and pour your tax money into the sewers of society.'

'Shut up, you,' said Kramer.

A couple of his men were glancing at one another. Was the bribe getting through to them?

Clare hoisted her burden. She was trying to lift it high, but she couldn't. She let go – she let it crash down on to the wooden floor. She reached for the trophy, the heavy shield, and wrenched it free.

Poised, she was about to stoop and pound the Qua.

'No—!'

Kramer swung his rifle. In through the doorway, Jack threw himself at Kramer, grabbing.

A different gun fired. Blood welled from Clare's back. Dropping the trophy, she pitched into the wall.

A shot from an M-16 hit the sentry who had fired.

Davis ducked behind a table to free his pistol from its holster. Soul had dived to the floor to protect himself. Kramer drove his elbow into Jack's belly, winding him, doubling him over. The other ALA sentry fired. The sentry was already staggering back, collapsing against the oak door, his chest bloody. Hit in the shoulder, Kramer cried out. He dropped the M-16, clutching himself. Davis was aiming his pistol.

'Freeze!' from somebody.

'Five million,' Davis called out.

Jack found himself doubled up astride the M-16. His hand closed upon it. As Clare sank down the wall, she swung round. Blood bubbled on her lips. The exit wound in her chest, so soaked. Feebly she tried to regain the trophy.

Had dropping the Qua to the floor been sufficient to wreck the cooling system, to spill liquid nitrogen inside the machine? Impossible to know.

'I'll go for five million,' said somebody. 'Who's with me?'

'Don't be fooled,' Kramer called out in pain. From upstairs, a blur of shouts.

Clare's eyes were still clear, yet she was surely dying.

Dying.

There'd be no medical attention. There couldn't be any in time.

She was summoning some reserve of stamina. Her eyes were imploring Jack. Her hand trembled towards the Qua. She struggled to frame words.

'Smash it—'

Bloody saliva frothed. She choked, she fought to breathe.

Smash it, and restore the world to a single reality.

A terrible realization came over her. Such horror was in

278

her eyes. She was begging him to delay. She fought to speak.

The words were a gurgly croak. She was staring at the rifle Jack had acquired.

'Kill me first . . .'

Kill her?

Suddenly he understood.

If he destroyed the Qua before she died, she thought her identity would evaporate.

She was facing annihilation.

Fists battered the door. A fallen body was blocking the door from opening. One of its hands was acting as a wedge. Pushing the door from outside only increased the resistance.

'*Colonel Davis, what's going on—?*'

Soul had risen. He was putting on his Rasputin act for those with the M-16s. 'You shall not kill me—'

Davis held his pistol steady. 'Five million dollars and sanctuary—'

Kramer bawled, 'Fire, damn it!'

No one fired.

Clare had to be deluded about survival after death in empty ghost universes. Hadn't she?

It was what she believed. It was what she was putting her trust in, fatally injured as she was. In this, and in Jack.

In him, to assure that for her.

He shifted the M-16. Hope seemed to well in her. Desperate impatience. He had never handled a gun before. Was there some trick to firing it?

The Qua was cracked, yet it must still be functioning. If he emptied this gun into the computer, probabilities should collapse. The world should become once again the original world.

Where would he be in it? What would have happened? If he shot Clare, as her eyes beseeched him to, would she necessarily be dead in the original world too?

The question was an impossible torment. He ached with anguish.

Her life ebbing slowly, she pleaded silently, unable to speak any more.

He shifted the muzzle towards her, and saw incredible relief – not a desire to end her pain, but something comprising everything that she was, her entire being. He was torturing her by hesitating.

He couldn't shoot her. She was deluded. He couldn't.

As he angled the gun away, she knew his decision. In her eyes there was such an accusation of utter betrayal.

Squeezing the trigger, he fired into the Qua.

112

The cellar and all within it rushed inwards – again and again yet all at once. All folding up around him. Volume into flatness, flatness into lines. Lines shrinking to a point. He was infinitesimal, he was infinite. He knew nothing, he knew everything – and everything cancelled out.

Except . . .

. . . for the black leather sofa colonized by files, the matching black armchair, shelves of books on psychology, neurology, anatomy, her desk, that window through which Orlando had climbed to ravish her, those geraniums still bloodily abloom in their terracotta pots on the small balcony!

'It's a terrible tragedy, sir. A young life cut short, and so promising.'

Jack swung round to face Rogers, who was putting on such a show of sympathy.

'If you'll remember to leave the master key at the lodge, sir, when you pick up your things? If I'm not there myself.'

A red plastic tag fastened to a Yale key was in Jack's hand. He could have screamed.

Maybe Rogers fathomed that Jack was on the verge of a frenzied outburst. Smoothly the man withdrew, shutting the door.

Jack lurched to the sofa. How his heart pounded.

He was in Cambridge, in Clare's room, and Clare was dead. It could only be her to whom Rogers had been referring.

Moments ago, he had been staring at Clare's agonized, accusing face. Instants ago, he had fired the rifle.

Those moments were utterly alienated from now. They were on the other side of some window of plate glass against which he beat in vain like a bird. And yet they were continuous with now.

No memories of other events which had brought him back here to Cambridge were receding, dreamlike, from his grasp. It was different, this time – so different. He had no inkling of how he came to be here.

The roofs and upper half of the second floor rooms on the other side of the quadrangle were in sunlight. All below was in shade. Late afternoon.

He felt insane.

Rogers had known what had happened. Such a tragedy. How much did he know? Maybe the Master knew.

And Heather – what would Heather know?

If only his wristwatch told the date as well as the time; but it didn't.

Jack nerved himself to sit at Clare's desk and lift the phone and dial.

Lucas answered.

'It's me, son,' Jack said.

'Dad – where are you?' Expectation, worry, concern.

'I'm in college.'

'When will you be back?'

'Soon.'

'Mum had to go to Cottenham about some bloody child-battering – sorry, I didn't mean to say that.'

'Have you just got home from school, Luke?'

'I took the afternoon off. Free study. I was on the Net till you'd get back. I've been on the Net a lot since you phoned.'

Phoned from where? From Heathrow? Had he landed there some time earlier today?

Jack fished for help. 'You mean when I rang from the airport?'

'No! Mum said you called to say you'd landed – but I mean the first time you phoned from San Francisco, when you told us what happened.'

What had he told his family?

How could he possibly ask?

Such a hollowness was inside. Such an ache. Such panic. And exhaustion.

Lucas had spent his time surfing the Internet . . .

Of course! Of course.

'Luke, is there much talk on the Net about what happened?'

'Lots, Dad. I've been trying to find out – beyond what you said, and what was on the news.'

'What exactly have they been saying about me?'

'I can show you it all on screen as soon as you get back.'

'Will you tell me now, Luke? I really want to know.'

'Um, Dad, you needn't worry about Mum. She's really sorry for you.'

'Please.'

'Well, okay.' His son was marshalling himself. 'Well, the attack on the QX place in San Jose. The quantum computer getting stolen. The thief kidnapping you both. Then Vietnamese gangsters finding that house you all went to in San Francisco, and the FBI turning up. All that stuff. Dad, I can't possibly!'

'*Please*. What are they saying about—?' About Clare. He he couldn't bring himself to utter her name. He tried to force himself. He choked. He mustn't cry.

Lucas seemed to understand, or at least half-understand.

'Listen, Dad, they aren't saying you were having it off with her.' Reproach? Or a sneaking hint of excitement? 'Were you having it off with her, Dad?'

'Never mind that. Are they saying who shot her?'

'Well, one of those Vietnamese. Isn't that what happened? Dad, there's a rumour about the security services

282

being involved. Did they botch it? Is there a cover-up? Is that why you're asking me?'

How this must appeal to an adolescent boy.

Maybe it was true.

'Are they saying much about Matt Cooper?'

'He's the thief. His death's blamed on the Vietnamese too. Dad, did something different happen? Something you couldn't talk about on the phone in America?'

'No, it was just like that. Exactly.'

Not exactly at all. The familiar world had paused in San Francisco, and had resumed, restored to itself, with probable events filled in . . .

Jack forced himself to concentrate on this room, the sofa, bookshelves, the geraniums on the balcony, Clare's computer on the desk. Taking stock. Identical, identical.

'Luke, are they saying anything about a man called Gabriel Soul?'

Such astonishment in his son's voice. 'Dad, that was on the news! All about the Soul Shelter and her being kidnapped and freed and – it was all on the news.'

'I'm sorry,' said Jack, 'I'm a bit confused.'

'I'm not surprised, Dad. What a trip.'

'What are they saying happened to Soul?'

'Most wanted fugitive – that's the phrase. And there's a lot of stuff appearing under—' Lucas clammed up.

'Under what?'

'I haven't really looked at it.'

'Under what, Lucas?'

'The, er, alt.sex addresses. Why are you in college?' his son asked hastily. 'Are you scared to come home? Don't worry. A Mr Newman from Matsushima phoned. He's anxious to talk. And reporters have been phoning. Dad, I think some of them are in cars down the street. Just you tell them to piss off. That's what Mum said to the ones who phoned. I think some of them offered money. Were they waiting for your plane to land?'

Had they been? He had no idea.

'Is that why you're phoning from Spenser's? Are you in

your own room? God, that's bleak ... It *doesn't* have a phone! Dad, you're in her rooms, aren't you?'

'Yes,' he admitted.

'You're, er, taking a last look? Don't tell Mum. I'll say you phoned from the railway station. No, we'll say that Clare's *dad* begged you to do this. He's half gaga, isn't he? He begged you when you were there. You felt you had to even though he's gaga. How did he take it? Could he understand?'

Jack must have gone from Heathrow to North London, to visit Clare's father on the way home ... Taking Clare's luggage and her ashes with him in a taxi? In a monstrous repetition of how Ivan had taken Miranda's ashes there last year!

How was Clare's father bearing up, indeed?

'Will you need to go back there for a memorial service? Will there be one in the college chapel?'

'Lightning strikes twice,' said Jack bitterly.

'What do you mean?'

'It's a saying, son. How's Crissy, by the way?'

'She got her money. She paid her fine. *She's* fine. Well, apart from the business about the draw, but that isn't too serious. Dad, are you okay? Well, you can't be. What I mean is: come home now, will you?'

'I will. I'll be there soon. Thanks, Luke, thanks so much.'

He cradled the phone.

Home, home indeed.

The world was almost identical, but he was not. And Heather was going to be sympathetic, compassionate. Shocked by what had happened. He must build on that. Heather, Lucas, Crissy, his family.

Clare – and it was almost a silent prayer – *are you out there?*

She was absolutely dead. What could he do but continue his life? In a more understanding partnership with Heather ... Maybe that was the meaning of all this. This, which no one knew about except for himself.

And Gabe Soul. Wanted fugitive. Unable to bother Jack.

Surely unable to. Why should Soul wish to, even if he could get out of America?

Soul might be killed resisting arrest. If he was captured, and if he blabbed, his claims would seem insane. Jack would deny those claims, if asked about them.

With the awakening of many quantum computers, unreal probabilities would all cancel out. The familiar world would continue onwards.

Just as Jack, too, must continue. He felt so old. He'd acquitted himself decently, hadn't he? Especially when he escaped on the motorbike . . .

Clare had done much better than he had. And he had betrayed her. In her eyes, at least. In those suffering accusing eyes . . .

A knock on the door. Rogers must have returned, or had told the Master that he was here.

A second rat-tat.

The door opened.

The blue velvet jacket, the floppy polka dot bow tie, the oily black hair lapping the collar, that smug sensual face wearing a diffident expression for once . . .

Orlando Sorel.

Behind him, a woman.

A slim young woman in jeans and a white sweater. Loose fair hair cascading. Dainty oval face, snubby nose.

Jack thought that his heart would burst.

Sorel idled forward.

'I'm utterly devastated about Clare. You have all my sympathy . . . Jack.'

Sorel was choosing his words with such sly care.

'I almost feel I bear a grain of responsibility myself. I happened to meet the lovely grieving Miranda in the lodge and offered to escort her, hmm? Since Rogers said you were up here.'

Clare's sister stepped past Sorel and gazed at Jack. As though for the first time ever.

'I was asking where you live. I had to talk to you.' The words tumbled out breathlessly. 'When I landed at Luton I phoned Daddy and you'd just left. I only heard yesterday

285

in Crete. I'd gone to Crete to be on my own and think. Did Clare ever tell you about Ivan? I had to think about Ivan and me, so I was out of touch, and then I read—'

She broke off, comprehending the shock on his face.

'Oh God, didn't you know I'm her twin? Identical. You did know, didn't you? She did tell you?'

The scar on her forehead, the pale blue eyes, the face . . .

'Yes,' he managed to say, 'I knew. But . . .'

'But what—?'

But Miranda was alive. Clare's perfect image. She hadn't been murdered by a mugger in San Francisco.

No one had killed Miranda. No one had flown her ashes home to her dad. The world was not identical.

A marvellous difference? No, a torment. A difference which pierced his heart – and which could be no comfort at all. Which could never be a comfort! Never ever.

'But what?' she asked again.

'It's just . . . seeing you.'

'I ought to have realized! I wasn't thinking. I'm sorry.'

'We're all sorry,' said Orlando. 'La chair est triste, hélas.'

If Jack had felt steadier, he would have risen and assaulted Sorel.

'You killed her with that *Scoop* story, you shit!'

'I already apologized to the Master as soon as I got back from France. It was just a joke.'

'You can't ever apologize to Clare!'

'I came up here in good faith to say how desolated I am—'

'What story?' asked Miranda. 'What's this about?'

'You were in Crete,' Orlando said smoothly. 'It's too complicated to put in a nutshell.'

Miranda's voice choked. 'I want to know how she died. That's what I need to know – exactly what happened.'

'I can't,' Jack cried out. 'I can't tell you anything.'

Miranda stared at him in astonishment.

About Soul, about QX, about Angelo's house he could perhaps force himself to speak . . . It would be such anguish when she was the image of Clare. As for how Clare had died: impossible. How could he tell about something which he hadn't experienced? Yet how could he lie?

He whispered, 'I can't bear to.'

'Because I look like her: is that it?'

Suitable words eluded him. 'I can't bear you near me. It was over. Now it isn't.'

'Christ!' cried Miranda. 'You just want it to be all over!'

'I say, old fruit, that's a bit shitty—' Orlando was suppressing a smirk.

'Shitty?' she echoed. 'You were having an affair with my sister. Now she's dead. You want the slate wiped clean. I'm just a damned nuisance. Even a provocation to you!'

Miranda, in the Holy Bagel, ikons on the walls . . .

Pissed off.

Thinking that they were messing with her mind.

Dead Miranda.

Alive.

Very pissed off. Furious. And deeply hurt.

No way to reach her, no way to tell, to comfort.

No way to answer her question.

Clare's Cardinal Newman was wanting to ask questions too. Questions about QX and the prototype. Jack had no obligation to Newman. Let him not try any sort of emotional blackmail. *Clare would have wanted me to know, Jack . . .*

'You seriously *are* refusing to talk to me?'

Jack said nothing. He must endure his betrayal of Clare – in her own eyes. He must endure disappointing her sister – her sister wondrously resurrected, so familiar to look at, such a stranger. He must never try to get to know her.

'I rather think our Jack is overwrought. Maybe I could buy you a drink,' Orlando offered Miranda. 'I can at least explain about the *Scoop* affair. I was extremely provoked, you see . . .'

Orlando mustn't insinuate himself into Miranda's life. She mustn't ever come visiting Cambridge.

'You leave her alone!' Jack bellowed.

Miranda might have rejected Orlando's invitation had it

not been for this feverish outcry, this endeavour to banish her.

'One drink,' she said guardedly. 'I need one.'

113

Jack opened the wrought iron gate into the Scholars' Garden of Dame Elizabeth's, shut it behind him, and lugged that old brown suitcase along by the river like some newcomer seeking lodgings. Really, he ought to have taken a taxi from college. But he had felt such an urge to walk this route to re-establish a sense of connection.

Red and yellow dahlias fringed the landward side of the gravel path. Orange clouds were curtaining the descending sun. The air was chilly, yet he himself was perspiring. The suitcase had become annoyingly heavy.

Wings swishing, a lone swan flew overhead, to find a roost for the night.

Might this world with Miranda in it be some kind of poisoned gift from Clare? Maybe everything was about to start again. Sorel. Miranda – her most passionate wish might be to visit the house on Telegraph Hill to see where her sister had died.

Nobody else was about. Stepping close to the water, Jack swung the suitcase, two-handed.

The suitcase flew. Not far – yet far enough.

It flew about as far as Orlando had been on that Sunday a world ago, in the punt with that sandy-haired girl.

For a short while the suitcase floated as it settled, but soon it submerged.

Jack began to trot.

Homewards.

To family.